SAINT ARETINO

A New Novel

From The Author Of

Invisible Cities

And

Scourge Of Princes

Paul Petillo

SAINT ARETINO

for my wife, Bonnilyn

CONTENTS

And would it have been worth it, after all,

After the cups, the marmalade, the tea,
Among the porcelain, among some talk of you and me,
Would it have been worth while,

To have bitten off the matter with a smile,
To have squeezed the universe into a ball
To roll it toward some overwhelming question,
To say: "I am Lazarus, come from the dead,
Come back to tell you all, I shall tell you all"
If one, settling a pillow by her head,
Should say, "That is not what I meant at all.
That is not it, at all."

The Love Song of J. Alfred Prufrock – T.S. Eliot

1

Santo Aretino was not self-aware. When he exited the elevator on the twentieth floor, front desk security had alerted the receptionist who had passed the information onto her company's security detail. She would later tell Marley in the break room, describing her reaction to his entrance as "like being in a vacuum. All the air wooshed toward the open elevator door. It was bizarre and kinda scary and definitely kind of erotic. Those green eyes. That walk. The feral look."

The way she recounted the incident made Marley smile. "It must've been something," she replied.

"I know what you're thinking, young lady."

"Do you, Denise?" Marley enjoyed the 'when-I-was-younger' conversations.

"When I was a twenty-year-old, I also harbored the notion that my generation had invented sex and sexiness, and matronly women like me could not comprehend the eroticisms I knew."

"I don't see you as matronly. Motherly, maybe." Denise smiled.

"You're sweet. So, as I was telling you, he says 'I'd like to open an account,' and he says this very seriously. As if he had done it a million times before. About that time, Todd and the new security guy step out of their little room and try to act as if they belonged. In their off-the-rack suits. Our boy Santo, he looks at them and ignores them.

"I've always thought of myself as a competent appraiser

of new clients. I felt as though I had to be." Denise was the first face visitors encountered upon entering one of the largest brokerage houses in Portland, Oregon. "He looked, I don't know how to politely say it, like small fish."

She knew small from large. Small fish, especially those not presenting themselves as having money, is, by default, given to a rookie broker. Someone like Marley. Big fish and whales had appointments, entourages that made arrangements in advance, arrived carrying essential documents, as expected and often late.

"So, I tell him I'll have somebody for you to speak with shortly. And you know what he says to me?" Marley shook her head. "He asks about the bell?"

Santo smiled. "Is this a Dotaku bell?" he asked, after a brief pause. He had seen one before at the library in Chester. That building housed all sorts of eclectic objects from a wide variety of historical periods, most of which had been hidden away for years for a long-dead industrialist's personal enjoyment.

"It is, I replied, attempting to not show too much enthusiasm." Marley thought this girl-talk was cute. She never had that sort of interaction with other girls her age. Denise was trying to fill that void.

"And then he starts going on about it being a mute object, and Japanese history and agrarian rituals, rice harvests, and I don't think I heard most of the rest of what he said."

"You always told me it was a conversation piece."

"You would think so, Marley. It's an arrogance meter. More than three-fourths of the people who come in here never say a word." Denise had told her about the bell, though. Denise's bell had been a gift from her father. She explained to her once, "It was symbolic and somewhat symphonic. Just as composers work the pauses between notes, the negative notes designed to give the work a certain balance most listeners take for granted, just knowing the bell was there helped me focus when I heard someone speak."

Marley's father had taught her a similar lesson. "Appreciate the moments in between the sentences of a conversation, Marls, it is a critical element of the speaker's intent."

"But this one, he wants to chat about it. Only, he wants me to chat about it while he listened. He's a man of few words, Marley. A charmer, for certain. I could sense that in him, in the brevity of our exchange, which, to me, spoke volumes. It was unexpected, the negative hush of man in control and yet projecting a willingness to bend in the slightest breeze. He lets you know it is not due to lack of strength but instead, due to a fullness of it."

"Poetic, Denise." And she let the silence continue without adding much more than that two-word response.

Marley had a brief moment to appraise the visitor she had been summoned to meet. A long glass wall separated the reception area from the inner office. One the other side of the glass, a hallway ran perpendicular to the reception area. She walked nonchalantly as if she was not the person called to the front of the house. She paused, shuffled some papers in her hand, feigned interest in what she was carrying while she looked at the young man waiting. Although she didn't have the same initial trepidation as the receptionist initially had, she wondered why this man, close to her age, was requesting a meeting.

Santo seemed out-of-place as he sat in what was clearly the bastion of white-collared businessmen. These were the stodgy yet opulent halls of the affluent Balvenie drinkers, an old boy's palace of financial transactions, where the pretension of European cut suits with wide lapels and shoulder pads was the uniform of the money warriors, where wealth had its own aroma. Marley's coworkers, all men except for the women in the office pool, dressed in the peacock fashion of the day. And it greatly amused her.

And yet, here he was. He could have easily passed as the quintessential hippie, the road tripper, and someone who had purposefully shunned a world that valued shirts and ties as the armor of their royal attitudes. Marley watched him sink into one of the leather chairs scattered in groupings. The expression on his face suggested the way it enveloped him was not comforting. He stood, almost bouncing from the seat and walked towards the receptionist.

From her vantage, the man standing at the desk looked like a beautiful amalgam of Peter Fonda and Dennis Hopper, rugged without the buckskin tassels or the biker leather, weather-beaten without being wind-beaten. He was clad in jeans and a crisp white t-shirt untucked under a thick brown waist-length coat, all of which seem to be clinging lovingly to his frame.

She greeted him professionally, introducing herself as she extended her hand. Her father had taught her at a very young age to engage in this male greeting, always keeping her right hand free, always stand to shake a man's hand and do your best, he would say, to avoid some sort of Victorian finger shake where the man didn't fully grab her hand. In the late seventies, her direct and firm grip still caught men unaware and disarmed them slightly, if only for a moment. Not this one, though. He returned her smile warmly, allowing her hand to slip into his, find its bearings, and grasp just firmly enough to show her importance.

As she led Santo back to a small desk at the far corner of an expansive open room. The inner office hummed with the hushed sounds of her coworkers, whispering, sighing, the sounds of exasperation, and a few urgent grunts, far different from the muted wood-paneled reception area. Marley motioned to a chair and waited for him to become settled.

Her desk was sparse, with no pictures, no errant coffee mugs, pens, and pencils in their holder. It was in sharp contrast to her coworkers who decorated their areas with family photos and sports memorabilia, items of conversation, and position. She had told Denise during one of their bathroom conferences that she intended the absence, so, as

PAULPETILLO

she put it, she could "move on to the corner office with nothing more than her briefcase and a purse."

Marley adjusted herself in the chair, leaning forward on the desk, resting on her elbows.

"What would you like to open the account with, Mr. Aretino? Did I pronounce that correctly?"

"You did. And thank you. But Santo works best." Marley's father had taught her that names were the first and most crucial hurdle to a longtime relationship with a client. Although he was not in the world of finance, his business dealings with other men followed unwritten rules, and he made sure his only daughter knew them, and more importantly, why they were important.

"Then, Santo, it is." What she didn't ask was written all over her face.

"I didn't always go by Santo. For the majority of my life, Sonny was what I was called. Some people say that nicknames are the ultimate sign of friendship, of belonging. There was the kid who had his father's name and his father's name before him, he was the third in line, and somewhere along the line, he was instructed to sign his name with three Roman numeral ones behind it. Kids called him Benny Three Sticks. And then there was this kid, a good friend of mine who had a really long neck, like a giraffe and they called him Raffe. I think when they called me Sonny, it was because of some deep irony I completely missed. Kind of like a joke they all knew, but they neglected to clue me in on the punchline. There was even a time when I thought Santo was sort of an inside joke."

"Sonny doesn't seem to fit you."

"And you think Santo does?"

She didn't answer him. "I don't exactly have a name the lends itself to nicknames," she said, thinking of how her father referred to her as Marls. Denise called her Lady M privately.

"Marley is an interesting name. I like it." Had anyone else said that they liked her name, she might have been offended. It would have sounded as if it had received some sort of

10

unrequested approval. But she was pleased that he said this, and that surprised her.

"And I think Santo is an interesting name as well. It seems to suit you. Anyway, Marley means pleasant seaside meadow." And although she immediately wished she had not told him that piece of personal information. It would have probably been received with a deeply furrowed frown if her father knew.

"You'll meet many men, Marls," he told her once. "You will have business meetings, many of them, and you will be the only woman in the room. Although the advice came from my father, you might consider it. He said, you never fish where you swim." Her father had instructed her on the possible pitfalls of the job over many weeks. These nuggets of advice, often delivered casually, surfaced as if the thought might have only dawned on him that moment.

"And this is important, Marls. There aren't that many women trying to do what you want to do. So, remember this in these instances. Always dress to convey sexlessness with as little exposed skin as possible, no earrings or small ones, hair up, and never ever touch it. You are already pretty measured in your delivery, but as a reminder, keep your voice, you know, even, moderated and definitely without that upward inflection some women use at the end of a statement. And always sit up straight." There was more. He had also instructed her to "Never linger if you do make eye contact, always have another place to go with your look as long as it is not down." She had long since stopped wondering about all these rules of the meeting, the parameters only she would have to live by, the lessons learned in his study as a child.

And yet, here she was, suddenly out of her comfort zone with a man she had just met, reminding herself.

Santo reached inside his coat and slipped a leather satchel over his head. He placed the bag in front of her, the sound of weight and metal.

"May I?" to which she replied with a nod. The way the

bag rested on her desk, the contents inside spreading out to meet the surface, it could have been liquid. Marley pulled back the flap. Gold Krugerrands. A lot of them. She wasn't sure what she was looking at as she opened the bag wider.

"How much is in here?" she asked, as she lifted one of the South African coins, holding it approvingly in her hand. She had never seen one in person. The full ounce of gold had an unexpected heft compared to the quarters and loose change at the bottom of her purse. The profile of Boer war hero Paul Kruger was minted to one side. She turned it and traced her hand over the antelope looking creature prancing on the flip side.

"It's a springbok," he said. She looked up at him; the suspicion on her face was more than evident. The fellow on the other side was a bit of a controversy in his day, a Dutch Afrikaner who didn't like British immigrants.

She quickly asked, "How many coins or how much is it worth?" she asked, stumbling over the question in her excitement. She would have instead inquired as to how Santo came into possession of such treasure.

He didn't answer immediately. In the long pause, he watched her struggle with the next possible move. "I suppose provenance is probably more than just a curiosity. I'm not sure how I can explain it."

Marley smiled, "You could try. You have to put yourself in my place Mr., er, Santo. A person walks in here with a bag of gold coins, and although it is possible, they are yours, and you came by them legally, consider the questions I might have."

"You know, I hadn't considered any questions. I've never been in a broker's office, and I think I mistakenly assumed that it would resemble the grandeur of the New York Stock Exchange, albeit on a smaller scale."

"That doesn't answer the question or even come close to me considering taking down the red flag."

"Where do I begin?" In the sixteen-month trip west, the young man had become a student of the investment world, for almost no other reason than curiosity. He had poured his attention into everything Benjamin Graham and David Dodd had penned. He found other voices, delving into critical economic books written by Veblen, Weber, Keynes, Freidman, and Jacobs. And all the while trying to view these works as if they were Pirandello's "Six Characters in Search of an Author." The world of investing amused him. He was amazed that an industry such as this could rise fashioned from the ability of one man to profit from another man's mistake. At first, Santo saw it as a sort of financial bullying. He found the exercise absurd, even somewhat masochistic. While he understood the principles of why it existed, he found it fraught with the potential for deceit.

The more Santo learned about the marketplace, or scheme as it was often called, the more he became concerned that he too would be complicit. He did not want to profit from someone's mistakes, even if they knew the risk and made the wager nonetheless.

This was how he arrived at gold. While it lacked the luster of stocks and the safety of bonds and real estate, the coins had the same tangible feel as cash. The only mistake he or the world could make would be to under or overvalue it.

"There is eighty coins total," he answered as her eyes widened. "A while back, I bumped into this old-timer in Denver. For some reason, he told me that if I had any money, I should buy gold."

"Go on," she replied, placing the coin back in the satchel.

"So, I did have a few dollars, did my research, and took his advice. I'm not sure whether it was a good thing I didn't buy more. Or maybe a bad thing. I was, I am mostly traveling on foot when I wasn't riding the bus, of course." This seemed to register as he watched her consider the weight of the coins.

She turned to her computer, a big boxy model that had just recently changed the way these salespeople conducted their business.

"A little over eighty thousand." He quickly added, "At

least according to the spot price this morning." When Santo took the man's advice, he bridged the gap between outsider and insider. Most of his education up until that point had come from books. He had built a literary castle, surrounded it with a moat of written words. He was also aware that this sort of consumption, the randomness of his approach, left him with only a macro view of the world. The result of this research left him in a position of distance. Santo became a bystander who became an observer of events, with a sort of fly on the wall perspective. His generally dispassionate nature allowed him to understand what he would do in a specific situation, not the lesson the author was trying to teach. This was when he discovered the value of the periodical and vibrancy of the daily newspaper.

Until he began reading these periodicals, Santo was a shadow in the fog. The country Santo was born into was in economic turmoil. Inflation was high, and interest rates were soaring. There was a war in Vietnam and a civil rights struggle. However, that was only part of the backdrop.

The New York Times and the Wall Street Journal, local and international publications, all forced him to unwillingly admit that he was part of something bigger. Even if he had not been aware.

"I paid about $97 a coin."

"We don't deal in coins, Santo," she said, her words trailing off as a question.

"I kind of figured that. Thing is, I don't want to sell them just yet. I'd like for you to hold on to them as leverage, so I can buy stocks."

She repeated his request. "You want to open an account with these coins, asking us to hold them while we loan you the money to buy stocks. That's not necessarily the way we do things, Santo."

She was not much older than him, although he seemed incapable of reading her age. "That's what I was thinking. In my opinion, the price hasn't quite topped out yet. Soon. Maybe even tomorrow. Maybe next month. As you can see, they are worth quite a bit more than that now, which should give you a better than average return should the bet go sideways."

Marley picked up her phone and dialed. When the person on the other end answered, she turned away from Santo to speak. He pretended not to hear her end of the conversation. A couple of minutes later, a man in crisp-white shirt sleeves and tie approached her desk and introduced himself. He, too, looked into the bag, turning the coin in his hand. He also made a lingering assessment of the coin's owner.

"We don't deal in coins, Mr. Aretino," he said, repeating Marley's statement. "A margin account will cost you twelve percent interest to maintain, and we can only allow you to buy up to fifty percent of the value of what you plan on placing in the account."

Santo stood and picked his up the bag. "Sounds reasonable to me. But not nearly reasonable enough. I was kind of hoping you folks would be a little hungrier for business and be willing to go five percent at ninety percent invested." He turned to leave.

"Eight percent and eighty percent," the man quickly added. Santo kept walking. 'Be reasonable, Mr. Aretino."

Santo turned slowly to him. "If I walked in with cash, would there have been the same problem?" The man started to answer but stopped short of actually speaking. He was now suspicious of how this young man, who by outward appearance showed little indication he had the financial wherewithal to make such a purchase or these kinds of demands.

Santo leaned into the man and answered the question that had yet been asked. "I have a receipt for the purchase. But I'm guessing you are probably wondering why I had that kind of money in the first place. Am I right?" The man stepped back slightly.

"I'm going to walk out of here and go sell them now. Most of them, anyway. And then I'm going to come back and

Marley and me," he said, smiling at the young broker seated at her desk, "we're going to make some money."

"I have some more experienced brokers, more senior than Marley that could help you with that plan, Mr. Aretino." Marley seemed relieved that her boss had said this.

"No. It will be Marley."

*****

She was born Janice Marley Abrahamson but had dropped the Janice on her own, and Abrahamson legally. Her parents had expected she would as soon as she had saved enough money. She was a strong-willed child that had grown into an opinionated young woman. She had developed an independent streak that her parents had both celebrated and feared.

She was their only daughter, and although by the standards of society, she was a good girl, her rebellion ran deep. It was not the type of revolt that caused parents anguish. Marley instead chose a gentler path and, once accepted, held fast as if her very breath depended on it. They had learned that her choices were never the result of some pre-teen fad or random teen fixation. Her opinions, statements, or conflicts had an arguable logic that was well-reasoned and even sensible. And she was an apt pupil of people.

"Where did that come from?" was her father's response when she told him, at the tender age of sixteen, that she would like to become an investment analyst. He knew better than to dissuade her choices, but like so many of her bold pronouncements, he was nevertheless curious about their origins. He leaned back in his chair and considered the young woman before him. She certainly had the mathematical wherewithal to do the hard work. He knew that she would be breaking new ground with her choice of jobs. He expected it. He had taught her to be the woman she was, how men would view her, how she could change the world with subtle gestures, and the rigors of excellent choices. He knew few women had survived the jungle of this primarily male bastion, and he was right to be concerned about his little girl. But he was anxious to see her unleashed.

"Where it always comes from, Daddy."

It was when she told him that she wanted to drop his surname that he showed some sign of emotion. "I would never do this if I was your son. You know that, Dad. But as a girl, it matters so much less."

"I'm aware of that, Marls," he replied, feigning disappointment. "Have you picked a name that suits you?"

"I have." At this, she wrinkled her face, the look of a little girl who was not so sure he would accept her decision or the reason why. "I would say it is a little less Jew, but it is probably more..."

"A little less me. Ouch and double ouch." Her father cringed, but he also smiled. While he went directly to thoughts about the old country, the ties, the struggles, the deep feelings that seemed to be as near as the last generation, and yet generations removed, he knew his daughter was not trying to dismiss her heritage. She was, instead, trying to gain recognition of her own, well removed from her father's legacy.

"Not that being Abrahamson is a bad thing. It's not that. It's not even the Jewish name. Even if I have questions. But it is a name that does have the dual impact of categorizing you in advance."

And there it was, he thought, his daughter without definition.

"I was thinking of your mother's maiden name. Cornish. Grandma might not have agreed, but I think it would have made her smile."

"You think?" His future polymath, recognized by her peers and celebrated by her fans, a woman of unheralded power and position, barefoot in his office, in jeans and her "I'm a pepper" t-shirt. She paced around his office, a light step that seemed at once girlish, then rise up onto her toes for a brief moment before gently landing on the other foot, hands clasped behind her back. It was her prance.

"Of course, she would've smiled. She would have been laughing and probably still is, pleased with herself that her curse came true. You are just like me; she would have happily pointed that out."

He got up from his desk and opened the French doors in his office that led to a garden area. Marley followed him to a park bench he had put on the back lawn. This was his silent place. When she would find him here as a little girl, he would pat the bench for her to come to sit. She was never the sitting type, a bundle of nervous energy always ready to explode, dazzling him with her vibrant thoughts, robust opinions, and youthful exuberance. From where the two of them sat, they could look south out over the Willamette Valley, a view that commanded awe on a clear day. She imagined herself the queen of this vast kingdom, a world that existed and hummed and went about its business oblivious of her reign, her protection, her will. But in need of her nonetheless.

They were good at silence. This, however, was not always the case. Marley knew her wish to distance herself from the family name would come as a shock to her father, and there was still the possibility he might not be on board. She was hoping the name change revelation was sinking in.

Her father sat, smiling, mostly at the rebelliousness of her youth. It was always expected, and yet, he was always surprised. He had learned long ago to simply do what he could to be part of her life while she still allowed him access and to let her run her chosen course. He knew she thought of him as her king. And yet, he often felt he was just a bystander, a willing pawn in her ascent.

"So," he said, unsure of what topic to choose to address first, "can I maybe help you with the job search?"

"Absolutely," she replied, expecting the first comment to be about the surname. "Of course, I'll need your help. Just like always, Daddy. I have absolutely no problem letting you open the door for me. I am a realist, after all. But you should be aware that if you do, you might get the blame for what happens next."

"You do know that no matter how damned smart you are, or think you are, there will be a man telling you that the steno pool is where you belong."

"At their peril."

He chose not to disagree with her on that point. He also knew that she was patient and kind. However, he was well aware that no one entered the world of trading stocks without paying their dues, cold calling for clients, and taking their lumps first. He knew she would use sugar rather than vinegar to capture the attention of senior partners because of notable abilities. He knew she would advance despite her sex.

"You do know that investment analyst is not a beginner's job, nor is it a woman's job." He would never suggest another path or career.

"I have Abby Joseph Cohen to look up to, Daddy. From what I've read, she now works as a financial analyst at T. Rowe."

"That's a nice Jewish name."

"And Mary Roebling. The banker in high heels, I believe she was called. President of the American Stock Exchange."

"Another nice Jewish name. I'm sorry. I sometimes can't resist. The point is, despite the trail that Ms. Cohen and Ms. Roebling cleared for you."

"Let's not forget Abigail Adams."

"Agreed. I know you'd like to think I could go in there and change the world. You have been given the gift of resolve."

"I blame you for that."

"I disagree, young lady. That is all your mother's doing." He sighed deeply, "Okay. I'll open the door, but once you're in, you're on your own. Deal?"

She threw her arms around him, and although she was almost twenty-two, it made him suddenly remember her when she was five. He swallowed the emotion, but she saw it.

"When I marry a man, if I marry at all, he better damned well be just like you."

"Really? And what would he be like?" He was more

surprised that the topic of marriage was even mentioned. He had secretly pegged her as being the type who would never find a man to suit her. He was increasingly convinced that her only equal stared back at her from the mirror.

"Someone who can't say no to me, strong, but in the service of the queen nonetheless."

"I believe that, Marley Cornish. I really do. I'm not so sure God has created your equal yet."

"Daddy, I don't have an equal."

Steven Abrahamson had amassed a sizeable fortune in warehouses. As Portland grew in size and businesses, found the area favorable, the need to create, store, and otherwise stage different enterprises allowed his foresight to pay off. He eventually added an insurance arm to his business as well as landscaping and janitorial services, building maintenance, and even took a role in refuse disposal. This fortune was now managed in a conservative portfolio of holdings by Morgan Stanley.

Making the call to his broker, one of the managing partners was unexpected, but because of the strength of his portfolio, the request received serious consideration.

"Good morning, Ernie," he said, brightly. The two had met a week ago. It was a monthly meeting that had resulted in most of his investment direction remaining on the same course.

"Steven. This is unexpected."

"My brilliant daughter would like to become an investment analyst, and she would like to work for you." His broker, who had put three kids through college on the commissions he earned from him, laughed. Steven, however, did not. The silence on the other end of the phone was, as they say, deafening.

"You're serious, aren't you?" The man on the other end of the phone leaned forward in his chair. "I'm sorry, Steven, we're not hiring at the moment. I wish I could be more help."

"I do, as well." There was another long pause. "You can

do something for me, though."

"Sure, what?"

In the evenest voice, he could muster, void of any inflection, delivered in as mild a manner as possible, he said, "You can close my account."

There was a pause as he imagined his broker examining his options. Steven Abrahamson had been one of his most successful clients, and not just in terms of money he brought to the firm. His investment choices often seemed unconventional and, as the office came to realize, wildly profitable. Soon, the Abrahamson portfolio was the model of a contrarian approach, using value as the core strategy. What his broker didn't realize when he dismissed the idea of taking a chance on his client's daughter was who had actually been managing his account for the last ten years, making the market decisions and directing her father on where to go next and why. While the broker did the actual execution, it was Marley, beginning at age twelve, who poured over her father's portfolio.

It was Marley who instructed which trades were to be made, when, and in what quantity. When she laid her reasoning to her father, it often came with a full report explaining her motives. At first, her father had humored his daughter, opening a small account for her to manage, keeping the lion's share of his hard-earned wealth in a separate, more conservatively invested account. But soon, in less than three years, the earnings generated from her managed account exceeded seventy percent, trouncing the average return during that period of just over five percent.

He determined her ideas were worth testing on a much grander scale. Soon, her father shifted the remainder of his portfolio to the same strategy used in her test portfolio.

Her deft hand with his portfolio had become legendary. His broker had tried on several occasions to warn Steven of the wisdom of some of his trades. In each situation, he ignored his protestations and instructed the deal to be completed as intended.

"You've been one of my best clients, Steven," he began before being interrupted.

"Oh, shut the fuck up. I am your most successful client, and I know full well you've taken my trades and extrapolated them to other clients, and even though they got in after my trade, they still made a butt load of money."

"Well, I..."

"I'm not finished. I think it's only fair to tell you that those trades were engineered by my daughter. Every single fucking one of them. For ten fucking years. She's smarter than all of you idiots. And better educated. If I wasn't an old school investor, I wouldn't need you to complete the trade. And, I wouldn't even be having this phone call." His voice remained as even as possible.

*****

She wore a smartly tailored tan suit, the skirt cut to just below the knee, a man-tailored white blouse, her hair harnessed into a tight ponytail. Denise, who had been at the reception desk for over twenty years, had been told to expect her. The office manager instructed her to show the interviewee into the number two conference room when she arrived.

"Mr. Abrahamson always brings me a truffle from the chocolatier around the corner." Denise knew who she was. Over the years, the young girl had accompanied her father on numerous occasions. Marley would often sit a read as she waited. As they walked towards the room, down the ligneous lined hallway, the two women pretended to be formal.

"He does?"

"He has, for the whole time I've known him. Your father is,"

"An extraordinary man," Marley said, completing her statement.

Marley reached into her purse and pulled a small white box labeled with the calligraphic signature of the famous confectioner. "Then, this must be for you." She had been asked by her father to make this side errand on his behalf. She did, and the results were as he would have expected.

Denise led Marley to the empty room. It smelled polish and varnish and wood, a motif that suggested Paul Bunyan was the decorator. The walls were deep mahogany on three sides with a large mirror encompassing a fourth, floor-to-ceiling. It was all very masculine and, as her father explained, very intended. She took a seat in the middle of the table, facing the mirror. She sat straight-backed and never once touched herself or primped.

The door opened to the conference room, and her father's broker entered. Marley stood.

"My name is Randy. I'm your father's account manager." He was a tall, angular man, almost scarecrow-ish in appearance. "We've met when you were younger." He extended his hand, and she shook it. Marley had never met him before this appointment.

"We've got a standard test for you. Mostly math and such, and we'll give you an hour to complete it. No calculators. Longhand only." He smelled of Brut cologne. Marley knew that scent would linger for an unspecified time in the closed room. "Here's some scratch paper for your work. Good luck and I'll see you in an hour." He left the folder on the table and exited the room.

She had a feeling that he was standing on the other side of the mirror, watching her work. She lifted one of the pencils and opened the folder. Twenty-five minutes later, she closed the folder. The scratch paper was unused. She folded her hands in her lap and waited, motionless.

Randy had been standing on the other side of the mirror watching her. No one was more surprised to see her close the folder. She had been writing furiously, never pausing to think or ponder, or even try to work her answer out on the extra paper. When she closed the folder, he assumed she had given up. He waited until the exact moment when her hour ended before reentering the conference room.

"How did we do?" he asked. Marley despised people who pluralized the work of one individual as if their presence had lent something relevant to the process.

"I think we did fine." Her father had cautioned her to be polite and to set aside her issues with people. He was fond of telling her that she could find a jackass ten feet from her front door, "So, don't look for them; they'll find you soon enough." When she was leaving for her interview, he reminded her of this salient fact, adding, "the workplace is where they all the jackasses gathered during the daytime."

"That was a hard one, Randy." She watched his expression as she said this. The info that crossed his face told her that he had indeed been watching.

"Give me a couple of minutes to review this, and we'll go from there." She smiled, declining his offer to wait in the reception area. She wanted him to examine her from behind her mirror, perhaps drawing his supervisor in for a look. She sat motionless for another twenty minutes, ignoring the small itch that had developed just below her right eye.

When he returned, he swung the door open dramatically, holding onto the knob as if to support his flamboyant entrance. "Can you please come this way, Ms. Cornish?" They worked their way past the receptionist's desk. Denise winked. The two of them moved through the tangle of offices. She did not look at the men on phones, some with their feet resting on the desk.

"Tim Wessel," he said, extending his hand. "Please be seated, Ms. Cornish." She did. Wessel dismissed Randy with a look, and she could hear the door close behind her, a silent whoosh as the frameless door returned to closed.

"This is impressive, Ms. Cornish. Can I call you Marley?" He had folded his hand over the folder and leaned in to speak. "No one has ever completed this little test in the time allotted." She waited without speaking. "No one has ever answered every question correctly.

"We can if you'd like, start your journey with the Morgan

Stanley family. We'll fill out the paperwork later. Of course, we'll need to send you to New York for your Series 7 training and licensing. That takes a little over a month. And when you return, assuming you passed those rigors, we'll start you on the call desk."

"That sounds great, Mr. Wessel. I already have my Series 7, sir."

"You are already an RR?"

"Yes, sir. I was sponsored by the insurance arm of Abrahamson Holdings. I have my Series 6 as well." He opened the folder looking for the documentation, but there was none. She handed him what she had carried with her. Randy had not asked for any additional documentation assured by his own prejudices that she would not pass the test.

He gave it a cursory glance and asked her, "Steven Abrahamson is one of our clients."

2

H e never looked back.

It was now in his nature to move forward. For most people, time is a measure of progress, one foot in front of the other. For Santo, it was more of a hurdle, a physical motion that resembled the gait of an antelope.

The younger Santo was born in and borne of a single minute on a Sunday morning. He would never look back on that decision to skip Mass and head to the bowling alley, the time before the incident whisked away.

The kids he was with on that fateful Sunday morning, the same kids he skipped Mass with to go bowling, had crumbled at the sight of the stranger lying in a growing pool of blood, looked back frequently, often in horror. These kids hadn't even seen the trigger pulled, the bullet discharge, the sickening thud of the body hitting the ground. None of them had seen the man pulling the trigger, the look on his face, the fear in the victim's eyes. His friends had not been there to witness the scramble to get away, the resolution in the shooter's look, the relaxed and casual way he withdrew the gun and fired.

They, along with the patrons at the bowling alley, had been inside the building when the action unfolded. They, unlike him, had seen nothing. Santo, although, had been made witness to the crime and a participant in the event. In that briefest of seconds before the life slipped from the wounded man, young Santo experienced the full display of how sudden violence can envelop a moment in time.

It took several long heartbeats following that incident for the gunman and Santo to lock eyes, create those weird marriage witnesses suddenly have with the scene. Of course, he would never forget it, but at the same time, he would never remember it.

His cohorts, on the other hand, could not stop looking back.

And when asked by the cops who showed up several minutes later, after the guy who rented the shoes found the wherewithal to call them, the crowd that had gathered couldn't recall any of the details. And with good reason: they hadn't seen anything. Instead, their experience devolved into a scarred mess of memories that left two of the three friends seventh grade Santo knew distraught and severely impacted by the event. Two of his three friends would not return to school, and eventually, their families moved from the neighborhood.

The remaining friend had been impacted but, for some reason, shifted his concern to his friend. Raffe was the first to notice the chasm between him and Santo. Things were different. The kids at school would forever whisper about what Santo saw.

Santo never spoke of it, to anyone, not even Raffe. In those days, they called him Sonny. In those days, he had friends, cohorts, people he knew he could pretend with, play with, and get into unnecessary trouble. That was before.

Unlike his cohorts, who suffered all manner of mental disturbances in the aftermath, Santo felt nothing.

*****

As Santo drove north out of the city, almost eight years later, he was the same person. His classmates had all grown and moved on. Santo had used the ensuing years to further isolate himself within his emotions. The incident at the bowling merely closed the door to this inner fortress, and he lived within its walls. Living there meant he both move forward and never leave.

Santo drifted in and out of the real world as if he actually belonged. His isolation would facilitate his excuses for any number of social infractions, not the least of which was his success at the business of drugs.

He peddled the soft variety, and he immediately realized the financial escape hatch this effort could provide. Santo fell willfully into this underworld. He took naturally to the world of dealing, ascending quickly to the status of a significant distributor before the age of seventeen.

Each level of the drug world required a different approach. Moving up demanded fluidity and resourcefulness. Much to Santo's surprise, convincing cautious and generally paranoid men to allow him into their secretive world was easier than he had anticipated. Like everyone else, they were subject to their own egos. If anything, Santo had become a student of the human experience.

He had discovered that people reacted in predictable ways. He felt as though he needed the key to people. His fascination with the human experience did not give him access to those feelings, however. Instead, he felt like a researcher entering field notes for a forthcoming white paper on the subject.

"Why do some people challenge me while others cower?" Santo considered that a reasonable query.

"Why do some people embrace others as strangers while some consider them to be equals?" and worse, the question he often asked of no one in particular: "Why are some people emotional, even to the point of foolishness while he felt nothing?"

Santo knew something was missing. One thing he was sure of, he lacked the energy to dig deeper into the people he encountered. And he worried he would throw their balance off; with nothing to offer in return, he assumed they would be changed. Santo would be forced to scribble something in the margin of his non-existent research paper. "Man is not what he thinks he is, he is what he hides," crediting Andre Malraux.

His success in the marijuana business amused him as much as it astonished him. Santo's trajectory to the top of the distribution chain had demanded he become fluid, intuitive, and more importantly, resourceful. He never succumbed to the paranoia; instead, he allowed himself to calculate the possibilities, creating a statistical analysis of his world where there was no real data.

So, when it all unraveled, he was present but not quite there. He knew the day would come, just not when or how or why. The arrest of the two partners, Santo's partners, was a significant victory in the war on drugs for Nixon and a well-needed boost to local law enforcement morale. He watched from the perimeter, like some fortunate sibyl, witness to an event that he should have been in attendance.

He assumed no one would notice when he left and yet, everyone did, in time, feel the void. His business partners never said a word about his involvement. Santo did not attend the trial, he was long gone by the time his two cohorts were arraigned. Neither of them mentioned Santo. The arresting officer would spend the remainder of his career in pursuit of the young man, for no other reason than to satisfy the suspicion of a friend. That 'friend' would die without knowing the truth.

Santo knew he had to flee, and he knew he could never look back. Ever. He was, however, not so sure he could ever ignore what he left behind would cease in their search.

He had not planned on stopping in Lititz, either. He supposed that no one does intentionally. In his case, it only served to set off another series of events that seemed wholly out of his control.

He had found a home here in this small rural Pennsylvania hamlet, dangerously close to the town he had fled. And yet, it seemed incredibly distant. And now, after eighteen months on a small farm with an elderly lady, after spending time in a world where he seemed to belong, a place he had never intended leaving, Santo was boarding a bus on a late spring day for points as-yet-to-be-determined. Oregon sounded nice to him, he told the lady at the station. Lititz had served its purpose. It had comforted the unrest in him and rereleased it to wander. He seemed to have always harbored the belief that three thousand miles away might be far enough.

His life had mainly been lived in the shadows. He identified with the absence of self. Santo had become quite comfortable with not having full knowledge of who he was. Although he would never acknowledge it, the young man had also grown fatigued with trying to find the answer. His parents knew but seemed unwilling to say. His siblings looked at him as the stranger. His experience at people was ambiguous at best, some treating him as the savior and others, the pariah, no medium, only extremes in which no one understood. The answer wasn't to found in Lititz either.

This time though, the leaving brought him out of the shadows: he had committed a crime, boldly, in daylight without any attempt to hide, a premeditated act of revenge. If he were caught, someone would press charges. There would be no mention of the heinous infraction he was resolving, how the interaction he had with those three college kids who kidnapped two Amish girls from a roadside fruit stand. It was a reprehensible crime of impulse. Santo did not take time to review what seemed to be both bad luck and misplaced fortune. He boarded the bus at the same time the three boys were found tied to their dormitory bed, with every appearance that something deviant had occurred. All three boys were shamed from the school.

And while he would never look back, while he seemed to be growing in a way that Santo never had, he was still the prey.

3

The injuries to the boys were not taken as seriously by the college as their parents had hoped. The dormitory RA had found them tied together on a single bed and because Santo had expressed his disgust with the young man assigned to that hall as he exited, the impression that something unbecoming had occurred in that room was the first conclusion that was drawn. The campus police were summoned and untied the boys. They expressed their disgust as well. The scene of three students, curious bound and tied to a curtain rod, laying across a single bed warranted some sort of explanation.

The boys were taken to the campus infirmary, the most egregious injury done to their egos. The crowd that had gathered in the hallway would ensure that whatever happened in that room would follow these three for the remainder of the days on campus. Their parents were called after they received medical attention for cuts and bruises, a broken nose and a bruised groin. All three boys made an embarrassing exit home soon after.

The local police taken statements from the three young men but despite the fact they had all offered stories that were similar in nature, they could not describe their assailant. They all agreed it was the same kid from the gas station but when asked for specific details, a description, they offered a variety of possibilities. They promised they would keep investigating.

But they didn't and decided instead to let the case go cold.

*****

Almost every trip, be it by road, rail, car or bus, or as Edward Payson Weston preferred, by foot, there is always some sort of plan in place, a sort of A to B mapping of the process, a timeline and a schedule at hand. A person might be walking for the sake of it, or driving to nowhere, or perhaps purchasing a ticket to city they had never visited. However, each trip demanded a beginning and an end. Journeys were different. They held the intrigue of possibilities and there was never an end. Santo had decided on a trip only to find himself on a journey.

Unlike Weston who made the dramatic journey from New York to San Francisco on foot at some point in the early twentieth century, Santo had no intention of walking the entire length and no intention to go to California. He enjoyed Thoreau's brief treatise on the activity as well but hadn't decided on how much wilderness he was interested in encountering, on purpose or otherwise.

His first encounter with the idea of a world beyond the one he was in came with the exploitive explorers hired by the royalty of Europe to look for treasures and passage. He imagined himself as a traveler from a very early age. But no explorer fascinated him more that Alexander von Humboldt. His efforts at chronicling nature in the years before Darwin, remained with him, even as he set forth into an unknown far less wild than this eighteenth century botanist encountered. He imagined the obstacles, the hardships that were overcome and the length of time it took to do what was considered at the time to be groundbreaking work. What he could find on Humboldt was dense and often dusty, books that had only rarely been visited. He had traveled to Philadelphia repeatedly as a teenager to read the only copy of his Personal Narrative, a travelogue based on a nine-month journey to Peru and Chile.

But Santo had no intention of traveling by way of boat, nor any inclination to spend two years before the mast.

While the allure of the railroad was certainly attractive, the method of travel seemed inflexible, as if you were destined to the tracks and the scenery some surveyor had mapped, regardless of whether it was dramatic or not. Large hunks of steel hurtling through the landscape, seemingly detached even as it depended on the ground it journeyed through. Not that the history of rail travel didn't intrigue him, it did. He knew the railroads had built in this country designed more for function rather than sightseeing, often traveling along the industrial corridors, the focus of which we the transport of goods. The romantic notion of hopping a train, the elegance imagined but long since passed, the passage through vast expanses of wilderness riven by metal, the small outposts that dotted the journey as if clinging to a lifeline, the mechanized hum of a previous century's progress was lost on him. Eva's husband had a copy of Christopher Isherwood's Berlin Stories amongst his war memorabilia. Trains, it seemed, relied on the openness of strangers to interact, create intrigue while hurtling through time, mysteries and murders and such. He was no Mr. Norris. It also felt confining to Santo, especially after his days on the farm.

Of course he had also indulged the possibility of a journey based on his reading of Kerouac and his journey in a post-World War II America, a linear course from New York to San Francisco in an automobile. But he had abandoned is car in Lancaster as a way to slow the possibility of being tracked by the local authorities.

While being trapped in a car did not immediately appeal to Santo, hitch hiking did. He promised himself that he would spend his time on the side of the road for at least half of the journey.

As the bus pulled from the surprisingly appealing bus

station in Lancaster, Santo contemplated nothing. He didn't reflect on what had happened during the last two days; He rarely did. He had always been able to leave the past where it belonged, stored away for future reference. Whether he would ever review the information that was stored there, reflecting on decisions he had made, the people he had impacted along the way, or on the events that seemed to herd him like so much happenstance into one situation after another was the subject for a later date. As he boarded the silver bus emblazoned with the words Continental Trailways, what had just happened had already begun its predictable retreat, filed away with barely a footnote of importance in his life. Lititz would prove a sixteen-month detour. It was nearly empty when he boarded it, choosing a seat about mid-way.

He had read somewhere that a true traveler is not the same person who began the journey. Somewhere along the line, a new person emerges, not different, but a much better version. To Santo, who was wondering who he was, when he gave himself the idle luxury of that sort of contemplation, entered this journey in search of a better version of himself, a freer version, less encumbered by the pull of society and the restrictions that he was often bound to bend or break. To do that, he imagined you would have to know from where you began and from there, who you were.

He was unfamiliar with looking back and although he was instrumental in the choice to travel at this exact moment, he never felt as though he was running. That would have been an act of tracing each step along that path and with the choices available, understanding each decision. If he had reflected on where he had come from, it would have presented a continuous ribbon of road, a path that while having numerous intersections and bridges, hairpin turns and gently rolling curves that banked and spewed you out onto wide valleys from dizzying heights. It was an atlas of a single life in isolation, and although he hadn't realized it at the time, a search for love in a universe of haphazardly colliding with the people he encountered.

His ability to approach each new day like a first day would have been disconcerting to most people. To Santo, who after almost twenty years, saw it as a suggestion of opportunity. While most people would reflect on the events of the previous day or previous week in an attempt to glean some insight for the time at hand, he chose to wipe the slate clean and start over.

As the bus rumbled beneath him, occasionally hitting a rough patch of highway on its way to Chicago by way of Harrisburg and Columbus, and any number of small way stations and rural outposts along the way, he allowed his mind to clear itself of the flotsam of the past few days.

He had developed a deft hand with the pencil and charcoal. He made no claim to its origins, in part because he saw his lineage as uniquely absent of the talents he seemed flushed with. He had drawn a wide variety of subjects, some with Cubism hints of the abstract, others sketched with delicate thought that made you more curious as to the artist's intent, still others held some harbinger of the darkness inside of him, a bleak landscape he refused to acknowledge. The sketches had first been done on walls, in pencil before moving to paper and then canvas. Dina, a former lover had gently moved him along this path during their afternoons together. He signed his works with a large A with an S dangling along the crossbar.

He continued to do studies in shapes and forms and on Eva's farm, he turned his attention to the moving form of animals. He captured the Great Pyrenees dogs, animating their muscles beneath the gentle motion of their white fur. The horse, the cattle, the chickens, the wildlife were all tested by the graphite in his hand. It seemed only natural that his eye begin to illustrate what his mind saw. Eva had given him a well-read copy of Watership Down. In the apocalyptic novel, as he brought Richard Adams' lupine characters to life, he saw a search for his identity.

He had likened himself to Fiver. He was in direct contrast to the character though: the rabbit was young, he was not and probably never had been, considered a runt, the days on the farm had only increased his vigor and sense of invincibility.

But Fiver had a sixth sense that had made him feel isolated from the other members of the warren and this appealed to Santo. While he could not foretell the future as his furry counterpart could, he was also loathed looking backwards at the past, further isolating his mind from the distractions often encountered by the world around him. Watership Down was a traveling adventure above all, a story of escape.

He worked through numerous sketches attempting to mimic every muscle move of the animals. With hours to spend on each drawing, and the otherwise listless scenery of endless of late autumn grey as the bus moved from rural to industrial to depressed and back again, he produced each drawing in exquisite detail.

"That's really good," he heard the voice say over his shoulder. She was leaning around his seat and smiling at him. He had not remembered her boarding and for all he knew, she was already on board when he embarked from Lancaster.

He thanked her for the compliment. She saw that as an opening to continue the conversation. "Where you headed?"

"Well," he said putting his pencil down and slipping the sketch pad onto the seat next to him, "the ticket is one of those one-way deals. So, Oregon I guess." She slipped out her seat and into the one across the aisle from him. There were only eight other people on the bus.

He had always marveled at the ability of strangers to speak to other strangers, even more so when he was the stranger. Although Santo never had a clear vision of himself, always feeling as though his image was in a state of flux, something that would blur and refocus and otherwise exist in a sort of absence of light, some people seemed to look at him without any fear. Because it happened so rarely, he was unsure of what should happen next.

"I'm Stella Blue," she said extending her hand. She looked as if she was a holdover from the free love of the sixties, a Woodstock hippie but too young to have attended the festival on her own. Her auburn hair refused to stay pinned, falling like jungle vines around a flawless face. Santo had never seen anything like it. The tendrils of hair were different thicknesses, thinner strands hanging lower on her shoulders.

He paused for a moment wondering which person she was about to be introduced to, the one from a previous life or the one he saw himself as. "Friends call me, Sonny."

She laughed under her breath as if amused by his name. "What?" he asked.

"You don't strike as the kind of guy who has a lot of friends. I'm mean,"

"You mean what? You could guess this in the ten seconds since you introduced yourself?" She shifted in her seat nervously. She pulled her feet underneath her and leaned slightly across the aisle.

"You look so serious. I mean, I saw you get on the bus back in Lancaster and you looked, I don't know, listless. Not stoned, although I did catch an organic whiff of something about when you got on. Maybe listless isn't the right word. Resigned. Like you didn't have a choice. Like the spirit force was drained from you." She paused for a moment.

"My spirit force?"

"Yep. You know. It's like we all have these forces, physical and spiritual, our terrestrial selves and our neshama, our souls, that's Jewish. The Hopi called it our maasauu. The Lakota called it wakan tanka. It's in everything.

"So, you're an animist?" She twisted her face slightly as if she had not registered that as a description.

"Do you mean, like someone who sees the gods in every rock and tree and stream and bug? Then yes. But, I'm also a consolationist."

"Like the Marx of Freud kind?"

"Yep. I was born into religion and have cherry-picked my way through my beliefs ever since. Do I believe in God the way other people believe in God? Nope. I don't need to make sense of things. Things have their own sense. They're dreadlocks by the way."

"Okay Stella. I'm sorry. Was I staring?"

"I think so. I know you were listening." An awkward silence followed that he often allowed to end conversations that he assumed would be doomed to small talk. To Santo, speaking was a cherished interaction, a sharing of thoughts that should be carefully considered, not so much to craft the words for the listener as to carefully choose the right ones to economically convey the idea. He had had long conversations with Arianne, but they had been more discussion than what would be typically referred to as talking. But here was a total stranger attempting to engage and he seemed unprepared.

Suddenly, she pivoted. "I'm headed to the Hash Bash in Ann Arbor and then I'm on to try and catch the Dead in Charlotte. From there, I'll just follow them up the coast to Amherst. That's where I'm from."

"What's a Hash Bash?" he asked.

She perked up with girlish excitement. "I have no idea

but doesn't it sound fun? I mean, if you're into that kind of thing." She leaned closer and looked at his eyes. "You're into that kind of thing, aren't you? I can tell. Anywho, it just started a couple of years ago on the University of Michigan campus. My parents told me about it."

"And Michigan turns a blind eye to this... bash?"

"It's a college campus. It's cool." Santo had his doubts. He had made a decision in high school to evaluate his options, which actually meant that he would probably never attend school. The experience was not all that appealing even though he excelled in every class he took. The fact that he had amassed so much money before his eighteenth birthday may have had some impact on his decision. Arianne had discussed this with him at length and agreed that this young polymath might have more troubles than benefits.

The dim lighting that came on inside the bus as the night ensued gave Stella a sickening hue of yellow, faded and travel worn. She had distracted him from his sketches and was speaking in excited phrases about her journey and expectations. The marks on the page began to shadow and blur as he wondered about what was missing from his own personal trip. She seemed so anxious to arrive at her destination, which by her own account, was only one of many. He caught various snippets of conversation: "Stella's not my real name; it's actually Audie. I changed it after the song Stella Blue" and "I never go anywhere to have a bad time" and "Don't you just love to be in motion." Her voice echoed around the near empty cabin, even when she tried to whisper.

At one point, she asked about his story. He never thought of what he was doing as a story, not in the linear sense. In all of his reading, amongst all of the pages of characters and plots, some chaotic, some angular, some about love while others lamented at the lack of it, lessons to be learned and habits to be judged in the court of public literature and all with endings, some neat and tidy while others were less conclusive, he did not consider each breath he took as worthy of such record. He could see Stella, in her excited demeanor drawing the world into hers and reshaping it. Santo on the other hand preferred the isolated approach to living, pushing those close to him away and rebuffing those that wanted access. The contrast of comportment seemed noticeable only to him.

Eventually, she fell asleep. He turned back to his sketch book. He could, if he squinted his eyes, see the lupine characters come alive. He had drawn Fiver with a slight smile, the knowing grin of someone who saw something the others had not and yet rising above the shadows he would have normally inhabited to warn his cohorts of the danger on the horizon. His brother Hazel took on a broader look, as if his shoulders were slightly farther back, pushing his chest and his embrace of bravery to the forefront of every movement he made. He gave Blackberry the black-tipped ears that Adam's had envisioned while Holly, Dandelion, and Silver seemed to lumber across the page with their military standing intact.

"Have you drawn Hyzenthlay yet?" she asked, peering at the sketch book on his lap. This was whispered and it sounded small, as if the distance was much more than the several feet separating their seats across the aisle.

He hadn't. But when he looked at her, he saw the essence of that character. The name Hyzenthlay was an imaginary creation Adams had fashioned for the story of these rabbits on the verge of their own personal apocalypse. It added to the well-woven story he had crafted for his daughters, essentially translating the name in his made-up tale as 'shine-fur-dew'. And if there was one word that described the girl sitting across the aisle, it was shine. In the brief time he knew her, he felt the need to reach out and see what she saw, even if it was foreign to what he was seeing. He imagined that this look opened doors and probably parted waters.

"I haven't as yet. I'm not sure how to translate sweet dissension into a ball of fur. Runts were easy. Powerful was easy. The gentle timidity that held a level of fear by the rabbits in charge would be much harder to capture."

"She should look like me," she said as she attempted to wrap her wild dreadlocks in a scarf. "Free but inevitable, adventurous but wise, and fearless. Yeah, fearless. That's me. It should be her too" He didn't reply. He closed the pad and threw it onto the seat next to him.

"I can't see anymore." She was right however, Hyzenthlay should be clever and troublesome to those that wanted control. Even as a rabbit, or in the form of the hippie girl sitting across from him, the power in their being should be more than evident, even if it was frightening to men. The road slipped into the darkened highway as they rolled through Ohio like passenger in a Trojan Horse.

"The real voyage of discovery consists not in seeking new landscapes, but in having new eyes." He looked at her. "That's Proust." She was now fishing through what could only be called a satchel.

Santo found the quote ironic. He had read Proust, a sickly momma's boy who couldn't seem to leave his parent's home. While he enjoyed the craftsmanship of his words, Santo was most attracted to his mention of involuntary memory. Proust suggested that it was a recall based on sensations, in his case it was the act of dipping a madeleine in teas, an act that triggered a detailed remembrance of a time long since forgotten. Santo wondered, as he read the dense "In Search of Lost Time" where his memories were. He had unconsciously refused to indulge in trying to revisit his past, if only to avoid the questions that those thoughts left unanswered. His discomfort stemmed from something Proust had that he did not: he knew where he came from. Was that essential, he had thought. He wished for new eyes but had no idea where to find them.

Santo had never felt a connection to the family the raised him. At times, he held this feeling at bay, wondering instead why his parents, even if he conceded that title to them with reservations, acted the way they did. He didn't hold either Sofi or Umberto directly to blame, believing that there was something beyond their control at play, something untold that they could not verbalize, some disturbance bubbling under the surface. At times, their discomfort was palpable and in other times, when other 'family' members were present, it was less present. Both of them went through all the right the motions, as if the fly on the wall was taking notes. Both did what parents are expected to do. Yet the emotional connection that a child and his parents were supposed to have, seemed to be absent in his relationship with them. When his brother and sister arrived, it was different. As they grew, he knew what he was missing. He now had a template for what a childhood should have looked like. And it was not the childhood he was living.

And now this young girl, he guessed at just twenty or so, who was traveling the country, following the Dead, quoting a long dead writer who barely moved from the confines of his own bedroom was suggesting what he had known all along: "If you don't live with new eyes, you perish."

He had no response to her statement. As she turned her backpack into a pillow, leaning it up against the window, he envied the fact that she had a theme, something she could use as an excuse to move forward.

"Do your parents know where you are?" he sounded older when he said this and immediately regretted the intimacy of the question, or worse, the condescension it might harbor.

"Of course, they do." Leaning up against her backpack, her tendrils of hair swirling about her face, the disarray resembling a tangle of ropes and strings giving her a creamy organic appearance, as if time would forgive all transgressions and never leave a scar in the form of a wrinkle. "This is how Mom met Dad, she on adventure and he was taking a break from his. The story has numerous details and nuances that got them together, she was traveling north from Baltimore and he was looking for inspiration. Romantic, huh?"

"I suppose."

"Of course, it was. Whenever the goddess inside points you in a direction, if you refuse to surrender to it, allow the flow to just take you, uplift you, move you into a place you may not have known existed, you will miss the call. Sometimes," and she lowered her voice, "it is just a whisper. Sometimes, it's a cute boy with a sketch pad on a bus to wherever." She smiled an infectious smile and closed her eyes.

Sleep never came easy to Santo but the darkened landscape passing by his window, the gentle hum of the tires on the interstate and the fact he hadn't rested since leaving Eva's ranch allowed it to tighten its grip on him.

He was standing just off stage with six men, all much older than him, pepper grey beards and the slightly worn look of men who had lived to experience the life he had yet lived. They were holding sheets of paper in their hands, rehearsing silently, mouths moving and hands gesturing, but without a sound. All six were doing this and although they were each ensconced in their own world, the motions had a choreographed look. He looked down at the paper in his hands.

It was a script, complete with directorial notes explaining when and how to gesture. He had the feeling he knew these words, the motions the script had instructed, where to stand on stage, where to look, all seemed familiar to him. A young man with crazy spiked hair instructed the group to get ready. Santo noticed that he was also as well-dressed men as the men, in a bespoke suit of dark grey, white shirt opened at the collar. He didn't own anything like this and the shine on his shoes as he looked down took him by surprise. Where was the clothes he had boarded the bus with, he asked with no voice. Where was his backpack? He whirled around to search for it and noticed a small mirror to his left.

He could see his eyes, green and his brow, furrowed like Eva had told him it tended to be, but that was all he recognized. Gone was the thick, rich auburn beard and so was the pony tail. Both were replaced by peppered grey and a closely cropped business-like haircut. Gone was his denim and t-shirt and newly purchased hiking boots. There was something circling his head, a small wire stopping just at the corner of his mouth. Before he could panic, an attractive blonde woman wished him well and disappeared into the shadows. For a brief moment, she looked like she wanted to kiss him, but didn't. The spiked-hair person, who appeared to be not much older than he was when he entered the bus, instructed all of them to take the stage.

He seemed to know where to go and found a mark on the darkened stage. The crowd applauded cautiously, unsure of what was taking place. Santo found the center mark labeled one. The other men found their marks and stood silently. Suddenly, the lights poured down around them, creating a half circle of reds, blues, and greens. The effect on stage was the same as it was for the audience. Suddenly, everyone was hidden behind a veil of light, the figures on stage with him became shadowy while the audience blurred, faces without details.

He spoke. "My name is Santo Aretino." The crowd erupted and stood. Some were straining to see which of the men had spoken. But they all had, but only he had said anything. He gave the crowd a half wave. The other men did as well. The script had told them to do so, a practiced motion done in perfect unison. When the applause died off and the crowd sat down, he spoke again.

"I know that you come to these TED talks for inspiration, for ideas, for really educated people to give you their unique take on the world or to sell you something they have yet to figure out how to sell elsewhere. I'm here to talk about the concept of good. Not great. Not excellent. Good."

He felt a touch on his shoulder. It was Stella Blue, leaning close to his sleeping face. She whispered, the slightest whiff of patchouli acting the way smelling salts did, bringing right back to where he had left off, "The bus stopped at this diner so we could get off and stretch, get something to eat. I didn't want you to sleep through it. You know, in case."

He murmured a faint thanks and she headed towards the front of the bus and out into the cool Indiana morning air. They were still a hundred or so miles from Chicago. He dug around in his pack for a pre-rolled joint. Santo hoisted the pack on his shoulder and exited the now empty bus. He nodded at the driver, who was sucking hungrily on a filterless cigarette, his blue uniform threatening to surrender to his enormous belly. The man barely gestured as he flicked the burning remains into an arc crossing the retreating night air. "We won't stop again for another three hours," he heard him say as he walked away.

The parking lot was empty with the exception of the bus and a couple of cars parked near the building. As he walked and smoked, the gravel echoed beneath his feet. The smoke filled his lungs and began to relax him. He thought for a moment that he should be sharing this with his new-found acquaintance. But she was not anywhere nearby.

It was then that he noticed another passenger, the skinny man who was sitting in the front row when he boarded. He was walking towards the shadows behind the building. He drew again on the joint, cupping the burning end in his hand to hide the red glow.

Then, he noticed two men approaching the skinny passenger, emerging from the darkest part of the lot. The kid didn't notice them. He was holding a long spoon in his hand, the kind of weird object restaurants attach to a key so patrons don't forget it. Santo realized that the young man was looking for the bathroom. The men stepped towards him.

Santo pinched the joint between his fingers and walked in their direction. When he was within ten feet of them, he noticed that this was not a friendly meeting. Even in the deep shadows away from the restaurant's anemic neon glow, he could see what was about to happen. These were petty thugs, the bottom feeders of the criminal world, the opportunists who sought to cull a living from the weakest. These were the people he had spent most of his life ambushing as they were in the process of exerting their strength in nefarious ways. This was his days in school, the alleyways of his youth, Kendris at the gas station and the three idiots who terrorized the Beiler girls. Santo mouthed the word "shit" under his breath.

By the time he crossed the lot, the two were fully in the process of robbing the kid. He assumed they were locals who would disappear into what was left of the night with whatever they could acquire. He noticed one of them push the kid, as if to reinforce their dominance. He stumbled and fell to the ground, his backpack falling off his shoulder.

The skinny kid was handing his backpack to one of the men at the same time Santo closed the distance between them. The other man turned. "What the fuck you looking at?" he asked stepping closer. He was used to people recoiling in fear, flinching or running. Santo didn't answer. The other man looked but continued rifling through the satchel. The man who asked the question walked closer to Santo and repeated his query, this time with a bit more malice in his tone. Santo remained silent.

Then he came straight at Santo, as if closing the distance

would give him the advantage that was not as clear with his tone of voice. The man was big, easily weighing forty pounds more than he did, farmhand muscular and moving fast. Instead of thrusting his fist forward, Santo brought it down in an arc, grazing the man's chin as it hit his throat. There was a muffled crack as his fist connected squarely where the man's Adam's Apple. The man dropped, clutching the point of impact. He squirmed for a bit, kicking gravel, holding his neck but otherwise choking for breath. Seconds later he fell quiet.

His friend turned and muttered something unintelligible. He dropped the kid's back pack and ran straight at Santo. The fact that he had a knife in his hand did not faze him. He adjusted his stance slightly and when the man lunged, he allowed him to pass without obstruction. Off-balanced he stumbled slightly. Santo struck him in the ear with a punch that originated from his waist, twisting it into a cobra-like thrusting. The man staggered and left his feet. He hit the gravel with a skid. Santo stood for a moment looking at him to make sure he was down.

He walked over the kid and helped him up. The kid had pissed his pants. He didn't ask him if he was okay. He looked back at the first man on the ground.

They both turned when the driver blew his horn. He told the kid, "You better hurry up and get cleaned up. I'll make sure he won't leave without you."

The kid, not much more than Santo's age but smaller, was whimpering silently as he struggled to his keep his balance. Slowly, the event came into focus.

"Is he dead?" The two bodies on the ground hadn't moved. In the drifting shadows, Santo couldn't tell. The boy's eyes were tear-soaked.

"I'll check but you better get changed." The boy picked up the spoon and hurried into the restroom behind the diner.

The man who had brandished the knife was alive, his chest heaving with great effort, he held his ear as he tried to unfurl from the fetal position. He always thought that retreat into the first position you ever knew when you needed comfort was curled up like a fetus. It was as if the pain contracted his spin, giving him the look of pill bug, the rollie pollies of his youth. Santo saw him move slightly. He attempted to get back to his feet but fell heavily onto the gravel unconsciousness. Santo just stood, the same way he had when he had approached the scene: hands relaxed at his side, backpack slung over his shoulder, his face embracing the shadows like a mask.

The kid jumped to his feet and ran towards the restroom. Santo stood there for a couple of additional seconds. The other man wasn't moving and he couldn't tell in the blue hour shadows whether he was breathing or not. He walked over to the driver, who was not lumped into his seat behind the wheel.

"It'll be just a minute," he told him. "That skinny kid sitting up front, you know the one that was keeping you awake, is on his way."

"He wasn't keeping me awake. He was boring me to fucking death though. We've got a schedule to keep." He heard the boy scrambling across the lot, backpack in one hand, still unzipped and carrying the spoon key in the other.

"I'll take that back for you." It was the first time he looked at the young man. He could've been much older that fifteen and was probably told by his parents to sit up front so as to avoid any danger.

"I'm not waiting for you." Santo didn't reply to the driver as he walked towards the diner. He could hear the door swoosh behind him as the brakes released, tires crunching on the graveled lot.

4

Santo dropped the key just outside the entrance. As the bus pulled out of the parking lot, he opened the door and entered. He took a seat at the counter and ordered coffee. The waitress poured him a cup into a thick scratched mug.

"Where was that bus headed?" he asked.

"On to Chicago." She stopped wiping the counter. "Were you trying to catch it?"

"No," he replied, which was essentially the truth. "I'm actually headed to nowhere in particular." He flashed her a large smile. She blushed knowing that he was too handsome for his own good. She was no longer the flower she once was but she was grateful for the warmth in his gesture.

"You can wait here for the next bus to come along," she said, assuming he had missed the previous one, "catch the connection in Chicago. It'll come in about five hours or so from now. I hear it's headed nowhere in particular after that." This time she smiled at him, offering just a little bit more of a flirtation than she might have given for a trucker's tip.

"Thanks," he said, giving her another warm, almost seductive smile. She hadn't had anyone smile at her like that in a very long time. She smiled back as she grabbed the coffee pot to refill his cup. "I was planning on walking?"

"Seriously? Walking? You do know you this little dive is

in the middle of nowhere, right?" She stopped midway through wiping the counter as she noted the pun.

"Then I've arrived." She mumbled "I wish" under her breath. Instead she asked him if he wanted to get something to eat.

There were only two other people in the diner when he walked in, a man sitting in a booth smoking Camel cigarettes, reading the paper, and a man sitting at the counter to his left. He was dressed in working blue, complete with a well-worn cap, the bill of which was black with dirt where his hand had adjusted the tilt. When he heard the waitress ask him how he was traveling, he looked towards Santo.

"I'm kind of headin' that way young fella. I can give you a ride, if'n you don't mind riding in the back of the truck with my tools."

"That would be just fine." The two men paid their bills and exited the diner. Santo turned and threw the waitress a parting smile. She smiled back, wishing she was younger and prettier and able to toss this apron and small town diner aside and follow this traveling Romeo.

The man, who hadn't bothered to introduce himself, had parked on the opposite side of the building where the two men were still laying in the growing daylight. They would have traveled almost an hour before the local police pulled into the lot, and another half hour before Sheriff Jackson Crow would be alerted to the bodies from a customer who almost ran over them. He would have had time to order his usual breakfast before someone came running in the front door wanting to tell someone about his discovery. He spotted the cop at the counter.

It was another two minutes until he swung himself around on the stool, shoveling another forkful of breakfast into his mouth. He would hesitantly leave his waffles and coffee, wondering whether the troubled looking man was telling the truth. He told the man to slow down and catch his breath as they walked towards the door. All the woman behind the counter heard were the somewhat garbled, anxious words "dead" and "man".

Crow followed the man out the door and towards the side of the building where the outside lavatory was located. He saw the two men; one was standing over the body of the other. He seemed as if he didn't know what to do. When he saw the cop, he ran. This, in almost every other situation would have given Crow a reason to chase him; although he was not the young man he once was and because of that, was not about to. He knew once he figured out who was on the ground, he'd find the other one. Which gave Santo over two hours and two minutes before anyone would even ask the question: "What happened here?"

*****

The bed of the Ford pick-up truck was comfortable enough. He used one of the folded tarps in the back as a bed and laid back to enjoy the brightening sky. He was a long-time fan of the moments of the day, when the most significant transformations took place, the way the sun moved through its dawn, astronomical, then nautical, then blue and finally, as the road rumbled beneath him, the golden hour of sunrise. His insomnia allowed him to witness innumerable sunrises, much preferred over the haunting death that sunset delivers, the same colors of autumn, the same throes of the end, the finality of the day. The sunrise over Indiana encountered no obstacles, no tall buildings save the occasional silo, no towering mountains with the exception of several rogue cumulonimbus clouds lumbering along the horizon.

He thought about the winsome smile the waitress had left him with, a warm promise that would never be fulfilled, a wish just out of reach. He had found the sunrise similar to the company of older woman: comforting. Like the sun, they provided some measure of evenness in a world that seemed just slightly off-center.

All of the women he had known, beginning with the older neighbor girl who thought it was her obligation to teach him how to have sex, his one-time tryst with the local librarian, Arianne, and then on to a many more encounters, each giving him as much as he took from them. They were comforting and kind and seemed to need to talk. He was a good listener and apparently, a tender and considerate lover.

Arianne, in all his experiences, remained different from the rest of the women he had been intimate with. She had slept with him only once. This was not his choice but he never asked her why it couldn't continue. She had tried to explain to him that she wanted friendship more than the physical contact. The explanation fell short, adding to the confusion he was careful to conceal. She had said that her world was not the one she had wanted and "To make it more complicated was not smart," adding that she was "not always prone to the smartest decisions."

Such lofty ambitions were foreign to him. No book he had read, and he had probably read well over two thousand by the time she had said this, explained what she meant. Most of the stories, even the bad ones had followed a predictable linear path that adjusted every now and again to new circumstances. How could you know, he wondered, what you needed in advance of taking the certain path?

She had alluded to Robert Frost's poem "The Road Not Taken" when she tried to explain her feelings to him. So, Santo read it, much more deeply that the high school curriculum had outlined. This was not a poem about a road less travelled, a path that was less trampled offering new adventures, sights unseen, vistas unwitnessed. To Santo, it was an ode to the obvious choices a person makes, a motion forward that should be both embraced and never regretted. Right or left didn't matter to Santo and he wondered why Arianne put so much pressure on her ability, or inability to make a clear distinction. He never had never pressured her to have sex, instead reacting to her invitations. And once that invitation was withdrawn, they retreated comfortably back to the relationship they had before: she as the confidante, mentor, friend while he became, despite his younger age and somewhat unwittingly, the same for her.

The other older women in his life also entered by way of circumstance, and they were all older. Some wanted sex, others wanted sex and conversation, and one became a good friend after a spell and while finding the sex compelling, decided the distraction was more than she could handle. They all mumbled something about his 'old soul' while taking his whatever part of his youthful exuberance to suit their own needs.

The girl he had met on the bus was the first girl close to his own age he had felt something for and laying here rumbling down some unmarked country road, he regretted not getting back on the bus. Audie, or as she preferred, Stella Blue was sweet enough to have become more. Had the incident in the parking lot not happened, he might have been on the bus north to Ann Arbor rather than rambling down Route 40 towards St. Louis. He had left his sketch pad and tattered copy of Watership Down on the seat, fully intending to only grab a quick smoke and get back onboard. He hoped she would have found it.

*****

Four hours later, as the truck closed in on the small town of Montrose, it stopped at an intersection to allow a large piece of a farm equipment to exit the road. Impulsively, he quietly slipped out of the truck's bed and dropped into the tall grass alongside the road. The truck pulled away without any acknowledgement of his departure. The sun was now headed for the highest point in the sky, promising a hot, sticky day. He decided to throw his thumb out to chance the random pick up.

Traffic was beginning to thicken on the old road. Locals mostly, in a variety of vehicles seemingly ingrained in the farming lifestyle, functional, dusty and driven with intention, and while preferring it to the interstate drove it with the same speeds. A late model F-150 pick-up truck slowed and pulled over on the side of the road just past him. This was Santo's first time hitchhiking and he was unsure of the etiquette. Should he approach the car on the driver's side or simply get in as a passenger, maybe hop in the truck bed like the last ride? He had barely been twenty minutes into the walking/hitching/walking some more process before the truck had stopped. The passenger side door swung open, answering his question.

The driver was just a little older than he was. "Where ya headed?" he asked, tipping back his sweat stained cap.

Santo thought for a minute. "The short story? West. The long story: Not really sure."

"Fair enough," he replied and pulled the truck back onto the two-lane road. The two rode in silence for a couple of minutes. Santo was comfortable in the silence and the driver seemed to be as well.

"What's you running from?" he asked. He didn't take his eyes from the road when he did. The road, called the National Road by locals had continued in a southwesterly direction, leaving the highway behind.

"I prefer to think of it as running towards. The place where I was kind of wore me out."

"I know what you mean. This place, well, it's fucked up." Santo looked around at the seemingly endless miles of agrarian landscape. The 'place' the driver spoke of had no anchor in the conversation.

"But I'm not going anywhere soon," he added. "My life's turned into a country song." This made him laugh. He looked very rural to Santo, a man who was born to the open skies and dirt and crops. His brief experience with rural life with Eva had somewhat prepared him for scenes like this. "It was all fun until I got my girl pregnant and now, not so fun."

Santo didn't know what to say. He had never been able to understand the ease with which people shared their emotional turmoil with each other and total strangers. In the briefest of sentences, in the shortest amount of time, the man behind the wheel encapsulated his entire life up until that moment. It made him wonder if he was wired incorrectly.

"I'd run," he said after a couple of minutes, head down to Texas and just disappear. Over the Mexican border eventually." He pulled a cigarette from his shirt pocket. He offered Santo one. He hadn't smoked a cigarette since leaving Chester almost two years ago. He hadn't quit; he just hadn't purchased any.

"I'm familiar with Lynyrd Skynyrd, Marshall Tucker, you know, the hippie country bands. But I can see where you should be a song."

"Oh, I'm a song alright. I'm all the loving and living and living some more and obviously, and especially now, because of Julen, I'm about to be all about family and God and raising kids." He didn't seem sad so much as resigned. Santo could be guilty of rolling with the so-called punches, adapting where he needed to and when. But this unnamed driver in this midwestern chariot seemed to be willing participant in a series of reckless decisions, as if he had no control. Santo did not believe in fate and he did not believe the options this kid was no burdened with were appointed to him. Instead of being judgmental, he was fascinated.

"Well, I'm heading to Mt Vernon, which is south. If west is where you're headed, you might want to get out up here and pick another driver. St. Louis is about four hours by car in that

PAULPETILLO

direction. Longer if you are walking." This made him laugh.

"Can I give you any money for gas?" The driver, who never introduced himself waved him off and told him to live the life he never would.

****

Sheriff Crow tried to piece the scene together as best he could. There was the dead man someone in the small crowd that had gathered around the corpse had identified as one of the Mason boys. They were, he was told, trouble a couple of counties over but mostly for petty crimes and never in his neck of the woods. Someone in the crowd offered the dead man's brother's name suggesting that the two always ran together.

He radioed the county medical examiner to come out and take a look but mostly to get the body. He roped off a large area for the crime scene but it was clear that whatever happened here happened quickly. There was no sign of a struggle and because the blow that Santo had leveled, almost no bruising.

Once his deputy arrived, he went in to talk to the waitress. Crow was well-known in this rural community as being fair handed, doling out a form of justice that developed slowly without any harsh leaps of speculation. He was known for saying "There is disorder in all of the universe" and adding, "It was his job to keep it that way." Locals knew what he meant but people unfamiliar had no idea. It was his way of saying that chaos kept him gainfully employed and if it stopped, he'd be out of work. Most of the crimes committed by the local citizenry were impulsive and usually fueled by alcohol. These were often easily diffused with a few choice words and a firm hand. However, there hadn't been a dead body on his watch for almost twenty years.

"First question, Emma," he said addressing the waitress, the only one who hadn't gone outside to see the body, "can I get my coffee warmed a bit? Please?" he added as he swung his sixty year old body on to the stool. She placed a fresh cup of steaming coffee in front of him. "Looks to be a long morning, so maybe I should eat," he said almost to himself. Emma, who was watching the gathering outside, asked him, "I got your waffles warming over here, Sheriff. I could get you some fresh ones if you want."

"Nah. I better just have some toast. And maybe a side of bacon." He took a sip of the coffee and sighed in relief. "You know, I like it peaceful, Emma but every now and again, something like this comes along to add to the excitement. Did you know him? The dead guy?"

She answered nervously, "I heard it was one of the Mason boys but I never met him or his brother." She was wiping the counter and looking out the window. The ME drove up in his sedan, followed by the hearse. People are funny, Crow thought. She desperately wanted to go out a join the people standing around the body, leaning into each detail that was related to her. Before long, she would be a credible compilation witness having gathered and edited the whole scene down to a single relatable story from dozens of 'witnesses'. Crow knew this and would depend on her to uncover some tidbit he missed. The one thing he knew about Emma made him smile: he would get fair treatment in her story if he followed her suggestions. Diners in rural areas of the country's breadbasket were meeting places, pass-thru sort of entities where folks gathered, left a nugget of info with somebody like Emma who would inevitably start a conversation as she poured coffee with, "I heard..."

"Anybody strange in here today, say within the last six hours or so?" This was a just a guess. He assumed that the body hadn't been there when the sun went down and because this place doubles as a bar in the evening, it probably happened after closing, when the place reverted back into a diner. State law prohibited the sale of alcohol after one a.m.

"C'mon, Sheriff. The usual suspects I suppose. The bus people but there weren't that many of them last night." She brought him his revised order, dropping the sodden waffles that were under the heat lamp into the trash. He thanked her.

"Well, you're the only lead I've got now so, for me, can you try and remember? Something? Anything?"

"The bus pulled in just before dawn. Four people came in. The driver, a hippie girl of about twenty of so, a scrawny kid who asked for the bathroom key. And he never returned it come to think of it. It's probably still out there in the parking lot somewhere. Oh, and some older lady." Crow had seen the mark on the dead man's throat but didn't want to draw any conclusions on how or even why it had gotten there. Anybody with a baseball bat could have struck him but there were two of them. That would, he thought, be a bit much for any of the people she had just described.

"The scrawny kid," he said, just thinking out loud, "he didn't come back in?"

"No," she answered, "you don't think?"

"If I was thinking, I'd be doing nothing but guessing but if I was, I'm betting he didn't do that. Not with a key tied to a ladle." He took a sip of his coffee and said, "He had help or a savior."

The medical examiner had made a quick assessment of the scene and came in and sat down next to Crow. The victim he told him, whispering in his ear, just out of earshot of Emma, was taken down by a single punch to the throat. This made Crow swear. He threw a ten dollar bill on the counter and turned to leave. He caught Emma's eye. "If you think of anything."

As he exited the door, she remembered Santo. He would

have been capable of doing what the medical examiner had said had happened. He certainly wasn't from around here and this was a good reason to make it known to law enforcement. She had no idea why she didn't mention Santo at the time but she still could. And as she watched Crow and the ME walk towards the scene, even though she still had plenty of opportunity to do so, she decided not to mention him.

Crow was okay with the delayed reporting. He knew that the time he needed to jump all over this was slipping past quickly. He found the key to the restroom outside, about twenty feet from the body. The medical examiner was his wife's cousin and the town doctor. He was a capable man with a curious eye for detail. Crow and he would talk for hours about the way people lied even in light of overwhelming evidence to the contrary. For him, it was often the "I wasn't speeding, officer" and for the doctor, it was "I've been watching my diet" which was typical of folks around here who wanted help but valued their privacy more. Or perhaps, like Emma, they were fearful of exposure to those private thoughts.

"So, some skinny kid needs to go the bathroom, gets the key from Emma in there and on his way, gets jumped by this guy, and maybe his brother. Maybe not. Maybe both. There's no car in the lot so these boys came from somewhere." They both looked at the wild tangle of overgrowth that bordered the lot. Crow then looked down the road in both directions. "But something happened in between."

The ME offered, "Maybe the kid ate his spinach, grew some Popeye arms and knocked this guy into the next hell bound train."

Crow wouldn't dismiss the possibility but it was doubtful that the kid had anything to do with it. Emma's emphasis on the word skinny and the obvious size of the dead man suggested that spinach or not, that he was not the suspect. He was, although, probably the witness. Maybe the Mason boy was jumped and the kid saw something, he thought. "We'll need to get that bus before it arrives in Chicago." Or maybe not, he thought. He figured that whoever had done this wouldn't have decided to simply wander into the diner with a dead man lying in the parking lot.

Crow walked back towards the diner, drawing a straight line in his mind from the body to the front door. Inside, he tried to see the body from every window. In both instances, it was just out of line-of-sight. You would have been able to see the bus under the lot lights, parked about fifty feet from the front door. It would have been impossible to stand inside the diner and not witness that, at that early hour with only a handful of customers, all of whom would have had their backs to the large diner windows. Only Emma would have been able to see who exited the bus. And if she was telling the truth, and he had no reason to not believe that was the case, then only the skinny kid, wandering towards the rear of the building to use the lavatory in back would have seen what had happened. Unless, the body had been there for several minutes prior.

The sheriff walked back outside, trying to capture all of the possible vantage points. He walked back into the diner and sat down at the counter. Emma wordlessly motioned to him with the coffee pot aloft and he nodded yes.

"You know, Emma. If you didn't see anything else and you didn't serve no one suspicious, then either that Mason fella, more specifically Deeker Mason, the oldest boy in a long line of troublesome youths pouring out of Bond County on regular basis these day, either was dead when the bus pulled up, which I'm thinking was not the case, because that would have been noticeable to any other patron coming in, and he was not exactly a small bump in the lot, which means, the person who did this was on the bus." He paused for another moment. "What time do you come on?"

She answered, "Right around four. After the bar stops

serving, it takes about an hour for the folks to wander out and home, or maybe they go home. The diner part never closes but their ain't usually anybody in here when I get here. Just the bar cook doubling as the diner cook. He is more like a placeholder. You know Cedar, right?" Cedar got his name from his reddish complexion and the fact his clothes always smelled like they had been mothballed in a cedar chest.

"I haven't seen him, well, since the last time I arrested him couple years back."

"He's been staying out of trouble. But he's the only one here then." For moment, he wondered whether he should consider Cedar a suspect but decided against it. Some people are runners and some people are fighters, even if they are wrong. Cedar was a runner. And Crow knew he was fast.

"That puts us back to someone on the bus. The skinny kid is a no, or so it would be assumed. He might be the victim. The hippie girl sure as hell didn't take out that Mason fella. The bus driver is out, just from a logistical standpoint. Cedar can be written off and I'm assuming you didn't murder the bastard yourself. So, our guy has to have been on the bus."

Emma looked at him and then away. With her back to the sheriff she commented, "But you don't sound so sure." She was right, he was not so sure.

"Does that bus stop here every day?"

"It does, that's the first bus; there's another one that comes by in the late afternoon."

"And if goes onto Chicago from here? No other stops?"

"I really can't say. We don't talk, except for the pleasantries of the job I'm obliged to participate in. The driver of the early bus is big, fat slob of a man who acts like a bad husband. So, he and I never really hit it off, if you know what I mean. You know, grumpy and in and out in a flash." Crow just smiled.

He had tracked a friend at Precinct 42 in Chicago and explained what had happened. The bus had a three-hour head start, based on his calculations and only had a little over a hundred miles left on the journey. He radioed one of his friends in transit enforcement at the bus station to check out the arrival. He was able to make his way over to the platform just as the bus arrived in Chicago. This was just fortunate. One minute later and the passengers would have dispersed onto other buses or disappeared into the big city.

The cop stepped onto the bus when the door opened and instructed everyone that he would like a moment of their time. The driver was unable to give the officer a head count but he thought it was ten, coming out of Harrisburg. There were only nine on the bus. The "hippie girl" Emma had described chose to leave her conversation with Santo out of her recollection. The scrawny kid was also questioned but said he couldn't remember anything. The cop could do little else but take their names and information, which was not verified and let them go. He had been instructed to focus on the skinny kid, the only one who might have been in the vicinity of the incident. He did adding, "that the skinny kid sure as hell didn't throw any punches." No one else remembered anything. Without a description and no one offering up any details, Crow had reached an investigative dead end.

When Emma "recalled" her side of the story, it was much later in the day. She called Crow at his office. She said that there was a young man who came in. "He was blonde." Santo had brown hair. "He was short too, kind of stocky and seemed brooding, not the kind you'd mess with." Santo was tall and athletic with a disarming smile that he could unconsciously weaponize with sexual accuracy when the time required it. She was lying but she seemed unable to help herself. She also failed to mention the driver who gave him a ride. Crow had a false description, no direction, no mode of escape travel and one less local criminal.

5

About the same time Santo was buying a fresh pair of jeans and two new shirts at Famous-Barr department store in downtown St. Louis, Sheriff Crow was discussing the case with his long-time friend in that city's police department. It was more of an exchange of ideas that anything that resembled an investigation. Four days had passed and the trail, what little of it there had been, had gone cold. Crow was wondering if he should let it just stay that way.

"Losing a scumbag like Deeker Mason is not what you would call much of a loss," he said into his end of the phone. The sun was just setting over Crow's small jurisdiction, a rural enclave encompassing about eight square miles. Each season had its own expression on this landscape on the eastern end of what was once the greatest prairie. Summer and winter were blindingly brutal in their extremes. Early spring, with the corn barely poking through the ground, the hope and promise of another bounty, the way the sun kissed the surroundings, both in the morning and night, made him glad he had moved here thirty years ago. But autumn, he realized, was just a time to gather what you could. As he grew older, he felt less inclined to venture beyond these borders. It was his hope that those borders would not force him to extend his reach. But this case was both a vexing curiosity and it cause him to suffer an ethical bout of ennui.

His friend in St. Louis, recently promoted to the rank of

captain asked the question any law enforcement officer might ask a fellow brother, except it sounded like a statement: "It's still a dead body, Jack." Donal McGuire knew his friend was not calling to tell him he gave up. Jackson Crow was not a lazy country sheriff. He had been elected over six times and for the last several elections, he ran unopposed. People liked him, even if he hadn't grown up in the area, he had become one of their respected sons.

"I know, Donal and it's still a crime. But this one is different. His demise probably ex-ed out about fifty to hundred future crimes, just like that." He sighed heavily into the receiver. "I'm just not so sure this is worth an active investigation. Mason gets killed. His brother is in the wind. And no one saw a thing."

"So, do you think it was planned?" The answer to this question had broader implications amongst police. Nobody thinks that rationalizing this sort of act should come with any mercy and the court system does treat premeditation seriously, more so than every other instance when a dead body results due to some other kind of bad action.

"I talked to the kid, the one who was a suspect until we laid eyes on him. The kid didn't look strong enough to open a jar of pickles and while we all know that is not a disqualifier, the officer who spoke with him said 'no way', which left us with him as the victim, or the one who was about to be the victim." This was the result of one of McGuire's cops even engaging with the young man was the result of a series of lucky events. The bus driver had talked to the kid, or depending on which one you asked, the kid talked to the driver for the entire trip.

"You know how some people position themselves so they can talk to the driver during the trip, using that front row seat as a way to see the road the way the driver does, or make sure he stays awake because they are scared shitless. I gotta hand to the driver of these buses, I couldn't put up with mindless chatter from just over my shoulder all night long."

Jack sat in his small office and listened to Donal. The two had met at a trade association meeting held by the just founded Indiana Police Association, when the two of them were working in Indianapolis. He could see the man on the other end of the line as if he were sitting across from him, flat top marine cut over a round Irish face, the kind that alternates from cerise to coral depending on whether he was enraged or not.

"The driver made mention of the fact the kid was dressed different after the stop at the diner. He said the kid, who has now been identified as Zek Rushtin told him he had 'had an accident and soiled his pants and had to change them', or so the driver said, one thing led to another and he told him about the guy in the parking lot."

Jack said, "Nice police work, Donal."

"Let's not get too far ahead of this. I only got pieces." He continued suggesting the kid definitely had help and when we finally tracked him down, hit was confirmed. "he told us that the guy who stepped in, and from what he told us, even though it happened fast, the unknown who stepped between him and we're guessing Deeker, came out of nowhere, as if he suddenly appeared, like some fucking guardian angel. He said he never even noticed him, said he was curled up in a ball on the ground, when he heard the first guy, the dead guy, hit the ground."

Zek reluctantly relived the moment for the officer who tracked him down. "Yes, he was embarrassed at having pissed himself but he was headed to the john when it happened. Falling to the ground like he did was a little bit of both shock and shame. All he saw really were feet, the dead guy hit the ground and the other one wasn't far behind. All he saw was fucking feet."

Jack sighed heavily at the fact they had nothing. He attempted to recap the scene, "So, if we are piecing this together, the next guy, who was Mason's brother, they call him Barty by the way, left the kid and tried to help his brother. And of course, the vic said at this point all he saw were feet and then the other guy drops. But something is wrong with that and unless he plans on telling the rest of the story, like, did the assailant help him to his feet or simply disappear into the wind, like he arrived, was he on the bus, had he ever seen the mystery man before, I can't move forward."

"The officer did ask him those questions and each answer was no, often empathic." He knew that the kid, who had returned to his classes at Loyola and was probably reliving the incident over and over in his head. He was certain of it.

"But until he has suffered enough mental anguish to give up his so-called savior, the trail is essentially ice."

"You think the kid is protecting the assailant?" Donal had seen it before, victim gets saved as the person who save them commits a crime in the process and they fear retribution for their champion.

"Wouldn't you if you were him? Two guys approach this kid who is trying to take a leak. I think the Mason boys were just using opportunity, we're still checking to see if they were drinking at the same place just a few hours earlier and were just hanging around outside when the bus pulls up and they make some spur-of-the-moment decision to jump the kid. The kid, the dead guy, the other guy who was also beaten hard enough to hit the parking lot and the kid curled up in the fetal position, four people, one who we have and he saw nothing."

Donal corrected him. "I think the kid was first jumped by Barty Mason who leaves the kid, who is already on the ground when he leaves Rushtin to see what's happening behind him, he sees Deeker hit the ground and Barty goes to defend Deeker. And then he's down. All the kid remembers is this man just standing there, looking all relaxed according to him. And then he just vanishes." Both men paused to let the information sink in, hoping that recounting it again, for the hundredth time, would have shed some new light on the incident.

"So anyway, that answers the change of clothes question."

The other witnesses who might have seen something, the passengers on the bus told the police that interviewed them that they saw nothing. "The other passengers all checked out, mostly locals, like the kid. There was a young girl who was probably lying but she sure as fuck didn't do it and there is no record of her traveling with anyone. She was the only outsider. She bought a ticket in Philadelphia and was headed to Ann Arbor via Chicago. That's all we know. Driver didn't do a head count after leaving Harrisburg. Said if they had a ticket and didn't cause any trouble, he could've cared less."

Jack added, "We spoke to the customers at the diner who might have been there around that time and they didn't see anything. The waitress confirmed that as well."

"What?" the voice on the phone asked.

"Yeah, I know. Nobody at the diner saw a thing. So, this guy just pops in and out, from fucking thin air and leaves us a dead body." Crow thought about this for a minute.

Whoever this person was, he did everyone a favor. Would not pursuing this case actively make him an accomplice or simply complicit? Should he follow his instincts and pressure Emma, a person he had known for decades? He believed she had seen something but he didn't want to ask her the same question, suggesting she had lied. There was something in her expression, the slight shift between the Emma he knew and the one the stranger had talked to, the one she claimed to have not met.

"Do you think the assailant was on the bus?" Donal asked

this even as the interviews his officer had done suggested otherwise.

"I do. Most everyone on that bus was sitting up towards the driver and the girl, according to your guy was in the back, or towards the back. She knows something."

"What makes you think she knows something?"

"She's in the wind now, Jack. Gave her name as Stella Blue, which I doubt is her real name."

"She knows something." Jack thanked his friend for listening. The girl on the bus knew something. Emma knew something. Barty knew something. The kid knew something. Hell, he thought, everyone knew something including him. "So, why," he asked himself aloud to his empty office, "do none of us want to do anything about it?"

*****

About the same time the two officers were concluding their conversation about the ghostly presence that was responsible for the first murder since Jack Crow was elected to the office of Sheriff, Santo Aretino was in the barbershop of the Mayfair Hotel in downtown St. Louis. The old black man had told him he couldn't cut his hair until it was washed. So Santo checked in to the hotel, paying with cash, and cleaned himself up before heading back down to the barber.

He hadn't been to a barber in over five years, occasionally trimming his beard himself but otherwise letting his thick hair fall down the center of his back. The haircut and shave made him look younger but for some reason, no different. He shied away from his reflection, preferring to avoid examining the person he presented to the world. He sensed that some people found him menacing, while others seemed to swoon and this was both disturbing and confusing. Interacting with people was unavoidable and he had more or less learned how to do so without attracting too much attention. Or so he thought. He was in fact, unforgettable and yet, conveniently forgotten. The barber, who had remained silent through the entire cut, handed him a mirror to look at the back of his head. He declined this view of himself as well.

The new clothes however, along with the haircut and shave made him feel better. He had grabbed sleep where he could, his insomnia keeping him from confronting the terrors of his night. This had been his demon for as long as he could remember. The dream he had had on the bus was still lingering as an unsettled haunting. He had bumped into the concept of dreams in numerous books, seeing it mostly as an author's tool to set the scene that otherwise couldn't be explained during waking hours.

He wondered why they did it. He knew that novelists were trying to mine some deeper hidden emotion that might be lurking below the surface, something only the unreal nocturnal wandering of the mind could uncover. Santo had always found the use of dreams petty and full of suggestion, the ploy of an atrophied imagination. He felt a little more empathetic when it came to the nightmares characters had. He had never had one that he could recall but he knew people that did. They seemed to be trapped in a very real place, enlisting their body to ward off some evil that was not there. Books with nightmares were easier to read but not by much. He still felt it was childish to include something that wasn't real inside something that wasn't real.

Some authors got it right. Shakespeare did but then he got most everything right in Santo's opinion. Kafka got it right with poor Gregor Samsa. Tolstoy got it right too. The dreams these writers gave their characters were nagging and relentless, as if they meant something and were not about to fade until the truth was told. Gregor became a bug and Anna feared childbirth. But the scene he witnessed on the bus was different. It was far into the future, in a place where memories had not happened yet, seeming nightmarish because it lacked any grounding in what he knew.

Santo did not yet believe it was a dream of premonition. As he thought about it, the details seemed to become less clear, as if fading with each review. There was nothing to hinge the thoughts on: why six men, seven including him; why did they look alike; why were they on stage; why did they appear to be a well-aged version of the man he might become?

While this was actively churning in his brain, he had made his way across the lobby, a luxurious affair that he was unaccustomed to visiting. His upbringing was blue-collar and hotels like this were not within the budget. In fact, his parent's idea of a dinner out consisted of fish and chips at the West End Boat Club, a small marina on the Delaware River. He never questioned this choice of restaurant, nor did he wonder why they went to a boat club when they owned no boat.

He slipped into the lobby bar and sat down. He threw a twenty dollar bill on the bar and ordered a Heineken. His thoughts were interrupted by a man sitting several stools to his left.

"Nice job," he said and raised his cocktail glass as if offering a toast. Santo took a second or two to drag himself from his thoughts. He didn't respond. He wasn't sure the man was speaking to him. He was dressed in a grey suit, his tie pulled loose over a white shirt.

The man looked around to see where the bartender was. He spotted him delivering drinks to a couple in a dimly lit corner. "You know, congrats on getting served."

Santo hadn't even thought about. His countenance was often seen as serious, deeply contemplative and as he often thought, framed with a certain kind of menace that often made any opening salvo in a conversation difficult for strangers. He was just as shocked when Stella Blue spoke to him on the bus.

The man had sharp angular features over an emaciated frame. His suit hung loosely over his shoulders, looking as if it was still on its hangar. Santo could see the man as a young man, cowering under the fists of those who sought to dominate the weak, encountering the school hall menacing that manifested itself as some kind of Darwinian rite of passage. He was the type of person that Santo found in situations he stepped in to save, to rescue from the threat of those who saw themselves as princes, the kid in the school hallway, the skinny boy in the diner parking lot. He was the one who would repel those who had an unhealthy connection to the most primal genetic code, the perversion suggesting that only the fittest survive. His natural domination depended on adaptation; these brutes refused to adapt, looking not at the act of brutality as unnatural and a socially impotent expression but instead as something that they simply did, without remorse or consideration, forethought or regret. The man sitting several stools away from him, drinking alone, was a man who had been, and quite possibly was still, a victim of the strong versus the weak.

"I'm Davis," he said when Santo didn't respond. "I just noticed your technique. Classy. Self-absorbed. You worked the part. I'd of served you." He stopped and looked down at his drink. This breaking of eye contact, the relinquishing of place as if he suddenly realized who he was, at least in his mind acted as an apology.

"I'm Sonny," he said deciding to break the awkwardness using the nickname from his youth as if it was alias, an also known as. It was a confusing reaction but he had seen it before. He felt compelled to apologize. ""I'm sorry. I was kind of lost in my own thoughts." He was amazed that the man would have even spoken to him.

The man relaxed and smiled. "I was saying or maybe

not, and now that I think about it, you getting served is not probably an issue with you. Folks don't see me the way they probably see you." This made Santo smile as well. He had been walking into bars since age thirteen and he knew part of his success was the swagger, an outward appearance that suggested he'd done this a million times before and of course, cash. What money didn't solve, his overly mature look fueled with hormones of unknown origin. He was still considered underage by the state of Missouri but the bartender never even thought of asking. He had been shaving with success since his last years in grade school at St. Rose and the hard shadow he wore before the beard grew in seemed to dismiss any additional questions the bartenders might have had. Now older, his beard aged him further. It was nicely trimmed, much of the last year coifed tightly around his jaw. It was still full of reddish hues and even though the barber had cut a considerable length from his hair, he had left enough to tie into a small ponytail.

"This is my last day in St. Louis," Davis began. "Tomorrow, this boy is headed to Wall Street to be a titan." He looked around at the empty seats next to him. "My so-called friends couldn't make the celebration. Work night, they said. Fuck them, I say. Can I buy you a drink?"

There it was: The vulnerability he often wondered about, the openness that some people he had met over his short life expressed with such ease, cast aside inside the improbable risk of a simple question. He was certain that the stranger was finding courage in the liquor he may have already consumed. Santo had seen his reflection and often wondered why, the way he seemed to appear to himself in the mirror, would anyone begin a conversation with him. It was a mystery. The world Santo knew beat those heart-on-a-sleeve emotions back without remorse.

Santo said, "Sure. I got nothing going on tonight." Davis

got up from his stool and moved closer to him. When he settled in and the bartender had delivered a fresh round of drinks, he asked him, "What's on Wall Street?"

Davis looked at him with the sort of expression that suggested he was in some possession of knowledge that bordered on condescending. That was one of those looks that some brute would have found too tempting to accept without attempting to wipe it from his face. He seemed to reconsider his response by briefly lowering his eyes. In a less abrasive voice, he then asked Santo, "You don't know about Wall Street?"

"The books I've read mention the place, and not always in flattering terms." He had found the portrayal of this hallowed place to be the venue of bosses and power, the place where the strong go to exert their will over money and those with a less rounded experience. Not being someone like that, he didn't do any further research into the place. He paused to take a sip of his beer.

"The stock market, my young friend. The center of capitalism. The place where the smartest people profit from the stupidity of other smart people and more than one dumb participant." He leaned in slightly, as if whispering some secret about the place often considered the financial capital of the world. "You see, Sonny, everybody is scared of something. Rich people, those bosses you mentioned, are scared of losing what they have. Poor people are scared they'll never have enough money. Wall Street is where these people go to a special kind of church, to pray for the advantage, the one win that has to have one loser, or thousands of them. It's where fear comes to roost."

"And why would you want go there?" He could easily understand the base emotion of dominance and when it came to money, he was aware that it was a quest that never seemed to be satisfied. He knew that power was not democratic but it was anonymous. You could look like anyone, come from any

74

background, or even risen from the ashes of your own mistake, but the power that money delivered was unlike anything before or after it: It didn't care who had it or what they did with it. And most importantly, it didn't care how you came to be in possession of it.

He laughed, his Adam's apple undulating grotesquely against the skin on his neck. "I got noticed for the work I did at the bank I work for, or worked for until last week, by an investor and he said I was wasting my talent. He got me a job interview."

"So you're off to greener pastures?" This made him laugh.

"Yeah, greener. No pun intended, right?" At this, he raised his glass to his new drinking buddy. "Not that I wasn't happy at Boatman's. I've been managing the investments for the bank and its mortgage company for the last eight years. And I've done some good work. The bank is growing. Got thirty eight branches and we're the oldest bank in these parts." He looked away at some point over the rim of his glass, as if he was recalling his role during those years. It was the look of someone second guessing. He pulled himself out of it and turned to Sonny, "You really don't know anything about investing?"

"Not really," he replied, which might have been considered a falsehood in some circles in part because he had read about the historical underpinnings of money and machinations of the people who developed great wealth from opportunity. People like Alexander Hamilton and Nicholas Biddle, William Jennings Bryan and of course J.P. Morgan played significantly as characters in the history books he had read, starring as real-life actors portraying the country's earliest financiers. There were Jewish houses and Yankee bankers and a world that grew on its own to finance the growth of the U.S. He found the stories interesting but failed to connect with their ambitions. So, by default he did know something about investing but had never found the idea appealing.

Davis seemed to smile at thought of making the stranger a convert. "A couple of years back, this book called the "Last Days of the Club" came out. Maybe you read it, maybe not. It was about this pivot point between what Wall Street was and what it was to become. Not the best read and if you ask me, sort of pessimistic and dense but if what the author said was true, even if he almost sounded as if he wished it wouldn't, did come true, then it was the ultimate place to make money. 'Her voice was full of money'."

Santo asked him if that line was from Gatsby. "It is and it also applies to Wall Street, a siren whose only purpose in life is to lure the smart and the dumb into the same pool and allow only the strong swimmers survive. So, I managed to get a job at Salomon Brothers, a big trading firm that is about to build a bridge over that watery abyss. This is a dream come true job for me. So, tonight, I celebrate." He turned to Santo and again, raised his glass. "I celebrate with you!"

Santo raised his glass in response and said "Congrats to you then, Davis. May you become a titan, I guess."

"King of fear," he replied lifting his tumbler higher, tilted in Santo's direction. "The scourge of princes." The last comment had come as a surprise and he looked closely at the man sitting next to him. Eva had called him that. The phrase, she suggested, described his foolhardy way of interrupting the natural order of things. He intervened, she told him when the princes felt as if they had no challenger to their birthright. She was talking about the gas station and his rescue of Kendris, a natural order disrupted, albeit somewhat heinous by its nature, and created an alternate series of events that led him to her front porch.

But more than Eva had used that phrase. St. Bridget at

St. Rose Catholic Grade School did as well, Brother Connors at St. Ignatius Catholic High School for Boys, who believed himself a prince, considered Santo's presence in his school a threat, a menace to his authority and under his brief, cynically would tell him "I will get you gone one day, you so-called scourge of princes." The beat cop cum detective cum narcotics officer, John Tell devoted his life to trying to understand and apprehend him for his disruption of the natural order in the city he had left.

That natural order was not much more than an activity that had manifested in a string of mostly coincidental beatings to deserving 'princes'. Was he what they had described? He chose not to reminisce. It was easier than looking back. Looking back meant reviewing, filtering it through some sort of ethical lens. Was it right, he refused to ask.

His most recent disruption of the natural order happened only days ago, at a bus stop eight hours outside of Lancaster, where, as if those disruptions follow him like a tailwind, he had boarded a bus to escape another recently delivered princely retribution to three college kids who had abducted Eva's neighbor's young girls, to the gas station, to a time not that distant in terms of hours or days or years, all the way back to high school, where he saved the same type of boy Davis once was or perhaps still is, to a time in grade school where he had come of age too soon. It all seemed so endlessly connected but Santo had yet to make the connection. He refused to. Do the saved become their own version of a prince, circling back on the same people who bullied them? he asked himself. Is this what happens when the righteous are saved? He had never given it a thought before this.

And what about him? What did this make him? Before he gave it much consideration, Davis began to lay out his plan.

"Salomon doesn't know it yet but they are only my doorway." His voice was gaining momentum and clarity, as if passion gave it depth. "My access point if you will. I have ideas that will change the way Wall Street makes money and in the process, make money myself. By the bucket load. No. By the train load."

Since Davis seemed to be conducting this conversation more as a monologue, Santo decided to say just enough to allow him to talk. He fancied himself a skilled listener and when someone like this wants to talk, listening was the only option, with the level of attentiveness adjusted for the topic. But he found this interesting.

According to Davis three things were happening or about to happen and he wanted to, as he put it, "Be on the crest of that wave." The first thing he explained to Santo had something to do with taxes. Santo had yet to pay any. His activities, which he would not have defined as criminal despite its status among law enforcement, had created vast sums of income for a kid barely past legal driving age. This was not the kind of money you could tell your parents about, and worse, not the kind of money that could be spent without alerting someone with just the slightest hint of curiosity as to its origins. Money he had found out was both a boon and burden and money gained through illegal activity was twice that and more. He couldn't upgrade his car or clothes without questions he didn't want to answer. He did have a job but the money earned from it was earmarked by his parents into some Depression era contract designed to make him give his paycheck to them and they would award him about twenty percent for his own spending. That was technically all the money he had and that was, for appearance's sake, all he could spend. He spent the lion's share of this stipend on albums and concerts and gas for his '63 Ford.

So he had his public money and his private income. Because his needs were small, he simply saved his drug money, tucking up into a drop-ceiling tile in his basement, alongside his growing stash of exotic weeds.

Davis had said that a couple of accountants in Philadelphia had uncovered a provision in the tax code that allowed wealthy people to save even more for their retirement than they currently were allowed by law to do. Santo knew the word retirement but not the concept. At barely twenty, this was so foreign and far away, knowing what it was became ancillary information in a world of more pressing matters. No one in the all of the books he had read, ever seemed to retire. Apparently, retirement is for those who lack both importance and imagination.

"These two guys don't know what they did. But when I interviewed for the job, I told them how a lot of money could be made. And you know what, the dumb fucks hadn't even heard of it. Right in the fucking forest and they were missing the money trees."

"What did they do?" Santo asked and before the question was finished, Davis jumped in with an excited answer.

"Not what they did; why. They did their job, which was to cheat the government for their wealthy employers. Poor people try to keep their money from running out; rich people spend money to keep their money from running out the front door and directly to the U.S. Treasury. Naw," he corrected himself, "it's more why they did what they did and the fact that this would change the whole pension system." Santo cocked his to the side.

Davis picked up on his body english right away and almost without missing a beat, continued to explain the concept that had him almost dancing on his stool. He looked around as if revealing a secret of great importance, lowering his voice, he almost whispered, "Right now, companies keep employees loyal and coming to work by promising to help them when they get too old to work any longer. These companies felt like they had some obligation and in truth, they might have, just a little bit, but hey, it's business.

"So anyway, these guys opened the door to that way of thinking and in the process, gave me an opportunity to show that misplaced benevolence the exit. I mean really, is your company supposed to care for you after you retired just because you showed up for work every day? Fuck that." Davis, the weak one was now speaking like a prince.

So far, he had introduced Santo to a world he had no previous knowledge of and in the process, was making complete sense. "Sounds kind of rude to me," was all he could think of saying. Princes, he thought. He knew that Umberto, the man who was considered by many to be his father had worked at the same place, a dismal refinery in Marcus Hook, a town that seemed to be smeared by the industry, one tangled array of pipes and silos, smoke and towers with flames igniting the ashen sky. He still did as far as Santo knew, with no intention of changing jobs. He wondered if he had a pension. Everyone he knew did what they did until they seemed to die or, and although he hadn't paid much attention to it before, retire. So, people like Umberto weren't looking for an opportunity to do better elsewhere. They stayed put, raised a family, and then what? Did those companies have an obligation to invest for their future after their years of service? Davis was talking about the foolhardiness of this concept and how he, without remorse or consideration, planned on dismantling it once inside a huge financial institution.

To help show his interest, which had yet to be piqued, even if he had never heard of what this man was talking about, even if the taste of the idea was beginning to sour in his mouth, he asked: "So, a company saves some money for the worker and gives it to him when he retires?"

"Exactly. These two accountants found a billion dollar loophole in that plan. Or should I say, billions. Here's what would happen: the worker would be allowed to save for his own fucking retirement and the company might help, enable, even contribute a few coins on their behalf, I haven't completely worked out the details, figured I'll do that as soon as I had a paycheck in hand, but that's it in a nutshell. Make retirement a benefit but not a benefit."

"And that's investing?"

"Oh, hell no." Davis let out a small chuckle as he waved the bartender down for another round. "It's corporate greed that will be colored as corporate benevolence. It is just genius." Each of those last four words were spoken slowly and deliberately. "The worker will go from getting a monthly check from the company to having to save for it himself. And that's where I come in again. First, it is presented as a big money savings for the company and of course, the poor schlep won't know what to do so someone like me steps in to help him manage the whole affair. On each end of the transaction, I make money. Or, the company I work for makes money and I get promoted, eventually to partner and become immortalized for my adaptation." He waved his empty glass towards the bartender, again, impatiently.

The two men were alone now. Santo slid two twenty-dollar bills on the bar, giving her some comfort that she would be paid. She winked at him.

"You said three things."

He moistened his lips with his whisky and continued, "Well, these corporate types are going to need someplace for their employees to stash that cash. Ever heard of mutual funds?" Santo shrugged his shoulders and shook his head no.

"It's a scheme. Love that fucking word, by the way. Anyways, it is a kind of group investment where everybody puts money in the fund and lets the fund manager do the investing because they're too scared, too dumb, or too lazy to do it themselves. So, we, my firm and I bundle up these funds and sell them to employees, for a small fee. Where the real money is, is inside the fund. We'll run the fund, charge fees and expenses and then charge fees and expenses for selling the fund to some company for their workers to use."

Santo smiled at the idea of some smug ass like Davis making money on both ends of the transaction. It seemed to be an endless loop of profit. "Sounds amazing." But the whole idea was making him nauseous. Here he was, sitting with a man of no discernable physical stature speaking as if he were the muscled brute in the room, all stag in rut, money as his oestrus hind.

"It is. Just remember this Sonny; there are three kinds of investing. The first is investing in things like cars, watches, gold, and real estate. These are illiquid assets for the most part. The next is ideas, which is essentially what Wall Street does best. A guy starts a business with some idea the world can't do without and Wall Street finds money for him to do so, and they make money by enabling. The last kind is debt. This is where you lend money to make money and all you need is someone who wants to borrow, what they do not currently have." He looked at his watch. "Shit. I've got to go. But you should look into it," he said sliding carefully off his stool. He began fumbling for his wallet but Santo waved him off.

Davis stumbling from the stool, his long legs protesting at the sudden request to walk. He took a moment to gather his balance and left the lounge. Santo, finished his drink, waving off the bartender as she tried to make change. She smiled and he returned the gesture and left.

As he made his way to the lobby, he thought of a question he wished he had asked. Davis was navigating the revolving doors, disappearing into the darkness outside. He began walking quickly to the same door Davis had left.

The man had turned right and was now out of sight. The night had brought a chilling rain that made the empty streets shine. He spotted him about a block away, just as he saw two men emerge from an adjacent alleyway. They grabbed the man he had just spent the better part of the evening with, discussing a world he had never even known existed, a world that seemed fraught with an imbalance of those too naïve to know better and those who acted as if these neophytes were just another passing meal to be preyed upon and eaten. But during that whole conversation, which was a peppered with Davis's grandiose plan to take on and eventually over Wall Street, he had found his curiosity piqued. But Santo had failed to ask how to get into this world without getting eaten first.

By the time he caught up, the men had forced the more than inebriated Davis to his knees and were demanding something from him. He could hear his voice, pleading and much smaller than the commanding tone he had taken in the bar. In one place he was king, or the future scourge of princes, soon to be a titan, and here he was back in high school, cowering, afraid and defenseless.

Santo walked up behind the taller of the two men and grabbed him at the base of his neck. With his hand hold and the sudden forward motion, he slammed him face first into the wall. Davis covered his head and folded onto the ground. The second man turned but was frozen, surprised by the sudden intervention. Four long seconds had elapsed before the other assailant whirled around at his friend's attacker, four long seconds where he was undecided on whether to check the condition of the man slumped against the wall or to take action against this intruder. If he were able to answer later, he would have told anyone who asked that he should have probably cut his losses and helped his friend.

He barely had the opportunity to mouth the words, "motherfucker" before the heel of Santo's hand drove his nose up into his skull. He dropped solidly to the ground.

Looking at the three men, one whimpering at the edge

of a puddle, one holding his forehead and writhing in pain, and the other making no motions, Santo had a full second to decide what to do next. He helped Davis to his feet and quickly moved the dazed man out of the alley. He tried to look back but Santo's grip under his shoulder elevated him slightly, leaving his feet to almost drag along the wet pavement. They turned the corner and exited the alley. They kept moving for another block before he decided to let Davis recover.

"So," Santo began, "where do I start?"

The question baffled Davis at first. He was still trying to piece together the last three minutes or so, the threat, the fact that the threat suddenly disappeared, and their hasty exit occurred so fast, his brain was not allowing him to process the events. It was however trying to focus on something.

"Sonny?" he asked as if he was only just getting his focus.

"So, if I want to begin to invest, where do I start? Reading books? What?" His question had an air of impatience. He fought the urge to look around for either the men or the police.

"I suppose," he said, spitting phlegm and wiping his eyes, "you could start reading the Wall Street Journal and definitely pick up anything Benjamin Graham wrote." When he coughed, it seemed to be painful.

"And then?"

"Find a broker, I guess." He let the "I guess" part pass without comment. It is amazing how certain a man can be until he is met with a crisis, something that challenges their bravado in ways they had not anticipated. The world allows us to grow up, Santo thought, but often doesn't allow us to go too far.

He started to walk away when Davis decided to add an unusual piece of advice, considering his circumstances. He said, "Buy only what no one wants." The two men looked at each other, Davis all angles and jutting elbows and knees, his suit torn at the shoulder, and Santo, looming like a shadow on the rain glistened street, large but somewhat ethereal.

"Sonny," was all he heard as he walked away, returning to the hotel lobby.

*****

Sheriff Crow had expanded his search area to points north of Chicago, and into Michigan and Wisconsin. The area of inquiry was now expanded as far as Des Moines and into Kentucky, but he doubted that he had gone south. He had contacted the bus stations in the major cities and asked that they looked at a sketch he had created. It was a composite based on the piecemeal information he had pulled from the young man the assailant had rescued, the driver of the bus who seemed to recall a passenger who had remained quiet about fourteen rows back, and the person Trailways had determined sold this suspect the ticket in Lancaster. Although the waitress at the diner had been the only one who had clearly seen Santo, she kept the vision of his face in her private thoughts. Crow knew she knew something, sometimes those hunches were worth pursuing, other times they were only seedlings in a rocky crevasse. She had looked at the sketch and commented that the man was handsome and she would have remembered that face. He thanked her but decided to not press her for the real truth.

He had decided to treat his search for this mystery man without the help of the FBI. In fact, he hadn't even reported Deeker Mason's death and his next of kin, Barty, who had died about a week later in a bar fight. There was no one to press charges in the case and no one to grieve the two men. At this point, the still unidentified man was simply a person of interest.

The man in the portrait was both handsome and at the same time, edged in a sort of roughness that seemed to be a composite of everything these people thought about in a superhero, chiseled and contemplative. His hair was long and although they couldn't agree on the color of it, or the color of his eyes, but they all agreed he was someone they would want on their side of the fight. That may have been due to an epic reputation that had emerged when there is scant information to refute. This made Crow wonder if they were, for some reason that seemed completely human to everyone but a cop, trying to protect him. The skinny kid may have summed it up best when he told Crow by phone, "He took on two strangers like he had been dipped in the River Styx."

As Santo boarded the bus in St. Louis, showing his one-way pass to the driver, the man examined a sheet of paper with a drawing on it. He looked at Santo carefully and punched his ticket. He was not the kind of person who was accustomed to helping the police catch someone who had every right to travel without the hassle of the law. He had failed to see the resemblance in the well-groomed passenger and allowed him to board.

Santo was not aware of that he was being pursued, nor was he aware that the St. Louis police would be adding their significant resources to the search once they found the two men in the alley. That is, if they could tie the two incidents together.

Davis, unable to sleep, had turned himself in before heading to the train station. Although he was essentially the victim, he was also a witness and this made him feel obligated in some way to do the right thing. In this instance, the right thing involved lying.

The police had encouraged him to stay for further questioning but he refused. He had told them he was drunk when he stumbled on them lying in the alley. He made no mention of "Sonny" or the drinks they had earlier. Eventually, they told him he was free to go.

The police had found the two men where Davis had told them they would; one dead and the other close to that point. The sun had barely risen and the shadows were still long enough that the two bodies would have gone unnoticed for several more hours. The interviewing officer could tell by looking at Davis that he was not the one who inflicted what was apparently a bare-fisted assault.

The two cops on the scene recognized both men and wondered "if a career criminal is killed, does it make a difference if you didn't pursue the person who did it?" It was their job to uphold the law and not to treat anyone any differently. It would take days for any sort of consensus to gel about what took place in the alley. They were certain that Davis had been jumped and that he was unable to defend himself. That meant that someone saved him and that someone didn't wait around for a medal to be pinned to his lapel. They waited to see if a pattern of vigilantism developed but it didn't. They visited all of the drinking establishments within a four-block radius, questioned all of the bartenders working that night and while one of them did recognize Davis by their description, she said he was drinking alone. The incident simply faded away. By the time Sheriff Crow's half-hearted inquiry reached the police department of St. Louis, Santo was with the bison.

6

He had taken Davis's conversation to heart and purchased a handful of financial publications in the bus station before boarding the bus. Finding a Benjamin Graham book took a little bit more effort but he managed to secure a copy of "The Intelligent Investor" at a small bookstore about a block from the depot. The older woman behind the counter also recommended a book called "Economics" by John Maynard Keynes and a used and very dog-eared copy of "The Theory of Investment Value" by John Burr Williams. Santo bought all of them and hurried to meet his bus.

He settled in with this incredibly dry reading about a subject he had previously little interest in, and knew nothing about prior to having drinks with a stranger. There were three dominant themes in the books he had read in the past: love, love lost and wealth. These three emotions moved the world and people to do things they may not have otherwise attempted. He also took note that despite what hope and promise and access those three subjects offered a reader, a person in real life, the people he knew around him, the core of each of these was isolation.

Wars were waged under the premise of power and land acquisition but at the heart of what actually occurred could be traced to one of those three subjects. History followed great unions and disenfranchised relationships. Science and philosophy sought to understand the universe not because it was there but because it was admired and even revered. Religion, a topic Santo had long since lost interest in was a belief that some sort of universal love was at play and if lost, so would be the person. Santo existed without love and therefore, he never experienced the loss of love. But as he read, he felt the pull of wealth and how it impacted certain men and eluded others.

As he read he could feel the tug of what they were trying to tell their readers. These authors were the sages of the new world order, Plato under Buttonwood trees. They had made their profits by understanding the emotional underpinnings of people, how those people reacted and in turn, how they should act in response. He had been a masterful dealer of drugs, cornering the entirety of Delaware County and beyond, managing to elude the law and profiting greatly. This was similar to what these men were suggesting even if their efforts were considered legal. And although he had championed an ideal of saving those who were weaker from their natural threats, he could not see how his advantage as the supplier was just as ethically ambiguous. The weak make mistakes, choose the easiest path, listen to their basest senses while ignoring the underpinnings of logic. People didn't need to smoke pot, they wanted to. And he had not yet confronted his own role in that process. What he did acknowledge was the end. And as he read, he was beginning to see a way to benefit from the money he had made without having to deal additional drugs.

Santo began with the six hundred plus page tome by Williams. Bringing nothing but the conversation he had recently had with Davis to the effort, he was open to what this experienced investor offered the reader. While the idea was foreign and some of the language seemed just as alien, he had followed enough characters in enough books to understand the concept of profit and profiting from another person's oversight or mistake.

Each word, each concept gave him pause. He wondered, as the tires rolled beneath him and the single dim light illuminated the coarse pages, had he ever examined what he was doing before he would do it? He had created a six-figure nest egg in an incredibly short span of time, juggling people and places and things all while dodging the law and barely acknowledging his paranoia. These pages suggested that only a fool would believe that everyone could profit. Was he a fool? In order to win, someone must lose. Investing seemed to be an arc that reached across the real and tangible to the abstract.

One could invest in time or in another person but in those instances, the profit was undetermined, hard to measure and difficult to manage. Santo had read about people who had invested in ideas and built businesses but they always seemed to be drawn to the risk rather than the reward. To these people, risk was both elation and destruction, elevated or defeated, winner or loser. While he saw the world as black and white, the perspective he had was perverted by so many morally ambiguous events in his past, some old, some recent. He asked himself if there was an acceptable medium, a place where everything was evenly dispersed.

The author in this instance was focused on something that he had yet to embrace: What the future held had value and that value could be determined by what happened in the present. This was not how he lived his life up until that point. His life up until this point was a complex algorithm that could be simplified for the sake of explanation as the sum of what happened in the minute before an event multiplied by how he felt after the fact. Because he felt nothing, no emotion, no connection and more importantly, no remorse, it was always something times zero, with zero as the only answer.

The book had plenty of what at first look appeared to be daunting mathematical equations, which if you gave this door stop sized book nothing but a cursory look, you might think these sentences were added to ward of the uninitiated. But the more Santo read, the more he felt a kinship to the text. He supposed, for the first time, that lurking somewhere on the pages was the answer to a question he had not yet asked. When he closed the book, most of the Midwest had drifted rhythmically beneath the bus tires.

Santo had always known that he stood on the thin line bordering between solitude and loneliness. Traveling left no distinction between the two, although he would have suggested that the act of moving forward was a journey towards something, and the interim moments were left to the traveler to determine how interactive their passage might be. He assumed that being lonely was no longer a choice once in motion but instead a place that someone might elevate themselves from, with something as simple as an hello to a stranger. Santo did not feel inclined but when the opportunity presented itself, he didn't shrink. For him solitude was how it is; loneliness is how it was supposed to be. He smiled as he thought about this, Eva and the talisman hanging beneath his shirt.

The more he read Graham's book on investing, the more he wondered why Davis had recommended it. Investing he was learning, seemed to be focused on the elements that Davis gleefully sought to master: how to profit from the stupidity of someone else. Davis had suggested that everyone knows something but not everyone knows something worthwhile. He explained it like this: "If I have a dollar and you refuse to buy it for a dollar, am I stupid for enticing you to make the purchase by lowering the price to ninety-nine cents?" He remembered the man laughing at that notion, his pointed Adam's apple jumping in tandem with the cackle that was emerging from his throat.

"The answer," he remembered him saying, "is yes, fucking yes. And no, fucking no. And that Sonny, is how the market works. You know the worth of something and wait until you can find some moron to sell it to you at that price. And you only have to walk ten feet outside your front door to meet one. But if you think about it, suppose the buyer knows something you don't? Suppose he knows that tomorrow or the next or a week later the value of the dollar is going to rise and be worth a dollar ten, or a dollar twenty and you, the one who sold it to me for ninety nine cents and laughed at your measly profit of one percent would have, had you held on just a little longer, profited by ten, maybe twenty percent, maybe more."

Graham seemed focused on the other side of the coin. He wanted, at least from what Santo had read, to keep his losses at a minimum. In other words, take a calculated risk. He wondered if that was what he had been doing in his own life. Each step he took forward, and he remembered telling Eva that was all he was looking to do, move forward to whatever the next step held, was not without its own risk.

And he had not calculated the outcomes prior to this urge to move. Was he taking too much risk by not considering whether to take the next step or not, or where that step might lead? Had he made any calculations about what he was doing, or why, before he did anything, what would happen if he had done what he had done? Davis had said he was "investing in myself", thrusting his skinny chest forward as he declared what he also described as his intrinsic value.

"What does that mean?" he remembered asking his growingly inebriated companion.

"Old man, you have much to learn," he had replied to the younger Santo, somewhat regally. He didn't mind the pompous condescension, reminding him of an emaciated Mr. Stryver, the same 'Bacchanalian propensities" but without the girth.

"Intrinsic value is what I see as my true value and what the rest of the world fails to value correctly. See, I know stuff that other people don't know I know and that is my margin for safety. Nothing nefarious, mind you. I don't intend to hire some sort of PI to find something worthy on my employer. No, no. My margin of safety," he says as he knocks himself on the side of his head with a boney knuckle, "was something I was born with."

"You don't have many friends, do you?"

"Why do you ask?" But Davis didn't wait for an answer. Nor did he answer Santo's question. He didn't have to. The ease with which he introduced himself and moved into his evening, intruding on a stranger's moment suggested he was more like he was. Where Santo was isolated, Davis seemed as if he had furthered his own isolation by insulating, adding a protective barrier of magnificence to his otherwise plain façade. "Being prepared for risk is not the same as planning for it. Planning demands calculation, will I win, will I profit, will I lose and if so, by how much? Calculated risk. I'm going to turn Wall Street on its ear by..." and his voice trailed off as he raised the glass to his mouth. He made a slight sucking sound as he tried to retrieve the last drops of liquor.

"By, doing what?" But the conversation had ended. Several minutes later, so would the lives of two strangers in an alley. The risks were outsized and demanded careful consideration but Santo had stepped in to help his new-found drinking buddy without acknowledging the risk or the value or the calculation or worse, how he happened to come along at exactly the right moment. What should have troubled Santo, was the absence of that event. He had already filed the moment in some mental shoebox, the memory ending at the boast Davis had made. By the time he had asked the last question, his recall had moved on.

As the bus sped towards the mountains rising ominously from the plains, he wondered how he could use this information about investing. He hadn't told Davis he had any money. He had simply listened to a man who probably made friends quickly and kept none of them. Was Davis the type that dispensed advice without regard, a soapbox preacher who knew prophets but had no provenance? Did this chance meeting mean anything? Was his advice easily transferrable into Santo's more realistic journey? Was that what Davis intended, to set him on some spiritual quest or was he just trying his best huckster on him before heading to New York? And in recommending the biblical sized missives from some old white men from another time, was he suggesting that Santo was supposed to pull some sort of life lesson from these pages?

The bus had traveled hundreds of mile across the paper flat terrain of the Midwest. If he had looked up from his window, he would have seen the heavens stretch across a cloudless sky, the black of dying corn fields against the brightly accentuate blackness of the night. Occasionally he would look up from the single overhead light, looking down the empty aisle at the bullet-straight highway. The few passengers that were on the bus with him could not be seen, the rounded shapes of their head now finding sleep more appealing than watching the nothingness slip past.

As the sun began to ascend in the back window, the bus slowed to a stop. This would happen with increasing frequency as civilization came into focus. First, small roadside gas stations, souvenir shops that doubled as bus stops and other random outbuildings with any purpose long since abandoned to the weather and then clustered dwellings where kid's toys lay waiting for resurrection and then to small towns that serviced a population of farmers and ranchers who lived beyond the white lined road. More people, people with purpose and destination entered the bus as they approached Denver. They looked serious and sleepy and disappointed. They would walk down the aisle looking for the right seat, one without occupants preferably and if not, one with an occupant they could feel safe sitting next to.

An old man sat next to Santo, entering after a brief stop in the small town of Bennett. He was dressed in a tan windbreaker and held a paper sack in his lap. He had folded his hands over the rolled closed opening.

"Hope you don't mind me sitting here," he said as the bus pulled back onto the two lane road. Over the last four stops, the bus had steadily gained passengers and was nearing capacity when the man sat down next to him.

"Not at all." Santo had never ridden on bus prior to this journey and was not aware of any etiquette in play for who sat where. He had noticed more than one potential seatmate size him up and look elsewhere. But the old man made no assessment.

"Irwin," he said, extending a wrinkled and well-weathered hand to him. Santo shook it feigning surprise at the strength in the grip. "Friends call me Hodgy. Last name's actually Hodgenson."

"Santo. Friends call me Sonny." He was unsure why at that moment he had pulled that old nickname out for use. He had promised himself to abandon it as he moved away from his past but it kept returning for a cameo. There was a long pause after the introduction so Santo returned to his reading.

"Santo? Is that eye-talian? Or Mexican?" There was a pause as Santo placed his finger in the book.

"Yes, I'm Italian."

"Graham, huh?" Hodgy asked as he looked at the book in his lap. "Brilliant man. All about value."

This comment caught Santo by surprise. He imagined that this book, although heavily technical through the middle chapters, was the kind of reading that would be preferred by the Davis type, profit oriented, well-dressed, and focused.

"You've read him?" The man was looking forward when he replied, an air of pride the seemed out of place with his wind-blown almost white hair.

"Of course I have. Came in handy in a previous career. I didn't always go along with everything he said, although, maybe in hindsight I should have had." With this he laughed, but uncomfortably. Santo sat looking at the man, struggling with the concept of the right comment.

He knew that the man had left the door ajar, a piece of conversational trickery he never mastered. He had read the great orators, the Ciceros and the Gandhis and the Websters. Arianne had loved the great conversationalists, the Gertrude Steins and the Catherine deRambouillets and the indigenous Iroquois who created the decorum of the talking stick that Franklin so admired. Where he retreated from the exchange, she relished it, encouraged it and as a result, taught him to listen. And yet, for all he knew and appreciated about words, Santo was not always comfortable stepping in through those openings. Rather that create an endless loop of possible outcomes, he simply remained silent.

The man sensing his curiosity that seemed laced with the manners not to pry, turned to Santo and said leaning in without looking at him, "So you know, the only reason I'm in this godforsaken part of the country was because my wife's parents needed help. No. I take that back. She needed to be with them and was probably going to go to them with or without me. So, I gave up a career managing other people's money back east, where it was comfortable and I was rich and all the amenities were at hand and moved here. And wouldn't you just know, a month later the father dies, a month later the mother dies, and here I am in the middle of butt fuck nowhere for the last three years." Hodgy laughed at this. "It's okay kid. I tell that story every now and again to anyone who hasn't heard it and you know what, it still sounds like I don't have a set of balls to call my own."

"Sounds noble enough," he answered. "Do you feel betrayed?" No sooner had he asked that question that he apologized for it.

"No worries, kid." The bus rolled forward toward Denver and Santo returned to his reading.

"You got people in Denver?" Santo was glad he hadn't asked the most annoying question he had found since he began his journey: "Where are you headed?"

"I don't. It wasn't necessarily the destination but it is right in my path so I will probably check it out. I have no real schedule to speak of. And you?" This was not the Santo that Santo knew. He found his inquiry into the man's affairs to be disconcerting and out-of-character. He immediately wished he could retrieve the question and end the conversation. Even as the people he had spoken to since he had rolled the old Galaxie 500 out of Chester had given him a perspective on the world around him that seemed as genuine as the author's he had read, even as his curiosity continued to grow, it always felt as though the world was not his business.

"I just go to make trades," he answered. Santo was once again confused by the conversation. He was young and he knew that he hadn't interacted with a lot of people, choosing to ignore this social aspect inherent in everyone else. So, when someone left the answer to a question dangling like bait for the next, he was unsure how he should respond. Should he simply let it go away, even if the answer had piqued his curiosity? If he said nothing, would this affable stranger, Hodgy, continue the conversation with him in his absence? Or would he be like Davis and be simply happy that someone spoke to him in a kind way?

These strangers were people with stories of their own who had no previous knowledge of who he was or better, what they thought he was. To a stranger, he was a clean slate that was only prejudiced by the way he looked. He knew that some of the people that spoke to him were just a little bit afraid, others were more fearful, the way a mouse might be in the presence of a hawk, and still others would nod and speak as if he were a peer to be respected. All of this without, in most instances, even speaking a word. Santo once found himself staring at his reflection wondering if he would speak to himself if he were to meet the person he saw.

Attempting to make light of the man's statement, he asked, "Trade what?"

"Excellent question," Hodgy replied smiling. Santo wondered if this was a hopeful response to a subject the old man had been wanting to talk about. "In this case, it is money for gold. Some might view it as a trade of one idea for another. Either way, I can't do this in Bennett." He gripped the bag just a little tighter but did not move it from his lap. Perhaps he suddenly regretted what had revealed to this man sitting next to him.

"Would you like to join me?"

"You don't even know me."

"I know two things about you. You're reading a book that is like an investment bible. Kinda like carrying Fromer's Europe on $5 a Day. Everybody knows you're on a journey and you speak a common language because you're toting this big book. It's human nature. You see this book being read in a café or on a train and you just walk up and connect. This is kind of the same thing. You and me, we have a common ground. Anyway, I think it is now up to $15 a day. You know, how much it costs to travel around Europe. Except for Paris, or any of the other big postcard cities like Rome or London. You should go some time.

"Where was I? Oh, yeah, the book. The other thing I

know about is a little more nuanced. I didn't read that book until I was at least thirty. I mean, think of the money making years I wasted. Or should I say, like a Grahamer, the money I wouldn't have lost." He was smiling as if laughing at the mistakes he had made in the past. "And besides, it's not exactly beach reading."

"You lost money?" The tone of the questions made Hodgy laugh out loud.

"Sorry. Everybody loses money. It is why you lost it that matters. Graham had all of these cool little things he'd throw out like, and I'm paraphrasing here, 'go ahead and trade, trade a lot, the more you do the more you'll lose' and he couldn't have been more right in that. Once you make a bad trade, you try to make another one to recoup and then another and another until someone comes along, you know, the guy I the mirror, and explains that you're fucked. Give it up. Start over."

Santo looked at him with a question on his face. Hodgy wasn't sure if he was going to ask it or not, and assumed he wouldn't. "Graham liked value and oddly enough, he liked to compartmentalize his life. That's two things that most people don't do and that's why stock brokers get rich. It's why I got rich from other people and mostly lost, at least in the early years, when I traded my own cash." The old man shifted in his seat and half turned towards Santo.

"Think of it like this. You like a company or a business for whatever reason. So you buy shares in it. Shares give you a sliver of the operation. As a broker I could care less why. I made a commission on the trade. Then the whole fucking thing goes south and you want to sell. That's a bit dramatic. Usually, it is your opinion that goes south and often too late. As a broker, I did what you wanted me to do and I made money again and again, I couldn't care less. I have some responsibility to care but unless the client, in this example, the knucklehead who bought shares without doing due diligence asks me but if no one is watching, why should I?

"Now, if you were smart and bought the company because you knew that they were a great operation, you would be buying more now that the cost is lower. Because you know something. Sure, I, you know, me as the broker would make money on the commission then too, or used to anyway, but now you have an investment. You've moved from speculation to investing. Graham said you should never confuse the two."

"So, when do you sell?"

"Never. Or practically never. Remember, you did your homework. You like the company and what it does. You own your idea and that means you like their idea. Never sell, unless things change. Stock is ownership."

"So, you're going into Denver to buy something?"

"I am. I am going into town to speculate. And if I'm right, I'll make some serious money. If not, I'll know soon enough that I shouldn't have but, hey, I'm using my mad money account." Hodgy turned and saw the expression on Santo's face.

"Do you follow the news at all?"

"Not much. More of history buff, you know, examining the events after they happened seemed more prudent than attempting to follow current events. The only thing I paid attention to was the draft."

"I'll bet," Hodgy replied, without adding his own conscription or the horrors of war or the comradery of his unit or the overall inevitability of conflicts in general. Sitting on his porch watching the Midwest sky roll across the flatness allowed a man to think about things he didn't want to think about. He was thankful Santo missed his opportunity to ask him about his experiences.

"I was still in high school when the draft was going on

and by the time I graduated, it was over. I didn't see any real reason to follow the events of the world as it unfolded. It always seemed like counting leaves in a windstorm. I like my news analyzed by time and historians, you know, the folks who got to see it play out in full who have turned it over, looked at the flaws and the risks that were taken and giving credit where its due and blame where it is deserved. What does that have to do with investing?"

"We're talking speculating now." He adjusted himself in his seat. "Couple of years back, Nixon decoupled gold from the dollar. And then even more recently, he allowed people to buy gold. And then the world started going wacky. I mean, it always has been but now we could hedge or bet against the collapse of the whole world by buying something that for the history of all time has had value. So I'm going into town to buy gold because I think the Iran hostage crisis is that trigger to make people wacky scared. Not that we as a rule always are. This is not even close to being important but gold," and he left the sentence unfinished.

A couple of moments passed as Santo absorbed some of the words the man had said. Was he an investor or a speculator? He suspected he was an investor. Most of his decisions had been good ones, even if they were abruptly made, instinctual and without the 'calculations' of risk he had been reading about before Hodgy sat down. They all seemed to have been analyzed for risk even if he could not consciously recall the effort. And that might mean something. But he had done incredibly risky things and had done so without the thought of or anticipation of the possible downsides. He wondered if that make him less an investor and more of a speculator?

"Can you be both?" he finally asked.

"Yes and no. There is risk in everything. So yes. But there is less in investing than in speculation. So no. The differences are subtle and unless you adhere to some basic concepts, like Graham did, you will not see the distinction." Santo didn't answer. He assumed the man was basically telling him to finish the book if he wanted the answers.

He was wrong though. Hodgy began to speak again, leaning in closer so Santo would hear what he had to say, as if there was a great secret he needed to share with him alone. "Never invest money you need. Never invest until all the bills have been paid. And never invest unless you have saved something for retirement. Cross those boundaries and you are speculating. Even good gamblers know the difference. They call it protecting the nut."

Santo smiled as he thought of his backpack full of 'nuts'. He was an investor who took unknown risks and he now knew that those risks can have unforeseen consequences. He had watched his two business partners taken away in handcuffs.

"Yeah," Hodgy said after a couple of minutes, "You can come with me. If'n of course, you want to."

*****

The two men exited the bus station in downtown Denver and began walking down Arapahoe St. The day was pleasant enough Santo thought, almost too clear. His breath seemed to labor as his lungs adjusted to the thinner mountain air. Hodgy didn't speak much and hadn't said anything to Santo since he had agreed to come along. He felt odd following him but did so in silence.

They entered a tall brick building several blocks from the station that stood alone and seemed to rise straight up like a spire. The lobby was polished marble with the receptionist on one side and small business that seemed to cater to tenants or visitors who needed a snack or a newspaper. The woman behind the counter didn't look up when they passed. On the other side of the otherwise empty lobby was a coin shop with a small sign in simple script above the door: Denver Numismatics.

The two entered and were immediately greeted by a noticeably armed Asian man who asked them how they were. Hodgy replied that they were anxious to do business. He smiled and politely nodded, his thick jowls rising up as he did. He reached behind and opened the door. Santo followed the old man up the staircase where yet another equally husky and well-suited man, making no effort to hide his firearm asked them again about their disposition. Again, Hodgy replied anxiously.

"Sir," he asked, as he turned to Santo, "can I look in your backpack?"

"Now, I'm anxious," he replied, looking more towards the old man than the doorman.

Hodgy said in a matter-of-fact voice, "He doesn't want your drugs or your money. He just wants to make sure you aren't toting any weapons." Santo stood looking at Hodgy, and apparently asking the question he was thinking with the expression on his face.

"Look kid. I made a living sizing up people. It's a skill that resides on a tree-lined street just beyond guessing and not far from certainty. I mean, think about it. You look like a resourceful kid and that means you know what you are made of. The haircut is recent and although it cleans you up a bit, it can't hide the rebelliousness of your age. It's a skill that doesn't involve using much more than your wits. You also strike me as person who keeps things close. So, I'd be willing to bet that all your worldly possessions are in that bag." He smiled as Santo relaxed. "Just let him look."

As they entered into the coin room, Hodgy turned to him and said, "Besides, I saw you blow a joint back in Bennett before you got back on the bus."

The room was lined with glass cases, filled with all manner of coins. Hodgy paid no attention and walked past them to a single woman at a desk. Santo wanted to look and as he leaned in, an employee not much older than he was asked if he could be of assistance. There were six people behind the cases, all well-dressed and all carrying sizable sidearms. They were the only two people in the shop.

Hodgy walked to the back of the shop, approaching a tall, statuesque woman in professional attire. She looked up from the journal she was writing in. She smiled. "Irwin. So nice to see you again." She looked at Santo appraisingly, who was still taking in the surroundings and nodded in his direction.

Hodgy turned and introduced him. "This is Sonny. I think he is interested in buying some Krugerrands." He was unaware he was interested in doing anything but accompanying the man and less interested in purchasing a coin he had, until that moment, never even heard of. Santo composed himself and shook the woman's extended hand. It was long and thin and slipped into his like a scarf.

"This is Sarnia." Santo smiled and tried not to be consumed by what was clearly a demanding erotic aura haloing about her. She pushed her chair back and led the two men into the room behind her. They followed her fragrance, a scent that Santo had never experienced.

Hodgy leaned into Santo and although made no attempt to hide what he was saying, spoke low enough to give him the impression that they had enter some sort of sacred area. "You might never find someone like Graham in here because he was smarter than all of this. If he had been able to buy gold as an investment he would have laughed at the concept. Gold is a commodity and there is only so much available, either above ground or below. So, because it is finite, the price can fluctuate wildly and Graham would have thought this to be foolhardy. And gold can't grow based on its potential. Stocks can. Gold, never.

"We are right at the point where gold is at a suitable price. He would have liked that. But he wouldn't have liked the idea that it won't always be. In fact, in six months, they'll be lining up at the front doors trying to buy whatever Sarnia has to offer." It sounded suspect to Santo but had he stopped to consider how many gambles he had taken, the risks he had mitigated, or the chances he had jumped feet first into, he would not have found this all that out of character.

"We, or should I say I, know that this is a purchase based on anticipation. Something's gonna happen and when it does, the price will rise and when something else happens, it will fall just as fast. And Sarnia will still be here like she was last week and the month before that."

She spoke as she opened the metal box. Each coin was encased in its own plastic envelope. "It is too bad someone did that to the coin around your neck." Santo was unsure she was speaking to him. Until now, she had focused her attention on the old man.

She repeated herself, "The coin around your neck. Had someone not drilled it, it would be worth several thousand dollars. A mint 1926 Buffalo nickel. Not that one."

He smiled. "A friend gave it to me. Apparently I am supposed to remember to do five good things every day. Not sure how having a nickel around my neck will remind me. Kind of cool though." She was not amused. In her world, untarnished and unaltered were considered to be the only way a coin could hold its value, often eclipsing the actual currency valuation. Her voice may have had the smoothness of silk, but her disdain had the feel of an unsheathed sword.

When the two men left, Hodgy had exchanged the ten thousand dollars that was held in the brown paper bag into one hundred and three shiny coins or a little over six pounds of nearly pure gold. She had offered to sell him bullion but he declined. Santo had purchased eighty coins, also declining the solid pieces of molded yellow metal. He was enamored by the deceptive heft of the coin and turned it repeatedly in his hand.

As they made their way back to street level, Santo asked, "How will I know when to sell?"

"That will be almost easier than buying. Pay attention to the news. I know you don't like to but do it. One day, those frickin' A-rabs," he said, splitting the syllables into two words, "will let those hostages go. Sell then. Or sell when it hits $800 an ounce. That'll be in the news too."

*****

It would be more than three decades before Santo Aretino would revisit that moment, or any for that matter. He was blissfully free the weight of what had happened up until that point, or any other point for years after. For many, this would be considered problematic. For Santo, it was a defense mechanism built into his genetic make-up, a construction of information that was lacking anything you might consider a source. He would wonder, for instance, and this is only much later, why he didn't just stay on the East Coast. He would wonder, that if he had, would it have been any different. As he would struggle with each minute, looking for some connection, it all required a beginning, and he had, as far as he knew, none. But that wouldn't happen for quite some time.

*****

The two parted ways at the bus station. "Remember," the older man said, "stay current on the news. You will have all of about a week to unload at the top." He got back on the east bound bus and left Santo wondering how he could track 'at the top'.

They had briefly discussed the remainder of his journey as they walked back.

"You have to see Boulder before you move on kid. The rest of the state is nice but poor. But Boulder," Hodgy had described as the town with more than its fair share of PhD waiters. "You'll see why when you get there." And that was it.

Santo wondered if that was the way it was in this big world outside of the city he grew up in. Do people simply swoop into another person's life and change the way you think that easily, passing off some mantra they had chosen to live by with the ease of sharing recipes between neighbors? What Hodgy left him with would impact many of his future decisions, giving him a scale with which to weigh whatever it was he was faced with. Was it an investment, something he was willing to lend time and energy to or would it be speculation, a passing interest that would fade as quickly as it was considered?

Santo flashed his one-way bus pass at the driver and boarded still thinking about these contrasts. The trip took about an hour skirting the mountains to the left and the prairie to the right. He could feel the road begin to rise as the terrain went from windswept brown to scrub forest and just as gradually, rocks and boulders began jutting from the ground in ever increasing heights until they threw deep shadows on the road. While the bus was near capacity when they arrived in Denver, this bus was mostly empty as it left.

Santo had no immediate plans to go anywhere in particular and no real schedule to arrive at that as-yet-to-be-named destination. His love of maps had created a de facto place he'd like to visit in Oregon. He had studied the topography of these maps, wondering what kind of decision was made by the people who lived there to stay. He imagined that many of the people in these towns did not have a choice. It was made for them, perhaps in the form of an opportunity or decision made by some distant relative to settle in a place that may not be the one they would have made. But still; why stay?

And here he was heading into yet another town he had not considered, another place in a journey that was always wished for yet unplanned. As the town unfolded, first in small plots of ranched acreage and then into more densely constructed buildings, he was taken aback by what Hodgy had left out of his description of the place. He had never witnessed anything quite like it. The way the high mountain beauty swept down onto the citizens of this college town, encircling them like a granite fence made him pause for the first time in his life.

Everyone seemed invigorated, almost lustily engaged in breathing the thin air. Despite its beauty, he felt out of place, more so than normal. It was as if everyone he saw got some joke he hadn't heard.

The bus, for all of its convenience and even methodical efficiency of moving people and their stuff, had grown tiresome. He had appreciated that the journey he had made up until that point as he made his way across miles of featureless landscapes, brushed with wind and towering storm clouds, evangelical sunshine and limitless nights was done largely by these huge people movers. He had decided that the ride on the Trailways chariot as he came to refer to it, needed to end. Sitting on a bench as the shadows grew, he realized that if he really wanted to see the rest of the journey, he would have to give up the comfort of being driven anonymously through the world. It was time for a change.

He had ridden the bus for almost the entire trip, seasoning the journey with the occasional ride he had procured with an extended thumb. That part of the journey, the random traveler extending their path to him, accepting his request, was how he should move from now on. He decided that this is where the stories of his life would occur, the pages of his novel or biography or door-stopping history.

*****

The car didn't exactly pull over when they had spotted him along the road. Instead, they slowed to his pace and the girl in the front seat leaned out the window and asked if he'd like a ride. The tires made a gentle crunch sound as it rolled half on the shoulder, half on the road. She immediately reminded him of Stella Blue, all warmth and welcoming, shining.

No words were exchanged as the back door swung open, the Stella Blue girl reaching into the back to open it. He crawled into the back seat with the boy they were travelling with, a girl with ridiculously large sunglasses was behind the steering wheel. The Stella Blue girl swung her arm over the seat and asked, "So, where ya headed?" They were all about his age.

"I'm not quite sure." The Stella Blue girl, who did not have the thick dreadlocks simply smiled.

"Okay, so why stand on that side of the road? I mean, how is it you chose to go west instead of coming from that direction?" The girl behind the wheel slightly turned to see him.

He was suddenly aware that he had not had anything resembling a conversation in days. Since the old man who got on the bus outside of Denver started talking to him, riffing on what he was reading and eventually taking him on his speculative errand to the coin shop, he had not spoken in anything other than clipped sentences exchanged with total strangers in stores and diners. "I'm kind of new at this travelling thing," was all he could think to say.

"You look like you might have been going on for some time." And again, he was unaware of how he presented himself to the world. As he wandered through Boulder, he did notice his reflection in storefront windows. But he didn't recognize himself. He had weathered somewhat and the man who looked back at him seemed even more elusive, offering a chilly distance as a barrier to anyone looking to scale his wall of isolation. He had never intentionally pushed people away. Instead, it was more like the way a person gives respectful distance to a well-muscled dog.

The Stella Blue girl offered some sort of non-answer for him. "We're all new at this. Every fucking day is new, my handsome friend." She quickly added, "I just didn't want you to think we were headed where you were going."

Santo laughed at this comment. "Do you know where I'm headed?" She squinted and looked at him closely.

"You're running, I bet. I just can tell whether it is towards something or away." She considered him more closely. "You're not from around here either and you don't look the university type. Am I warm?"

"You mean like, are you getting close to the truth? I suppose. Isn't everybody one or the other?" Without answering him, she turned and reached for something on the front seat. When she turned back to him, she was holding a joint in her hand. "Wanna get high? Or are you new at that too?"

He smiled and realized that there was a reason he remained quiet in so many social situations. People, he had decided were unpredictable, often given to reactions he was not expecting. He lacked the ability to anticipate, even incorrectly, their responses. He was still surprised when people picked him from alongside the road, for two reasons. One, he could not fathom how anyone could allow someone into their car without any prior knowledge of who they were. This was not a fear question; he was not emotionally equipped to experience many of the hardwired reactions everyone around him experienced. And secondly, he assumed that the person he saw in those representations was the person they saw as well. Although he avoided those reflections as often as possible. When he did find himself unable to retreat from his image being mirrored back, he would laugh at the way his brow furrowed, darkening his eyes, sending a long, ominous shadow across his facial expression. He imagined he was handsome enough, or so he was told by the women he had slept with, but he couldn't tell whether that was just talk, a compliment of passion or a comment made to reassure them he was a suitable, if temporary partner. He never stopped to consider that maybe this harsh self-assessment of who he was had a flaw.

She first lit the joint and handed it to him as she exhaled, speaking with smoke pouring from her words, "Surrender to the wind and it will be the ride of your life." She coughed and began introducing her friends. "That's Zach. He hates being called Zacharia." This made her laugh and Zach, who had been handed the joint by Santo, cringe. "Driving this winged machine is the very pretty, very talented, and very much a prude, Zephyr. So, that surrender to the wind does not apply to her. She only surrenders to cute girls who don't know they like girls. And I am your sarcastic hostess, Emily." She had taken the joint from Zach and handed to the driver.

"So," she said, "do you have a name?"

"I do," and left it there.

"You know that would be funny if we were standing in line for a beer but we picked you up so it's kinda creepy."

"Sorry. It's Sonny. Like I said…"

And she finished the statement for him, "You're new at this."

The weed had a dirty taste to it, possibly homegrown, dried in the late summer sun. "I'm more or less headed to Oregon. I set out with that as a point on the map and decided to see where it would take me."

"How's it been so far, Sonny?"

"It's been interesting enough. The trip through the midsection of the country was not very scenic, unless you're reading, which I was. I got off the bus every now and again and I liked the smell of the air. Certainly not like the east coast." He was reaching in his backpack when he said this. He had pre-rolled about twenty joints of his own. He had smoked whenever possible, at bus stops, while he was walking along the road, whenever the opportunity presented itself. His joints were perfectly even from end to end and although he would credit the rolling machine he had borrowed from his now-jailed friends, he wouldn't offer the information unless he was asked. He brought the joint to his lips and lit it.

As expected, the car became hushed as the joint was passed. He had been a dealer for one reason: He wanted the best available pot for his own personal use. If it meant dealing, if it meant having to travel in a circle of criminals, if it meant having to interact with customers, he was prepared to do so to own the very best the world had to offer.

He recognized the taste of the pot in the joint as something he had procured from Cambodia. It was smooth and expansive and everyone coughed. Soon his car mates were smiling stupidly and humming to the country music blaring from the AM radio.

Emily was the first one to find her voice. "Where the fuck have you been all my life?"

"That was rhetorical, right?" This made her laugh, with the contagion of chuckling washing over the other two. Santo just smiled. The four of them sat in silence for the next twenty miles or so. The radio began to lose its signal as they left the city, the static growing louder as the music hiccupped. At one point, Zephyr pushed a Deep Purple eight track tape into the deck. Santo owned several of their albums, or did, but had lost interest in the band as they adopted a more heavy metal standard. Listening to one of their better releases, Machine Head endlessly spin on the eight-track loop was not as bad as it could have been.

Unlike the roads he had been traveling on, this blacktop seemed to climb into the surrounding mountains. Santo had never seen much more than the geologically worn hills of the Poconos. These forested slopes gave majestic rise to the first snow of the season, the white in stark relief to the piney greenness and the jagged rocks. He found himself lost in the sight as Space Trucking played "We danced around the Borealis, we're space truckin' around the stars."

Emily turned in her seat and looked at Santo. Her eyes were bloodshot and if eyes could grin, they were. "Where did you plan on staying?" she asked as if this question had just dawned on her.

"Because you were thinking?" Santo answered, half asking the question and partially making the statement that he was certain would follow. He was always amazed at the what happened to people when they got high, the impact of the same drug had on different people was endlessly entertaining. He didn't care for the people who endlessly chatted, unless of course it was cohesive. His drug-dealing partners Matty and Sal could converse about almost anything. He had also encountered laughers, those who seemed to do so until they cried. While he could appreciate their glee, they were just as annoying as those who needed to fill the air with mindless words. The list could go on and if he had ever do so, he would have realized that he did not see himself as a social smoker.

Like so many other situations he had found himself in over his short life, his reactions would be different. Santo, no matter how much he consumed, Thai or Cambodian or Afghani, weed, hash or oils, he never lost his lucidity, never staggered, and certainly never looked like he was as wasted as he was. Instead, it seemed to sharpen his focus and allowed his brain to compartmentalize his thoughts, giving him a crystal clarity that he supposed everyone else simply resisted.

"Yeah. I was thinking." She paused for a long moment as she struggled to regain traction on the thought. Santo knew that if you were this high, any interruption would be sudden and final, any thought you might have had was lost until it was jarred from its mooring again.

*****

The thought it seems centered around another opportunity for her to get high. Santo had found that most people fall squarely into three categories when it came to drugs. There were the people like Zach, who seemed to be noncommittal when it can to getting high. If it was there and easily available, he was amiable to the experience. He was not the type that would spend his Friday night in search of the right high to accompany the event. If he couldn't find any weed, he would make due with beer. Many of the kids Santo grew up with fell into this category. To these kids, drugs represented a counterculture that was more California than Pennsylvania, more flower power and tie dye than street thugs and leather jackets, more Woodstock than West Side Story. When he talked, it was only to add color to what Zephyr was saying.

Then there were people like Zephyr, who, once she had found out that her passenger had never passed this way before and even better, had never seen a mountain, decided she would offer her experienced comments on the scenery. Like her name, her stories about that trailhead or this particular peak existed on a breeze, winding its way around obstructions and leaving no trace aside from the rustle of her words. Santo enjoyed these types of people the most and many of the women he had slept with fell into this category. All older and all more experienced than he was, every lover he had ever had, whether he slept with them or not, found a verbal freedom in his presence. They talked, no more than when they were not stoned, but always unencumbered. Both Louise and

Eva suggested it was because he listened without prejudice. Dina had said it was because his expression made them less hard, not softer she had said. Zephyr's descriptions were part of her ongoing memory rewrite, editing the experience on the fly, adding a nuance, deleting a character, describing the trees and sun and the people differently each time she revisited the scene. She had long ago turned down the music, allowing her voice to become the instrumental.

Zephyr would always have the advantage of having drugs near her. Whether it was simply a fortuitous arrangement or excellent positioning, she would probably be in the same room as the drugs she enjoyed more often than not. Drugs would always be where she happened to be. And because of this free-flowing nature of this access, this cute coincidental-ness suggested she would likely remain on the fringes of being either a Zach or an Emily, a sort of neutral zone bridging want and need.

Santo knew the Emilys of the world. They were the hunters, the aggressors, the alphas in search of some sort of release. That release could be from anything but in most cases, it was an illusion. She would actively pursue the next high to such a degree that it would become an obsession from the moment she woke up. There were times when supply would slow down, or even dry up. For the Emilys, they would not allow no to be an acceptable answer. Santo may have seen himself as an Emily at one point and would, if any one dared to confront it head on, deny it. His focus on weed and all of its subsidiaries was a curiosity, an unscientific survey into his own desire, each exploration as an experiment, answers creating questions and on and on. He was fascinated with the substance, the varieties that had developed and of course, the networks that brought the products to his doorstep. He needed weed and understood that it would never seem to command him if he had more than he would ever need. Emily though, wanted weed. It completed her, added to her presence, gave her depth and dimension and she applied it the way make-up is applied, daily, for the public consumption.

It was no accident that Santo had found all three of these drug types in one place. Zach was along for the ride, Zephyr was where the drugs are or would be and Emily was the one who kept it cohesive, the one who allowed these two to feed at her table, or in this instance, smoke on her couch. If she were to drop from the picture, Zephyr would find someone else. Zach would just move on.

Santo also knew something else about these three: Zach would not do anything he was skeptical about; Zephyr would use an excuse of some sort and no one would pressure her to try something she was not interested in; Emily would try anything.

"I remember," she said excitedly. "I've got a friend who has a ranch about twenty miles from here. We should go." Zephyr shrugged her shoulders as might have been expected.

A half hour later, the car was kicking up a huge cloud of light brown dirt as it headed down a long drive.

*****

Their birth names were Gregor Strakeljahn and Joe Nguyen. The two men could not have been an odder couple. Gregor was a tall, lanky and blonde Norse type while Joe was short, much darker complexioned and Vietnamese. Together, they lived on a small dusty ranch nestled along the North Foothills Highway. Far from the road and able to see any approaching vehicle, the two men lived off the grid, a term that wouldn't be invented for decades, in a ramshackled grouping of buildings and sheds. On three sides, the foothills created a scree wall that triangle out towards the road. From a distance, it all seemed abandoned. Up close did not improve a visitor's perception.

When the car approached, Gregor stepped onto the

porch to greet them. He was introduced to Santo as Mr. Poppy. He hugged Emily and gave the other two a smiling nod. He was clean cut compared to Joe, who had arrived at the group from somewhere behind what appeared to be the main house. He was dusty and layered in all sorts of clothing, or the remnants of what was once serviceable articles. Even though the temperature was approaching eighty degrees, he was wrapped as if it were much colder.

Mr. Poppy extended his hand, offering a disarmingly strong grip. Joe simply nodded. Emily led her two car mates into the house leaving Santo standing on the porch with the two partners.

"Not to be rude, but I didn't catch your name." Santo told him it was Sonny, once again reaching into an identity he thought he had jettisoned. "Well then Sonny, why did Emily bring you round here?"

"Not sure." The three men stood silently sizing each other up before Joe spoke, at first to his friend while looking at Santo, and then directly to him.

"Me thinks he's made an impression, Poppy." He swayed and pointed towards the house where his traveling companions had entered. "Did you make an impression?" Santo debated whether answering was worth his time.

"Joe," he scolded his friend, "let's offer our new arrival with a bit more courtesy and less skepticism. If he came with Emily, he can't be all bad." Poppy turned and waited until the three people who had picked him up entered the house. "You're not all bad, right, Sonny?"

"Not to be rude, but I think I'll bail on whatever you two guys got going on here. Nice to meet you both." He turned and started to head back to the long stretch of driveway. He could hear the two of them speaking but a sudden gust of wind had drowned the voices. Mr. Poppy had received his name because of his cultivation of the plant and the extraction of the milky forbearer of what some turned into heroin. His house was a place where people could come and partake, people like Emily and her two willing followers, isolated and remote, the three could fall into the drug's trance like state, a state of awake but comatose.

He first heard the footsteps, running on the dry gravel. Then he heard the voice of Joe. "Wait. We was just bein' careful, Sonny. We ain't exactly doin' legal like things out here."

Santo turned and looked at him and never for a moment reconsidered his exit. Something about Poppy that made him feel uneasy, as he was seen by the two men as an opportunity, as if a wealthy person suddenly found himself in a less affluent neighborhood, dressed too nicely for the surroundings. The natural, hardwire reaction was to flee any danger, real or perceived in a situation like this and Santo was not that different when it came to this wiring, even if he was not one to flee. He often found himself confronted with these types of situations, most recently in St. Louis, and before that in Ohio and in those instances, he actually stepped into the fray. If he thought about it, he would not be able to tell you why and nor would he be able to recall the exact moment when his reaction outweighed common sense. And while Santo did not really acknowledge fear as a viable emotion, he wasn't a fool if he had a choice. He wasn't fleeing the unknown; he was following the instinctual voice in his head, the trusted voice in his head.

"C'mon back," Joe beckoned. "We'll get high, smoke a little opium and maybe cooks some food." His eyes were pleading. It would be an error to suggest he didn't trust the shabbily dressed Asian man, who leaned in with his shoulder, almost winking. It had nothing to do with trust; as a rule, Santo trusted no one.

"I'll pass but thanks." He was barely two steps beyond Joe when he felt a hard kick to his ankle. The leg sweep had failed as Santo took the blow but didn't fall. He was a low stepper, his feet barely leaving the ground between each foot fall, his balance evenly distributed between each step. He turned quickly and clipped the man along the side of his head with the back of his hand, balled in a fist. It was enough to knock him off balance but not down.

"You mutherfuckinassholesonofabitch," and he lunged at Santo. There were two things Santo knew about people: When they were angry, they were stupid, and when they were stupid, he was their intellectual superior. The small man's motion was direct and would have made contact with someone who was standing in his way. As Santo stepped to one side, he dropped to one knee and punched him squarely in his kidney as he passed. Joe dropped to the ground but not before vocalizing his pain. He was stringing another thread of curse words together. Santo stood up and for a moment looked at the man on the ground. He was breathing and would probably be pissing blood the next time he urinated. He picked up his pack and started to head down the road again.

"Hey, Sonny," and for some reason he would never be able to explain, he heard the wind split as the baseball bat broke through the dry air. He ducked as Joe's cohort, the previously polite Norseman stepped into the swing, the bat extending his wingspan by forty inches.

As the bat passed, Santo came up under the man's arm. When he was eight, long before he saw the man murdered in the parking lot, long before he took it upon himself to avenge all of the bullied kids in his school, long before he saved the asthmatic man in the gas station in Lititz or the kid trying to take a piss at the bus stop or the thugs in the alley in St. Louis, Bobby Aiolo had taught the local kids in his neighborhood how to fight. It was a simple lesson that centered around three basic concepts. The first being: "Get a punch in". The kids were warned that if he had ever found out that no punch was ever landed, he would find you and land a lesson of his own. The second lesson was much more helpful: "if they have a weapon like a bat or tire iron, hit first." The last thing he told them was an on-the-spot judgement call: "If they're crazy, run. Never ever fuck with a crazy person." Bobby never considered what would happen if there was nowhere to run from a crazy person, or two.

Poppy dropped the bat and Santo completed the act of dismantling his aggressor. He was able, where Joe had failed, to sweep his foot along the ground and take the man down with a kick to his ankle. He dropped on his back and Santo landed a punch in the middle of his chest.

Ten minutes later, Santo was walking down North Foothill Highway. The two men, although he could barely see them, were still lying in the dirt, small whirlwinds of brown dust, devils of dirt circling their bodies. He suspected they might be there for a while.

Thirty minutes later, a truck driver picked him up a mile from the ranch.

*****

Santo was lost in his own thoughts, or more accurately, the thoughts of the landscape around him. He listened to the gravel under his feet, birds rising from the grass along the highway, the wind, which swept passed any obstacle in its path with sonorous impact. What had just happened was all but forgotten. He focused almost no attention to the approaching sound of the old Ford pickup lumbering down the two-lane road. It slowed as it approached him and stopped. The dust had turned the factory red paint to russet. He could see the man behind the wheel as he reached across and began to lower the window.

"You have a long walk ahead of you, son." Santo had not considered the distance when he walked away from the

120

opium ranch. He wasn't even sure he was headed in a direction that would lead him to some place he wanted to be. He was still coming to grips with the concept of distance. Someone other than him would have asked questions of great depth and meaning, wondering if time still existed, pondering the lack of ambition or even the overabundance of it, contemplating each upcoming prospect, each singular experience and their role in reshaping it. Not so Santo. No one would ever confuse this young man with purity of soul but in some respects, he was among the purist. He was an oxymoron of sorts, an innocent criminal.

Santo stood there for a moment looking at the driver. His skin was deeply colored and lined with the look of folded leather. He seemed ancient to Santo. "Would you like a ride?" he asked, his voice perfectly aligned with this appearance.

Santo looked at the truck bed. There were several bales of hay. "Should I ride back there?"

The man popped the door open, the hinges moaning in refusal. "Na. I'll take my chances." Santo slid into the front seat and pulled hard on the door to close. It finally closed with a loud metal on metal bang. The old man eased the gear into place and the truck started to move again.

"The name's Anthony." Unaware he was doing so, Santo sat staring at the man. "Actually, the name is Antonga, or Black Hawk depending on where I am and who I'm with. White folk seem more comfortable with Anthony. I'm pretty sure you're not from around here but with you staring like that, I'm wondering just how far from home you are."

"I'm sorry." The act of hitchhiking was not as random as it is often portrayed. It involved some mental preparation, the anticipation of what to expect as the car, truck, whatever rolled to a stop, the driver having made their assessment and the hitchhiker, the other half of the event, had little to no time to make a similar judgement. Only moments were allowed to pass.

While still relatively new to this process, Santo had now done enough of it to understand that some of the people that stopped did not want to talk. This often made him wonder why they even stopped to pick him up. Some wanted conversation. He had learned that he had to do nothing more than listen to whatever was on their mind at the moment, whatever the time alone on the road had allowed pushed to the forefront of their thoughts, whatever trouble they were trying to work out, whatever angst weighed heavily on their psyche. Some told stories that were tales of being alone even as they described the people that made them feel that way. Some acted as de facto tour guides, willing to point out the land of their birth in vividly painted tales of local lore both present and past. Some asked direct questions, often personal and many without really needing an answer.

Each ride was different. Throwing your thumb in the air as soon as you heard the vehicle approaching from behind you, turning, allowing the driver to see what you wanted them to see, sizing you up from the safety of their metal box. More cars passed than stopped, some drivers never removing their eyes form the road. Until one pulled to stop just beyond where you were standing.

In this instance, he did not have his thumb in the air, not even haphazardly. But the truck stopped anyway.

"Are you an Indian?" This made the man laugh.

"Have you made it all this way without seeing one?"

Santo shifted in his seat. "I've read about Indians." The man took a long look at the young man sitting next to him. Santo still had some of the manicured appearance courtesy of the old barber who had cleaned him up in St. Louis. His beard had grown back, the auburn on black complimented the thickness of his hair, which the foothills wind had whipped into its own artistic disarray.

"You've read about Indians?"

"Every kid I knew watched the Lone Ranger. So, every kid I knew thought Tonto was an Indian. But I was curious and I found out that he was, but not really. I mean, Tonto is Spanish for moron, or so I found out and that had to be the handiwork of someone who had," he paused, looking for the right word when Joe interrupted, "never met an Injun."

Something about the man broke his uncharacteristic quiet. Santo continued, "So I found out that he was an Indian. He was from the Great Lakes, or his people were and I thought, how did he end up in a Western? Everything I read about Indians from that point on left me with this weird combination of guilt and sadness." Santo had taken his research in both directions, asking where Indians had come from and where did they go. He questioned the whitewashed texts he found. Not a single mention of this race of indigenous peoples had been made at his almost completely white school.

The more he uncovered about the invasion of the people from Europe, discounting any blame that could be placed on the late arrivals that he supposedly sprung from, to the displacement of these nations to less desirable locales like the west and southwest, the more he grew to disdain this part of the history of the United States. These first people were mentioned often but mostly as historical novelties, a part of the tale of the land but not a part of its history. At one point, he felt an emotion for the first time: a sadness that he was unable to explain.

"You know that Indian on the coin you're sporting around your neck ain't really an Indian." The engine made a sound that resembled a complaint. Joe looked at the dash through the steering wheel. He gave the dash a gentle caress that Santo found amusing. He didn't respond to this comment.

"It's a composite you know. Don't ask me why but apparently he couldn't find an Indian that looked Indian enough. Like me." He smiled broadly at this notion. "That don't mean the white guy is forgiven."

Santo remained silent. It was his habit to avoid coaxing conversations from people, focusing instead on listening. Although he was naturally curious, he had found his assumptions, his personal suppositions, about the people he met were often just as accurate as the colorful words that they spoke, or better, hide behind. The men he knew differed greatly from the women he knew. They were frequently caught in their own pretense, attempting to be someone that they were not, or an actor in a movie they wished they were in. They were character sponges, soaking up the qualities of the men they idolized. Simply observing them, watching them interact, excluding the language that was washed over every scene, gave Santo the impression that most of the people he met were looking for the next best character to become. Some of these characters were genetic replications of the fathers they knew, the father figure, carrying events they didn't experience with them as if they too had been part of that time and at other times, attempting to be as opposed to those influences as possible. It might have been older kids in the neighborhood, or simply someone who took an interest in them, a teacher, a priest, a coach.

Women were different. He remained silent in their company speaking only when he felt as though the time was right. They thought of him as an excellent listener, commenting that he was not like any man they knew. But when they prompted him to speak, when they phrased the question the right way, wrapped in the obvious weakness he had for them, the comfort he enjoyed in their presence, he would unfold his thoughts the way a sheer piece of fabric would fall to the floor, gently relinquishing itself to the impact of gravity. They found this attractive or as one of his lovers, an older woman he had met in what seemed like a distant past called charming. In reality, all of his lovers had been older. And even though he carefully chose when to speak, he found these women more likely to look like a character than to actually be one, nurturing a façade intended for public consumption while saving the truth of who they were, what they wanted, and how they hoped their lives would be to the private moments that Santo was invited to share. They had a surface, a veneer revealing just the outward appearance, and he seemed to be the one they felt comfortable with, enough to reveal something beyond the show they put on for the world. This was their substance and depth and uncharted territory and he became the intrepid voyager, the explorer, the discoverer.

"Do people ask you where you're headed?" This was something else Santo had found fascinating. The world he knew so well had unfolded itself to him within the covers of great novels, historical expositions, scientific journeys and musings, through voices that had experienced something he assumed he would never do, visiting places he might never go. As soon as he turned the key on his old Galaxie 500 and pulled out of his parent's driveway on the musty summer morning, fleeing the reality he was just shown, the sight of his business partners in his drug dealing world being hauled away, he was thrust into the another place beyond what he knew. As he drove away, he reminded himself that this is normal, this is what the people in books did once everything was lost, fleeing the broken reality, the shattered hope and the unattained dream. Once you realized it was over, the protagonist was left with only one option. They fled. The fled love scorned, trouble brewing, and the voices in their heads. This exit was nothing like that.

Santo didn't answer. "That's okay," Anthony said. "Some people don't really know that answer. I wasn't prying mind you. It's more of a conversation starter." He didn't look at Santo when he said this, his wrist draped over the steering wheel despite the hard ride the truck offered.

"Really?" he replied sounding as if this was the same beginning to the same question, just with a slightly different verbal lob.

"They know you don't know but they don't know why. I mean, they see you doing something they could never do but really, really wish they could. People, most people that is, never venture into the great unknown." He looked at Santo, who was paying attention to the man driving. "But they're afraid to ask you why you're on the road. They're just hoping you tell them."

"What did you mean when you said you'll take your chances? You know, when you offered me a ride?" Anthony smiled, creating deep canyons along his eyes disappearing beneath his pepper grey hair.

"Who gave you that coin?" he asked.

"A woman I stayed with for a couple of months, more like a year, back in Pennsylvania." Eva had given him the coin with great ceremony. He assumed it was because her husband had made it for her.

"She knew."

"Knew what?" Anthony ignored the question. So far, they had seemed like the same kind of linguistic salvos he had always encountered, queries that attempt to pry into the inner workings of a person's thoughts and deceptively lifting a rock here, searching behind a tree there, a secret hidden somewhere.

"Ever seen a buffalo?" he asked. Santo sighed. Joe added, "You should. We could take a little side trip."

"Last time I was told 'we're going take a little side trip', I had two drugged out hippies try to roll me. I think I'll pass."

"I'm guessing that didn't come to pass?" Santo didn't answer, looking straight ahead at the road. The way the truck rumbled, or perhaps complained gave him the idea that the tarmac had become tacky. "I'm guessing you're talking about Poppy and Old Joe. Not what you'd call the kind you'd take home to mom."

"What attracts people to those kinds of, I don't know what you'd call them without insulting somebody by comparison, is beyond me. How do people make wrong turns like that?"

"Says somebody who has made a few wrong turns." The statement hung for a moment as Santo wondered about what the old man meant. Without looking, "You know what I mean."

"I think I always treated people fair enough." And he believed that. In a compartmentalized brain, this was easy.

"Ever heard of a totem?" Santo sighed again, more audibly than the first time.

"I've read about them. It's when some cultures attach animal spirits to the living. Kind of like a form of religion. A talisman or an idol. Am I right?"

"You are. For someone who has never seen an Indian, totems are kind of our thing, that's not bad."

"I recently left a friend who was a big Louis Lamour fan." This made Anthony laugh, the deep kind of all-knowing laugh that leaves no doubt he knows more than he is telling. "What?"

"You know, and I've read him because I was curious and for the most part, he was realistic, even authentic. We weren't always hostile. Once we figured out what Manifest Destiny was, it kind of pissed us off. White folks, well, they came west to find themselves. I'm guessing you never read 'Butcher's Crossing'. It's okay if you haven't. It was a good one if you like…"

"Like what?"

"My people never really got the best, how do you say it,

portrayal." The sudden jolt from a crack in the road changed the conversation. Anthony said, "I think I'll be needing to tighten some bolts real soon. Where was I?"

"You were about to tell me is that my totem is a buffalo."

"Was I now?" Santo shifted in his seat and turned to face Anthony. His profile was not so dissimilar to the carving on the coin. Except when he smiled. He had never seen such a genuine grin. It was as if he had dropped all of the armor people usually used to hide a feeling or mask an emotion. It had the disarming genuineness of the surrounding landscape, windblown and authentic, like a man who has lived the previous thousand years, inherited the teachings and the songs and the spirits, breathing the same wind and smoke and fire.

At the exact point that he thought walking would have been better than riding with this stranger, replied, "I would love to see a buffalo, Anthony." He heard the slight resignation in his voice. He wondered if the old man driving could and if he could, whether he cared. He suspected not. Then he heard the words of the girl in the car: "Surrender to the wind and let it take you for a ride."

The rising heat in the foothills swept through the windows without conviction, whirling around the cramped cabin and dropping off its intensity before taking its leave. The truck had not been traveling much faster than thirty five miles an hour. But the turn was still sudden. The truck protested again as he pulled across the highway and entered a small road. It was unmarked, dropping into a small culvert before turning. They drove up a steep incline, the machine groaning under the driver's bidding, until it crested a hill. Lying before him was a large pasture with over fifty of these grand animals, insouciant beast full of their own awareness. Many of them raised their heads and looked at the stopped truck, the dust settling, and then returned to whatever it was they were doing when they arrived.

They exited the truck and stood at the two beam wooden fence separating these majestic animals from the human observers. Santo wondered if the fence was adequate. A large bull, with a hump Santo could only think of as something of unimaginable power, moved closer to the spot they were standing. His approach was languid, almost nonchalant, as if his reputation preceded him. He stopped less than ten feet away.

"You know this fence won't be much of an obstacle," Anthony said, quickly adding, "But he doesn't really give a fuck about you or me."

"Why does he stay here? I mean, if the fence isn't a barrier to his freedom."

Anthony laughed. "Let me tell you why I think this animal is your totem." Santo was beginning to find Anthony's habit of ignoring the questions he asked annoying. "Just look at him. Is there any reason why my people wouldn't have considered him sacred? I'm speaking generally now because my people, the Utes didn't really hunt these creatures. They are more of a plateau or plains animal. When we first got here thousands of winters ago, there were tens of millions of these beasts roaming around. And we pretty much sucked at hunting them. It wasn't until the next wave of invaders brought us horses that we really start to make some progress. But that's not why I wanted to show you this beast."

"I get the impression you are going to tell me that this animal is just like me." Santo was not comfortable with the direction of the conversation and his impatience came through in his tone.

"You, my young friend have done some bad things." Santo turned and looked at the man. He did not return his gaze, instead staring at the animal methodically chewing its cud.

"Anthony," he began slowly, almost defensively, "I

probably have. Everyone does, don't they?" Anthony cocked his head in semi-agreement, a half-nod.

"The fact that you have yet to introduce yourself to me tells me more than you might think." Santo began to speak but Anthony held an arthritic finger to his wind chapped lips. "It doesn't matter. I don't need a name. In the big picture, you are a big player. But those bad things will haunt you and give you pause to reconsider your purpose over and over again." He smiled. "The funny thing is you don't know that whatever happened to you or because of you was bad. You were doing something good when the bad thing happened. Like when I picked you up. You had done something bad but you didn't want to but it wasn't like the other bad things. No. Those were good deeds. But when you did whatever you had done before we met, it probably had some good in it somewhere."

"Look, Anthony I'm sorry if I seem as if I don't care. I wasn't trying to be short with you."

"Oh, I know. Otherwise I wouldn't've picked your ass up." The buffalo that had been watching them from a safe distance began to move slowly closer. "You know my people look at that animal as something that can only save them. It meant life, survival through the cold winters that descend on this place. It gave us substance, substance and hope. There is even a Blackfoot story about fucking the animal. Calfboy I think it was called." He laughed at this thought.

"But what makes this animal so important and so much like you is its disaffection. It does what it does without thinking. Like you. You are majestic in your conviction. They are majestic as well. They are feared. You are feared as well, but not by everyone, just like the buffalo. You will survive in spite of yourself and even though the buffalo barely survived the white man and the rifle, they did, even if it is behind these fences, protected for their own good. Just like you will be."

He turned away from the animal and faced Santo. "I have

a friend who lives over by Peyton. They pay him to keep his buffalo and every now and again, some white family will pull up in a car when they see one of the animals near the fence. They all pile out and one of them will climb the fence to get closer or take a Polaroid or something and the buffalo will just stand there like he doesn't notice or doesn't give a fuck. He waits until the person is really close. And then he stamps his foot. He says it's funny to watch. You, my young friend draw people closer and closer cause they're curious and just want to get close enough to see the great beast you don't see in yourself. And then you stamp your foot. And then you find out who's scared and who isn't."

Santo didn't answer. The buffalo stopped close enough for him to feel the heat of his breath. He looked at his eye, the cold blackness of it seemed to be without fear. He turned away and started back towards the truck. Anthony watched him walk away before he too followed.

"People call me, Sonny."

"Pleased to meet you, Sonny. But what name do you call yourself?" He laughed at this as he walked toward the truck. Santo decided not to say.

Anthony reached into his shirt pocket and removed an unfiltered cigarette, He offered one to Santo. He had all but stopped smoking tobacco during his time on Eva's farm. He drew heavily, the first puff that filled the lungs had an expansive quality, as if the blood flowing through his veins was energized, and unlike the first rush from the hit of a joint, it made him dizzy. Weed had a blanket effect, washing him in warm. Cigarette rushes stung like a cold wind.

"You know, we didn't meet by accident."

Santo turned and looked at him. The reddish hue of his skin seemed a stark contrast to the surrounding grasslands, his face was chiseled and somber when he wasn't speaking, adding additional contrast to the wind-blown surroundings. He wore his pepper back hair in two long braids that disappeared beneath his coat.

"As if the Indian and the buffalo weren't cliché enough, I was hired as a tracker. Actually, more of a private investigator but the white folks like the old west image of Indian sidekick being able to find what the white man can't seem to find." He extinguished the cigarette with a pinch between his finger.

"You know that girl Emily? The one in the passenger seat of that car that picked you up. Her rich daddy hired my partner, the comforting white face in the front office to find her. It wasn't too hard, especially after she added those other two to the trip."

"So, you followed…"

"I was sitting on the ridge above that drug house you drove up to, of course, I had no idea who you were but I did know Poppy and Joe. I've rescued a few other clients from that outpost. But you, not you. You didn't need any rescuing, did you?"

"I have no idea what you're talking about." And this was true. The encounter in the dusty foreground of the dilapidated shack was forgotten almost as it unfolded.

"Really?" Anthony asked, looking squarely at him. Santo didn't answer.

*****

John Bates had just enough polish to be accepted into the upper Main Line community without drawing too much attention to who he was. He dressed better than he could afford but the end game was higher end clients with incredibly robust checkbooks. The only drawback to this ruse was the amount of maintenance these privileged people required.

He had come from a long line of private investigators

stretching back to his great grandfather, who chipped away at an honorable living digging up dirt for solicitors in London. His son made his way to America when his father died at the hands of an adulteress, dragging his family and John's father. Each found their own way in this business, each choosing not to piggyback on the success of the previous Bates investigator, but each benefiting from the experience that was passed down.

John had resigned himself to the notion that he might be the last in line of this investigative house. He was well into his forties, spending most of his income on bespoke suits, leather and wood grained office and car, and small apartment in downtown Philadelphia. This left him too broke to attract any woman worth his seed, and too self-absorbed to share his life with any one he had met so far. He was not optimistic that this situation would ever change.

He was always under the impression he was being watched. This was an odd trait in man who made a profession documenting the lives of others. As he waited for Jules Harding in the library of his twenty thousand square foot mansion, he sat absolutely still, back straight, legs crossed, positive he was being observed from a distance. He never adjusted his clothing in public and never touched his face, an all too frequent exercise people engaged in without thought too often for him to consider anything but disgusting. He believed that if a man chose his clothes smartly and dressed for each occasion with care, his appearance should require no adjustments.

And as much as he despised shaking hands, when Jules entered the room and extended his hand, he took it as naturally as possible. Not only was he always under the impression he was being watched when he was alone, the feeling of being judged by people in person made him avoid as much contact with others as possible. Meeting clients was an unavoidable downside to his business. He preferred the job to the arrangements that could only be made in person but silently suffered through it. And then there was the client update, the meeting that justified the expenses and determined whether the flow of investigative money continued; he suffered through this as well.

Jules took a seat across from where he had been sitting, motioning for John to be seated. He also disliked the affectation of courtesy and the regal air so many of these less than regal people seemed to think they possessed. Inherited wealth does not make you royalty.

"So, what do we have Mr. Bates?" If Jules Harding had not been rich, the result of wealth created two generations ago by a Philadelphia industrialist, he would not have been noticed, or married, or have a mistress, or have an idiot son like Trevor. John took great pains to ignore this ordinariness and pay attention to his every word as if being rapt would placate his uneasiness.

"At this point, I have a few more leads that suggest our boy went west."

"Our boy? This is just a manner of speaking, correct?" John smiled and called him a prig under his breath. They were all like this: Powerful and pretensions but so fucking fragile, as if the very world outside their gilded compounds was a constant threat to the sanctity of their money.

John laughed. It was fake but he sold the action. He instead began his recap. "The police in Lancaster had not even heard about the incident at the school. The campus police at Franklin & Marshall had treated it exactly as it was explained to them: As a disgusting sexual activity gone horribly wrong. They were, in the words of the campus chief, disgusted and chose to ignore it. If they hadn't, they explained to me, there would have been a dismissal or two or even all three boys." Jules was the father of one of those three boys. Trevor Harding and his friends Sid and Harry had been found tied to the bed, hands and feet bound with curtain rods, half naked and as the repairman who had found them explained to the dorm RA, involved in something kinky. Sid and Harry had dropped out soon after the incident. Trevor finished the semester but came home to his father's house. Whatever happened in that room, the boy would never have children. And this was why John was here. Jules Harding was not going to have an heir but he would have his revenge.

John's father had shared how he felt about the concept of revenge as he was beginning his career. "Revenge," he had told him, "is mostly wishful thinking. Only idiots and wealthy people actually follow through, wanting their pound of flesh. The average dolt doesn't realize the burden it carries. It demands that the wronged be accuser, judge and jury and in some cases, the executioner. Those that have any money hire a detective like us to do the job of finding the target. And then they use whatever we dig up to justify their actions. Rich folks are just too lazy to do it themselves so they count on us to be the judge, jury and the person who leads the guilty party to the hands of the executioner. Don't do it, boy. Of course, we don't care to speculate why poor people think they'll get away with it any more than their wealthy counterparts because, they can't afford our services. Just don't get wrapped up in it. Stick to something our family is good at: working for lawyers or insurance companies."

He does remember asking how to handle the situation when and if it ever arose. His father was clear on this point: "I agree, life is sloppy and unpredictable. Fate, though is the arbiter, the last say-so in too many conversations. But they don't believe it if you tell them that. They want comeuppance. They want the score settled. Except they don't realize that whatever they paid you doesn't allow you to turn your back on a crime no matter how bad the person was or how bad they were wronged. Karma doesn't work that way. It is a come-around but it always takes time."

And then he added the final line that made sitting across from this narcissistic, callous, and vindictive prick more tolerable. "The money, John. We do it for the money." Thinking of this final conflicting comment he remembered his father saying made John smile. In John's mind, taking his father's advice was smart but if the paycheck was good, take it. Jules was shelling out $200 an hour to rectify the situation his son had probably deserved.

"First off, I believe the repairman mentioned in the campus police report was our boy," he said and then quickly corrected himself, "our suspect. I found the car," he continued without explaining how he had made the leap from finding out who did the deed on the man's son to identifying the car, "so I had to first back track and see if he was still in the area."

Sid, the weakest member of the trio had put it all together and was more than happy to tell Bates everything he had concluded. The boy had apparently lived in fear of the suspect after the gas station incident but had never told the more powerful member of the group, the now sterile Trevor about this concern. He also excluded telling Trevor's father why the visit had been made, leaving Jules to believe that this had been a random act.

"Turns out, he had been staying on a farm just down the road. So, I go there, to someplace called Lititz and talk to some fucking bogtrotter named Seamus and some older gal. They weren't a wealth of info except I was pretty sure the kid had been there and was now long gone."

Jules shifted in his chair. He lit a cigarette. At this point, John hated the man even more. He would have joined him but the clear delineation between employer and employee prohibited such commonality. He waved his hand suggesting John should continue.

"I caught a break when I realized the best way out of that shithole was by bus." John flavored his conversation with the appropriate profanities, if only to make them uncomfortable. His father had told him that swearing was simply a lack of good word choice. He had said every use of the word fuck, or damn, or shit, had a real live word that fit better, with equal emotion. He disagreed. Profanities allowed him to ignore protocol for the sake of his own amusement. So, he treated the words as a well-placed seasoning that would make his wealthy clients feel as if their station in life made them above than such language. And perhaps he had a fatalistic tendency towards getting fired.

"Has Trevor been able to remember any more about what the kid looks like?" He knew the answer but he asked anyway.

Exhaling, the smoke drifting around him, he said quietly, "No." He knew the man was suffering. Trevor was his only son and the boy had returned different. He was angry and at times impatient. Tucked away in his father's house, he could only harm himself and this John believed was the real fear Jules was experiencing. His helplessness was palpable.

"I had some additional information but it is tenuous at best." The man leaned forward in his chair, the universal sign of attentiveness. "There were a couple interesting events along an almost parallel line from Lancaster west."

"Such as?"

"I spoke to this cop at some one stop light town about a hundred miles outside of Chicago. Some small-time criminal met with an untimely demise while mugging some passenger taking a leak. There was no big deal made about it because, and I'm speculating here, the local sheriff was glad to be rid of the guy. No charges were pressed and apparently no next of kin that cared ever came forward to claim the body. That might've been because the next of kin didn't last too long himself.

"The cop had a friend in Chicago stop the bus and

interview the passengers. They found the kid who got mugged but he said it happened so fast that he didn't remember a thing. But they were one passenger short but they couldn't confirm one way or the other that it was our guy, suspect, I mean. If you'll consider, the situation was similar to the gas station incident that Sid described and Trevor would, could not recall: A stranger swoops in and saves some helpless kid and disappears.

"But then, something else happened in St. Louis. Same sort of thing. Somebody saved some guy from getting his ass kicked or killed in some downtown alley. This time both guys ended up dead. Swift dispatch. Like the diner death. The math, at least in my mind was beginning to add up. No witnesses could describe the guy, not even the guy he saved. Cops there did some due diligence and checked all around, local bars and hotels and such. It happened in the business district at night, and once again, nada.

"Fast forward about a month and a couple of drug dealers who ran an opium house somewhere outside of Boulder turn up dead. The drugged-out kids who were hanging out there eventually called the cops but waited until they sobered up a bit. I think they also stole what they could, too." At this point, Jules raised his hand.

"So, I've been expensing your cross-country trip to do what? Chase cold cases that don't actually point to the motherfucker who did this to my boy, my legacy, my..." His face redden when he told Bates this. He had expected it though. And he had questioned his own methodology in the process. It is difficult to explain the process to a client. Understandably, they were more focused on a swift and immediate conclusion, something they can act on.

"I wasn't actually there. Seems that our boy, I mean, our subject arrived at the ranch in a car. He'd been hitchhiking and was picked up by some girl who was being tracked by some old

Indian."

"He actually found him? Did he know what he had found?"

"I think he did but he let him go." Anthony Black Hawk had decided that the boy was not finished, although he didn't articulate it in so many words. "He said he might have met him but that's just code for 'I wasn't being paid to find him, so, therefore, he wasn't actually found."

"Son of a fucking bitch. So, the motherfucker is holding the information hostage, for some sort of payday?" Yes, Bates didn't answer. He talked to Mr. Black Hawk on the phone because the small caravan that the subject had joined had been questioned at length by the authorities. It was a messy scene that Mr. Blackhawk had called in long after he had parted ways with Santo.

While Black Hawk may have had something, all of the other people Bates had spoken, not the pursuers but those who actually may have seen him, they did not offer anything specific to his investigation. Instead, they offered something less tangible: an impression. All of his interviews had been impressed in some way by this elusive quarry. The police did their job, albeit halfheartedly. The people they had spoken with, so-called witnesses, never admitted to seeing Santo. But they had seen something. And this Indian fellow was no different, choosing instead to simply let this scourge make his way west without interference. This made it harder to connect those random dots. But not impossible. And the timeline and the trajectory were right and now he more or less had confirmation.

"What's next?" Jules asked, hoping that at some point this mystery would unravel favorably, although he had no idea what would happen when it did. His resigned sigh suggested something else: The end to the relationship. He didn't have a next step. He expected to be fired and the father of the emasculated boy would have been well within the rules of logic to do so.

"We wait." And that was really all they could do.

NOW

The cornel-buds are still white,
but shadows dart
from the cornel-roots—
black creeps from root to root,
each leaf
cuts another leaf on the grass,
shadow seeks shadow,
then both leaf
and leaf-shadow are lost.

Evening by Hilda "H.D." Doolittle

7

J anet Esterhouse was making every attempt to keep her hands warm and clean. The temptation to thrust them into her heavy blue overcoat had to be consciously dealt with after each blustery gust of wind. The blue surgical gloves they were given before their walk on the beach did little against the biting cold. What the team leader had told them in advance of their search was simple: "We need to keep the turtles as clean from the junk we carry on our hands as possible." The boy sitting next to her leaned in at this point and whispered something about urinating in the ocean. She smiled. Zach had been on these volunteer jobs for the last several years and she enjoyed their reunions. When he said this she thought of her own parents, the warm day-long summer outings at Crane Beach outside of Ipswich, instructing her siblings to "just go", impatient fingers pointing toward the surf's edge.

But she did her best to do as he asked. The job was too important to ignore his expertise.

She had arrived on the beach with two other volunteers on that early November morning to collect young sea turtles, many of whom were endangered, from the stunning impact of the cold water that swept into New England. All three girls were in their first year of college and had been participating in the turtle rescue since they were freshman in high school. The focus of their efforts were small juvenile chelonians who had ventured forth in the summer from warmer waters to the south, to fill their bellies with the bounty of marine life along the northeastern seaboard of the U.S. Some turtles would get caught in the change of season, paralyzing their warm bodies as the water temperature dropped. That drop in ocean temperatures was sudden and judging from the amount of turtles needing rescue, happening sooner every year. What once was a handful of turtles had turned into beaches littered with the small animals, many who had lost the struggle. Her job was to collect every specimen she could find, both living and dead and return them to the Aquamarine hospital on Cape Cod.

Walking these rock strewn beaches at this time of year, even when the weather was pleasant was challenging. Today the wind was whipping the grey skies, threatening their efforts with a seasonal squall. On this cold morning, they were busier than they liked. There were four times as many assumed dead turtles as there were noticeably living. It was not their job to pronounce the animals alive or otherwise; just to gather.

She had partitioned her towel lined banana box to house those that would be saved, the ones that appeared alive and those that would be studied at a later date by the Audubon scientists at the Wellbay Wildlife Sanctuary, the animals that appeared dead. They weren't always. In the days following the gathering, Janet would be part of the group that would focus their efforts on the gradual warming of the survivors. On this day, the dead turtles outnumbered the living turtles three to one. She silently prayed that those numbers would change, that some would survive and be revived from their frozen comatose state.

She heard the shrill whistle of the team leader over the angry wash of the waves. As she turned in its direction, she saw him waving his arm several hundred yards away. She removed her gloves and replaced them with warmer wool mittens, picked up her box and headed back towards the highway where the group van was parked. Her two teammates, who had been working this stretch of beach for the last nine hours, breaking only for a brown bag lunch, were waiting in the van when she arrived. It was blessedly warm.

The girls remained silent on the ride back to the aquarium. Janet looked at her cache of near dead animals, most of which looked like Kemp's Ridley turtles. This incredibly rare turtle was no stranger to Janet or the other girls. She was saddened not so much by the endangered status of the animals but the harsh cruelty of a world that saw this beast hatch on a warm Mexican beach, travel north after spending a year or so in Sargassum seaweed beds. Most traveled no further than Louisiana; others venture as far north as New Jersey. Animals who ventured farther north risked the greatest chance of encountering a sudden change in the water temperature. She held a box of turtles who had followed a warm opportunistic current to this unfortunate fate.

It was fully dark when they entered the parking lot. There were two other vans being unloaded, carrying box after box of turtles into the low-slung brick building. Once they were inside, the beachcombers made their way to the small table to the left of the main lab. While the turtles were assessed, gradually warmed, and sent to various stages of rehabilitation, the volunteers were given warmth in the form of hot soup and coffee. Hugging her cup, Janet read the small handwritten memo asking everyone to attend a small update meeting in room 7.

By the time she arrived, the meeting was underway. Dr. Emile Branstown was speaking in the front of the room. Dressed like a seafaring captain, the sixty-something man smiled as she entered the room. She spotted Zach in the far corner of the room and sat next to him. He had once told her that Branstown got his gravelly voice after a near-drowning accident when he swallowed a barnacle that had since lodged itself to his voice box. She loved an inventive lie and sought him out whenever he was on the team, if only for his endlessly witty chatter.

"Not counting what the late arriving groups have brought in, we have about 750 turtles in rehab. And the prognosis is good for what appears to be the vast majority of them. It's been cold but not as bad as it could have been, or was predicted. And it's late in the season so I suspect we are nearing the end of this effort, kids." Branstown took a deep breath and leaned against the whiteboard which listed the different types of sea turtles rescued and in rehab. The deceased turtles were simply represented by a number: It was twice as many as living.

"In past years, we could drive over to Boston's Logan or sometimes to T.F. Green in Providence. There was always a pilot who would tuck a little bundle of reptilian joy in the cockpit, taking it south if they were headed that way. Not this year though. There have been just too many. I've got a call into the Coast Guard and we're holding onto hope we might be able to wrangle a flight on a south bound commercial plane. But it'll have to be soon." There was brief murmur in the room. The hospital needed to get these turtles to their destination before winter set in too deeply. New England weather could be fickle but the latest Artic Front seemed to have settled in for a stationary nap. The water temperatures though were really what concerned this young group of environmentalist as a cold-water blob, possibly the least scientific name for the slowing of the Atlantic Meridional Overturning Circulation, a much fancier name that suggested the way the ocean mixed warm with cold, was now parked off the New England coast. Zach always nudged her and made a B-movie horror face whenever the name was mentioned.

Branstown answered the unasked question. "This is not for naught people. We'll find a way. We always have. As long as you find a turtle with a heartbeat, we'll find a way to get it back on course."

Janet related this scene to her aunt during her monthly conversation. Louise was not really an aunt in the sister of her mother or father sense. She was actually her grandmother's sister. Janet had taken to Aunt Loozy from her earliest age. They were kindred spirits.

"And how is my little green goddess?" It was after midnight when she called but Louise made no mention of the late hour. She was gifted with entering awaken fully functioning. She had no idea why and was often cross with her own internal clock when it went off at 4:00 a.m. Louise would have blamed on farm life and the never-ending obligations of what is often archaically referred to as chores. "Why," she would ask Seamus, the young man who had been with her almost forty years, he no longer young, just younger than she was, "do they call farm work chores when it is more of a job than any city slicker ever had?" Seamus would not answer but instead poke at her use of the description of urban dwellers. He'd remind her that she came from the city as well, quickly pointing out that "just cause it was a lifetime ago doesn't make you less" and they'd laugh.

"I didn't wake you, did I?"

"Of course you did. I'm an old woman and find the soft side of ten o'clock a good time to call it a day." Janet apologized. "I'll sleep when I'm dead," she said. "I'm more than happy to wake up to make sure that now isn't that time. And of course, to speak with you."

Louise listened from her darkened room, sitting up in her bed. A late November moon was illuminating the Pennsylvania countryside, giving the room a soft luminescence. She listened to the vibrant youthfulness of her quasi-niece's voice, the passion that is often bubbling unpredictably like butter melting in a microwave for too long, fat to liquid to foam to overspilling in just a minute. These calls were always welcome and more so as she got older. Regrettably, they were growing less frequent and that Louise knew marked the bridge into adulthood, the repossessing of new experiences and people and dispossessing of the childhood trappings.

"I might be able to help your little group, Jan. Let me call a friend I know. He's got a plane." They made promises to get together over the Christmas holidays, although she probably wouldn't go to wherever Janet was spending the holiday and she knew she wouldn't be coming to her. Another dispossession: The disregard for time which usually meant as you get older, the argument for convenience. Throw the unpredictable nature of the weather around the holidays and the phone became the connection. They said their goodbyes.

When the phone was answered, the man on the other end sounded concerned. "Louise?"

"Hi Sonny. Nothing's wrong," she added quickly. It was 1:00 a.m. on the east coast and she knew the first thing he would be thinking. Louise was now in her late seventies, although she never let on exactly how old she was. He knew she was about ten years older than Seamus and Seamus was a year older than him, so the math, albeit general was better than nothing. Nonetheless, a phone call after midnight Lititz, PA time was a reason to be concerned. She heard him exhale. He was not the type to worry or even overreact but it was a lot later than he was used to talking to her.

"Okay," he said leaving the rest of the sentence unspoken: what's so important that you had to call now?

"I need a favor, kind of a big one and actually not for me at all." He didn't respond. Louise was well-acquainted with the cadence of his speech, the gentle manner that he spoke each reply, almost as if he had done a quick rewrite of the possible answers and only just approved the current edit, and even his silence. His pauses were like atonal miniatures, the quiet accentuating the words, much the way Haydn did during his "Joke" Quartet, intended to be silly and annoying and comic. Each liminal silence held its own mystery and for those familiar with the man, of whom there were very few, his method. "I may have mentioned my great-niece Janet, maybe not."

"You have. She's a tree hugger like you. She's your favorite if I recall."

"She is." Her answer made no attempt to mask the smile on her face, which poured through Santo's phone three thousand miles away.

"Your green goddess. Am I right?"

"You know I stopped long ago asking no one in particular who the fuck you are, but really, who remembers that stuff? Yes, my tree hugging protégé if you must. Actually, she needs the favor although she didn't know who to ask. She's up in Maine plucking half dead turtles off the beach."

"Really? Saving the planet one reptile at a time?" Santo Aretino was in his library. He had never been able to shake the feeling walls of books gave him, as if the warmth embrace of so many stories, so many voices all attempting to get and hold his attention, holding him hostage with their words and thoughts. When the landline rang, he looked at it as if the interruption was unwelcomed. Marley had not yet arrived home from the office so he answered.

"Actually, her little group has about 700 or so of them in an aquarium up there. But the work is only half done." She paused hoping he would ask a question, although she knew he wouldn't. Those silences were disruptive for the speaker, who was forced to listen and wait, as Debussy once quipped that "music is the silence between the notes" or something to that effect. "The turtles need a plane ride south." Another three second pause with dead air. "And I was…" He cut her off.

"Which airport and when? I can send a plane to Barnstable Municipal in the morning, or whenever she needs it. Will that work?" Louise rarely called these days and never asked for favors. Her history with Santo had spanned decades, long before he became the man he is today, before Marley, before the farm. He had met her first when her lunchtime-tipsy girlfriends had bumped into his car at a stop sign. Although he had developed a relationship with each of the women in the subsequent months, with each passenger in that car that day pursuing his favors separately, Louis refused to sleep with the young Casanova. Despite his ridiculously dashing looks, far too handsome for a boy his age, a topic none of the women ever chose to inquire about, his relationship with her was built on the art of conversation and her hopeless history with men. He had asked her, along with another childhood acquaintance set adrift by the cruel fate of life, to maintain the farm he bought three decades ago.

It was often Seamus who called with updates, usually in the morning as he oversaw breakfast. He could see the big man moving around the kitchen with deft motions, as if each one had been honed and habituated to free his mind to think of other things. The farm had saved Seamus from the grief of his mother's passing and at the same time, opened his world.

"Can Barnstable handle the jet? I think that they have some tiny biplane airports up there." Louise was almost wishing she could retract the question. Of course he would know where a plane could land.

"I'll check again but I know Jet Blue is flying small jets out of there. Let me know if you find out anything different." The rest of the conversation involved small talk about the farm and Seamus. The two had lived on the eighty acre spread for over thirty years, taking care of each other and filling in the gaps in their lives. Their relationship was more like that of a mother and son; she never had one and he needed one.

Louise hung up from Santo and called Janet. She fumbled for her phone in her coat pocket as she put the keys in her car door. Her aunt's ringtone was the opening notes of her favorite Phish song, Weekapaug Groove. The news was exciting, so much so, she left the keys hanging in the door handle of her old Subaru, running back into the building to find Dr. Branstown. She never knew what to expect when she spoke to her aunt. The last thing she had expected was a solution to the group's transportation problem.

Two days later, Branstown, Zach and Janet arrived at Barnstable airport. The guard at the gate knew the doctor from previous visits and spoke to him by his first name. "Your plane is right over there, Emile." The U-Haul pulled onto the tarmac and the group began unloading and then loading the towel lined boxes onto the plane.

Janet had walked over to speak to the pilot. "I want to thank you so much for this."

"I just fly where I'm told." He was a handsome man of about forty, his looks accentuated by his insistence that he wear a uniform at all times when in service. He had been told that it was not necessary but he had insisted.

"You rescue more than turtles?"

"This is a first, missy. Usually it is kids and their families. My boss is good that way." Santo had several planes in his fleet, primarily using the plane on that New England tarmac to transport sick children to various treatments around the country. The other planes were used for international projects.

"Who's your boss?" She asked, now wondering not only who his employer was but how her aunt came to know someone that would respond this quickly with a private plane with just a phone call.

"You mean, who do I work for? It's actually SA Corp. The boss, well, I never met him." He began to walk away from her, doing a quick preflight walk around the plane. She followed him on is inspection.

"What did you mean kids and their families?" She increased her pace to keep up with his long strides.

"Story has it, a long time ago he started this business, only it wasn't really a business, more like a philanthropy endeavor called uCareBNB. It's for families that couldn't afford to visit their kids in the hospital. He ponied up this huge chunk of change and began this network where he'd subsidize the cost of someone staying in a local house near the hospital their loved one was, you know, for a couple of days. Kinda like a friendlier version of Ronald McDonald house but open to everyone. You know, more than just kids. If a wife has a husband in the hospital, that sort of thing."

"You don't happen to have a name for this amazing benefactor?" She said this with the belief that no one really had secrets anymore. Even the richest couldn't hide from everyone and in fact, she believed that people who hide, really, deep down fully intending to be found. How they were outed, either by design or happenstance always seemed staged to her. Even if you hide from the public view, she thought, eventually a disgruntled relative would give the media what they wanted, often for a price that would have been gladly paid for by the person wishing to keep their secret safe, or they would fabricate a story to manage the curious. She was young enough to know that when the tribe gest this big, no matter how much of recluse you want to be, you'll be found. Either way, being a recluse was simply not possible in the world she lived in.

"I have a name: Santo Aretino. Nobody's ever met him. He's like one of those Howard Hughes types but not a nutcase. But I hear he's just as, if not richer." So who was Santo Aretino?

She pulled her phone from her pocket as he walked away and typed the two words into her browser.

8

Getting out of receiving the award was easy. Marley simply sent a very nice handwritten note to the Conrad Hilton Humanitarian Prize Committee saying that Santo Aretino, her boss, would not be able to accept the award on the night it was to be presented. Because the $1.5 million prize was not awarded to an individual, only to an organization, by default he had no obligation to make the effort. But many of the people in his employ were just as anxious to see the man behind the multibillion dollar business conglomerate that was now being given what was essentially pocket change for the good work he did – or instructed be done.

Marley Cornish was accustomed to collecting various awards for her employer. She was one of the few who had inner access to the man and knew exactly who he was. The company was private so he had no shareholders or board to answer to and if some other source inquired, Marley handled it.

*****

It was Marley who made the arrangements for the plane to arrive at the small municipal airport and cleared the way for the pilot to refuel his Learjet in South Carolina before heading on to New Orleans. It was she who politely thanked the Hilton group for the award, posed for the cameras and respectfully declined the cash award, suggesting they pay it forward to the next year's recipient. It was also she who told him that he needed to do the Ted Talk.

It was Marley who had fallen in love with the man who had wandered into her office thirty plus years ago, who had been unlike any boy or man she had ever met, not that her dating was so extensive as to be an expert in what men were like. Not even her father seemed as even handed and well-mannered as he was.

It was Marley who embraced the single quirk he had arrived in Portland with, who had learned to live with this oddity, and even adapt. They didn't actually date, at least not in the traditional way. Santo had told her he didn't really know how and preferred to avoid what he assumed was the awkwardness that seemed to be standard procedure. She found this particularly odd, imagining that women threw themselves at him. While that assumption was not far from the truth, it was not something he openly acknowledged. He seemed shy for a man so beautiful, and when she would think back on those early days, she couldn't describe him any differently. He had a handcrafted handsomeness that made her breathless. He had a cowboy coolness without the hat. It was so much as a swagger, the kind of walk she could find driving a hundred miles in any direction away from where she was born in Portland. She considered herself a city girl. He had a dusty, weary look, road tanned and dispossessed of the normal trappings.

She never asked him why Portland. She was afraid to inquire, not the kind of fright that might uncover some hidden truth, some past he was running from, but instead, she feared the answer would not be because of her. Santo shows up in her brokerage office with a bag full of gold Kruggerrands wanting to open an account. She was instantly caught in whatever feeling love at first sight might feel like. It was tantalizing. She never asked why Portland because she hoped she would have been the reason.

She remembers walking him to the elevator. It felt

comfortable to be standing alongside of him. They shook hands and he smiled at her when they said goodbye. She was still standing looking at the closed door, in the heavily wooded hallway, when it reopened.

"Marley, I know this isn't maybe one of the things you do, but I was wondering, since I'm new here, hell, so new the shine hasn't worn off, that maybe you could point me to a good hotel, or someone renting a room in the short term, maybe."

At first, she stood there silently. Her first thought was that this was just a conversation she wished she was having. When those doors opened, she was sure it would have been empty, a wide maw in which she allowed him to disappear. It took her almost three beats before she answered.

"I'm sorry," was all she could say, not sure what she was apologizing for. Once she regained herself, a feeling she had never had prior, the always-in-control girl who amazed her father with her adult-like witticisms, her indomitable curiosity, her strength of self was now wishing for that girl to step up and say something.

"It's okay. I'll figure it out." He smiled as he reached for the elevator button. She stepped on.

"Of course, I can help." There she was she thought. Here was the Marley she knew herself to be, the woman she gave for public consumption, the woman her father had said they would be looking for every time she opened her mouth, the one they wouldn't expect. Her father had kept abreast of feminism throughout his career and wanted his only daughter, his only child to be the change. He also believed that the change would need to be subtle. He had groomed her to consider herself equal and yet, prepared her for a world that would not treat her that way. By the time she met Santo, a different type of feminism was embracing the workplace and she already had the foundation of deference in her constitution. She was not equal to the men she worked with; she was better. But he cautioned her to let them think otherwise.

Santo just smiled. "Thank you," he said, not thanks, not aw shucks, not even the exited slang of the eighties. Just a simple, fully formed thank you.

So, they would walk. Sometimes he would meet her for lunch in the park across the street from her building. Sometimes they would meet on a Saturday and wander the wet streets of Portland, ducking into specialty shops to browse the wares. There was no pattern to speak of when these meetings would happen, just a call from him asking if she was busy. Even if she was, she lied about it and said no. She at first thought she was being too accommodative but quickly dismissed attempting to play the hard-to-get role. She was not good at being coy and his soft, gentlemanly approach made her swoon.

It was Marley who suggested they rent a car and drive to the Oregon Coast. He agreed and showed up punctually. The day was delightful, unusually warm and windless. He had never seen a coast line like the one they visited. It was rugged and majestic, wholly unlike the reclaimed beaches of his Jersey shore days. She always referred to it as 'the coast', while he always referred to the place where the Atlantic met the sand three thousand miles removed as 'the shore'.

It was Marley who agreed to the request that came at the tail end of that pleasant adventure, only one of three he ever made of her. That request came just as suddenly as the other two, but set the stage for the rest of their lives.

Unfamiliar with the road, Marley had left Highway 30 as it approached the Northwest Industrial District, a tricky fork-in-the-road interchange. It had grown dark, the rain falling in an annoying mist that streaked under the wiper blades, water reforming with each sweep, aqua diamonds her father had called them. She had been driving and although she thought about waking him when she chose the wrong exit, she didn't. She had never seen him sleep. The weeks that had passed since they first met gave them time to share some intimate secrets. Santo could not remember anything and had to really consider himself to play along. He was unused to that and offered his insomnia as worthy of sharing.

She had asked him, "What do you do, I mean, with all that awake time?"

"I don't really give it too much of a consideration, really. Summer is easier because its lighter longer, but I mostly read, consider, you know, that sort of thing."

"Consider? Consider what?" He didn't answer her and she quickly backfilled the question. "That's none of my business. I should have asked you what you read." His "not a problem" response ended that conversation. She chided herself for hoping that he was considering her. It would be years, even decades before this made sense to her. But seeing him now in the most innocent of states, made her feel happy.

She was lost but decided to keep driving east. At an intersection, she pulled the car behind one already waiting at the light. Several seconds passed before a second car pulled behind her, so close that she could barely see the headlights. Then the car in front eased back slowly, effectively pinning the automobile between the two. She gently touched Santo.

"I think we've got a problem." His reaction was unexpected, in part because she had no idea what to expect.

"Lock the door and stay in the car, no matter what." This directive was almost whispered and seemed to be a good idea. She rolled up the window and locked the door. When she turned, he was gone. He had quietly closed the door on his side, locking it as it shut.

The driver of the car in front of her slowly exited his car. She noticed the traffic light turn green, a million emeralds on the misty windshield, then wiped away. He walked slowly towards her, his face hidden. From the corner of her eye she saw Santo slipping alongside the passenger side of the car in front. He was crouched low and unseen. She noticed a man in the passenger seat of the car in front. He was turned looking at her, arm slung over the seat, a sinister smile on his face. Suddenly, his head jerked back hard, Santo's hands wrapped around his forehead. He pulled him back squarely on the window track and caught the protruding door lock. The man slumped in the seat.

She saw him reach through the window and throw the idling car into drive. It slowly inched forward. The man approaching her turned when he heard the tires slowly crunching on the road gravel. As soon as the car had cleared Marley's, she saw a flash. It was Santo charging straight at the man, in front of her car. He hit him so hard his feet left the ground. He carried him several feet with the momentum and threw him hard to the blacktop. The man did not struggle, his arms dropping lax at his side.

He got up and gave her a small sign, a finger in the air signaling her to wait. The driver in the rear car was looking at his friend lying in the road and for a split second, lost Santo in his headlights. He jumped onto the hood of the trailing car and squarely smashed the windshield with the heel of his shoe. The man put up his arms but Santo's foot was moving too fast to stop the blow. With the window out of the way, he pulled the man from the car. She tried to see using her rearview mirror. It was over before she could determine what had happened.

Santo jumped off the hood of the car and walked to the passenger side. "You okay to drive?"

"No," she answered emphatically. He didn't hesitate. He closed the passenger door and walked around to the driver's side. She slid across the seat. She started to speak. He held his finger to his lips as he put the car into gear and slowly drove off.

"What the," she began before he had gone too far.

"Do you have any idea where we are?" She looked at him and then at her surroundings. She could see the Fremont bridge. She pointed. He turned the car in that general direction. Soon as they were in what appeared a less abandoned looking section of the city, he pulled over.

"I'm not sure what you saw back there. Whatever you did see, never tell anyone. Please." She touched his arm. He smiled and put the car into gear.

*****

Her logic was, as always, unwaveringly linear. "You need to do this, Sonny. Not for you but for the sharks. They know you exist but no one has an idea of what you look like."

"I disagree," he said, leaning back in his office chair. To further confound not only the media but also his employees, he conducted most of his business in a windowless office in the middle of the seventh floor. It was mostly machines on this floor, the gentle hum of their electronics did a good job of drowning out his conversations and the door was there for the same reason. The only extravagance he indulged himself in was his chair. There were no pictures, art, or otherwise personal items in the room: just two computers, a phone he rarely used on a plain laminate desk, and his Aeron chair.

Marley was also a mystery to many of the people in the company. They knew she welded enormous power and at some level, they thought she might be more than just the "boss's" liaison. She was a tall, elegant woman with a purposeful stride. Her blonde hair hung about her shoulder in what might have been called cocktail curls, softly cascading down to the middle of her back. She took several elevators to arrive at this floor, first going up, then down, then up again. It took her ten minutes to get to his office one floor away from hers.

"You can disagree all you like." She said this with the

familiarity of a long association with the man.

*****

Less than a month after the incident in the industrial district northwest of downtown Portland, they married. They drove north to Vancouver, exchanging the promises that would give him the first commitment he had ever made. She had never considered getting married and Santo didn't fit into her perception of what a union might look like.

She had never considered getting married. While she had centered feelings about who she was, she wondered if she was capable of sharing herself with anyone. She had no partitions, no boundaries between the public Marley and the private one. She was even willing to accept the second secret he asked her to keep.

"Why?" she asked as they drove to the small cottage.

"Why, what?"

"You know what." They had found the address and sitting outside the unassuming little house, the place where they would exchange vows of trust and intimacy, promises Santo had never made, she wanted to know more about this man who had stepped into her life. She turned in her seat and faced him.

"I feel like this is a saving, Sonny." As much as he wanted to drop the nickname of his youth, he liked the way she said it. It was as if the name offered her something personal about him, something no one else knew in this new version of himself, the liberated man, the man without possessions. "I mean, I've never met anyone so supremely conflicted and yet, at the same time, so confident. You never question why. Not that you're not curious. No one reads as much as you do without a generous helping of it. It's just," and her voice trailed off as if searching for the words she had rehearsed privately.

"Just what?" he asked, his voice taking on that causal late-night FM radio cadence that made her literally lose her breath. It was glorious and golden, the words slipping slowly over her like a warm summer day. He was looking right at her, giving her the kind of rapt attention that made her wonder if he was an apparition, part of a schoolgirl infatuation for one of those 'dreamy boys' that smiled on the cover of Tiger Beat. When he was close, he could feel his breath and as much as she looked for comparisons, the gentle breeze of a summer's day or the waft of scented flowers, it was more like the gentle sway of an animal's back, tasked with carrying each syllable, each tonal reference, the staggered and musical silences.

"I've never met a man so intrigued by what most of us never even consider. I always thought that each day was a precursor to the day that followed. Like each one was some kind of building block. You know, the way science works, one discovery leading to another until you have this endless ladder into the heavens. You, no you on the other hand: It's like nothing that happened yesterday mattered. You just move forward."

"And that concerns you?" He was wondering where she was headed with this thought.

"Yes, it concerns me. Will you remember what we're doing right now ten years from now? Will you remember tomorrow when the sun comes up the following day? Will you always remember me?"

He knew he was in unchartered territory with her. He had lived his whole life on the whim of his internal compass. Each new direction seemed to send him to the next place and inevitably, it was always unexpected. And without family, or friends, he had no possessions by which to bookmark the time passed.

"Yes, I'll remember you, Marley." His capacity for recall was a legitimate question. She was the first person he had actually conversed with, sharing things about himself that he hesitated to revisit. Arianne began by listening to him, what he carefully chose to tell her and then, he became the listener. And this pattern repeated itself with every person, specifically with the women in his life, listen to him for a short period and listen to them thereafter. Marley was different. She was always listening. He had told her how he felt about remembering, the uncertainty of the memory of any person to recall without editing. She had called that reflection. He disagreed.

"Nope. You pull a thought forward, any thought, fond or otherwise and depending on who you are telling it to, you will recast the situation to suit the listener. Nothing criminal about it by it is heavily employed by that element." He could see her thinking of a memory she could use to dispel his theory. "I know what you're doing and it's not a theory. It is my practical internal conclusion and it has served me well, I think. Except in times like this."

"There was th..." He stopped her.

"Marley, this is me. I'm the oddball. Not you. You are my perfect and I didn't even know I needed one. This is my experience." He leaned closer to her. He realized that neither of them had unfastened their seatbelts, sitting as if they were prepared to turn away this opportunity.

"And who knows." He sighed. "I don't know what I'll be like from this day forward. But I will know I will have someone who will remember, eh?"

He had come a very long way so far. He had told her about his parents, Umberto and Sofi, his doubts that they were who they said they were. He had told her about the first time he saw someone murdered, an event that he had never relived. She quietly listened to him talk about the women in his life. He told her about Arianne. He told her about Eva. He told her about Louise, and Dina and Suzy, all of them beginning with his first. He told her what he could remember, which he worried was becoming less accurate the longer the memory styed hidden.

"So, is it the weed?"

"Maybe, but I don't think so." He had filled her in on his smoking giving her an overview of his life, just enough to keep her fascinated in the story but without the details of how successful he was. Marley was like most people. She understood smoking, she indulged in it when it was available, which almost never since college, and held no disregard for those that did. She had watched him as he smoked, the way it washed over him, slowed down his thinking so he could tolerate the onslaught of curiosity. It did not slow him down enough to help him sleep, and that fascinated her the most. The he told her about Mr. X.

Santo had described him as a significant influence in his life and something he had happened upon accidentally. Mr. X had extolled the virtues of smoking pot. He had found a kindred spirit in his essays, a description of heightened appreciation for art and culture, music and sex. As Mr. X described the often-devastating insights that would carry over long after the high wore off spoke to the young Santo. But, as he explained to her, he felt isolated in his enjoyment. His cohorts were more interested in the disabling effects of alcohol, often mimicking the same stupidity of the adults they grew up knowing. But marijuana was different and to those kids he knew, the people he envisioned as trapped into the life that their parents had lived, it was another fun thing to do on a Saturday night. It became a solitary experience for the most part, a choreographed indulgence that required just the right surroundings, an uninterrupted place that required he be alone to achieve. He told her that he had been social with it but it was not his preference.

She remembers the childlike excitement he had as he told her who Mr. X was.

"Did you ever find out who Mr. X was?" she asked.

"Carl Sagan!" he said with more excitement that she was used to seeing. "Mr. X is Carl fucking Sagan. Or was." For Santo, as it was to Mr. X, pot was a creative scholarship. It was also a salve, keeping him comfortably numb, able to withstand the things he could not understand. As much as he held trapped in his mind, she knew the insight he was hoping to have, or avoid perhaps, surfaced occasionally, sometimes involuntarily. "Weed," he told her, "keeps the beast at bay."

She would find, over the years, that his interests were varied and wide flung, often difficult to keep track of. He mentioned almost nothing of his past without concerned prompting, and that kind of gentle interrogation was available infrequently and could be exhausting. Mostly, she just let him be whoever he was in that moment, always kind and gentle and soft-spoken but with a cautionary stance. His recall of arcane facts, long forgotten poets and passages from dusty books was enviable. Everything he seemed to have read and researched was all conveniently filed away in the great expanse of his brain.

As they drove north that morning, crossing the bridge that connects the two states, he allowed her the time to think. She had her head turned away from him, passing the huge Waddles sign which simply said, 'eat here', over the grey wash of the Columbia River, into the city of Vancouver, a place she seemed to affectionately call Portland's attic. He remembered her telling him that getting married was all that she ever heard was any good about Vancouver. This was his first visit.

She thought about the people he came from, the people most would willingly call their parents. They held something different for him, a weird abstract of what they could have been had they been what they said they were to the world outside of their house. Over the months leading up to this journey to finalize their love legally, he had mentioned them only when questioned. Each time, it seemed painful. These were memories purposely tucked into the darkest corner. If Sofi and Umberto were his parents, she wondered, why then did they act as if they were not?

She understood that she had only his side of the story and a child's recollection of who his or her parents were was often clouded in their own perception. Not so Santo. He thought about them but not fondly and not with disdain. It was more confusion that was unresolved, his own questions and suspicions left unanswered. Would he want children? Would she want children with him?

And then there was the women, all of his lovers or pseudo lovers, whatever they were to him. Did they create viable stand-ins for the mother and father who had abandoned him even as they gave him shelter? While he had the characteristics of Oedipus, both the good and the bad, the abandonment at birth, the blindness to the reason, the guilt and shame he kept hidden seemed to offer her a glimpse into her lover's tragic life. He told her he hurtled forward but each time he had revealed something additional about himself, it seemed as if that journey was not planned or contrived. He may not have suffered the hubris so often associated with the Greek king, but she couldn't help but wonder if he was also running. And would his journey stop with her? Unlike Oedipus, he took the counsel of the wise men and women in the books he read. Did they offer him the counsel he needed now as he drove to his wedding vows? Could this dispossessed man begin to possess? Would she be the one to save this tragic hero from himself? Could she prevent the fall of the morally good man with the outsized personality that no one but her knew?

She thought about those women and the way he retold their stories. He had known them but did not know them. She wondered why the women he told her about seemed to swoon but at the same time, keep him at arm's length, as if he were a barbarian at the gate? Why did Arianne, his best confidante push him away at the point when he seemed ready to bridge the emotional divide he had never attempted to cross? Did they find what they were looking for in the personality of this sinner/saint that helped them carry on? Would she be able to? "Alas, how terrible is wisdom..."

She wanted to know how he came into her life. He had no answer to this question. Instead, he told why he left the town he grew up in, the drug partnership gone sour with the arrest of two friends, his many months in Lititz, the reason he left Eva's farm. All of these were, in Marley's terms, dragged out of him in piecemeal fashion. It was as if they were tidbits of memories floating in a gelatinous ocean, visible but isolated in their own membranes. And because of that, huge pieces, important details were left adrift, the way a boat falls as a swell rises, hiding it temporarily from view.

He had not made a conscious decision to withhold other more disruptive memories. But these hidden events, how that violent departure from Lititz had seemed to set the tone for his journey across the country would remain untold and unremembered. To Santo, the unconscious version of himself, these were moments not to be revisited. They had taken on an instinctual nature, much the way a beast might fail to recall how he was trapped or why. He would not test her emotional fortitude by describing the incident at the bus stop, the encounter in St. Louis, and the unfortunate mishap on that dusty ranch outside of Boulder. He made no decision to not tell her; it was simply no longer part of the narrative.

She would be the caretaker of those memories, recollections he cared little about. She would promise to keep his secrets and adapt to his fears. She knew this marriage would never be made public. Her parents would never know, at least not in the traditional sense. "He needs me," she would explain to them and comfortable in the child they had nurtured, they let it stand without question. "Yes," she would reply to the longing in their eyes, "I am very happy." She gave her parents the only photograph of the ceremony and the only photo of Santo.

She agreed to allow him to recede into the shadows as she became the face of his ambitions. Somewhere between running from one thing and ending up at her desk at Morgan Stanley with a satchel full of gold coins, he had become enamored with the world of investing. He would, through her create a vast fortune built on the mistakes of others, intuitively moving from one investment to another with such mastery, as the face of these decisions, Marley became a celebrity amongst the investment community. He was the eminence grise and she executed each of those decisions with her own savvy and intelligence. It wasn't so much a ruse as a convenient deception: It was none of their business.

She acted as his proxy as he carried out Eva's wish. She wanted him to do something good and eighty percent of every dollar he earned went to his various philanthropic pursuits. When he arrived in Portland, he used the profits from the gold to make additional investments: First in oil, then in local real estate and small companies, and then on to currencies. He channeled those profits into helping homeless people, financing art preservation, and helping families of terminally ill patients. It was this last endeavor that prompted the award.

*****

"You can and should do this. That fucking award didn't help and they're starting to circle. It's time to get out in front of this." This was Marley speaking as the business woman, the logical counterpart to his soaring ideals. He wasn't arguing the necessity of how it should be done and why. What concerned him was a flaw he might not have seen.

"You know how they are. They have your name thanks

to the goofy blogger which traces itself back to the kid you helped, Louise's niece, with those turtles who got your name from the pilot, what do you call him, Wind Pirate, although I have no idea how he deduced you were who you are."

"He calls himself Wind Pirate." This sounded sheepish when he said it.

When Santo had agreed to send the plane to Boston to save Louise's niece's turtles, he had not foreseen the series of events that would arrive at his doorstep. First, a blogger, probably the niece or a manipulated boyfriend started digging. He had made a serious digital effort to find out who this person was but lost interest when he realized the potential outcome of knowing. When he couldn't answer the question of what he would do if he did uncover the author of the post, he stopped searching.

Some paper trails are difficult to hide even when there is no intention of doing so. Santo had no digital presence and he felt safe hiding behind this anonymity. While both Marley and he had decided years ago, at the advent of the internet, that he needed to avoid creating a presence. As an early investor and a successful one, he was well aware of the technological downsides of adding this new medium to the places where the world's information would be stored. He saw any activity from anywhere eventually becoming footprints in virgin snow. Marley and he had worried about the eventual interconnectivity that information could have. Through Marley, he had recognized the description of the internet would aptly be a web, capturing known and unknown, intentional and happenstance.

The trail was there. Santo, for all of his technologically hidden efforts to try and connect any accidental dots so they could be removed or hidden hadn't anticipated this trail being revealed. By researching the flight plans of the plane he had sent to transport the turtles, the blogger had simply followed the information to the uCareBNB business Santo had created. It was one of those quirky ideas. It was built on the notion that people were inherently charitable and would be willing to open their homes to people who couldn't afford to stay in the same town where their loved ones were hospitalized. The pilot mostly acted as an airborne taxi driver, shuttling people to and from their loved ones, free of charge. The concept grew virally and quickly spread across the country.

At some point, the pursuit took a dark turn when the blogger enlisted a friend to do some digital espionage. The donor's list was hacked and eventually the trail led to the name Santo Aretino. Santo didn't blame anyone but Marley still offered apologies.

"I know how you feel about the public, Sonny."

"And how do I feel about them?" he asked, a smirk crossing his face. His isolated inner world involved as few people as possible. He lived like a ghost in the machine. He had let his guard down with uCareBNB. It was his flaw. He wanted to hide and did for most of the time however he had his moments when he slipped away from his own self-imposed prison.

His habit of involving himself as a middle manager with these charitable efforts along. She had suggested that this might be a mistake but she knew he couldn't help himself. Reclusiveness was his idea and if he chose to break with that, she had little power to sway him. She silently welcomed it.

When the SEC focused their investigations into his company's investment success, where Marley was the face in front, she thought he would step up. They had taken a dim view of his magical touch with the markets. She handled all three inquiries with an adept hand and while he thanked her, he still chose to shadow the whole process.

His name had appeared deep within the company's tax

filings which allowed the hackers to make several Olympic leaps of deduction. Marley had no need to apologize for his own mistakes, plural.

Marley walked across the expanse of their bedroom and moved into Santo's arms. She marveled at his strength and in other times, his vulnerabilities. "You're a good man, Sonny. Just because you want to hide that fact from the world doesn't mean the world wouldn't like to thank you." She leaned up and kissed him.

"Yeah, but," and she pushed her index fingers to his lips.

"I have only the vaguest inkling of why you chose to be a ghost and for all these years, I never bothered to ask. And I don't intend to now. And you never offered. You've done so many positive things, uCareBNB for example, that people feel as though they need to respond somehow. You're like water in an empty vessel. You see a problem and you solve it. You fly the families of little kids with cancer all over the country for no other reason than you saw a void and filled it. You reunite wives with husbands, children with parents, turtles with their intended habitat and most people can't accept that kind of charity without letting all their Facebook friends know. So, you don't have to apologize and I don't either."

"Fucking Facebook. So, remind me why I have to go public now? Won't it just fade from the collective consciousness in a couple of days, hell, a couple of hours? I've read enough about the world's short attention span to..."

"To what? Assume that you're not some as yet to be discovered treasure found out by people who earn their money with subscribers or are simply stoned trustafarians who have nothing better to do." She could see him over her shoulder in the reflection of the mirror. His mind was racing, the furrow on his brow was noticeable from twenty feet. She knew better to ask him where whatever he was thinking about was taking him. Often, what came of those tense moments of silence was the brilliance of a flower blooming in a sidewalk crack, unexpected and impossible.

"Trustafarian? Did you just make that up?" He was smiling. He was back in the bedroom with her, wherever he had gone in those brief moments would be revealed when he wanted it to be, and no prompting from her, no 'penny for your thought' question would force it before its time.

"Are you ready for your audition?" She smiled ignoring his question when she asked him this. The absurdity he had concocted was, in her opinion a fine work of smoke and mirrors, and if things went well, lights. She knew he had been compared to Howard Hughes with increasing frequency since the blogger had made his speculations public. But he wasn't and he wondered if anyone would ever know. Where Hughes began in the public eye as a record breaking aviator, her husband had slipped in under the cloak of darkness, as if the man that showed up at her office that day had been invented only moments before, a well-represented fantasy of the man she didn't know she needed. His reclusiveness was handcrafted and for no apparent reason, she went along with it, never asking the questions why.

This had bothered her in the beginning. She didn't need a man; she needed this one. She was self-sufficient, independently intelligent and a singular force to be reckoned with, all because of her attentive tutelage at her father's knee. He had not shaped her in anyway. If anything, he kept pushing back the boundaries, moving walls if it was in his power and always, without question, supporting whatever and however she needed it. But her reflection kept seeing him over her shoulder, just like now, sitting comfortably in a world of his own making, asking only that he be left to his books and his garden and her. If he had to become a public figure, it would be on his terms, not hers.

He had changed into jeans and simple black dress shirt.

As he headed for the door, she simply said, "Watch?" He removed the sixty five thousand dollar Phillipe Patek from his wrist, slipping it into his front pocket. As much as his life was unbounded by time, he favored expensive time pieces. "You remember where you're going?" she asked. They had discussed arriving with as little fanfare as possible.

"I do," he answered. She wished him luck with a kiss, which he insisted become a hug. He would grab her arm and flop it across his shoulder, and then the other one, their bodies pressed tightly against one another, his arms encircling her waist.

"Don't worry, my paramour," suggesting something illicit in their affection. He buried his face in her hair, in her scent and the softness of the skin on her neck. She knew what he was doing and she felt her body warm. He had told her he was memorizing her. This made her feel both safe and concerned. They kissed three times, quickly, one for love, one for goodbye and the last one, in case we never see each other again.

Santo headed crosstown to a small warehouse in the southeast part of Portland. The words CastRight was artistically spray painted on the wall above the barn door entrance of the otherwise nondescript warehouse. He was told to be there at 3pm and he arrived early. He waited for Marley to arrive in her chauffeured Escalade and enter the building before doing the same.

He heard voices echoing in the huge soundstage and moved towards the makeshift reception. The young lady sitting at a folding table checked off his name on the screen in front of her, a fictional moniker he had found amusing. She looked up at him and quipped, "You don't look like a Laslo."

"Really?" he asked, giving her a charming smile, something she mistook as an older man hitting on her much younger self. She didn't answer with anything other than a sigh. "What does a Laslo look like?"

She ignored him. "You're the first here so you can grab a seat over there until the director calls you."

The director was told that the first person to arrive was how the rest would be cast. Six additional people had been selected from a pool of headshots but were told to arrive no earlier than 3:15pm.

A small woman with a tattoo of an ocelot on her neck intercepted him and guided him over to a photographer. Head shots were taken from a variety of angles. Soon, six other men entered the building and were instructed to do the same thing. Each was handed a two page script to review. The ocelot girl asked them if they wanted anything to drink. They all took water.

Santo/Laslo was asked to read a small script, mostly for the benefit of those in the building. It was an excerpt of the actual speech he was to give at the TED Talk. As an acronym for technology, entertainment, and design, born of a single conference, these talks drew hundreds, sometimes, thousands of eager listeners to hear some otherwise behind-the-scenes geeks and nerds, thinkers and hypothesizers, survivors and dreamers make their obscure work public. And the public ate it up. TED had since become synonymous with raising money or as some like to refer to it, awareness for things that matter to the world, but the world didn't know mattered. It was founded in 1984, the first year Santo Aretino earned his first million.

All the men were all his age, build, and with similar coloring. Marley had helped cull the headshots from thousands of stills. They all read, even if Santo knew that the words he had written would not be uttered by a single one of them. But if the illusion was to work, they did not need to know that detail at this point. These men were to be copies.

9

She reached over to gently touch him. It was in the pre-dawn hours, the time of day she was accustomed to making this tender gesture, but he wasn't there. It was still dark outside and she knew she had another two, maybe four hours before she would even attempt getting up. In almost every night since their marriage, and before they decided to do so to make their union legal, he would go to bed with her, perhaps make love to her or just fall asleep. Marley was a slow sleeper, always inventorying the day's events, making mental notes on how tomorrow might unfold and using those thoughts to gently drift into slumber. Santo on the other hand, was gone in seconds, enveloped in a deep murmur of a man with a satisfied life. But that quick retreat into a hard sleep was short-lived. Sometimes she heard him rise, but that was in the early days, as she watched his shadow quietly, almost ninja-like, leave the room. As time went past, and the years of this nocturnal habit continued, she woke less often when he departed. Instead, she would slip towards his side of the bed, reach out to touch him if only to confirm that he was gone.

He made no excuses for this behavior, nor did she question it. He could be found, book in hand, in the later years wearing glasses, thermos of coffee and cup that had grown lukewarm, just the way he liked it, sitting in a tufted maroon side chair. Most of the time when she found him, there would be the gentle wafting of marijuana smoke around the floor lamp behind, a seductive fog, an ashtray nearby with a half burnt joint. He'd look up, tilt his wire-rimmed spectacles to the top of his head and motion for her to join him, tapping his lap. She would, they'd kiss and she would go back to bed, leaving him with wherever his brain was journeying, alone. As a small girl, she would wake at night and stare out of her window. If she timed it right, she would see a large raccoon cross the back lawn, the shape of a small VW Beetle but with short stubby legs, never looking at the little girl in the window. From the edge of the forest on one side to the forest on the other, oblivious of its audience, it would walk, purposely and without regard. That was, she realized, her husband, a nocturnal wanderer who could have cared less about the oddity of this habit. Wake and bake and read was how he'd describe it to her, something he had always done.

If that was his habit, she was his routine. She would hear him coming and roll away from him. She was waiting for what would happen next. Santo would make her arrival to each day as pleasant as possible, something he called the most important five minutes of the day, arriving at her bedside with a pot of ginger lemon tea in a thermos, softly sitting on the edge of the bed, he would rouse her with a gentle back scratch. She would smile, gently moan and let him ease her into wakefulness.

There was no startled arrival. She simply opened her eyes and spoke to him, "You were dreaming last night." She said this in a whispered tone but the concern was clear in her voice. She would not ask what it was about. She didn't have to.

"I was?" She was facing away from him, his hands gently scratching her contours, a very sensual and intimate gesture that she never took for granted. If she had any really close friends, she would not reveal this to them, certain that they would try and kill her to have him for themselves.

"And yes you were talking. Rather clearly," she added, rolling over. He looked at her and even though the room was still mostly dark, she was illuminated by the faint light from the hallway. "I'm just kidding. I couldn't make out a word."

He didn't sound relieved and she could see, even if the long shadows he wasn't hiding that fact from his expression. "I was staring at that buffalo again. I could hear that old Indian standing behind me saying weird ass shit."

"Anthony, or Antonga or something like that. I heard you say."

"When I turned around, he was speaking to Eva, not to me. She playfully slapped the man in the arm. Like they were sharing some inside joke. And then the buffalo snorted." She had never met Eva, who had passed away shortly after they met. And he never fully explained the Indian or the buffalo or why these characters were all in the same dream.

"Should I have woke you up? Or should I have let you finish that boring dream. Jeez, Sonny." This wasn't the first time he'd had this same dream. In the early days, they talked about it, how it was the result of something unresolved, something that had meaning that was not understood. He offered no background and he seemed to be really trying to figure out the importance of those people and that animal. As time drifted on and the familiarity of their relationship grew, the dream became less concerning. It was, they assumed, something that would always be there. Sometimes he'd moan, other times he'd speak and still other occasions he'd weep. This was the only time she'd ever seen him use that emotion. He was warm to her but she knew, he was mostly cold inside, crying was not something she thought he was capable of. "Can't you at least have a fun dream every now and again, or a wet one?"

"Can't have one of those, you keep me too drained. That's the domain of some blue balled teenager." She rolled away from him and stood to go to the bathroom.

"And we all know you were never a blue balled teenager."

"You don't know anything about me," he responded playfully. She laughed. When she returned he had stood up, peering out the window at the deserted street below. They were staying at their in-town condominium, a simply decorated loft space that had only the essential furnishings. They never stayed there alone.

"You're just nervous about the speech." She slid back underneath the covers. "Your animal totems don't help much, do they?"

"I'll be fine," he told her, rounding the bed and kissing her on the way out of the room. But in fact, he was wondering if he would be fine. The months leading up to this event had not been as stressful as he imagined. He had, apparently, written the speech over thirty years ago. This was another dream, one he hadn't had in quite some time. As cliché as it seemed when he finally typed the words from that memory, it was a speech to a crowd of people he had never seen. They didn't appear to recognize him though, squinting as if trying to discern a facial feature. The words he was speaking seemed to flow as if he had memorized them, which he found himself reviewing in the days prior to the speech.

Over the years, he had told her about the buffalo incident without telling her why he was talking to the old Indian, or even what significance Eva played in the scene. He had never mentioned the recurring speech dream, in part because it always came in clipped pieces, the people staring at him but unable to see him, the other figures on stage, the vibrant illuminations and sometimes, back stage, and of course, the speech.

His dreams disturbed him and for the most part, remained untold. He had, for want of a better explanation, sequestered every event in his life into a locked space and refused to revisit it. He explained this to her as 'moving forward'. Perhaps he was not a reasonable man, refusing to adapt to the world around him. Progress, which George Bernard Shaw once quipped, was the realm of the unreasonable and moving forward to Santo suggested progress.

Santo had told Marley about the speech, the recurring segments he was supposedly spoke to a crowd, "for whatever reason." She would prod him gently to write it down. "Some of the greatest books have come from dreams," she said, hoping to encourage him.

"Or nightmares. Lovecraft didn't write love stories and Jekyll and Hyde wasn't exactly the kind of story that conjures a smile." He knew that Poe pulled some of his best works from the terrors of the night. But these were not terrors, even as they concerned him. It wasn't fear. It was the fact that he had no recourse, no way to combat them, aside from staying awake.

"There's Bronte and E.B. White," she replied playfully, returning to bed and pulling the sheets up to her chin.

"Shoot me if I have Stuart Little dreams."

"I'll do nothing of the sort. I think you'd be a great writer if you ever decided to put some of that brain of yours on paper." He knew he had only to mimic what he had done in his sleep, sitting down at a keyboard and typing. The six thousand words speech came out eventually and needed no editing.

It was early summer and the city would shine from an overnight misting, yielding to the morning sky, the clouds would retreat. The sun would caress the flanks of Mt. Hood as it climbed into the sky. She watched him slip out onto their fourth-floor balcony. The only sound was from a garbage truck. It made disingenuous comments as it rumbled past.

*****

179

Marley had hired a young indie filmmaker named Bertrand. She had discussed with Santo how he thought the talk should be staged. He hesitated explaining what he saw in his dreams, unsure if the colorful machinations his brain presented were even possible to reproduce, and if they were, how would he put them into words. Marley did her research though and narrowed the choice to one young man. Over coffee, she explained what she wanted. It felt instinctually right.

Bertrand was excited to be producing a TED Talk stage show that, as she had explained, needed to be innovative and memorable. Bertrand used no last name but insisted on the moniker as part of all of his film titles. Gifted with bringing distinctive lighting to otherwise shadowy settings, he had gained a local Portland reputation with his film "Bertrand's Oblique". True to its title, the camera angles were arranged in such a manner as to give each character a different age. Parallel twists, often from the view of a child, made otherwise younger adults seem old. He swooped in shots from above, angling them with such precision, critics had written that "[it] was if he had conspired with nature, timing even the sway of the branches in the background to provide a provocative dialogue when no words had spoken." He was "a director on the verge" they often said and yet he was determined to name his fame and shape it in his own liking.

His excitement came without the ego of success. This was unexpectedly refreshing. She had anticipated an artsy conflict as she imagined he would do, hoping to put his signature on the project. As Marley explained the premise, using the same details that she and Santo had mapped, Bertrand seemed confident he could pull it off. He didn't change a word of the script.

By design, Santo had been the first one the two of them had met during the initial audition. Marley had leaned over to him as Santo stood in front of them and whispered to Bertrand that he was the prototype, the character that everyone needed to match.

"I like his menace," he replied in a voice hidden behind a cupped hand. "There's something else too, like that threat is somehow measured, coiled even."

All of the men chosen to audition did not need that look, but Marley remained quiet. She had experienced that menace the first time she had met him over thirty years ago when he walked into the office of Morgan Stanley and asked to open an account. That "menace" provided a safe comfort even if they rarely ventured into the public domain. She smiled as the young director mentioned what everyone her husband had met felt.

All six men had been told to grow a beard, which was then expertly trimmed and retouched to match Santo's beard and its peppered appearance. All six men had been given the name of a tailor for their suit and had been told it could be kept by each of the actors. None of the six men had ever owned a bespoke suit.

All six men had been told to memorize the script and pay particular attention to the directorial notes. These were added in collaboration between Marley and Bertrand. Ad libbing would not be permitted. All six men were told they should do this but be prepared to only lip sync the part. When they rehearsed, they did so in unison, each speaking aloud, making the same hand gestures and moving in a carefully synced choreography. They did this for three weeks prior to the speech, harmoniously mimicking each other word for word, attempting to hit the same notes as if the same music was amplified six times from six different speakers, each tonally identical. They were similar to an acapella ensemble but with only a single note being achieved.

All six men were told that only one would be selected on

the given night to speak. No one knew who that man was. All six men were handed a hardcopy of the script and a recorded USB drive with the speech on it, narrated by the director.

Two days before the actual stage appearance, the men still had no idea where the stage was. Marley showed up and later told Santo that seeing six imitators was creepy.

"Creepy how?" he asked playfully.

"You perv. Not like you're thinking," she answered just as playfully.

"C'mon, Marley. Seven lovers, although none of them as skillful as yours truly." She threw the folder she was holding, papers scattering. He shielded himself in the same way a person would do if the object was intended to do physical harm. He even said, "ouch" quickly adding, "elder abuse!"

All six men were promised a professional New York agent and twenty thousand dollars for the acting job. They were also told that this performance would not be credited, promoted or otherwise made public. Each signed a non-disclosure statement.

"I know that won't be easy," the director said when they had gathered after the first introductions. But after spending several weeks together, the men seemed comfortable with the oddity of the situation.

The one thing Santo found the most curious about the arrangements that he and Marley had made in preparation, the choreography included, was the idea that he could examine what other people saw when they looked at him. Not all people; just the handpicked director who, along with a casting agent chose the living doppelgangers of him. Granted, they would be made to look as a close to him as possible, dressed and rehearsed with all of his affectations, but the question remained in his mind: what do people see when they see him?

*****

After the incident with the carjacking in northwest Portland during those initial weeks in the town, Santo felt that he needed to move on. This was what he had done before and as time wore on, he was beginning to feel as though this state of constant motion was not only safer for him, but for those he may have gotten to know.

He left Chester to protect Umberto and Sofi. He was unaware of that motivation until thirty years later, when Marley questioned him about it, offering a weird psychoanalytical approach to his invisibility. Even though he had harbored lifelong doubts about his genetic lineage to the two who had provided for him, he knew they would be devastated if they knew what he had become. He had sensed they probably already did but remained quiet, the same silence you entertain when confronted with an avoidable danger.

He left Lititz to protect Eva. The night he had visited those three boys and did what he could do to leave scars that would be theirs for the rest of their lifetime, avenging two innocent Amish girls and a pacifistic father who sense of parenthood was being challenged by a society that did not value his beliefs was, he believed as an act of someone who needed to exit.

He moved through the Midwest meting his own version of response to an increasingly violent world, one that encroached on the weak. In each instance, just like high school, the saved were not inclined to accuse their savior of any wrongdoing. And his victims were not in any condition to seek retribution. In school, the defeated strong used their fear to turn inward, a sort of self-examination while at the same time, the school authorities took umbrage. Although This changed after school, after Chester, after Lititz, he would fail to recollect how he left this new group of defeated strong, who, rather than self-examination into why they preyed on the weak, he ended their reign of terror.

As in his school days, his drug dealing days, his attack on the boys in that college dorm, the kid he saved outside the bus stop, the wanna-be stockbroker in St. Louis, and the opium peddlers in Colorado, he unwittingly attracted the attention of law enforcement. But they too were struck with the difficult place he put them in: his crimes, while still criminal, helped cull the world of some of riffraff they dealt with on a daily basis. They were inclined to search him out, follow his trail, and bring him to justice. But they couldn't bring themselves to do much more than promise to get around to it.

John Tell, the detective responsible for the largest drug arrest in Delaware County history and the jailing of two of the area's largest dealers, one of the first big wins in Nixon's war on drugs, did not net Santo Aretino. He knew he might never get the chance but he always wondered what it would have been like to get the kid, find out what his role was, and how he managed to do what he did while eluding the police who had focused an extraordinary amount of energy on getting him. The only break they received was from a disgruntled girlfriend, and she refused to mention Santo.

Sheriff Crow had let the trail run cold as well. The St. Louis police department was not interested and essentially suggested he did the City of Arches a favor. The kids at the opium ranch did not report that crime either. One of them saw the opportunity and talked his fellow druggies into cleaning out the stash and never coming back. The bodies of Dr. Poppy and his Vietnamese sidekick rotted in the hot sun. Their corpses were eventually portioned by a variety of desert animals that thrived on those who did not. What was left of them was discovered about a month later. The Colorado State Police had known about the men and the drugs and did not pursue the case, essentially calling it cold from the onset. Anthony never said a word, even as he wholly witnessed the situation. Instead, he let his quarry get away as he drove Santo to meet the buffalo. It wasn't his original intent. He kept thinking of what his Scottish boss always said, "Confess'd faut is half amends, chief so's we be need'n to be prov'n it" as he drove the boy away from the scene. He was convinced the boy had acted out of mind and could not recall the disposed of men laying in the dirt.

The police in Portland had a similar reaction to what happened in the industrial district. The three men they found at the scene were well-known by local authorities. They had rap sheets as long as the summer solstice and had been known to try this car-blocking-robbery maneuver before. They had been questioned in the past but without viable witnesses, the victims, weighing the potential of retaliation, something they promised with such clarity, no charges were ever brought. Whomever had delivered this justice to these thieves was welcome news for the cops assigned the investigation although they admittedly were not going to try too hard to find the person who had 'taken the law into his own hands'.

10

John Bates was different. He had an expense account. He had a client who felt violated, even if it was his son who had borne the brunt of the punishment. He had time, patience and a special tenacity that he deeply believed was genetically hardwired and was handed down to him from generations of investigators. Had he lived in a different time, they would have novelized him, his British charm wrapped inside an American veneer making for the perfect investigator, like a brilliant shadow, they would have used him as a template, a character that would illustrate the greatness of writers like Christie or Poe. He had no cold cases, no unsolved mysteries and this robust resume gave clients no pause when he was retained.

Armed with only a description, he had followed the path west and then retraced his steps back to Lancaster, to Lititz and eventually to Chester. The picture was getting clearer but not by much.

The word ghost would come to mind as an apt description of the man he was pursing as he drove from one location to another. He knew that it was possible to become invisible. Some people have a gift for plain sight disappearance. Sort of the way the color grey could make a person less memorable in a frozen fog. Ninjutsu masters could be stealthy enough to exploit a person's sense of what was real and what was not, forcing a person to deny what was obvious because it was less so. But this person was different. He wasn't a ghost or the fog or a Ninja. He was flesh and blood who left a trail that resembled Burma Shave ads, each advertisement bringing him closer to Santo Aretino, sometimes known as Sonny. True, he was as obvious as he was forgettable, as memorable as he was ephemeral, intelligent enough to take advantage of those that were less so. But John Bates, he told himself, was different as well, a mantra he repeated like a worshiper with a rosary.

He reviewed the man's activities, hesitating at times to consider him a man, estimating his age at the time of most of his crimes at around nineteen or twenty. He had the sophistication of someone much older, someone much more experienced in the world around him and understanding how that world would react to various situations. He was the kind of person that would turn heads when he entered a room and if he played it right, and in most cases he did, he would leave unnoticed.

Men couldn't describe him expect to say he was big and they would sometimes add, quick. And those recollections were mostly dismissed for their completely masculine take on hearsay, or in this instance, post-witnessing and projecting. They saw a man capable of taking down multiple opponents and they supposed a very quick dispatch. And of course, because of the relative size of the men he had killed, these pseudo-witnesses and crime scene cops naturally concluded power generated by size. Those characteristics were not to be dismissed, Bates thought but they did not help to narrow down who his quarry was, just what he looked like.

Women, on the other hand would lie. Bates did not attempt to read the common tells other investigators relied on, no matter how unreliable those techniques were. Sure, the white lies were easy. For those kinds of lies you could watch her touch her hair or her lips, blink, shrug, think hard and do any number of things that were physically distracting. To him, the body language was not always an accurate read and may have been simply an indication of their own infatuation with him. Bates regarded himself as 'dashingly' handsome and needed to ignore the motions that a woman might make to support this version of what they saw.

The women he spoke to though clearly had seen him, talked to him, perhaps even fantasized about him, in the moment of encounter and probably under the veil of darkness. They were hiding their embarrassment and the intrigue that deep inside each of them, they had flirted with the devil they had all been warned about. And this unsettled all of them. It was easier to say they 'couldn't help', 'sorry' or 'I wish I could' than to admit they had felt something they had never experienced before and it scared them. At night, they'd embrace the thought and wonder what could have happened and why, if they had been the kind of girl that took risks, they didn't dive head-first into those green eyes. The tell was one of missed opportunity.

Bates knew they were lying and after talking to everyone that had proximity to Santo, he knew why. He was unable to call them out on the fabrication because he didn't know the truth. And he was not inclined to fish for answers. Bate's father, a private detective like he and his father was, had told him that you can ask any question you want of a suspect, adding that the only one worth merit though was the one you had all or part of the answer to already.

His grandfather had discussed this at length one day. It was not a lesson about being a good detective, having excellent observational skills or even blending into the background. As he drove west, some of the key tenet's of that afternoon seemed come back to him. He remembered him suggesting that "...disappearing is not necessarily the purview of the coward. No, Johnny. Some people are simply independent of the way things are. In our profession, you will find people who will leave not so much as clue and they will do it without an inkling of forethought, completely without thinking."

He couldn't help but argue with his grandfather's outlook on this specific case, even if he had been dead for over a decade. It must, he thought, take great effort to simply go about your business and not be noticed. But he felt as if he had adequately addressed that as well. The old man was adamant as he advised his grandson, replaying of the conversation as vivid as the day he told him. Beneath the whine of the car's tire, he could hear his grandfather's voice: "Everybody wants to be seen, remembered, and they do all sorts of things to stand out from the crowd. This is why we costume ourselves the way we do. A man who wears cufflinks for instance thinks more highly of himself than the man who does not. Bot can wear the crispness of a starched white shirt, but the man with the holes sewn to allow for jewelry makes the shirt-wearer more conceited, aloof. And all because of the difference between a button and a cufflink. One suggests superciliousness while the other wears a cloak of diffidence. Even the wallflowers stand out in that context. But there are a select few who see the world the way everybody else does and know, maybe with great skill, maybe instinctually, how to slip between those visual cracks."

Nature was full of invisibility. Artic foxes, walking sticks, leopards, even squirrels, all blended into their environments and did so without trying. John knew that was evolution at work but with people, it was different. Everyone he had met thought anonymity was too humbling to be a lifetime commitment. At some point, you would have to speak to the checker at a grocery store, get their haircut or interact with their landlord. Isolation took more work than one might imagine. Even conformity was not for the complacent. But here he was wondering if the man he was pursuing could keep up the effort for much longer.

He did.

*****

Thirty or so years later, Santo Aretino had maintained his invisibility. His wife of almost as many years, Marley Cornish, the face of his company, one of the richest women in the United States according to the latest Forbes survey, kept his secret as well and did so without verbally lying about it. She deserved a great deal of credit for that effort and she was the person who received all the credit for his behind-the-scenes machinations of their lives.

She knew and therefore became his cover story. And although it all seemed to have been a calculated move on Santo's part when seen from a distance, each step well-orchestrated, the timing and the considerations all thought about in advance, she knew differently. As she had come to know, he never questioned himself.

He had made a simple gold trade at the insistence of a man he met on the bus. Marley knew where that money came from and no matter how he had painted the harmlessness of his wealth, she was not convinced illegally obtained cash should be dismissed that way. But she never argued the origin of the money because his crafted accumulation of such wealth at that age was an enviable accomplishment.

Then there was the insistence of New York bound broker he met in St. Louis to redirect his intelligence towards investing. Had those two seeds not been planted into his fertile mind, they might not have meet. It began simply.

At first, they dated over business, meeting to discuss her work and his ideas. He never came back to the Morgan Stanley offices after that first encounter. He was her personal success and as a client who was also in the throes of something he had never felt before, a sort of connection he had imagined he'd have one day, they rode those investments to new levels. It was Santo who had manipulated the whims of the market in ways that had not been anticipated by anyone before him.

One successful trade after another, one idea leading to another grander notion, and of course, his lack of interest in kudos pushed her to leave that firm, marry the financial renegade she had fallen in love with, open SA Holdings as her company and ride the whole adventure to the forefront of Wall Street and national attention.

His indefatigable pursuit of the next day, the tenacious effort to just move forward was soon redirected to funding the first infrastructure bank ever opened. He ponied up the first $500 million, or his wife as his proxy did, and she managed to get a handful of other billionaires to do the same. Santo, the invisible would rebuild America.

His ambition became her lie, crafting a fabrication so complete that finding the truth seemed to verge on the impenetrable. Marley had been on Bloomberg television with an elegantly tall anchor of show originating from Sydney named Ai Zhao. She was describing her husband's latest brainchild, and taking full credit for it. Ai had flown to Portland for the interview and was walking the grounds of their exurban estate when she spotted him mowing the lawn.

"That's my husband," Marley had said when she saw her looking. Ai turned back to her, the question written on her face but unasked. The cameraman who had been following them as the strolled across the lawn panned towards him. "He likes to work the grounds himself. He says it helps him think."

"But you're one of the richest women in America," Ai stated, somewhat bemused.

"I never think of myself as that, Ai. It helps me stay focused. Sure I could hire an army of people to help out around here, but he likes it."

The anchorwoman smiled back at her, "Oh, like Warren Buffet still lives in Omaha?"

"More like behind every great woman is a supportive

man." Ai laughed at this. It wasn't the first reporter, and not the first female reporter who celebrated the success of a woman but at the same time was amazed by it. She was to be forgiven though. Marley had become a unique persona among the business community elite. She had no glass ceiling to crash though, no male counterpart in competition, and certainly none of the other interoffice politics to interfere with how she conducted herself. The company had grown in the shadows, guided quietly by their partnership and in the process had developed its own set of ethics and acceptable behaviors without having to force the culture on anyone. Marley once said to a reporter that "It had evolved without." The reporter almost had asked her, "Without what?" but did not as she seemed to suddenly get the cryptic nature of her reply. That reporter sold the story to Inc. and that publication emblazoned their cover with the caption: "How to Evolve... Without!"

Santo had told her that every accomplishment would come with a certain celebrity. "If you're a successful investor," he told her, "it gets noticed eventually and people want to elevate you to the status of guru." He was right on that point. Those people, he had explained, seek the magic elixir and they would hound her until they found it. "You should consider yourself fortunate," he told her, "you can't as Graham once said, become your own worst enemy."

She remembered him explaining it to her: "Even Buffet with his Coke-and-smile personality enjoyed being called an oracle. You could see it in his boyish, almost impish reaction to young reporters. Lose enough weight," he added "and everyone wants to know how you did it, what's your secret they'll ask. Even criminals idolize better criminals. Everybody wants the answer you've found," he told her adding, "and you have only one secret: Me."

"Actually, you have many secrets, Sonny. How can you be so sure you wouldn't be a celebrity if they found out who you are, what we're doing?" she asked.

"I don't but that would mean something would change and I like things the way they are. It needs to stay the way it is."

Ai continued the interview asking about a host of things that bordered on the exact thing Santo was attempting to hide from. She wanted to know what it was like to be such a powerful woman in a man's world or what domestic life was like. She even wanted to know if she could interview her husband. "How many men successfully play second violin to such a talented woman, need I mention rich?" She asked this as she swept her arm at the backdrop behind her and her subject. The interview on the back patio was chosen because inside the house was off limits to anyone from the outside world. The day had cooperated with an impressive crispness and brilliance. Marley just shrugged and smiled. "He prefers his anonymity."

*****

John Bates had retired from the business of sleuthing and since he never married, he would have no one to pass his knowledge of people, how to delve into their weaknesses and discover their secrets. This did not distress him as it might have in a previous time. it was vast wealth of worldly interpretations and conclusions that would have to rest between the pages of the book had had promised himself to write. His lifetime achievement of having solved every mystery to cross his path was tarnished by one elusive character. Santo Aretino remained the only mystery he had not successfully closed. For man who had been able to capitalize on the shadows that other people cast, this single figure lingered just beyond his expert reach.

He was watching Bloomberg television on July 4th, a holiday for the markets and a nonevent for his British blood when he saw him. It was on this day that business channels usually ran all day shows that fell comfortably into the category of 'how rich people live', exposés on wealth and travel that was restricted to those earning vast sums of disposable income. It was background noise as he read the paper and drank his coffee. But the Asian markets were trading and the feed from Sydney was being hosted by a Chinese anchor.

The editor of the show had decided to leave the long shot of the man mowing the lawn in the article profiling the richest women in America. The sound was turned low as the host narrated. She had long, angular features that made her seem regal. He was not disappointed with her 'on location' story, strolling the grounds in front of what appeared to be a modest structure. The long drive and sweeping vista suggested the approach to a castle, exactly the kind of opulence the show boasted.

Bates mumbled, "what the fuck" to himself and rewound the show, a feature that only three years ago would not have been possible. The two women, the host and a much shorter blonde with the kind of tight curls straight haired women seemed to envy were walking on an expansive front lawn when the man entered the shot pushing a mower. The picture was not as crystal as it could have been but he froze the screen just as the man turned and waved.

The following day he called the New York offices of the station and asked to speak to the producer of the show. Four people and seventy minutes later, he got an assistant of an assistant. The producer had once hired Bates to investigate his missing brother, a tragic story of a brain injured soldier who had simply wandered off. He did not intend to use that affiliation to get what he needed but did nonetheless. "Just tell him who is on the line," he told her carefully pronouncing each word to emphasize his intent while tempering his impatience. Bates had been unable to find the man's brother in time to save him from his own hand but the producer was grateful he had found him.

The hesitation in the man's voice as he answered made

Bates wish he had dug this hole elsewhere. "I'm not asking for an address, although that would be helpful. Just a ballpark location," he insisted gently, knowing the man's ethics would be challenged by this small favor. The man, who had almost forgotten that chapter in his life answered after a long pause: "Portland. Fuck. Fuck. Fuck." The phone was slammed into a cradle on the other end as the line went dead without a closing salutation.

He sat for a long moment to think about what he now knew. After a focused search that lasted over two years and more than fifty conversations and several thousand miles, he had seen the man he was looking for. It was not so much elation as it was regret. If he had been doing what most Americans were doing on Independence Day, if he had developed more of a life with other people, if he had been reading the book on his lap, he would have missed the two second snippet over Ms. Zhao's shoulder.

He pulled himself from the chair and wandered over the deskin the corner. He shuffled a few folders and papers until he found what he was looking for. He dialed the number not expecting an answer.

John Tell, the retired detective who had pursued Santo Aretino just before he had been hired, answered. Dismissing the usual greeting, Bates simply stated, "I found him John. I fucking found him. This is John Bates," he finally added to the silence on the other end.

Tell sounded a bit slower than the last time they had talked. "Found who?"

"Aretino. I found him."

"That's good news." He suspected that Tell hadn't fully grasped what he was talking about but he declined to reintroduce himself. Then it seemed to click. "Bates? I forgot all about you and now I wish I hadn't. Fucking old age. I should have called you sometime back, couple of months or so. I had a young reporter visit me asking about him. Out of the clear blue. Apparently, our boy Santo won some sort of award, some humanitarian thing or another and get this, no one knew who he was."

"Shit. So I'm sitting here watching this television show, some business thing, and in the background I see him mowing the lawn."

"He's a groundskeeper?"

"Not at all. Seems he's married to one of the richest women in the country. And he mows the lawn. He was mowing the fucking lawn. We gotta go see him, John." When the two had met, the promise had been made to keep in contact, sharing anything they might uncover. But that was decades ago and age had taken its toll on the elder cop. Tell agreed that he should go but declined his invitation to travel west to have a face-to-face with him. He said it was too long ago and he was too old and it was no longer as important to him. Santo Aretino had been for him the same open question that Bates had grappled with: Where did he go?

"So you think this reporter knows where he is?"

"That's hard to say. He was doing background and didn't seem any too happy about it. I told him pretty much everything I told you when we talked. He told me he worked for some free weekly in Portland. Nick something or other," he said and quickly added, "Heath. Yeah, that's it. Nick Heath. Nice kid. Knows how to eat a steak and drink. We spent a very rainy afternoon getting drunk."

*****

He asked her how the interview went. Marley told him she was tired of lying. "And someone will eventually find out who you are. Time to fess up, big guy."

"Wow. What brought that on?" He looked at her sitting at the edge of the bed. Her shoulders were slumped. Had he failed to notice this coming on? The events of the past several months had brought just as many decisions to the forefront, most of which he had dismissed as noise. But his wife apparently had not shared the same emotional dismissiveness.

"For thirty years you have been in the background and I just think it is time for you take credit."

•

11

Che was not her real name. It was Charlotte, named by her father after the actress with the surname Rampling. Her father had delivered her mother to the hospital with more than enough time to spare. The maternity nurses told him that he should "go make himself busy" as they prepped his wife for their first child. He had driven forty miles from rural Vernonia, through the lush rain forests of northwest Oregon to Portland and according to the attending nurse, she was only at the beginning of process. He remembered looking dumbfounded at the idea of "making himself busy" and asked the nurse where she thought he should go. "You've got lots of time," she had told him. "Go catch a movie. Enjoy your last moments before your whole world changes. 'Farewell, My Lovely' is playing at Cinema 21," adding, "Philip Marlowe is my favorite." He remembered feeling odd about going to the movies with his wife about to give birth. She reassured him again that it would be hours before their baby came into the world.

She was right about when the baby would arrive and about the movie. It was a classic that made him think of what his life would have been like without his wife. She was his rock, the only piece of his sloppily arranged puzzle that made sense. While he acted more like Moose, the erratic and impatient felon who propelled the story forward, he wanted to think of himself as Robert Mitchum. But there was no doubt that his wife could have stood in for the movie's femme fatale, Charlotte Rampling. Her looks were European, sultry and discreet, wholly out of place in the small town they called home. The characters on the screen began to fade as he thought about her. He remembered how she looked moving around their small farmhouse, hair tied loosely back, smiling and humming, and somehow cosmopolitan in this provincial of places. The baby, she had told him would be prefect, something she said that would complete us. He felt helpless as he watched his wife grow with the life inside of her. He told her he was worried at the thought this new addition would change everything. She had disagreed saying it will make him more of a man that he was already, quickly adding that as impossible as that might seem to him, it would.

The baby had barely waited for the credits to roll and the lights in the old theater to come up. As he hustled across town, feeling guilty for having enjoyed the movie, his wife's blood pressure unexpectedly spiked. Even as the baby was born unaffected by the emergency occurring just a heartbeat away, her mother died without hearing her first cries.

*****

Customers loved her as her hairdressing skills became legendary in a city with more than its share of professionals plying their trade. She had eventually decided to rent a chair at a salon called "Mish" and began to build her clientele.

Moving to the city was inevitable. The man who had raised her, attempting to ignore the guilt he felt, had done all he could have done. But the dark cloud that he wore began to wear on her. Worse, she had grown into Ms. Rampling's good looks, much like her mother's and her father seemed to be on the verge of tears every time he looked at her.

Her hair was swept back into a tight ponytail that was a rainbow of colors. She preferred cut-off jeans and mesh pantyhose and looked very much like she belonged in the city. That was six years ago and although she could still see the tears well up in his eyes, she never went back to that verdant swath of what she called "green hell".

Che had received the call on her cellphone earlier in the day asking for an off-schedule appointment. These were usually reserved for local celebrities who did not want the public to see them with their hair wet or twisted in odd ways. Bertrand was quickly becoming just that sort of celeb, so she agreed. She accommodated him in the hopes that he would bring her along on one of his projects. Like all young stylists, she wished her nine-to-five life snipping blue hairs and wishful cougars would be over in favor of the glamor that only movies can provide.

The last of her coworkers was leaving when he arrived at the shop on Broadway. He seemed giddy as he sat in the chair. With the motion of a matador, she whipped the bib across his body.

"We're in a good mood." she stated as she stood behind him, both of them facing the mirror.

"I am," he responded with theatrical flair. "Tomorrow, I premiere my first TED talk."

She looked at him as he adjusted himself beneath the cover. "Kind of a departure for you?" The sentence came out as a question. Her voice, unlike so many of her cohorts, didn't fluctuate. There was no uptick at the end of a sentence, the sound making the speaker appear unsure of what they were saying, as if they were leaving themselves a verbal bridge to escape in the event that whatever they were speaking about was wrong, or made them seem foolish. Instead, her voice was even and sure, a paved highway moving into the distance.

"It is," he said, still adjusting, squirming nervously beneath the bib. He was looking at himself in the mirror when he said, "Tighter on the sides and just a smidge off the top please. This might be my big break and if it isn't, it is definitely my opportunity to woo a benefactor into sponsorship. If I'm to be a true Renaissance man, I'll need a benefactor."

"So," she said, dragging the word out for several syllabic seconds.

"I can't say any more about it. It is very secret and very exciting and I am outrageously over the top thrilled." She was not about to pry it out of him and he knew he could sit in silence for the remainder of the trim if he chose to. This seemed to disappoint him but he added, "Do you want tickets?"

"Sure. Do I get two? One for me and one for Nick?" He produced two from beneath the cover and handed them to her. "Were you going to invite me or make me beg?"

"I knew you'd never beg. You're too, what's the word?"

"Bitch."

"Yeah, bitch. But no one makes me look better."

*****

Nick Heath had boyish good looks that were often a compliment to his boyish attitude. He could, in his job as a reporter for the Portland Riverfront Weekly, or affectionately known among the hipster crowd as PurDub, gain access to otherwise off-limit interviews with a simple change of expression. He had also gained an enviable reputation with his succinct and sometimes challenging prose. She knew he was wasting his talent but did not suggest he should reassess the job he had. He had told her that it was the best proving ground he could have and when the time was right, he was sure he would be able to tell exactly when that happened, he would move on. She worried that he might be calculating her into his equation and ignoring the very impetus of that change.

He was working on his laptop when Che entered the room. He didn't look up when he asked, "If you saw timorous in a sentence, would you skip it or bother to look it up?"

She leaned over and kissed him but kept walking into

the small studio kitchen. "So I'm your target audience now? Do you think I don't know what it means?"

"No. Not at all." He looked up long enough to accept the beer that she was handing him. She flopped on the couch beside him. He no longer mentioned how worried he was that one day, despite her small frame, when she dropped on the furniture like she was inclined to do, they would end up in old lady Castone's apartment below. She still fell onto the cushions with a satisfying thud.

"Not at all what?" she asked, wondering which question he was answering. She knew she was the free weekly's target audience: young, brash, inclined to spend more money on beer and pot than on food, likely to be barely employed and lastly, looking to keep Portland the way they liked it, which was incredibly difficult to describe to someone who hadn't been there.

He leaned back. He thought about answering her more succinctly but stopped short. This was one of those "does this make me look fat" questions married guys with fat wives feared. She was neither.

"And I don't know what it means smartass. Didn't your editor tell you to write to the least common denominator? And Mr. Nicholas Heath, you won't get a Pulitzer jotting notes in PurDub."

"You never know." Their banter was friendly, almost affectionate, and to an outsider, platonic. They both had a firm grasp on the life they were living, even if it wasn't they life they would have chosen above all else. And they were madly, desperately in love, the kind of affection that was seldom on display for the general populace.

"Oh, I know this: People who read the paper are mostly looking at the pictures. They peruse the ads, read the captions, look for a live show, but they don't read the in-depth articles that you sometimes write, Nick. I mean, the Oregonian does but they don't really matter. So how exactly were you going to use it?"

"In reference to Metro's land use boundaries." She just sat and looked at him.

"Really? Couldn't you just say they lacked confidence and be done with it? Timorous might describe Mrs. Castone down stairs on her way to the market after dark. But Metro doesn't fear anything."

"Okay. Fine." She leaned over and kissed him again.

"Wanna go out tomorrow night? Like on a date?"

"Sure? Where are you taking me? Dinner? A movie?" adding quickly, "or for a steak at the Acrop?" The Acropolis was a local strip club that was a cut above what strip clubs were normally. The owner raised his own beef. It had a salad bar. And Che knew a lot of the girls who danced there.

"To a TED talk." He just sat there looking at her, more stunned than excited. "Once again, a look like I'm not the kind of girl who has an intellectual side?"

"You knew what timorous meant." He knew that was weak retort but didn't add anything to the comment.

"You've got an opinion. Spit it out." She waved her hands as if coaxing a small dog trapped in a pipe.

He had thought about leading with a question, such as 'have you ever seen a TED talk" but thought better of it. He thought better of it, not because she probably had but because he had to tame his condescension. She always amazed him, the sort of rapturous insight she brought to almost every conversation they had and that often left him wondering if she could see his social myopia. She knew everybody and was incredibly popular. She was the polar opposite of him and because of that, she always a surprise. He had learned in his brief time with her that people see something different in her than he saw. He saw a warm, tender, and sometimes fragile woman who was perhaps a little timorous herself, struggling with an intellectual angst. What everyone else saw depended on who was looking. Little kids stared at her in a wishful, come-play-with-me way. Older people seemed to look past the leather and the roughened black edges as if she was the daughter that had just returned home, improvident and random. Everybody else just wanted to be near her orbit. It never ceased to amaze him.

He sighed first before responding. Che impatiently and coquettishly, with a smile and hands on her hips said, "And…"

"I think TED talks are overbearing hype delivered by hucksters looking to make a buck on the backs of gullible wanna-be intellectuals. Although," he added quickly, "I did like that neuroscientist who had a stroke and told us about it in excruciating detail. But I think even she must have fabricated some aspects of the event. I mean, who chronicles an injury or an event they didn't expect and after a stroke?"

"There's more, isn't there?" She asked this settling back into a corner of the sofa, pulling her legs underneath her. There was always more and she never tired of hearing it. Open Nick's mind and whatever popped out was either funny or smart or smartly funny.

"I mean, smart people like to tell you how the world is changing, how they'd like to change the world, how the audience can participate in the change. There is too much pressure to be inspiring, to be a cut above or simply make a cut differently. The audience is and this is no offense to those who attend them in person, creative dolts. They are creative but just need to know what to be creative on or with or whatever."

She waited several additional beats before responding. "You done?" This was delivered in a tone of both patience and as someone who was often on the receiving end of these streams of thought. Nick seemed as if he was always coiled with the perfect response to the imperfect world around him and more than willing to release it. She would listen, not in the sense of waiting for him to finish, but to actually pay attention to the words that would spew forth in such organized, free flowing manner, a breathless stream. He had never ceased to amaze her with his knowledge or his curiosity.

He smiled his response. "I'm sorry." He always apologized although she rarely accepted it. He had nothing to be sorry about, she would tell him. Not all of his monologues took on the critical air as his feelings about these TED talks did. Sometimes, he delivered some of the funniest strings of consciousness she had ever witnessed, looping and riffing as if he had taken the stage on open mic night at the comedy club.

"So, do you want to go?"

"Of course I want to go. When?"

"Tomorrow night." She got up off the couch and leaned over to kiss him.

"Who're we listening to?" That wasn't the question he intended asking. Nick actually wanted to know who was doing the shoveling.

"This guy, a local film director on the verge of big things comes into the shop, usually just around closing, was hired to direct one and he thought I might be interested." She was looking in the refrigerator for something easy for dinner.

"Film guys don't direct TED talks. At least I didn't think they did. People just get out there and talk, with jumbotron power points." He was now standing behind her as she leaned into the appliance. He held his hands on her hips and gave her a slight push.

"Well, this guy was asked to direct this one." She turned and wrapped her arms around him. "Take me out. I am so fucking hungry."

"I've got a food assignment. You want to go?"

"Oh hell yeah," she replied. "I love going to other people's houses."

Nick shook his head. He thoroughly despised this part of his job. "You never answered my question."

"Santo Aretino or something like that." She was slipping into the small bathroom as she replied. "Just give me a minute."

Nick had heard the name before. "The recluse billionaire?"

*****

Nick wore numerous hats at his job with the Portland Riverfront Weekly. He did features on a number of topics that often allowed him to do in-depth research on a wide variety of issues that impacted the people of the Portland metropolitan area. It was, at least in his mind, important work and was worth reading. But he often wondered who was actually spending the time to read through twenty thousand words on the inner workings of the city council, even if it directly impacted them. This city had adopted a slogan embracing weirdness and attempted to live up to it. Much the same way they lifted it from the city of Austin, Texas, their weirdness was practiced and at times seemed to require more effort than it was worth.

But his job also involved writing two other columns, both online with content added daily and a wholly separate piece for the print edition. One column dealing with the most inane questions imaginable sent in with all seriousness by the readers. These queries were answered with a sort of professionalism he brought to every word he wrote even if the column was called Simpleton. He had to be jocular and ironic while delivering information that was both grammatically correct and the end of the discussion. He had exactly two hundred words in which to insult the questioner, relate his own albeit fictional experiences with the subject, and answer the question in such a way as there would be no reason to follow-up. It was by far the most popular blog-type column in the Pacific Northwest and beyond. He received a percentage of the click-throughs and an additional stipend to ease the disgust he was forced to hide beneath the surface.

The other column had been given to him when the previous food writer had been waylaid with a serious food borne illness, ironically not related to the column. His departure was not without an upside: No one liked the fat man with the food stained shirts, even if his prose was worthy of much better publications. That column named The Kitchen explored the world of food sharing, a culinary offshoot of the sharing economy. Old ladies looking to share a casserole with company, any company, or wannabe caterers attempting to ply their craft in an already burgeoning food scene, opened their homes to dinner guests. The previous columnist was an affable guest and most of the homes he visited enjoyed his company.

The homes he and now Nick would pick were random choices. The paper did say he would not need to visit home cooks who had received less than three dinner plate, the cutesy version of stars. There were hundreds of choices on the app called "Eat with Us" that fit that criteria and each promised a culinary adventure.

Sometimes he took Che to these reviews, which his editor didn't mind. Zoti liked Che, and she encouraged his flirtation. He was an excellent editor/owner who had created a well-run publication. He also fit the stereotypical description of the mad Greek, and often with great flourish. Che was a wonderful distraction which allowed him to observe without notice the details he might have missed. He was mostly hesitant about taking her on these assignments to visit home mealer, a derogatory term he called them under his breath, for no other reason than it was work and he liked the clean line between his offtime. And he never really liked sharing her with the public, something he was convinced he would always struggle with. But at least the neighborhood was upscale.

"Where are we headed?" She sounded excited and she smelled delightful. He had tried to do some work while she got ready but he simply found her too distracting. She moved with random chaos, beginning one thing and before finishing it, starting another. Make-up was combined with outfits and the artistry that was the love of his life was constructed before his very eyes. But when she announced she was ready, he had the same feeling he always did when they were headed out: Selfishness. She would steal the hearts of every man, most women, and ironically, every child she met. He knew he had to share her with the world and he also knew it was easier when he wasn't witness to the theft.

"There's a couple in the Pearl who do a thing called 'Seating for Six'. They do it about once a week and according to the dinner plate rating on the app, these folks hit it out of the park every time. We're only in because of a last minute cancelation." He stood by the door and waited for the inevitable second review. She checked the mirror one last time and turned to present herself to him. He responded in the same way he always did and probably always would: "Do we really have to leave?"

"Take me out and I'll take care of you. Later."

*****

"You'll have fun," she said after catching him staring at his reflection in the mirror. Santo wasn't checking his appearance as much as he seemed to be exploring something only he could see. His brow was furrowed, a look he often had when deeply engaged with his own thoughts. He hadn't heard what she said. She stood at the opened bathroom door watching him for another minute. She repeated herself as if she hadn't spoken.

He seemed to rouse himself from the image he was looking at and turned to towards her. She was leaning against the jamb, her arm's crossed. He ignored the urge to ask her how long she had been standing there. "What makes you think so?"

"It's not as if they are total strangers. I mean, the woman is my admin and her husband does these underground meals which, I hear, are exquisite."

"So why doesn't he have his own restaurant?" It seemed like a good question. Marley didn't answer. He suspected she knew the answer to the question but was reluctant to debate the decision to go based on his reservation about the chef's reasoning. Santo turned back to the mirror and gave his hair a few pats, improving nothing before pronouncing, "This is the best it is going to get."

Marley knew this would be difficult on him. He had a big coming out party tomorrow night when he delivered his speech at the TED talks and she thought this would ease him into the event. Tickets for the talk had been sold out for weeks in anticipation of the event. She had decided not to mention this. She knew these people were curious, not about the intellectual tidbits and commercial promise these presentations often held, but instead, the chatter was more about the story of a reclusive man who had taken such great effort to wall himself off from the world, for whatever reason, and a the same time, insisted on inserting his philanthropy on those who chose to be part of it.

As they headed for the door, she stopped him, turning him to look at her. "You need this, Sonny. You've been in the background too long. I know why and you know why and no one else has to know. But they'll want to know why. And in case you haven't noticed, the world is a much smaller place these days." She reached up and kissed him. "It'll be fun."

"That's the third time you said that."

Santo Aretino's decision to simply step away from the world was only possible because of Marley. If she had dreamed of a large wedding and the public display such events are often are, they were dashed by his unwillingness to thrust himself in the public eye, no matter how small they promised the wedding would be. She had opted for a simple ceremony at a Vancouver Justice of the Peace, inviting no one but her parents. At some point, she would have had to explain the reasoning why their only daughter had acquiesced to her new husband's wish to remain private, but she never recounted the conversation. Her parents liked him for whatever reason and they had been well versed in her off-center antics.

It was not a disregard for their hopes. She had known since she was small that she would be the author of those dreams. Her father as much as said so. "You might be anything you chose, Marls," he had said, "but it will be you that does the choosing." She was their only daughter and they respected her choices. She had always sought their counsel and this time was no different. Even as the little girl who grew up and changed her name from Abrahamson to Cornish introduced the man she would allow to change her life, they saw the spark and believed her beau did as well. She had simply assumed the front-and-center role his reclusion required, which she told her father did not compromise my principles, and that following led to more than enormous wealth.

He wasn't the type of person who hid because he was fearful of the public. Instead, he was concerned that he was not afraid. Unlike the Salingers and Brontes and Goulds of the world, artists who offered their talent and then chose to spurn the adoration, Santo had adopted his seclusion as a safeguard, a way to control what he didn't understand about himself, almost from his first interaction with people.

His seclusion had taken on different appearances since

that night in the industrial district. He had begun this new phase of his life by doing what he could to ignore the people around him. He had experienced a world that existed in two planes: One of innocence lived without consequence and the other, an evil one that preyed on the ignorance of the innocent. But Marley, who had been witness to what he had done had also seen the man who had successfully walled himself off from that reality. Over time, he talked about Sofi, specifically and Umberto in passing. Never did he refer to them as Mom and Dad, or anything other than by their proper names. He could never say how or why this had evolved into this sort of relationship and that lack of understanding worried her. And she reminded herself of what her father had once said about worrying, "Don't, if you can't change what you are worrying about." She knew she couldn't change what had happened to him; it made him who he was. But something lurked deep inside of him that needed her to be attentive and she was. As he unfolded in so many different ways over the course of the time she had spent with him, more than half of her life, she was comfortable she had made the right choice. She was, as she told her reflection time and again, unused to being the savior.

Marly would occasionally make him walk with her on the downtown streets as she pointed out the architecture of the city, how it seemed to glisten in the rain. Their collars pulled up against the chilliness, her arm entwined with his, steps in unison as if choreographed within their DNA. She would explain the buildings the way Goethe had, as frozen music, a symphony trapped in concrete and glass and steel. She loved the hard angles and soft ideas turned to solid forms, art for the weather. He would listen and occasionally murmur in agreement. But otherwise, he would let her talk.

They walked the neighborhoods of the city as well, the streets where the people hid in their houses, their lives framed against the backdrop of wide living room windows that offered a portal into a life that he knew nothing about, a childhood that he either refused to remember or perhaps hadn't existed. There was the occasional look of anguish on his face when they would pass by one of these Rockwell scenes, framed for the public wandering down a darkened sidewalk. She knew better than to ask him what he was feeling.

Sometimes they would venture into a crowd but he found the experience deafening. It wasn't the sound of places like Saturday Market, a two day affair that ran from spring to mid-winter where artisans sold their wares so much as what was not heard. It was in places like this that he saw the anger and the innocence played out in the theater of the obvious. People milled around the stalls munching on various types of street fair foods but something was amiss and Santo felt as though he was the only one who could see it. He would see a man sitting in the back of a booth lean over a whisper something that was accompanied by a sneer. For some reason, he could see them at home, where this anger played itself out as if she were in some sort of servitude entered into via marriage vows. This wasn't art to his eyes but instead commerce at its basest level. Booth after stall he saw it.

The crowd was more than just the sellers of medieval wares. It was the look of disappointment that some mothers had in their eyes as they looked at their children who had done nothing wrong. He could see the thugs he was used to dispatching that were hidden behind the civility of the crowd, blending with the density. The bullies he had interrupted throughout his life as they tried to oppress were masked behind the public space. It was as if he could hear the rage bubbling beneath the surface and his body yearned to react. She could feel him tense.

Marley knew this about him but worried nonetheless. It wasn't, she assumed, a healthy thing to do. Hiding came with its own consequences and she assumed that at some point they would manifest themselves in some way. But thirty years had passed and nothing. He was still the same affable and totally loyal person she had met and married. To the outside world, a place he insisted had no quarter within his home, it would have seemed odd. To him, it was that outside world that was the oddity, uncomfortable in their own skin, always seeking social validation, forever pursuing an abstract of the world and of themselves, all with a vindictive and angry undertone.

So she had decided about five years ago to push him gently into small gatherings. It started out as a small birthday party, which wasn't small enough. She watched him interact with these strangers, a handsome stranger to them, and marveled at the way he wrapped them around his voice, a late night FM sound that seemed to exist without breathing, a soft modulation that fell on the unsuspecting with hypnotizing intonations, words wrapped in their best Sunday-go-to-meeting clothes. But she knew he was uncomfortable. She could see the slight bead of sweat gathering on his brow. She would side up to him and force him to lean down to her. She would utter one word and he would apologize to his small audience and they would leave.

After apologies to the host, which were unnecessary considering how entertaining he had been and how much they would talk about him after they left, after they had safely exited the door and were on their way to the car, he would always ask her, "What'd I do to you to deserve that?" With her arm wrapped in his, she wouldn't answer. He had feigned a good time on her behalf but only because of her.

This time would be a little different. "What makes you think I'll have a good time? You know, better than the time I'd have here?"

"You're going. End of story, Mr. Aretino." Aside from the hostess actually working for her, Marley wouldn't know anyone present.

It was she who had been the social one, the light that would enter a room, the sort of presence that made mediocre women shun her and attractive women criticize her. But in the world of women, this was not the path to anathema. Instead, given a moment to acclimate to her endless charms and wit, they would love her as much as they initially despised her. She was ultimately there for them, the public, the world beyond her door.

They were the last couple to arrive. Akiko answered the door and bowed slightly to her employer. Her smile was as pure and sweet as anything Santo had ever seen. Even though she acted as his wife's personal assistant and had been in her employ for almost twenty years, and even more ironic, owed her paycheck to his investment acumen, she had no idea who he was.

"I am so pleased to meet you, Sonny," she said taking his hand into both of hers.

"I am as well," he replied. "Were you born in the autumn?" Marley looked at him.

"I was. Do you know Japanese?"

He shrugged. "Not really." He stopped short of explaining how he came to know her name meant bright and autumn, in part because he was unsure exactly where he had come across a tidbit such as that. Marley no longer asked. In the beginning she did, almost as if he needed to cite his source for each arcane reference he would make. He would but he always told her that it would take longer to pull the exact source of the information. And it usually did, often resulting in him blurting out the answer, sometimes days later, forcing her to ask why she needed to know that.

A tall man with reddish hair joined her at the door, extending both an enormous hand and an equally large smile. He was not a handsome man but one who seemed very comfortable in not being one.

"This is my husband Ryan," Akiko said whirling first towards her husband and then to Marley. Her movement was almost a pirouette. She said to him, "This is my boss, Marley and her husband, Sonny." He gave Marley a half shake, allowing her to slip her hand into what amounted to two large fingers. The movement was subtle and always welcomed. Marley had shaken the hands of countless men over he career and was never offended when they treated her hand with a gentler touch. If the handshake demanded strength, she could easily convey that impression. Santo had developed his hand strength over the years, doing yard work and small maintenance jobs around the house. The men shook with vigor. "He'll be our chef for the evening."

"I've heard you've got quite the talent," Marley said.

Ryan responded with humility. "I cook. She says chef but I don't have the degree or the debt or the experience for that matter." He looked at Santo who, by his own admission, had a terrible poker face. He answered the question that apparently was splayed across his face. "Sometimes you have to cook for more than just the two of us in order to make some recipes work. So consider this little endeavor a leftover avoidance technique. A side benefit is the social aspect. Akiko just loves people and this keeps it fresh, light, and to a degree, distant."

"I am so looking forward to it, Ryan."

Ryan turned back to Santo. "There's no money in it," he told him in hushed tones, once again answering a question he was telegraphing.

He smiled and responded, "Doesn't always have to be a payday to make it worth the effort." Ryan agreed and turned to go back into the kitchen. Santo followed his wife into the living area, a wide open space with an easterly view of Mt. Hood. It was a nearly perfect peak and one of the landmarks of the area he had spent more than half his life. It was sporting a deep reddish purple shadow as the sun set, giving it the dominance of a formidable shadow.

"This is Nick and Che," Akiko said introducing them to the guests that had already arrived. "Nick is a senior writer for Portland Riverfront Weekly and his girlfriend is a hair stylist." There were handshakes and pleasantries exchanged, wine was poured and a small appetizer was offered. Ryan disappeared into the kitchen while Akiko added some additional touches to the table, leaving Santo and Marley with the young couple. Santo recognized the name and Nick seemed to notice this recognition.

"Is this your first time?" Marley asked turning to Che.

"For me it is. He never takes me on these things." She leaned in to her boyfriend with a gentle nudge. Nick had visited almost fifty of these app-related endeavors and was mostly disappointed. He always arrived biased and was expecting more of the same this evening. "I think it is fun to invite people in your home and cook for them, whether you are doing for fun or a little extra spending money." Marley agreed with her and turned to Nick.

"You write for the PurDub? Are you on assignment?" she added with a slightly hushed tone. Nick was about to answer when Che interrupted.

"Do you read the Kitchen?" Her voice had a certain girlish excitement that belied her tough exterior. Santo had seen that look on other young women in the city and wondered if it was more defensive than real.

"I would have expected a food writer to be," and before she could finish, Nick added "fat?" It was a safe assumption. Both writing and eating tend to be sedentary and when combined might lead a reader to believe he had achieved Paul Prudhomme-sized stature. "Let's put it this way: She won't let me get fat and most of the time, the food is terrible."

Akiko had made it clear when she told Marley about this that she had wanted it to seem more like a small dinner party than a financial undertaking looking to capitalize on the burgeoning sharing economy. She had also told her how much she would respect her opinion of what her husband was doing.

He had rehearsed his introduction with Marley in advance and decided that his career of choice for this evening's festivities would be botanical researcher. It was just arcane enough to give someone the opportunity to ask vague, 'isn't-that-fascinating' type questions that he was more than qualified to answer. His reading over the years had taken him far and wide, across so many various fields of study that Marley wondered about whether the insatiable curiosity of his mind had boundaries. She would never ask the offhand question of who would care about this or that: She had married a man who did.

The reporter in Nick made a note of this tidbit of information even though the topic never came up again. Santo, now introduced as Sonny was well aware that every question a reporter asked seemed as if was more interrogatory than just conversational curiosity.

Fortunately, they seemed more fascinated with Marley's job. It wasn't every day that people who labored to stay middle class got to eat with one of the richest women in the world. The young couple was polite and kept the conversation light, even though he was sure Nick would have liked otherwise. Santo saw the young man as more than his outward appearance and wondered why this triggered something inside of him to be cautious.

Akiko reappeared and requested they come to the table. As they sat, they looked at the first course in front of them, unfolding napkins on their laps as the attempted to catch a whiff of the food. Ryan stood at the head of the table and announced the first course.

"We'll be doing a tapas tonight consisting of several courses but no main dish. The first course might remind you of a gazpacho made of tomato and garlic, served with ham, hard boiled eggs and crispy eggplant for dipping. If you're keen on names, this is a classic Andalucian salmorejo." It was during this course that Nick asked Santo what a botanical researcher does.

"Truth be told Nick, it isn't as fascinating as you might assume. In the early days, I became a charter member of NORML."

Che interrupted him. "The pot people?"

Santo laughed. "Kind of sort of. Our group just thought the laws surrounding weed were a little harsh, not in this liberal state, but thirty years ago back east. It was there that I began to research the potency of weed and began to refine the strains, mostly to my own tastes. One thing led to another and next thing you know, I'm helping school kids identify plants they found on field trips." They all stopped and looked at him.

"Wait," Che said, holding her fork mid-air, "You helped school kids with weed?"

"No, Che. That came out wrong. I got interested in botany because of weed and when I found out I was good at it, I branched out to the rest of the world of plants. It's a long story but in short, I gathered a bunch of fellow enthusiasts into a research group with all sorts of curiosities, all of us nerds, and made our useless information useful to minds that wanted it."

"Seriously? That is so cool." She turned to Nick and asked, "You ever hear of such a thing?" He shook his head no.

The second course shifted the conversation around the table and away from Santo. What he had told them was true however, he was not inclined to share any additional details.

His reclusion was not as absolute as some might one day wonder. Instead, he moved through the shadows of everyday life, avoiding the kind of contact that would unleash emotions he was not equipped to handle or define, or for that matter defend. This was a huge social leap for him, the involvement in disguise, the anonymity of his efforts. Marley watched him closely, disguising her concern with the look of admiration, the appearance of having been incredibly fortunate to have met this man. Which, if anyone knew the whole truth, she was.

The next course was described by Ryan as Esparragos Peruanos, a grilled asparagus served with chimichurri. Following that delightful dish, Ryan introduced his Yuca Croquetas served with cotija cheese, delicately balanced with a rich huancaína sauce. It was during this course that Ryan revealed that he had been the author of the app that had brought them to dinner this evening. Nick broke his secrecy and revealed that he was the writer behind the Kitchen.

"You are not a fan," Ryan said as he gathered the plates from that course. "I've read your criticisms. Well said, but still critical."

"Nothing against what you have going on here Ryan. But you have to admit, eating with someone, getting into someone's car or sleeping on someone's couch all come with a degree of risk, or better yet, dismissal of prejudices, or even better yet, being more adventurous than the average person. It is as if we understand the support we are giving people who chose to be on the fringes but still, it takes a certain amount of looking-the-other-way, not seeing the cat and wondering if it wandered across a countertop, is the driver stoned or who slept here before me. And most of the places I've eaten were somewhat," he paused reluctantly deciding to not take what were, until this moment, comments written under another name and quote himself. "Let's just say, most of the food was average and overpriced. Somebody told someone, 'this is delicious Harriet – you should open a restaurant' and even though it was just smoke up poor old Harriet's ass, she didn't know it. So, Harriet lists herself on your app and doesn't what criticism, just the same old smoke-up-your-ass praise." He grimaced as if he was not explaining himself well. "The Uber-like stars aren't always a good indication that you'll get a five-star dinner." Nick could feel Che looking at him. "But you my host, are a decidedly good exception to all previous encounters."

"Sonny can really cook Nick and I tell him that all the time. Open a restaurant, I tell him. All he ever says is he doesn't want to work at night." Marley had a way of diffusing difficult topics and making people feel at ease. That and Nick's reversal brought some enjoyment back to the table. Akiko was now smiling proudly at the success of this little party.

Ryan returned with a tartare of filet mignon he called Acebichado. The richly colored meat was seasoned with capers, olives, and cilantro. Che actually moaned. This made Akiko laugh. Dessert was a morado pudding served with a coconut brittle.

*****

"See, I told you you'd have fun." They had parked several blocks away and a light mist was falling.

"It was delicious, Marl. Dude can cook. But fun?" He made a look as if he had experienced a small pain. He stopped her and turned towards her. "You know why I just can't take this people thing, right?"

"Yes," she answered sliding her arm into his, "But I never tire of hearing it."

He started to explain but caught the sarcastic underpinning of her comment. "Hey," he said, bumping her hip with his.

"You are a grown man and I fully understand the issues you think you have, but, you're a grown man and it's time to get over it. Think about it. I have been the face of this company for thirty some odd years while you hid in the background like some resident of Oz."

"Okay, so what makes you think I should be out in front of this? Now of all times?" He was well aware of what to say when this debate came up, in part because she occasionally revisited it after reading something in some business magazine or attended some conference on leadership. She would, albeit gently, bring up the topic and he would, just as gently, explain why he chose the life he did. These conversations always ended with him thanking her, scooping her up in his arms and speaking quietly into the nape of her neck. But he knew this time was different. He had agreed to this public outing on the night before the biggest outing of his life.

"I know you're tired of having to be in charge. But I'm not a leader in the sense that people think of themselves as leaders."

"I'm not sure what you mean." They had decided to stay at the condo in town. The streets were quiet, the streets glistening and reflective.

"Don't confuse ideas with results. Leaders are essentially the reverse of what I am. You're a leader. Me? I'm indifferent to people and this is well chronicled." They had had this conversation numerous times over the years. He had always deflected her suggestion. But this time was different and they both knew it. "And lastly, I care about the process more than the people."

"You are such a fucking liar and not a very good one." There was no anger in her voice and no frustration. On the eve of his TED talk, the day he walks out of the shadows, on his own terms, in front of a full house of curious onlookers, she gave him the benefit of arguing his point one last time. She wondered if he could see the irony. This time she playfully bumped his hip.

12

Apprehension is the clouded horizon, blurring the hard line between sky and ground, loosening the grip on the reality we treasure. And like that storm on the horizon, it is difficult to tell at a glance what's in store, where it's headed or even if you should care. The fearless will suggest that it will be dealt with when it happens. Yet fear doesn't necessarily translate into preparedness. The mouse caught between the cat and his escape will be afraid but not apprehensive. But a person caught between fear and safety will be apprehensive. For all of our repulsive attributes, our multitude of defects both mental and physical, even our ungainly physicality that relies wholly on our brain to protect it from the elements, from danger, from other people, and from the threat on the horizon, most of us are mice frozen in indecision, unwilling to indulge our passion and less willing to ask why we are fearful in the first place.

As Santo approached the concert hall, he saw the dust brown horizon envelope the building. He stopped to clear his vision, pressing his eyes tightly together and opening them in rapid succession. On the fifth try, it was gone.

He was on foot, and had fallen in with a crowd of well-dressed people headed in the same direction. They seemed excited. He overheard questions: "Have you ever been to one of these?"; "Why do you suppose he decided to come out of hiding?"; "Will he discuss why he's been hiding all these years?" He would often miss the response to the questions, catching only snippets. "I've been to quite a few and seen a bunch online," one person replied but he lost whatever was added after that. "He was caught no doubt," which was speculation on their part and only half true. "He's our generation's Howard Hughes," and something that was added after that was lost to the sound of traffic at the crosswalk.

On the opposite corner he noticed his dinner companions from the previous evening. He turned away from them even though they were engrossed in their conversation. The woman, more a girl in his opinion considering he was at least thirty years older, caught his eye. She was hauntingly attractive and Marley had pointed out how she had seemed to hang on his every word. The conversation the previous evening had been expansive and even he was surprised how engaged he was with what was being discussed. Her boyfriend seemed confrontational and not at ease with the way evening had progressed. Santo supposed he had good reason: He was, as near as he could determine, working. Add to that, he was also sitting at the same table with the man who developed the app he had loathed in the weekly ghost-written column. In spite of the surprisingly delightful food, he never seemed to warm up to the situation. He seemed to be silently wishing it would all go away, the app, the column, the sharing of food with strangers. But Santo also sensed that this was not his usual demeanor. He had one of those talk-to-me faces, the kind of look that had him on the receiving end of more information than a typical reporter might garner.

He had memorized his speech. It was after all his speech, words penned decades ago that had taken up residence in his brain, some might suggest to fester while others might suppose that something of such clarity would surely need to be nurtured or protected, wrapped in soft cloth and stored where it could not be found, harmed, or as what now seemed the case, unleashed on an unsuspecting world. The words were not the problem.

His biggest fear, if Santo Aretino, the scourge of princes could have possessed such an emotion, was adding something to the direction. Bertrand had made it clear that every man on stage would gesture in unison, a chorus line of middle aged men who would make the same motion as the man next to him. This strange choreography was rehearsed more than the actual script. He knew they could mouth the words and the staging of the talk would hide most of those mistakes. What it could not hide was a missed motion. He knew audiences could only be deceived to a point and after that, once they thought the trick was no longer magical, the effort of these past weeks would have been for naught. And now he knew that there was a reporter present and a woman with him who memorized more about him than he would have liked.

It was unnerving standing offstage with six men who looked almost like him. These doppelgängers would he thought be useful in the future if it hadn't been for their explicit direction to return as quickly to the personage they were before they were hired. For Santo, this meant hiding for another couple of months behind the gates of his home as the fallout fell where it would, unpredictably. No visits to the office. No surreptitious trips to the museum or library. Both of these he would miss but not too terribly. No trips to the condo, no quiet dinners out with Marley. None of this would phase him, but in a way it did. This was an event of his making and all of whatever happened should have been an acceptable consequence.

Marley walked past him and tapped him on the ass. He wondered if this ruse was as effective as he thought it might be. It apparently did not fool his wife.

Bertrand had lined them men up single file. Santo was the third in line. Each man was fitted with a wireless mic that wrapped around the right side of their faces. Six were dead.

Only Santo's device would be live. He was wondering how they knew which one to turn on when his wife walked on stage.

She walked through the shadows to emerge on a spot marked by a single overhead spot light. The crowd applauded with enthusiasm. TED audiences were like that: engaged and curious and always prepared to be shocked with some new idea or presented with some global or personal conundrum. This made them open vessels for whatever content the speaker had to offer, even if they wholly disagreed after-the-fact. They respected opinions of people they assumed were more thoughtful and better educated than they were, had experiences they had yet to experience or lived lives, suffered traumas, endured life-changes from which they emerged newly formed or able to recant with awe inspiring detail. This crowd was simply more curious than most. This event was about a man emerging from seclusion and entering into the spotlight successful beyond their wildest dreams and this was an attraction. They collectively hoped for some sort of insight on how and why and if.

Marley was a recognizable figure both locally, nationally and to some degree, internationally. "Good evening. My name is Marley Cornish. I am the CEO of SA Holdings. We're a for-profit and a non-profit company, although we don't take the later tax status. We pay more than we should. Willingly. This is not my idea. But our founder has said that taxes are proof we are alive." The crowd laughed uneasily at this.

Santo could have easily taken advantage of the complex tax laws and the loopholes they provided the oligarchs of the twenty-first century. He could have created a charity, which would have obligated him to account for a certain amount of each dollar that was spent. He could have created an LLC, a charitable way of dodging taxes by transferring what would have been capital gains to the company. Instead, he had instructed no evasions or inversions or any other accounting games to take place. No other company, public or private was more transparent. With the exception of how market-traded investments were conducted, all of the businesses financials were published online, much to the chagrin of his publicly held counterparts and to the loathing of private businesses. And yet, even with that look-at-us posturing and the billions anyone could see, no one knew who was really at the helm. Marley was the face of SA Holdings.

She waited for the crowd to compose themselves before continuing. Che leaned into Nick's shoulder. "That's the lady from last night." Her voice was excited and she sat straight in her seat. He knew how she felt, surprised and now curious. "Do you think?" she added, her voice sounding as if was about to see the wizard and she knew in advance that he was as handsome and now as great as advertised. He looked around at the fellow audience members. Did they know or have any idea what he knew? There were no companions nudging one another as if sharing a complicit I-told-you-so. Were they the only ones that knew who was about to be introduced?

John Bates was also in attendance. He had traveled from his home with the single intention of seeing the man he had hotly pursued thirty or so years ago, to perhaps see the man Detective John Tell had described, to maybe catch the ghost of Lititz, the angel of some bus stop in central Ohio, the savior of a hapless drunk in an alleyway in St. Louis, and scourge of princes who descended on some dusty ranch outside of Boulder. The trail had gone cold somewhere in west but not his investigative desire. And when the name had suddenly surfaced, he did whatever he could to get to this place.

The whatever-he-could cost him almost eight thousand dollars. The ticket to attend the event alone cost six thousand, which he gladly paid. TED Talks charged this kind of sum he had found out because they could and because it "weeded out" the riff raff who would show up at a low price point.

He assumed that everyone in attendance would be dressed in their Sunday best, an antiquated assumption that suggested to him that for a high price ticket of this sort, a person would up their attire, much as if they were attending an opera. He was incorrect in that assumption. Portland's moneyed crowd and the intellectually curious who could afford such tickets paid no mind to upper class prerequisites dressing as casually as they wanted.

He found his seat in the upper balcony, looking all the part of an octogenarian uncle in a bespoke suit. Unlike Nick and Che, who had seats close enough to see the dial on Marley's watch, John Bates would need binoculars.

"...and as many of you know, our non-profit arm recently received the Conrad Hilton Humanitarian Award, which is given to an organization and not to a person. We declined the million dollar prize for two reasons: We felt as though there more deserving and less adequately funded groups out there who could use the money and because we have never accepted a single contribution from a single donor. I say we in error. In truth, our founder, the man you came to see tonight has made that his mandate. You may think anything you like as to why: He's never told me why and I have never asked.

"For thirty years, he has given eighty percent of every dollar he's earned back to the foundation and to date that has amounted to almost twenty billion dollars." She paused for effect but did not move from her mark. She knew that her public speaking strength was not wandering around the stage. So she stood on her mark, under a single overhead spotlight. The effect was angelic.

"Because you know so little about the man behind this movement, or even his existence, which he's managed to keep secret for so many years, I can give you just a bit of a resume." Both Bates and Nick leaned in, along with half the audience.

His emergence into the public curiosity was just as odd as this presentation was. How the simple act of saving some misguided turtles brought him to this point spoke to the power of social media in a hashtag world.

Marley spoke in even tones, perfectly pitched and even hypnotic. She told the audience about how she met him, how he made his first million and what he did with it – "He had arrived in Portland at a time when homes were cheap and the money to borrow them was expensive. Santo bought sixty houses and sold them to sixty families with two conditions: They had to pay him two percent interest on the loan and if they sold, they would get half the profits above the purchase price."

There were whispers in the crowd as some people remembered the program he had begun quietly. But few realized that this was the first charitable endeavor of SA Holdings. "That worked out well for everyone. No one defaulted on the loans we made and no one moved. The following year, he made a sizable profit in the stock market and when he sold his positions, he took eighty percent of it and bought one hundred homes. Within six years, he had placed twelve hundred families in homes. All of the mortgages are current, even in the post-2008 debacle. Because SA Holdings was on the title with the family, and the interest rate was incredibly favorable, no one thought about refinancing so no one was exposed.

"During that three decade stretch, he poured money into a variety of other charities, from preserving Peruvian antiquities to alternative energy to saving turtles. He commanded," she paused again and corrected herself, "directed is a better word. And yet, it might even be better to say suggested it from the privacy of our home."

She heard the crowd whisper again and answered their murmured questions. "A recent article in Psychology Today suggested that no one choses to be a recluse. The author points to our need with a very cliché description, calling us social animals, or even sexual ones. But then the piece decides to argue for the reasons why someone would decide to throw off the conventions of intermingling. Santo fits none of these generalities. We've been married for thirty years, and his reasons for not being a public being are enviable and not easy to afford. He had told me he wished he could have done it differently but did not regret doing it the way he had."

She was prepared for the following responses to follow her part of the presentation: Would people think she was lying? Santo said in response to that question, "Who the fuck cares? We're not a public company and until we are, that question is not worth answering." What would social media say? He also had the same feeling about that as well. "It isn't social media Marl; it is the public acting like paparazzi. Talking about someone in the public domain isn't less harmful to the subject of the chatter." And lastly, she worried about the media. For this he held her close, and asked her quietly, "What have we done wrong?"

"I would like to present the man behind the company you may not have known existed, Santo Aretino."

13

She hadn't seen Santo Aretino in over thirty years. She had an exact count of the days but if she were asked how long it had been, she would use the rounded number rather than the seemingly odd calculation she had maintained. Even though she knew no one would ever ask and no one but here was marking the passing years, she still kept track of the last day she had seen him, the number of letters she had written and in doing so, blurred many of the experiences that occurred in the interim.

He had answered her last letter, the first time he had done so. It was as if all of the time in between the tears she cried both visibly in front of him and in private had slipped away. She had that freshly showered feeling, as if everything that had happened was not as real as she had perceived. She had never been in love but imagined that if she had been, this would be how it felt.

Her letter was similar to the two hundred and forty two that had preceded his reply. It began with no salutation and often closed with her signature in the form of a single letter A. It was a conversation she was having with a friend, a continuous chain of events beginning where the last letter left off and ending in an ellipsis.

When the first bundle of letters arrived from the farm in Lititz, the discussion about what to do with them could have escalated into something more than a correspondence with an old lover. Marley knew about Arianne or had heard him mumble her name in his sleep. When Santo was confronted with this, gently mentioned on a quiet Sunday morning five years into their marriage, he gave her a glimpse into a past that he had chosen to sequester into the depths of a past he never acknowledged. He had arrived in her life and accepted the person that was molded by all of the events that shape a life. She had seasoned their conversations with stories of who she was, as most people will, adding nuance to an opinion, sculpting shape to a personal trait. But Santo never responded in kind. She knew the man she loved, the man she embraced, had something to say. Telling her about Arianne was the first opening he offered and she did her best to withhold her excitement.

Opening the bundle, cutting the rough twine Seamus had bound the chronologically letters, gave Marley the slight chill that often precedes something ceremonious. He had agreed to allow her to read them and she had insisted that he listen. It was a shared oddity; her reading letters from an old friend, lost lover, whatever she was, in her voice to the man who knew the author well.

None of the letters required a response. Each handwritten page was a snapshot of a moment in Arianne's travels, sometimes personal and more often, simply expositional. The latest letter took a different tone.

"You have to write back," she said laying the letter in her lap. The wine glass he was holding seemed poised to slip from his hand. They had fallen into the habit of sitting in the library of their home, the room illuminated by the reading light behind her chair. Santo would sit silently, almost stoically across from her, shadows failing to cast any clue of what he was feeling as she read. But this letter attempted to change that.

"I could, I suppose," he said after regaining his balance.

She wasn't asking him to write Arianne, she was telling him that it was necessary.

"I have known something about you that I have never shared Sonny. Now might be the time I should share it with you, beyond the words on this page, revealing it to you with you in front of me, to see your reaction, which I expect will be muted, but who knows, and when I tell you, it will solve one of the great mysteries of your life that you never thought to pursue or even care to. I would like to tell you in person…"

His response, written the following day seemed to acquiesce to the will of the two most important women in his life, one from a distant past, the other from the present.

"Why not? The more I try to hide the more they try to find me. I am getting weary of what I don't know, tired of what I do because of it, and according to my lovely wife, I need to man-up to the obvious. She hasn't exactly explained what the obvious is and I am hesitant to ask. But sure, Arianne, come and see me make a fool of myself at a TED talk. You will find everything you need enclosed. SA"

His letter was delivered by courier to her small apartment in Boston. It contained a ticket to the TED talk, five thousand dollars, and a pass to an XOJet. Three days later, she found herself in Portland and seated in a darkened hall watching her former lover's wife introduce him.

*****

If her relationship with him thirty-five years ago had occurred now, she would be harshly judged by the law, her peers, and society in general. She would be called a rapist and he would have been called a victim. They would have been right too with one exception, an argument that would not have held up in court: he had been older than she was in everything but age.

She had resisted his seduction for months. It was

subtle, without the juvenile bumbling common to what was commonly known as a "crush". There had been no long distance staring, no anonymous gifts, and certainly no fumbling conversations where one party was unaware of the amorous underpinnings. His approach was much more insouciant, as if he cared little to pursue her. And yet, she knew that if the opportunity presented itself, he would show some interest. For years she had tried to review those moments in her head. Did she lead him on in any way? She didn't think so, even putting herself as outside of the situation, attempting to view their relationship from a distance. She felt as though she was nothing but proper in her approach. She was a librarian, caretaker of the archived words of thousands of voices, muted only by the covers the enclosed them, arranged throughout the cold marble halls of the historic building. He was nothing more than the hundreds of others who wandered those aisles in search of the right sound for their hungry eyes.

But her relationship emerged from a different situation. More than inquisitive, the young Santo would pause at the sculptures, study the enormous scenes by artists of modest historic value, and hold each book he discovered with a reverence she had rarely seen. Most visitors had a purpose, looking for something specific. Santo didn't so much wander as he explored, as if everything here meant something to him.

Their conversations were always kept professional, Arianne going about her business of checking books out without prejudice. Most visitors kept to themselves, almost as if they were embarrassed by the choices they made. Others sought engagement, which she happily did. The library was where she had thought she belonged and willingly shared that enthusiasm for her good fortune to have landed her dream job. She had earned her MMLIS from USC.

What would her peers say, she wondered, if they knew she had crossed the line? Would they judge her actions, the ones she believed she did not commit, as something bordering on invitational, or worse, flirtatious? He was different, she told herself, without ever attempting to define what made him so.

And then she would see herself in court, imagining the situation played out under an evolving sensibility where every transgression was played out with far less scrutiny. The crimes were not lessened; they were still crimes. But in the early to mid-seventies, the rabble was less likely to become roused into what the present would whip into a social media frenzy.

She had been in a position of authority, the prosecution would have argued and as the adult, she should have been able to exercise the knowledge of right and wrong that comes with that experience. He was a juvenile they would tell the jury of her peers, some of whom would have convicted her of being attractive before one word was uttered while others were secretly wishing they could have traded places with the victim. And she should have known better. Not only that, she knew how old he actually was when it, the big IT happened. There would be no consideration for the fact that it only happened once and that she had stopped it. One of the attorneys would tell the jury that it was "Sex. Plain and simple. You can't take it back. You can't put the toothpaste back in the tube." She always imagined the man with speak with the authority of Atticus Finch. At this he would turn to her in obvious disgust.

He'd continue with a majestic wave of his arm, "There should be no careful weighing of her situation, which by her own admission was crumbling, against his, which was as yet still emerging. She was not a port in his storm. Instead she was simply a tempest, a churning anxiety of emotions that she could barely control and allowing those roiled feelings to sweep the young man away in a swell of her making, your Honor." The dramatic pause would ensue. "As Miles Davis once said, your Honor, 'It is not the notes you play, it is the notes you don't play'. Ms. Roberts did what the court suggests she did, even unwittingly."

She had said no and he was good with that. How did it move forward after her refusal? Would the prosecution take that into account? It was a moment of emotional weakness and she was hoping for something the good people on the jury would consider abnormal. The prosecution would ask that, she thought, and she would not have a very good reply. Was it then that she decided to recant her refusal? Did she accept the crime knowing it was one and simply acquiesce?

Did it matter? She knew that had she left it at no, it would have been nothing but infatuation. Her problem was not with his feelings but with her own. She felt helpless. Would it matter? Would it play out as him taking advantage of her? Would the courtroom treat her as a victim even if she was eight years older? It would not because she had slept with him once and in the eyes of the law, once was enough to prosecute.

Thirty-five years ago, it was a Mrs. Robinson fantasy of every boy. Except, he was only a boy by age. Once again, the courts would not consider the life he had led and her inability to resist his too-adult-like charms, already matured far beyond those of any man she had ever known. Men, she had found out after she had married her high school sweetheart, were incredibly high maintenance. They required constant consoling, frequent strokes of their egos, and an ongoing adaptation to the damage their mothers had emotionally inflicted on them, a gift that was passed on to every women they would meet courtesy of the woman that raised them. Some would claim to not be momma's boys but their attitude displayed quite the opposite. And what characteristics they adopted from their fathers was manifested in a churlish actions directed at the mother figures they supposedly didn't worship.

But Santo was so wholly different, almost as if he was asexual, devoid of the emotional baggage she had known and portered. But he was so sexual it unhinged her morals and ethics and anything else that grounded her to the society she had been raised in. Time ripped itself from the real world when he spoke. She found herself looking at the mirror, not wondering what she was doing, but when she would do it and what would happen next.

She had been a librarian in his home town. She had guided his reading and appreciation of art, opening his voracious mind to a world that awaited. At first, she thought he was merely feigning the actual reading of the books he checked out until she had more lengthy conversations with him. During these interludes, it was her that spoke. He listened patiently, asked tender questions, and made references to the books he had devoured. They discussed philosophy and science, history and music, and whatever he had recently been exposed. And despite the long list of authors already consumed by him, both shared a love for Michener.

The distance between that first conversational intercourse and the moment he suggested they become intimate seemed to span decades. He had matured with such immediacy, she had lost track of who he was. No longer was Santo the young man on the cusp of an intellectual breakthrough; he had grown, almost as if he not only broke through but did so in such a way as to leave no doubt about his stature.

They had slept together only once, hence the crime she had carried with her for over three decades. It was for her, a magical time-out-of-mind, carefully arranged by him as if he did this professionally. He was tender and considerate and unlike anything she had ever experienced. At first she passed this off to her own limited experience with men. Thirty five years removed from that 'one time' and he was still the standard by which she judged all men.

They had arrived in separate cars to a motel five miles

from the place they first met. He had arrived first, checking in and decorating the surprisingly spacious room. It was, he had told her, the presidential suite, explaining that Henry Ford had stayed here visiting a long since closed auto plant and he was, he explained, a president of the company. Veils were laid over lamp shades, candles placed around the room and wine chilled in a bucket. It was all beyond the scope of what she had anticipated. There was so much forethought involved in this seduction, she lost track of what she was doing. It both frightened her and excited her.

The mysteries she had hoped would be revealed with each lover she had had were instead unveiled in one lost afternoon. It was then, in the afterglow that she felt the stigma of what she had done.

Worse, he understood. He didn't balk when she said she had to go. He didn't try to stop her and made no attempt to seduce her again. While she felt the immediate weight of their intercourse, he stood naked, the smoke of a joint wafting up his muscular arm. He smiled, unsure of whether she wanted to kiss goodbye or flee like the criminal she thought she was.

As she drove back to normalcy, leaving began to make her feel as if she had made the wrong decision, that she shouldn't have left at that moment, that she should have let the affair take its course, even if it was judged by society as unnatural. Thirty-five years removed, she still replayed those moments as if they would reveal something that would assure her that she had made the right decision, even if she was unsure which decision had been right: before, during, after, or all three.

In the days and weeks and months that followed, he made no attempt to avoid her. Nor did he go out of his way to make contact. In her mind, this emotional absence he seemed to have harnessed was the single characteristic she admired and loathed. She wanted to scream in desperation and mostly in anguish. Her mistake was she had experienced it, as he did but differently.

Her decision as a result was to leave, to run, to blend into the background of the world, be the forest, be the clouds, to be gone. But life in those last days had been messy. Her father had been slowly dying over the previous six months and her marriage disintegrated in tandem. She was steadfast in her resolve to leave the city, to tie up any loose ends and never return. Her father's death had made that decision easier. It was that event that brought her to this auditorium. It was what she had learned in the waning weeks of his life that obligated her to meet with Santo one last time.

But he left first, without a word, without warning and without saying goodbye. Her tearful announcement that she had to leave was usurped by his abrupt exit. And in the weeks that followed his hasty departure, she had uncovered the truth he had been seeking his whole life.

14

The seven men were still more or less strangers, even after rehearsing and choreographing their motions for well over a month. They had been instructed at the very beginning of the project, which was how they referred to the practice leading up to and eventually performance of the act. Bertrand and Marley had emphasized the need for total secrecy, suggesting that the handsome pay package would make the effort worth their while. Still, they didn't wholly trust them. A team of social media experts had been hired to monitor every text, post and phone call they made. They used sophisticated eavesdropping techniques to monitor live conversations and surveilled their activities when they weren't in the huge warehouse practicing. There was no need to do this to the one man they were all portraying.

All of the men had a vaguely Mediterranean look although two of them had no traceable lineage to the area. Medev Krus and Hans Urlich were near perfect matches for the man they were to mimic. Bebe Isom had lost all telltale traces of the accent from his Israeli upbringing and with his hair cut short, colored in the same pepper mix, he made a convincing doppelganger. Ryan Reese was the youngest and tallest of the seven men but Bertrand assumed that this would be less of a problem than one might assume. He had worked with Ryan in several films and knew him to be a gifted actor. Stephan and Sylvester Chaino had the advantage of being twins. The make-up person needed only to thin their eyebrows and lighten the dark circles under their eyes.

The mistake both Bertrand and Marley made was hiring the Chaino twins. They were happy to sign whatever promise of non-disclosure required for the job and lucrative perks that went with it. But they were equally vested in the disclosure and because of their relationship, they could openly talk about the situation amongst themselves. About a week into the rehearsals, just as the performance began to gel and the actors realized what the part entailed, Stephan turned to his brother and shot him a "what the fuck?" look that he knew would break that agreement. Sylvester was older by a couple of minutes but much less inclined to step out of the boundaries the world set for him.

"Let's follow them?" he turned to his brother as he cranked their old blue Saab to life.

"Follow who?" Sylvester asked.

"All of them. We know that Aretino isn't us so it has to be one of the other five and I want to know who the rich guy is."

"I'm not so sure that is a good idea, Stephan. We've got an agreement with that producer and I don't want to fuck it up. This could be a career," but Sylvester cut him off mid-sentence.

"Yeah, yeah, yeah. Whatever. A career changer is hardly what this is. In fact, if this guy comes through and there's no guarantee there won't be a cash payout and we'll be back to doing local theater and standing in the background of Grimm. Maybe we can squeeze a little bit more out of Mr. Santo to keep us quiet."

Sylvester sat there for a moment considering his options. And even though he looked exactly like his brother, Stephan could see facial expressions that didn't belong to him. He had long known that his brother possessed empathy whereas Stephan felt devoid of any such considerations. They have shared the same womb but the end result was almost a departure from the fraternal bond most twins claim to have. But years had taught him to be silent, to let his brother work his thoughts out, even the thoughts were half formed and somewhat unhinged to the reality of Stephan's world, a place where he was king because he would take what kings demanded. He would however protect Sylvester along the way. His brother sighed and turned to Stephan.

"Which one first?"

"Good question, brother. We'll just have to eliminate them one by one. Let's start with that one." They followed Medev to his family home in the Sellwood district, greeting his wife on the front lawn as she watered the flowers. The house was small but comfortable looking and both of them looked as if they belonged. The next night they followed Hans, who lived in an apartment over a bakery on Hawthorne. They watched him from the car for several hours as he fed his cat, ate and watched television until around ten, he closed the curtains. Ryan turned out to be a heavy partier, giving the two brothers a much longer pursuit as he went from bar to bar and finally to the back seat of an old Coupe DeVille parked in the basement of a 24-hour grocery store. Bebe offered no outward signs of a disguise as he walked to his apartment building near the warehouse. Stephan had considered getting out of the car as Bebe entered the building and disappeared but reconsidered. He imagined trying to describe the man who had just entered when in fact, he looked exactly like the man he would have been describing. It took several more nights before Stephan wrote him off as a mock-rich guy.

Santo first thought it was slightly more than coincidence that the car following him carried two people who bore more than a striking resemblance to him. He turned left and they turned as well. He pulled into the parking lot of the 7-11 and the driver almost followed. He waited and exited taking the road the Saab had taken. He saw it pulled sloppily into a parking spot of a windshield repair shop and drove passed it. It pulled out a couple of seconds later.

Santo had had thirty-five years of being invisible, a ruse he never showed any signs of dropping. He had created a labyrinth of buildings that held no relationship to him, cars parked in odd places, and of course, no electronic trail to follow. It was the stuff of spycraft and he did it without thinking.

The car tailing him came as a surprise but, with all of the preparations he had made, was not unexpected. Moving through the normal world would always be fraught with curious eyes and questioning looks.

He decided to continue as he had, arriving at a brick-faced building on the inner southeast side of Portland. These buildings were located in the warehouse district, not far from the rehearsal studio. He had rented a room here under the name Sonny Prince. He parked the car and entered through the main doorway, passing several men who were sitting on the steps in the late fall sun. These low cost rooms were the mainstay of single men who had jobs but no other tether to the world of success, no matter how mediocre. He followed the long hallway to a fire exit door and left the building.

He broke into a light jog and quickly went to a parking garage two blocks away. He waited for a moment to see if the men had followed him into the building before he left the shadows of the parking structure. He would repeat this at another location in the northeast, entering an apartment building where he had rented a room he would not use, and exiting through the rear to another car.

His overly cautious demeanor would appear to be rooted in paranoia but he didn't see it that way. From the moment he had decided to remove himself from the world he felt he didn't belong to, it was, in his mind, a natural progression of movements designed to protect that decision. When he stayed home, as he often did, he was assured that he would not be disturbed. He had ample wealth to make this happen. On the rare occasion when he went to the office, he would enter through the main entrance and show a name badge with Sonny Prince on it. He enjoyed the irony of using an unnatural nickname for Santo and the description Eva had used, calling him the scourge of princes, a term that took on meaning after the fact and moving forward. If he ever felt he had a mission, which he, if he did, never vocalized, he might have been inclined to agree: He was put here to disrupt the status quo. To Santo Aretino, the status quo represented the conquered, take-no-prisoners ground of someone stronger and hence, he made the rules of what was acceptable.

He felt the same about faith and religion, or as he often told Marley it should be called, hope and harnesses. Marley had grown up with religion in her life but had waited to fully abandon it soon after she met him. Changing her name had occurred long before she met him, so as to allow her to go through the world without the assumption of Jewishness. Her father had argued his legacy and hers but she told him it was not a betrayal, it was only a tool. Perhaps it was his logical argument against the organization of worshipers, a debate he was willing to have with anyone and had since he was in high school. Then it seemed rebellious. Now it seemed to be a sort of adult anarchy, the chaos wholly under his control. He had told her that people need faith to get by, which he found sad, and religion to keep them law abiding. He assured her that he was present tense.

And it was in this present tense, Santo noticed the car in his rearview mirror.

Stephan motioned for his brother to pull over. Sylvester parked the Saab in a no parking spot in front of the building and had barely pulled the hand brake tight before his brother jumped out. The men sitting on the stoop stopped cold, one with the bottle still pressed to his lips. Stephan, looking exactly like the man who had just hurriedly entered the building a minute ago, bounded up the steps and into the long hallway. He stood for a moment looking at the long corridor, lined on either side by numbered doors. He looked at the exit door at the far end and slumped.

They repeated this tactic again the next night, convinced that this elusive figure was the Santo Aretino they would all introduce themselves as on stage, that the man they were following would be the one who would be chosen to actually speak the words while the others mimicked the action. Santo expected their curiosity to be piqued and it was and despite explicit directions to remain anonymous and quiet about the production and their role in it, he also knew that there would be one man among them who would succumb to his curiosity. To Santo, the consummate investor, it was a simple law of numbers.

It wasn't until the next night, after managing to avoid them again, that the brothers thought they would become cleverer than their prey. Instead of following him, they raced ahead and waited, Stephan positioned himself in the alley behind the building while Sylvester waited in the Saab a block away.

Sylvester was paying close attention to the door, exactly as his younger brother had instructed he do, when the car door opened and Santo slid onto the front seat. He simply said, "Go" and in his panic, he turned the engine over, choking to life with a billow of black smoke. He drove off. Santo was looking out of the window at the building and uttered only one word: "Hurry!"

Still looking away from the unsuspecting driver, who had assumed that his brother was his passenger, he instructed Sylvester to pull over. He did as he was told. Soon as he turned off the engine and before Sylvester could ask any questions, Santo grabbed the keys from the ignition.

As he exited the car, he turned back and told Sylvester, "Stop following me." He gave the keys a toss into the open field and began jogging away.

The following morning, Stephan and Sylvester were told that the rehearsals and staging were being moved because of scheduling issues. The man at the door of their small apartment was well-dressed and polite as he asked them to pack a bag of personal things. Stephan was not as cooperative as his brother, who eagerly went to his room to pack. The man remained polite answering his questions with a simple "I only know what they told me" and left it at that. He wasn't lying in that sense although he was also instructed to not leave them alone if they refused to leave. Finally, after the futile interrogation, Stephan packed a small duffel bag.

The driver of the town car held the door open for the two brothers. The messenger slipped into the front seat. Sylvester excitedly asked where they were headed and the man told him "the airport." Stephan continued to be skeptical but wanted to let this play out a bit further before making any decisions. The deal they had signed was lucrative and did entail the possibility that there might be some traveling involved. There had been no indication that this contingent would actually be engaged; the rehearsals all seemed so mundane. They pulled up to the private jet and were boarded in a couple of minutes. They did ask the attendant where they were headed and she smiled saying "Seattle." That was indeed the destination. They were whisked to a downtown Westin hotel, both were handed an envelope with a thousand dollars, and told to stay close-by for further instructions.

Bertrand was told of the two brothers by Marley the next morning. He shrugged his shoulders but did not ask why. Five actors would provide enough of the illusion he was hoping to create.

*****

With the average TED talks, the stage was often given the library or den treatment. Bertrand wasn't sure why. Perhaps to give the speaker a more scholarly appearance, much the way some comedians use industrial backdrops to portray their edginess. When they asked about the staging, he simply replied that he only wanted a single curtain of any color. He had brought in a local rock band technician to do the lights, which were key to keeping the concept alive.

The stage didn't go to immediate black as Marley walked from her mark on the stage. He instructed the lights to go down to black over the course of a minute, gradually creating less light and not giving the audience any direct tie to the beginning of the program. Once the room was almost completely black and the ushers had made sure everyone was seated, the lights went down totally. Two seconds later, the stage was illuminated with a curtain of red overhead lights. The effect was to cut the audience off from the depth of the stage. It also had the effect of forcing people to lean in.

The men walked on stage in single file and positioned themselves on the mark resembling the item marked on their script. Bertrand had found the use of Monopoly pieces fun and even gave Santo the top hat, an irony he would have enjoyed. Two empty marks, the thimble and iron had been removed.

The audience politely clapped, not really sure what they were supposed to do. They were expecting the reclusive Santo Aretino, the man behind one of the biggest philanthropic efforts never heard of. The men were barely visible to the audience and they all collectively leaned in further, as if closing the distance by a couple of additional inches would help the faces materialize.

"Good evening," Santo said and with perfect

choreography, all five men half raised their hands as if to wave. "My name is Santo Aretino." Together, the upturned hands returned to their sides.

Nick leaned to Che and uttered a muted "What the fuck?" Twenty rows from the railing of the balcony and off to the left, John Bates cursed as well but more at himself and his failure to bring some sort of binoculars. Arianne, sitting twenty rows behind Bertrand, smiled just like he did. She was smiling because she understood the ploy right away, the illusion that he was there and then not, a tactic he had used since she had known him as a teenager. Bertrand was smiling because they nailed the first ten seconds.

"I would like to speak to you tonight about my thoughts on the word good, probably the most maligned word in the English language, relegated to a subtext that assumes there is room for improvement or as a mere waystation on the journey from one extreme to the other. As a descriptive, it is more than adequate without words like 'really' accompanying it." He stepped to the right and the other four men mimicked the action. The lights gradually changed color, moving from red to purple with the seamlessness of a rock show choreographed to the music.

"But first, I want to bring up your eulogy. Not your resume or your goals and aspirations, but the final words someone will say about you. As a younger man, I thought the goal of life was to attain two thousand words on the obit page of the New York Times. I was never going to achieve public stardom through movies or music or celebrity so that was in and of itself a grandiose dream. I have talents, mind you, but they are more personal and enjoyed by me, and sometimes my wife. I was not destined to be a scientist, not that I didn't have a fascination for any and all sciences. It was just not something I was cut out for. As every scientist will tell you, their work is built upon the backs of people who had already been eulogized.

In many cases, those eulogies and subsequent obits fell short of what they could have been, because whomever came along afterwards, took that body of work and made it something it should have been, if, of course, the person had lived a bit longer or even at a later time. I applaud the rigor of getting up every day only to leave the work you're doing half done, to be completed at a later date, to be credited with discoveries that might have been right in front of the previous scientist, until they were eulogized.

"I never fancied myself a writer either. I knew and love words and the power they possess, but I harbor no need to get inside your head and fabricate my thoughts to your literary weakness. The thought of massaging your inner thoughts to my will did not appeal to me as a young man and even decades later, still does not. To write is to manufacture legacy where there was previously none. Oh and to tell the same story again differently and hope for critical acclaim. Although many writers who are successful could not care one whit about critical acclaim and that is sad, in part because their eulogies won't dissect why they wrote, only what someone thought of it, someone they may have never met.

"So how is one eulogized if the public never knows you, if the person never sought the so-called limelight? And which kind of eulogy will be produced and by whom? Will it be a friend who tells cute stories about an incident that may or may not have defined you? Or will it be someone else who looks at your body of work, your life lived, and make the determination of what you intended and if you made a difference. Most of us won't and most of us wish otherwise."

The audience was forced to focus on the words, even as they strained to get a glimpse of the man who was speaking. Because they all wore wireless microphones, and as instructed, moved their mouths to the sound of one man, not only did the people in attendance not know who was speaking, the actors were also unaware. Actual body movements were done only for impact and none of them moved much more than a foot or so from the spot they began the performance. Bertrand had been certain that there would be some digital recording, where some geek would try to filter out the lights and grab a clear image.

"Our friends would certainly have something different to say about us than our colleagues, who I assume get the image of who were are from a carefully crafted edit of our true selves. You know, the old 'best foot forward' approach to public opinion.

"None of us begin the day with the intention that we will be bad. Yet few of us begin the day with the intention that we will be good. The reason is quite simple: we have a low opinion of good. I've seen book titles suggesting the good is the enemy of great. Cosmopolitan magazine will run on about how to have great sex or a great relationship or great make-up suggesting that good is, well, not great. Leadership is not good if it's not great. Some have suggested that the difference between good and great is intent, or the amount of heart invested, or the amount of loyalty, or context, or any number of other things that seem to dissect a perfectly acceptable attribute as less than the possibility.

"The trouble with great is everyone has a different description of great. But good is really what we should be striving for and great should be relegated to a modifier for good, as in greater good. And to react to the greater good, we must feel awe. Not awesome, but in a state of wonder, a place where we feel inspired, reverential, even the kind void of religious belief, the type people suggest we try to achieve with the simplicity of a walk through the forest, the experience of magical and the mysterious and the unexpected. Awe is good. It should be all we seek. It is the absence of self-importance and narcissism, the elegant feeling that Sagan once called reverential, what Kant told us is the morality in us and the universe around us, what Thomas Aquinas believed was the birthplace of philosophy. Awe can only be good. It cannot be great because it turns us into a comparative critic: This is good but this would be great and no longer will be in awe, we'll be wishing for what was never intended.

"I am fully comfortable with the fact that people will call some leaders great and they will remain that way until sentiment changes, the fluidity of human emotions begins to weigh their true feelings, of course only when we allow someone to explain those feelings to us and what they ought to be. Then we will no longer be in awe. That leader will no longer be great. Their fall from our grace will be further, passing good without so much as a pause.

"So are awe and good the same thing? Perhaps in the same way night and day are part of the same cycle. Good is what you do, awe is what happens when you do it. Good and awe lack individualism, they are void of materialism and only have value for someone else. You may feel good when you are good and in awe when you experience that good first hand, but it needs to be felt in order for it to have significance.

"Now this flies in the face of what every employment situation tells you. You must excel or grow or do both. You become politicized and confused and unfortunately, good people get left by the wayside because of some perceived pomposity in a co-worker is considered great.

"My wife described some of the achievements I have done but not why. I don't know why. I never even gave it a thought. I have been gifted with a unique form of memory that doesn't allow me to recall any past reaction to the minute I'm currently living. I'm not abnormal. What I have found is that if I did engage a moment in time that has already happened, it would not serve me well. To me, memory is sort of like an unfinished movie. Each time you yank it from its reel case and thread it on to the projector, you run it and look at it and edit it, adding subtle changes, it is no longer the same. Perhaps the original version, caught in all of its raw glory was adequate. But what is it after the first or second or third viewing? Is it memory if it has been altered? So, I can and am able to recall but choose not to. I am in awe of every single minute I live, for one, because I'm alive and two, I probably shouldn't be.

"I took risks that were probably not wise. I'm gifted that way. Every day of my early life, before coming to Portland some thirty-five years ago, was like a dare. I wonder if you feel that way. As you drive, do other cars, bikes, pedestrians dare you to do something that is against what you know to be good? Do they dare you to step outside of the person you know you are, the one you'd like eulogized by both friends and media? Of course you do. Every time you go to work, is every interaction a dare? It is and you navigate them with caution but sometimes, maybe infrequently, you take the dare and say something hurtful or harmful or career ending or quite the opposite.

"We operate under the presumption that we have control. We don't really. We have a choice: To take the dare or not, to avert our eyes or look at it and face the consequences, run or stand your ground and do so without any thought of what that decision might result in. We are genetically wired to flee danger but our temptation to take the dare, stay one second longer than would be advisable, is often overwhelming.

"But suppose it isn't temptation at all that triggers us to take the dare. Perhaps it is something good inside, some moral compass that is set at birth or maybe reset later in life, some influence of art and history and science and a combination of that. And no, moral compasses are not set by faith or calibrated by religions. They are benefactors of violence.

"In some sense, the world is not full of the opposites we think of. Hate is not the opposite of love; indifference is. Just like the opposite of good is not bad, it is violence, the usurping of a person's place, an interruption of their well-being and comfort, a crossing of a barrier between what would be comfort and not-so-comfortable. Violence, as Susan Sontag once suggested is not a thinking person's activity. You can't do both at the same time. I can personally attest to this. Once engaged in violence, all thought is vaporized inside of the first second and then the second and by the end of the action, you are incapable of thought. Or as Gandhi said: "Poverty is the worst kind of violence." And that is how good evolves; through violent subjugation.

"Suppose for a moment, a man is attacked, mugged, his space is invaded and the attacker shows little regard for that space. If someone were to violently intercede on his behalf, is that violence or is it good? We spend a lot of time these days talking about bullies, in schools and wherever weaker people are vulnerable but there is little talking can do. Back to our attacked man. Suppose the violence that steps in on his behalf, you know the stuff that wars and conflicts around the globe are made of, will it make a difference? Will good come of it? Will it be as Malcolm X suggested: "You have to pick up a gun in order to put a gun down?" Probably not: But if one man helps another and the victim is the person who was violent, should he be described as anything but good, even if he used violence?

"Personally, I have no idea why you folks are even here. I suppose you're curious at what a rich recluse looks like. And we duped you with the light show because reclusiveness is a choice you cannot invade. I suppose you want to know what drives me to give away eighty percent of my fortune before I make a fortune and then a big deal about giving it away. I've been giving it away for thirty years and only the people I helped noticed. But save a couple of turtles and suddenly I'm on a stage like a specimen to be examined and dissected. That's fine. This is all you'll get.

"I will continue to do what I have always done. And

you will continue to ask why. Because good is without equal. Great is reserved for the over performing, those that push themselves and expect you to provide the accolades that their achievements warrant, or so they think. Once you attain greatness, you will have detractors who will suggest you did it on the backs of lesser people, and maybe that's true.

"But good has no equal, no downside, nothing but an elegantly written eulogy that is delivered with a head bowed, in reverence, in awe. And that is what we do it for or should do it for. Because good is the highest achievement any woman or man can make. Any higher and someone will be hurt.

"I'm going to leave you with one final thought, or five actually. An old German woman gave me a buffalo head nickel on a leather strap once long ago. It was special to her but she told me I should wear to remind me to do five good things.

"She told me I would be the scourge of many princes. She was right and I suppose I have made that my life's work. I never really categorized it as such, but for the sake of understanding, you could say it was true. Because the first tenet of good is eliminating those that are violent. What she told me of course is open to interpretation.

"You're a serious young man she would say and I was, still am I suppose. But Eva believed I should toss a smile someone's way, toward some innocent, and maybe occasionally in the opposite direction, aimed at some maleficent. So I have tried even though it is not necessarily my nature to smile, or it wasn't in those days.

"She quickly followed her encouragement to smile more often with the somber observation that I should be alone but not alone. You'll get married she said but I doubt you'll have kids. I can hear her saying that I shouldn't just think that once I found love, and I did, that I might not have enough love to go around. But if you do, she said, it'll be your wife's idea and she'll be your guide.

"Eva also added that I might never actually love them the way the world suggests you do, but you'll protect them and her; you'll protect her from them. Kids can be vacant when it comes to the hand that feeds them and nurtures them. You'll make them know that she is all that matters and they'll fear you enough to remember that."

*****

One and one-half billion heartbeats before he stepped on this stage, Santo was sitting on her porch as the late autumn Pennsylvania sun drifted into the tree line. He just sat there looking at her when she said this. "Let me clarify. You have love in you somewhere and when you find it, there won't be enough to go around. So don't try."

Eva also felt as though she should mention that he should never take the evil in the world personally. He was pretty sure that he hadn't. "It's not what you think that means," she said. "It is more of an affirmation that the world needs silent warriors like you, with no agenda, to deal with the random acts of invasion that happen to far too many people. You are gifted that way and if I could see it, so can everyone else. People will tell you things Santo and you'll have to decide what's important and what isn't."

"Do you remember when I told you everyone lies, Santo?" They hadn't been discussing falsehoods or their impact on her or even him when she had first talked about this. It was one of those 'clear-blue', 'out-of-nowhere' comments. "Considering how well-read you are, you already know this. But I'm not so sure you're convinced of it. But, consider this: if everyone lies and they do, then there is no truth or anything concrete." Eva had suspected that he had never told a lie in his life. His frankness, often uncensored and sometimes cold and objective made him a conversational outcast and a favorite of this old Teutonic widow. But she enjoyed it. It was too late in her life to have any worth. She knew that speaking to someone who is incapable of lying is not much fun. But she found it invigorating, void of pretense. She imagined the look on the faces of the people who would encounter these purest hearts, these shining beacons, these emotionless sculptures of reason and rationality when they realized that this is not who they would want to talk to. "It's okay," she added hastily, "no one will feel right lying to you either."

The fifth platitude this old woman, the one her Hessian friends had referred to as a hexe, a witch, a seer, or soother of pain and discomfort, came directly from something Plato had said. He knew the saying and was impressed with her recall.

*****

"Human behavior flows from three main sources or so says Plato: Desire, emotion and knowledge. No man has all three in equal quantities. Some smart people have no emotion. Some emotional people have no smarts. And desire, well, everyone thinks they have that but in fact, what they have is a need to have desire. Eva told me that I have all three but I don't know it. She said that it's what makes me exceptional, without descriptors, and certainly an enigma. I don't have to be aware of them and within yourself, you don't have to either. They'll just happen. Just don't turn your back on them."

*****

In tandem, all the men on stage unbuttoned the top button of their shirt as they loosened their ties. All of them reached inside of their suit coats and pulled a small object out. Bertrand knew that the audience would not be able to see the small totem but the effect was perfect and gave the men a funhouse mirror effect.

"This fine woman gave me a 1926 Buffalo nickel as a reminder of those five things."

Nick turned towards Che, who had leaned forward on her elbows. "We should go." His voice was monotone and one she knew well. He would often take a deep breath and sigh as he exhaled when his voice hit that specific pitch. It was as condescending as he could get without adding the insults. He would explain his reasons later, when they were clear of listening ears and often they were concise and even shared. But tonight was different.

Santo's voice had taken on a hypnotic tone that had pushed more than just Che to lean forward. It rhapsodized like a late night, big city FM disc jockey, taking on the tone of someone familiar and yet, with the fleeting thrill of a one-night stand, both seductive and elusive. It took on the tone of shared indignities: You were listening to the radio and in your aloneness, he shared your frustration with why. It was hypnotic with no trace of a breath between words or phrases or sentences, each silence in between truly without sounds. It was both friendly and empathetic while being just out of reach.

She turned slightly without taking her eyes off of the man she was sure she dined with the night before and whispered, "No." She had focused on Santo and was certain in her identification of this man of mystery. In between wishing she could meet him after the speech, she toiled with the regret of not engaging him more when she had the chance.

Nick slumped back into his seat.

*****

Arianne was simply smiling. The complexities of his speech were delivered in short words and with vigor. She knew he was capable of showering a conversation with practical language that was easily understood by those listening but on the other hand, there were times when talking to him felt like a game of Scrabble, loose thoughts replacing letters and those words transformed into long forgotten SAT vocabulary.

Tonight he was simply elegant and easy. She knew which

one he was from the moment he had entered the light curtain. She was surrounded by people enraptured like Che was, hoping to grasp a shred of the air he was slicing with his words, clean, bloodless swipes that slipped easily into whatever vessel was available.

The letters she had been sending over the last thirty-five years were going to the same farm in the Lehigh Valley that he was talking about. He had only been there sixteen months, according to Seamus, the large hulking caretaker left in charge of the operation after Eva died. An older women, slightly more so than her, also lived there but did not like to talk to her. They shared a common love in their lives and they both knew the friction was stupid but it was palpable nonetheless. This was the first she had heard of the nickel and the invective that accompanied it. Arianne was pleased.

*****

The woman sitting next to John Bates turned quickly when he swore. He had hoped it was under his breath, the kind of whispered curse you might make in the company of more sensitive ears. He tried to avoid those situations. He considered swearing, if done properly, to be the focal point of all emphasis in a conversation. To some, it was a sign of failure, the inability to choose the right word when speaking emotionally and inserting the first four letter word that came to mind. Bates never struggled with this. He cared little whether there was a better, more socially acceptable word that was right for the situation. Swearing done correctly was an exclamation without argument. He ignored her though because the word he uttered came out louder than he thought it had. He sheepishly smiled at her, a sort of embarrassed apology that was more than she deserved.

He had made the off-color comment as soon as his memory aligned with the description of the nickel the man was wearing around his neck. One of the kids at the college had mentioned a coin on a leather band and another mention came from the victim of the mugging in St. Louis. Both had been offhand and unclear remarks that didn't connect. Now, he thought they did.

15

The applause was much more enthusiastic than Nick thought was warranted. People were standing, something he dismissed as the will of the herd, even if they seemed to reach their feet simultaneously.

It lasted several agonizing moments that John Bates used to exit the auditorium. He had hoped he could quickly circle back to the exit and perhaps stop one of the men exiting. If he was fortunate, it would be the right Santo Aretino, and not one of the sleight-of-hand fakes they had paraded on the stage.

John had barely listened to the words being uttered on stage. He had been consumed by the history he had gathered on the man and was not interested in what his life had become. One of the hallmarks of forgiveness is penance and to get to that point, one either asks for the infraction to be forgiven or sentenced by someone who took the payment for the wrongdoing with a pound of flesh, and or years in prison.

The Santo Aretino on stage had done none of this. He had not admitted to any crime but then again neither had he been formerly accused of any activity related to the crimes. He had instead acted like an innocent, a wholly good man who valued privacy while at the same time, valued the plight of his fellow man. It was an irony and a conundrum.

John Bates had a relatively narrow view on the path

a violent act should take. He had always seen it as a three stage endeavor: the belief that one could overpower someone else, the ability to block the morality of such an act from the present, and the last and most important element in the act, the illusion that whatever happened had happened for a reason and you were the sole remedy of the fate of another individual. It didn't matter whether it was deserved or not. In John's mind, it didn't matter if you had a pocketful of supporting reasons or the person who was on the receiving end deserved it: Violence is not an end and it sure as hell did not blossom into good like a weed growing from the crack in a sidewalk.

Nick on the other hand had listened to every word. He found it pretentious and less inspiring that his fellow listeners did. He found little worth in a man telling people how he did what he did, even if he had been forced into advancing his ideals, concepts that were, until this evening, private. As Nick powered up his phone, he watched the faces of the people leaving the building. They were engrossed in their conversations and from the look on their faces, enamored with the presentation. The first message that crawled onto the screen came from his editor.

Che had been doing the same thing, the bright light of her newly revived phone giving her the eerie upglow that only accentuated the perfection of her face. She touched his arm.

"I've got to go."

"Go where?" Nick asked. He turned to her and watched as she read the message.

"Seems our actors need a haircut and Bertrand wants me to go backstage and barber them." She had not made any logical leaps forward when Bertrand gave her the tickets but his message made sense: You couldn't very well eject five identical men onto the streets without someone recognizing, or seeming to recognize one of them as the speaker. "Says he'll give me $200 a cut."

"Should I come with you?" He hoped she would say no and she did, gently adding that she was sorry but the director had specifically asked she come alone. He acted disappointed and kissed her. He tried to leave without looking too anxious.

In the lobby, he called his editor.

Robert Zoti had founded the Portland Riverfront Weekly to have a job. He had been disillusioned with the obvious political bent that so many newspapers around the country seemed to be adopting. Journalism was being driven by the editorial page and that page was driven by the politics of the owners. He found that unappealing. Known to his friends in the newspaper business as PurDub Bobbie, an affectionate moniker that abbreviated his pride and joy and the harmoniousness of two names ending in vowels, Nick's editor was the newspaper. He was only called Zoti in the newsroom.

He had seen a great deal of himself in Nick Heath and hired him based on his limited resume. The qualities he recognized were similar but were wholly different in how they manifested in the two men. Zoti was older and more cynical, always believing that people held their goodness close while giving the world the side they'd rather conceal. It was human nature: Hide what you are and become the crowd instead. Unlike journalists in television and radio, Zoti enjoyed the handicap of an interview without a microphone, a crutch akin to buying a drunk the next round. It was a prop that elicited an instant interview and although it did have the net effect of getting people talking, soon as they thought they were being recorded, even the most quiet person suddenly became verbose, even surprising themselves in the process, what came out of it was almost always unusable. It was as if their brains were running two stories at the same time, bumping into each other as they tumbled from a person's mouth, one side telling the story, the other telling how they felt about it.

Print journalist had no such prop and relied wholly on first impressions and the opening line of the inquiry, the face-to-faceness of the conversation giving each word more nuance.

Zoti had the knack. He could get people to talk but he had to show them that he had just ignored their survey of his face. He had, as he often referred to it, "a face for radio", scarred from teenage acne and because of those cratered shadows, a damaged and darker look. He used empathy to pry the information from his interviews and by standing alongside of them instead of face-to-face, gave the impression that he was looking in the same direction, walking the same mile. Expressing empathy always helped. Nick had external empathy but struggled with the emotion of it and that's what Zoti liked best.

Nick was more visually comforting to those he interviewed. He had boyish good looks, was twenty years his junior and was blessed with a disarming, almost seductive smile. He too used empathy but when he did, his subject easily forgot their own pain and discomfort and began worrying what the effect of sharing it with someone as innocent as he looked would incur. The guilt of that commingled incestuously with whatever incident he was asking about made them reveal what they knew in more detail but with softer edges. Every story he had written captured this innocent exchange, as if his ability to get them to talk was a transfer of trust. His writing as a result had wide appeal.

"Yeah, boss," he responded when Zoti answered the phone. His voice sounded rough.

"You saw that Aretino guy tonight?" he asked, phrasing it as a question.

"I did," adding quickly, "Please don't make me write about him. I don't think there is anything there. Just some rich guy who..."

Zoti cut him off mid-sentence, "Oh there's something there, Nick. I just don't know exactly what it is but it's there." He had done a variety of searches and the name Santo Aretino turned up during a probation hearing for a drug dealer convicted in 1976 and serving a lengthy sentence in Pennsylvania. The question had been asked at the hearing of a man named Matteo (Matty) DeSilva who had spent his prime years at Bellefonte Prison. The best Zoti could determine from the transcript was the question was asked during at least three other hearings at the behest of the arresting narcotics officer. The prisoner answered the question the same way each time, according to the documents he had been able to find: "I don't know Santo Aretino, or Sonny Aretino or any Aretino." What, thought Zoti, does the arresting officer know about this person that he would travel upstate for each parole hearing just, apparently to have that question asked?

Nick walked the six blocks to the office of the newspaper. He listened to the crowd's reaction as he wandered with them. Most of the reviews were positive and polite. The criticisms he did hear seemed to be coming from the men. He suspected the women had been hypnotized by the tonality of the voice rather than the concept of his speech, even if it had what Nick could only describe as 'saccharine appeal'. Che certainly seemed to have been among those who viewed the event as energizing. Just the brief conversation he had with her as she salmoned her way through the exiting crowd suggested she was now a believer. Nick would later write that *the talk resembled a homily, a verbal story riffing on a written story, and with the ecclesiastical lighting, the flanking of acolytes masking the speaker and the reverential hush that seemed to envelope the audience, one could almost wonder if the conclusion would include a pipe organ and a choir*. The crowd thinned out over the course of the trek down Broadway, peeling off into parking garages and restaurants along the route.

He found his boss tucked in the corner of his office, a

small cube that diminished his importance at the paper. Zoti had founded the paper after a Pulitzer prize winning stint at the Los Angeles Times. With a pocket full of cash attained through a distant relative's untimely death, he started the Portland Riverfront Weekly in the un-renovated basement of an old retail building that had once sold furniture. The owner was fine with leasing the space but made it clear that they would have to evacuate if a better tenant signed. That never happened.

The paper had grown quickly under Zoti's direction. It truth, it thrived. He knew free was a very good price and in those early years it seemed more like volunteer work for those writing there than an actual job. The paper quickly adapted and adopted to the social norms of the city, acting as an alternative lobbying group for those who refused to belong to the regular machinations of the town. It was the thorn in the side of the established newspapers and its opinions gradually began to sway voters, who increasingly took the paper's review of the voters pamphlet as their own. By the time he hired Nick four years ago, the paper had a city-wide circulation of over 200,000 and had spawned sister papers in Eugene and Salem. But Zoti remained in Portland.

"I still disagree," Nick said as he entered the office.

"That's what makes America great, Nick. It can also make you unemployed." It was a typical Zoti remark, tucked inside a hollow threat. "Pack your bag. You're going east, young man."

He stood there for a moment, as if composing himself. His expression was something different and his boss waited as Zoti watched his young protégé gather his words. He liked him for this: Stop and think and if you put your foot in your mouth, it will be because you intended to do so. He opened his mouth and almost spoke but stopped.

"So who's going to do my regular assignments?" Zoti

smiled. This was typical Nick. He knew that Nick had many awards tucked into his future and when he hired him, he had hoped that one of them would be won while he working at the Weekly. The circulation would get him the notice but his writing, often concise but passionate, would be his ticket to bigger and better paying assignments. He was determined to send him where he needed to go and expose him to the opportunities, even at the risk of losing him too soon. So, he tended to treat him badly while he still had him.

His first assignment was doing a column called the Simpleton. It was one of those Q&A sections where readers would write inane questions about life they had experienced in Portland. Goofy queries like "do the walk buttons really work?" or "I live in a studio; would it be okay to put my friend up in a homeless shelter when he's visiting from out of town?" Nick was given two hundred words to chastise and ultimately educate the readership. What started as a tongue-in-cheek column tucked in the first couple of pages became a huge hit. Nick's wry responses prompted more queries than column inches allowed. The online version was widely read prompting the two of them to compile the most compelling questions. Zoti had hoped that Nick and he could one day publish a definitive, book length answer key to life courtesy of one of the weirder towns in the country. Nick just seemed to gravitate further, or better, elevate away from the concept over time.

There were meaty stories as well and Nick handled them with great ease, delving into the impact of every situation with a deft hand. People talked to him and for some reason, told him things none of the other reporters covering the same story found. His global approach to the story, his wide angled, wide-eyed curiosity made each of his feature pieces, many of which ran well over 10,000 words, touchstone contributions that forced the other media in town to not only reference but frequently quote the paper and cite the author. This sort of attention Zoti knew, made the editor of the Oregonian throw up in the back of his throat, and that made him laugh.

Nick could make something as controversial as a bridge across the Columbia River interesting to people who would never even cross it if it was built. He had a gift of passion filled dispassion. Everything he submitted was print ready and on time. Zoti had given him numerous additional assignments to challenge his acuity and each time he surpassed his journalistic expectations. He should have been writing for the New Yorker or the Times, he was that good.

The one assignment that found him sitting across the table from the very man whose past he would soon be chasing, was the one he disliked the most. It wasn't the idea of reviewing food that he often found repulsive in the project Zoti had named "The Kitchen", an ongoing review of homestyle dining from people who offered food through a sharing app called "Eat with Us", it was the idea of eating where the kitchens hadn't been vetted by inspectors that gave Nick the most trouble.

"You know that half the restaurants in town are barely passing those health inspections, right?" Zoti had told him once.

To which Nick had replied, "I don't want to eat there either. These people have animals and no kitchen should have animals. Not that I have anything against animals but don't act like they don't matter. I know they think of their pets as family but you shouldn't be sharing your food with people who think that might be an issue."

Zoti had settled back in his chair, assuming his stoic face in the light on another rant from his star reporter. "Perhaps you should mention that the app developer should add a little dog or cat icon so people like you know in advance, you'll still have to go no matter what, and people like them, who don't care that Fluffy has sniffed the chicken or that Fido violently scratches his ear in the middle of the kitchen floor, you know, they could gather as one big animal loving group because they do not care." He said this to rile the young reporter and it was working.

They had a good relationship, not paternal, but accessible. Nick would talk and Zoti would listen. And when it was done, no matter the home-based restaurant, the article would be written in edible prose that made it impossible to avoid and hard to plagiarize. He had become the make or break review for those hoping to gain some traction and a few extra bucks.

He handed Nick a small folder. "What's this?" he asked as he opened it.

"It's your jumping off point, plane tickets and a few bucks to spend. You can keep what you don't spend."

"What if I come up short? There's not a whole lot of money in here and this card looks like it has a limit on it." He knew Zoti didn't give him a card without fixing the limit.

"Then you'll probably be spending a night or two in the car. You've got four days from touchdown in Philly to figure out why this guy ran from his hometown and never looked back. I'm sure there's family there and I know that old cop is still alive. Write yourself into an award boy."

There was little use in arguing with him. He wanted until he was dismissed, which he knew would come if he stood long enough in silence. The "get the fuck out of here" was the signal to leave he was looking for.

*****

He had left Che at the auditorium and when he sent her a text, she told him to come back and walk her home. It was an unusual request. She was the kind of girl who had a street savvy that helped protect her from most of what the city could throw at her. But Nick didn't ask why.

John Bates had left early in order to situate himself in what he believed was the best vantage point to watch the comings and goings. He had scouted this spot prior to entering the auditorium. He could see several unmarked side doors and a freight entrance from his corner post. He was hoping he hadn't missed the exiting subject of his long-term investigation. The crowd had thinned to the point of non-existent. He sighed loud enough for the man standing near him to hear.

"You okay mister," Nick asked, surprising himself with the question. The man looked only marginally better than Aqualung and only slightly better dressed. Not that Nick wasn't empathetic, he was. But in small doses, and selectively. While his job involved interviewing people who would not otherwise be of any concern to him if they hadn't been witnesses to some transgression, which he thought was the worst way to access the so-called fifteen minutes of fame, he always managed to keep a physical distance from them. He could spin the words he would write in such a way that it gave his editor chills. Nick would capture the scene like a photograph that bled with emotion. But if he ran into some one he had interviewed last week, he would struggle placing them in any memory. And he avoided homeless people. This man looked like maybe he was, even if the coat he was wearing suggested otherwise.

"Yeah. I'm fine. I was just hoping I'd catch a glimpse of the guy who spoke here tonight?" His voice had a resigned and defeated tone to it, a slight hint of British was still available to certain phrases.

"Santo Aretino?"

"Yeah. You know him or of him?" He turned towards Nick. His face was lined with great age but his eyes looked alert and did not have the rheumy appearance of some of the people he knew that were this old. He guessed the man was at least eighty, if not older. He was lean but not skinny and even though he was leaning on the traffic light, he seemed to be in good health.

"I was in there tonight." The man looked at him and then turned towards the direction he had come. Nick smiled. "I had to run an errand. I came back to pick up my girlfriend."

"Why's she still in there?" He fully turned toward Nick. The man must have been formidable in his youth, his shoulders still square. "Does she know him?" The question seemed anxious and hopeful.

"The director asked her stay and do a haircut."

"Son of a mother fucking bitch," he uttered hanging each syllable out for inspection. Then he repeated the word fuck three times. Nick smiled. He always smiled when people swore, especially when the swearing came from an unexpected source. "He got the fuck away. Shit. Shit. Fuck."

"What's your interest in Aretino?" Nick asked, suddenly interested in the man his editor had just told him to investigate and amused by this older gentlemen's emotional outburst.

"I've been quasi-hunting that SOB for three decades and when he surfaced in a Google alert, I emerged from retirement to catch him. Not really to catch him so much as interview him." Bates was certain that the girl was in there making each one of those men on stage look less like the men on stage. Despite the trickery with the light, he knew they were all grey with beards. But only one had that coin, the real one, around his neck and that was all he had to put him near two crimes and possibly more.

Bates had developed some plausible theories about this mystery man and in his lowly methodical voice, he explained what he knew about the man. He assumed he wasn't that bad of a man; just circumstantial. He could see revenge as the reason for the first crime, or even well placed vigilantism.

Those boys deserved everything they got, he had concluded, even if the punishment doled out was a bit over-the-top and perhaps even a little theatrical. But he let them live and did whatever he did in almost plain sight. What he couldn't figure out was whether it was something he had always done or was that a trigger that started him down the path from circumstantial vigilante to circumstantial criminal.

The cop from Chester he had spoken to suggested that Aretino was always a bit suspect and was definitely capable of heinous crimes. "I've looked at that gaze and I don't want to sound, you know, religious," the detective told him, "but you can see the evil in there even if I didn't get the impression that any of it was directed at me."

Bates was intrigued. "What do you mean by evil, John?" Tell was not the kind of man who, at least in Bates estimation of him was the type that had much tolerance for fear. He might have been careful not to confront it as most police he had met were, carefully weighing their options in split seconds with one goal in mind: Getting home to their family in the same condition they left that morning.

"Maybe evil is the wrong word. Maybe more than capable is what I meant. I only knew him as a kid but he was clever and steely and you could imagine him as man. Not the kind of man you'd want to confront." But Detective John Tell of City of Chester Police Department was retired and Bates doubted he had a very strong recollection of the man as a boy. It seemed his deceased roommate, a teacher who knew him better as the Dean of Discipline at an all-boys Catholic High School would have been a better source of information as to the state of Aretino's mental disposition to violence in his youth, however justified. The cop and the lay brother were close friends and in old age, roommates. "Connie could have told you so much more," he added referencing his late friend.

But even then, the pattern was only forming and those

early instances might have been only the seeds of what would become.

The incident in Ohio proved a dead end and he could find no one willing to add anything to what was unofficially reported as a mugging gone bad by a couple of local thugs, one of whom ended his string of terror in a bus stop parking lot. Although the sheriff had done his due diligence and interviewed numerous witnesses or people close enough to have been witnesses, Bates could see that his heart was not into the investigation. He was free of a two person crime wave that moved without consideration across four counties and as he admitted to his wife, albeit sheepishly, he was happy the stranger had passed through.

Bates had taken a map out at that point and plotted several potential routes his quarry may have taken. He doubted that there was a method to what he was doing. He had a young drug lord who managed to evade capture, heading north into Amish country on what seemed to be a whim, stayed for many months in a pass-thru hamlet, terrorized some college kids in the nearest big city and then headed west. It all seemed so happenstance, almost windblown.

Even though the next crime also involved bottom-feeding criminals, the cop in St. Louis seemed nonplussed by the whole scene he had been working on, adding at one point during the conversation that he wouldn't mind it if whomever he had been looking for would come back and finish the clean-up he had started.

The incident in Colorado would have been equally as baffling for Bates had it been reported in a timely fashion. The two drug dealers laid in the hot sun for days before the local authorities arrived. The anonymous tip was phoned in several days later. No one was there but the two dead men; everyone had left carrying away whatever they could. The cops found two obviously murdered corpses had been worked over by the mid-summer sun, the vultures and whatever vermin chased about the world for the next dead thing.

"And now I'm here."

"Jesus," was all he could think to say. Nick was now intrigued by the notion that maybe all of the answers were not still back east in some grimy old city. He did not want to go and his first thought was perhaps he had found something equally as good, and an argument to Zoti's crazy idea. "Then maybe you can help me?"

Bates slowly, somewhat dramatically turned towards Nick. "I'm guessing you're a reporter," was not the next thing he expected the old man to say. Despite his age, he seemed vibrant, his gaze taking a quick inventory of the man sixty years his junior. "Ever heard of broken symmetry?" Bates asked this as he pulled his collar up against the cooler night air. "Judging from the look on your face, I'm guessing not. So, no one in journalism school took the time to explain it to you." This last line seemed to be made for some sort of spittle as a show of disgust and disappointment.

Nick began to say something but stopped. He didn't like interviewing strangers for his work and he disliked speaking to strangers even more when he wasn't getting paid for doing so. But Bates continued, he voice bordering on condemnation: "You're a reporter and you live to create broken symmetries, creating your own version of the God particle, that elusive truth that something someone has never seen exists." Nick wondered if he said "what the fuck?" aloud.

"There was this Japanese physicist, I forget his name. I have it my notes and wouldn't you know it, I don't have my notes with me." Nick stood there watching this man speak; Bates's eyes still hoping for one of the stage doors to open and his elusive prey of thirty years would appear. "Anyway, he used to describe broken symmetry as the time when everybody in a group looked in the same direction at the same thing. He believed that symmetry was when a group of people looked around for their own path. But when one person looked at the stage, like tonight, everyone looks in that direction as well, ignoring their own desire to take a different path.

"Your job as a reporter is to get everyone looking in the right direction, essentially breaking the symmetry of the average idiot's life. Right now, no one is looking."

"So you'll help?" Nick looked anxious.

"What? Did your editor send you off looking for background on him and, oh wait," Bates interrupted himself when he turned towards Nick. "He did tell you to go dig up something. That's hilarious. And you don't want to go. Where? Back east?" This made the old man laugh, a deep and satisfying cackle that was usually reserved for people who received a justly deserved comeuppance.

He drove his hands deep into his pockets. "I've got a car rented for tomorrow. Thought I'd tool around the countryside and see Mt. Hood. You know, let the dust settle a bit before I start hunting this fucker down. I leave in a week. If you're back, we can talk." He handed him a card and walked off. He stopped suddenly when the stage door opened. It was Che. She waved at Nick. Bates turned and for a brief moment, Nick thought he would come back. But instead he kept walking.

*****

While most people would describe the Benson Hotel in downtown Portland as elegantly decadent, a throwback to an era when visitors bringing money to the northwest needed an opulent landing spot, a place to be seen, a worldly traveler staying in the haunts of presidents and kings. Nick found it quite the opposite. The beautifully carved wood interior, beveled glass and arranged seating that blurred the lines between lounge and lobby had no appeal to him. He disliked public places almost as he was repulsed by their occupants. But

Che was buying and he was more than happy to accompany her.

She was almost skipping as they made their way down Broadway, dragging him along. They seemed as if, at least from a distance, to be polar opposites. And in many ways they were. He would not have been inclined to spend a pocket full of cash before it had a chance to warm that pocket. Che on the other hand, was more than willing to part with what she referred to as free money. This is where many of their definitions departed. If you work for anything, and are paid for that service, Nick would argue, it was not free; it was earned. Che saw any unscheduled, unexpected, or otherwise unanticipated influx of cash, earned or otherwise as free, unplanned and always welcome. With her pocket full of haircut money, an unexpected windfall tossed her way by her good friend Bertrand, was, in her mind, free money. And as was always the case she wanted to do something she would otherwise have not done.

She draped the cloth napkin across her lap and sat with her back straight in a chair he knew she would rather curl up in, knees drawn close. It was a sexy as it was unladylike. The waiter introduced himself to both of them, letting a slight frown of disdain and criticism cross his face. While the introduction was a formality that Nick both understood and detested, the waiter still looked towards Nick for the order.

"She's buying," he replied not making eye contact with him. He turned and briefly hesitated before offering a pretentious "Ma'am". Che never noticed and ordered a Manhattan, "And a menu too. I'm hungry." The waiter nodded and took Nick's order for a Heineken.

"So, I'll tell you everything because I know you want to know but first, either wipe that bitchy look from your face or tell me why it is there. I mean, this is kind of a date and dates don't bring baggage; just a good time." He had fallen in love with this attitude that was, at least as he saw it, more show than actuality. It was her Portland persona, a street-wise affectation that he found humorous when she used it on him. A moment passed before she said impishly, "Please?"

"I've got to go back east for a couple of days. And I'm not that happy about it." He sighed heavily at the thought of going and worse, the idea of leaving her.

Che smiled, buoyed mostly by the thousand dollars in her pocket but also because she loved his funky moods. They were in her words, genuine. People were often not as real as she would have liked, and despite their thinking that they were, they often fell short. Superficially, they placed barriers between others, acting happy when in fact they were pursuing a 'honey over vinegar' strategy designed to disarm and calm or they were outwardly disengaged, acting angry and distant because they were more afraid than they wanted to share. Nick was almost pure in his emotions, a blank slate that allowed the moment to take its rightful place plastered across his face.

"I couldn't tell," she replied, blowing him a kiss. The waiter arrived with their drinks and a menu. Che smiled at him because, as she had told Nick countless times, "There are really only two classes of people in Portland these days: those who serve and those who expect to be served." Nick found that applicable to any major city but the one they called home was in the middle stages of that particular flux, an ethos he was unsure followed the city's description of itself or preceded it.

He smiled and tried to right his sinking mood. "So, tell me about the haircuts."

"You know we had dinner with Mr. Aretino last night, right?" Nick had arrived at the dinner with the intentions of a man on assignment. He almost paid no attention to the other guests at the table.

*****

As the plane tilted its nose skyward, Nick was lost in thought. His passive approach to the guests on the evening he visited Akiko and Ryan, the proprietors of Seating for Six was still haunting him forty-eight hours after Che had said that he had dined with the mysterious Santo Aretino. He had he recalled, introduced himself as Sonny. He could barely forgive himself for not asking for his baptismal name. He failed to make the connection to Marley, to the company that held his initials, even when she said she was introducing her husband. Sonny was Santo.

He was instead projecting a series of potential scenarios for the next several days. He had a short list of people to search for, courtesy of his Zoti and now, John Bates. The old man bothered him. He had kept his information close, claiming that any additional information was in his notes. But if he was anything like him, notes only reinforced the information and cemented the memory, creating a visual reference over a cerebral footnote. Bates knew something that may have been valuable, possibly even defining how his investigation would have gone. Perhaps Nick thought, it was why he let him go on this trip without.

Nick had had a professor in college who discussed the state of subself, a grey area where, as he called it, we make a mental choice to be social or not. It was, as he taught, only healthy to have a balance between solitude, aloneness where we are in control of the quiet and social companionship, where the exposure to the public forces a person to succumb to the norms of that public.

The professor had called the need to be alone as a "guardian" self, an internal protector against the influence of the world outside, an often chaotic place that to those who crave the solitude take refuge from, some to a greater degree than others. The true self was described the ability to do more than follow or congregate; it was meant to also lead. Years later, as he wondered why the opposite of true in his example was not false, but a guardian, he began to wonder why he had chosen a profession that was premised on telling the truth while prodding people to reveal someone else's false.

Aretino's reclusiveness seemed different. To be truly reclusive, it would need to be voluntary. But if he was hiding, from someone or something, it was not by choice.

16

He answered the phone the same way for over thirty years: "I-O". It always made her smile as she imagined his large hulking body holding the hand set of the wall mounted rotary phone, standing in the kitchen of an old farmhouse in central Pennsylvania.

"Seamus," she said, the grin on her face leaking through her half question. "This is Arianne." The next words were also always the same, deeply respectful and guarded. He knew Arianne and he knew Sonny and what had taken place between them in the past, was not his to understand. He paused before answering.

"Nice to be hearin' from you, Ms. Arianne. Sonny's not here." This also made her smile. All of her phone calls, totaling about eight over the last thirty years were begun with that basic piece of information. He was never there but this was the only number she had. It was also the only address.

For almost thirty-five years, she had written Santo. Those correspondences now numbered in the hundreds. They were often short letters describing what she was doing, even if it was simply sitting on the wall of a garden or in a crowded café somewhere in Europe. Each letter contained a detail of what she was thinking, a line of verse from a poet she was reading or a snippet from a novel that she said reminded her of him. Each note acted like a map of her journey, first across free Europe and then as she drifted behind the Iron Curtain. She was living a Michener novel and she knew he'd get the irony.

The letters were mailed to the farmhouse in Lititz and unopened, were then sent to a P.O. Box in Portland where Marley would retrieve them. These letters contained hopeful requests that her former, and only one-time lover and friend was doing well. Arianne would mask her regrets in prose designed to inform her recipient of her doings while wishing he was there without ever actually making the lament. She knew, or harbored the thought that if things had been different, he would have really enjoyed the skyline of the old Umbrian village she resided in for almost a year, the peaceful lakeside retreat in the Balkans, or the bucolic, rolling greenery of County Mayo. In each note was a germ of hope that she knew would not be seeded in his lifetime.

She traveled with great ease on the money she had garnered from the dissolution of her brief marriage and the untimely death of her father. She had married young and thoughtfully, loving a man who had exhibited similar characteristics to those of her father only to find out that those attributes were not the qualities that garner long-term success. They were both simple men, complicated only by the distraction of the real world, which they managed to wall themselves off from, her father with his bar, her husband with his research. Those barriers proved to be insurmountable. Arianne had found she neither had the energy nor the inclination to break through those walls. She would reflect on whether that effort would have been worth a try. Eventually she decided that it may not have been. But every now and again, often when she was stopping to jot a note to Santo did she wonder, if she had, would she have been pleased with what she found.

Divorce, it turned out was easy. Her husband didn't put up much of a fight, giving up any financial stake he had in the marriage. Without the burden and complication of children, the glue that might have kept them together, the social stigma of the act held less sway. But as life will be ironic, the end of her marriage came at the same time her father's health had taken a turn for the worse.

Known only as Sam to his customers, he ran a small bar in Parkside called the Edge. There was little mystery in why it was not so cleverly named. It resided directly on the line drawn between Chester and Parkside and the border on the vast park that separated the two small cities. It was a meeting place for working men returning from the shipyard or the oil refinery, catering to them at the end of their blue-collar work shifts as they headed home to cookie-cutter homes lining the adjoining streets.

This is where Arianne's father met Umberto Aretino, a small old country Italian man with an intensely furrowed brow and radiant smile, a contradiction of features that often disarmed those who met him. As young boy, he was nicknamed Kid Smiley and occasionally he would hear it called to him from across the street. He'd wave and in doing so, show the menace of being reminded of a past he had no fondness for revisiting and a present he saw no way out of. He would often sit alone nursing a Rolling Rock, almost invisible at the end of the bar.

Sam and Umberto had one of those typical patron/bartender relationships: They would talk only if they had to, exchanging pleasantries, but otherwise they were silently absorbed in their own lives and the myriad of thoughts that accompanied them.

That changed one day when the blinding light from an early summer day knifed through the murky shadows of the interior. Umberto knew that those initial seconds of refocusing, as the eyes adjusted from the bright sun to the lack of it rendered the person blind. People accustomed to crossing this threshold did so with certainty. The inexperienced stopped, not wanting to take another step until they were certain the next one wouldn't drop them into some unseen abyss. On this day, the figure was as large as a man, but the pause suggested otherwise.

One second and then another passed, the retina straining in the young man's eyes to see in the absence of light presented his brain with what was literally a blank, black space. He stepped in and moved towards the lit glass door cooler that held six packs and quarts of beer. Without hesitation, he slid the door open and removed a six pack of sixteen ounce cans and placed it on the bar.

Sam, who had not been paying any direct attention, caught the surprised look on Umberto's face. It was his oldest boy, all of about thirteen but now fully matured into the body of a man. He was at least a foot taller than his father. The boy placed a ten dollar bill on the counter and made direct eye contact with the man behind the bar. Sam snapped a brown paper bag open and slid the beer inside. When he did, he glanced briefly at Umberto. He simply nodded. A minute later, the boy was gone.

"Would you have carded him if I wasn't sittin' here?"

"No," Sam replied. "But if you had made any other gesture, I would have. Does that make sense?" He stopped what he was doing and leaned close to his only patron. "You know him?"

Umberto sighed deeply and thoughtfully. He was about to bridge the distance between the two, turning what had been an arm's length patron and tender, acquaintance type of relationship that Sam had with hundreds of other people exactly like Umberto, and venture several inches closer towards the treacherous and cumbersome world of friendship, a trek neither man ever took. "He's my son."

"Come again?" There wasn't a single feature on the boy

that would have placed them in any sort of genetic parallel. The boy was serious looking like Umberto but not with the granite features. He could, even in the shadows see the menace in the boy's face, but he understood how the ruse was played. Sam prided himself on being able to read intent, the meaning behind the words, the caution conveyed in a single glance or the guilt that seeped into a person's voice. The man/boy looking to purchase that six-pack was absent those tells.

"Or at least he was my son." His face crinkled in anguish as if reliving a painful moment that was without cure or explanation. Like a good bartender, Sam just listened as his patron explained the world of the young Santo Aretino in detail.

"I love Sofi but her family, well, you know what they say: When a son takes a wife, he leaves his family for hers. So, my say so was not even asked for because I married Sofi and her family. I might be the man of the house," he said with a slight laugh, "but she just lets me think it's my house."

"I hear ya." Sam knew enough to not add any additional words to the conversation than was required by this sort of relationship. Agreeing was the only real role these two men. He turned and pulled a bottle of Irish whiskey from the shelf behind him and poured each of the men a shot.

"She had this cousin in the old country, Sofi did," he said adding which old country, "Italy. Keep in mind, we were only just married, just getting a start. Anyway," and he paused to finish what was left in the bottle, "This cousin, she was a novice, you know, a young nun," he paused again. Umberto was now working at the edge of the bottle's label, where the moisture had loosened the glue, swallowing back an emotion he was not familiar with. More than growing up when men didn't cry, more than his deeply Mediterranean roots would allow, he seemed to be redirecting his strength to fight back the unfamiliar emotion that his confession was uncovering.

"It's alright," Sam didn't say. Instead, he wiped nervously at the counter, finally deciding on pouring another round of whiskey.

Sighing heavily and for some reason Sam could not comprehend and Umberto would not be able to describe, he continued, "...when she was raped and that rape produced a son she couldn't keep in the convent." Sam leaned in as Umberto muttered angrily, "Is there no fucking protection for the children of God, for Christ sakes?"

"Apparently God lets shit happen to good people. The bible's full of these tests." Sam was beginning to wonder what the story about Sofi and the bastard they had rescued early in their marriage meant, when he realized, the stories were connected. The boy who walked into the bar just thirty or so minutes ago was the boy in the story.

"Still. I mean what the fuck?

"You a believer, Umberto?" Sam asked, surprising himself with the intimate tone of the question. A man's faith was always under pressure, tested by the reality of life and he knew that this man had carried just this sort of test. He knew better than to try and soothe the man's angst with his own comparisons of his own life, stories that would not even come close to paralleling itself with his tale. He had no relationship with the experience like what Umberto just revealed and could not imagine how that moment, frozen in the long line of decisions that followed, was finally out in the daylight. The man spoke as if he was uncovering something tucked away in a chest in some ancient attic, a memento from long ago. The only thread that connected them was religion, the only common denominator in the relationship, both worshiping at St. Rose of Lima for decades and although knowing each other for all of that time, had never had much more than a nodding acquaintance. Sam's wife had been the more religious. She had been the one driving his participation. He told himself he did it for her and her illness. She had prayed and prayed for the sickness she had to go away, often with him kneeling alongside her in church, at the foot of their bed as they did rosary novenas, eventually at her casket. Right up until the end she professed her belief that her Jesus would save her and when it was apparent he wouldn't, she switched to something she referred to as "It must be his plan" for her.

"Not really. But I didn't have much of choice."

"I'm sorry I interrupted. You were talking about the novice."

"Yeah," he replied, his voice resigned to finishing the story. "They let her stay in the convent just long enough for Sofi to go fetch the bastard and bring him home." He bowed his head and looked at his beer, as if trying to divine some truth hidden in the diminishing suds. "It wasn't the way I intended to start a family but it was the right thing to do I suppose."

"It was the noble thing to do Bert. Fuck. You've been raising that boy as your own all this time? You sure as shit will get past the pearly gates without a question." Sam placed another shot of whiskey in front of him and one in front of himself. "To noble actions," he said raising his glass. They both drank in one gulp.

But Umberto hung his head. There was a great deal of time between the time the infant landed on the shores of the United States and his appearance in the bar. Sam knew that time took odd turns, even when it was your own kid. He couldn't imagine what kind of struggle it must have been to raise another man's child, the child of a crime, the child of a child of God. The distance was vast between those two points and it appeared as if Umberto had long since tired of the journey.

*****

Her father's eyes were moist as he told her the story, as if he had harbored the pain for his friend and customer for years, reliving the conversation on his death bed. Arianne watched him struggle with the thoughts and the words to express himself. He was never an emotional man and this show of empathy made her heart ache. She knew that this was difficult for him but she also knew she couldn't interrupt him, even as she wondered why he was telling her this.

"Bert was a really nice, hard-working guy who was completely at a loss. I tried to be strong for him but all I kept thinking about was you, Arianne. The more he told me about that kid, and it wasn't just then either, the more I thought about how lucky I was with you. And your mom. I was lucky with her." Here he was, in the final throes of a life that seemed half-lived, where somewhere a decision was made to not chase this dream or that hope. Here he was, in those final days talking about a person she had never met, a figure who weighed heavily on his mind, a man he seemed to place on a throne above himself. She didn't know what to say. So she said nothing.

She wondered if she had put him through any undue anguish growing up. Arianne was convinced she had not. Her progression through life was without highlight, perhaps bathing in the mediocre of middle class, living the dull bits that fiction often left out. She knew her divorce would wreck him so she simply didn't mention it. She would lie to him instead, suggesting her husband's absence was due to some unnamed phobia about hospitals. It didn't matter because he never asked. She could keep secrets in the name of his comfort, the way all children do, judging their parent's tolerance for the truth in advance.

She was certain she had been a pain to him once in a while but she couldn't remember why or when and he never reminded her if she was. This was not the time. Instead, she let him talk about this man and his son without asking him for any missing specifics. As he spoke, she began to recognize the boy he was talking about.

She knew Umberto's kid too well. She had been a mentor to him, a friend to him, a one-time lover, and in the end, enamored with his maturity and intelligence. Umberto's boy had respected her when she didn't respect herself, loved her when she needed it and kept the distance she had asked him to keep. More importantly, he never held any of her craziness against her, perhaps, as she tried to venture backwards down the history of herself, was only that way since she had met him. He kept telling her, when she needed to hear it, "That everyone is crazy in a way" and doing so without implying that she was the craziest person he had ever met. He simply wondered why he wasn't. It was the first inkling she had that he was struggling with his own emotions, as if the cool exterior was not a veneer but a shell.

"What else did your friend Umberto mention?" she asked feigning interest but roiling inside with curiosity. Here was her father talking about the father of the man whose son she had secretly cherished as the most important man she had ever met and never told anyone about. On the eve of her departure, in the aftermath of Santo's disappearance, her father was telling a story of lost hopes and dashed dreams, misguided loyalties and harnessing of a life within the shackles of marriage.

"He told me all sorts of things," he said softly and then paused. It lasted a long time, making her wonder if he had lost his thought, dislodged by the nearness to death and the slow IV drip. She waited as he started to speak and then caught himself, finally deciding on what to say, editing the memory for her specifically.

"I let the kid come in the bar for the next couple of years and then he stopped. Bert said he was up to no good but couldn't tell me what happened. There was a considerable distance between the two of them by that time and once something like that opens up, there is no real crossing on your own. It's be like building one of those Inca rope bridges. Remember that trip, babydoll. We went all the way to freakin' Peru and chickened out. You remember that?"

"I do." She let the moment linger until she saw his face return to the pain of the story he had been telling.

"The boy would have to meet him halfway, and we both knew that wasn't going to happen."

"Was he a good kid?" she asked softly, hoping she could find some tidbit to offer her friend should their paths ever cross again.

"He was super smart, or so Bert said. He stood out because he called out his teachers on stuff they didn't know and Bert and Sofi, that's his mom or should I say, the women who acted as his mom, hell, the woman who let her moral fiber save his ass. Anyway, the two of them were always going to the school for meetings and such. And it wasn't because he was in trouble but because, according to Bert, he was trouble for them. You know, a non-conformist."

She asked him to clarify that, "Smart like smart ass or like book smart?"

"Book smart and a kind of smart ass. One nun, he told me called him the scourge of princes, whatever that meant at the time but the more Bert would tell me this story, not looking for advice mind you, just talking about stuff he didn't understand, I figured out that the kid was beating the shit out of tough guys. Once some kid attacked a nun, he told me and he said that he found out about it second hand from someone at the refinery. He was quick to add that it was not physically, just disrespectfully, and Santo literally threw the kid out of the classroom and pummeled him in the hallway."

Santo, she thought. Her Sonny?

"Must've been something to see. But no one knew what to do so they just left him alone." Arianne felt her jaw drop. She could see that emotionless reaction in the Santo she knew but she was quiet.

"He was in some trouble with the cops too but they didn't do anything either. Bert told me that once he was walking up to get a paper at the 7-11 and right in the parking lot, two cops were searching Santo's car, pulling seats out and ripping through the car. Bert said he just froze. He told me that he wondered if he would have reacted differently if the boy had been his but by this time he was sure the boy knew he wasn't; so he just watched from across the street. He said Santo just stood and smoked a cigarette and never seemed to care, even when the cop swiped the smoke from his hand. He said he knew tough kids like that growing up but had never seen something so," and his voice trailed off.

"Nonchalant?"

"That's not the word Bert used. He said, let me think, something like *non mi interessa*, like the kid was made of stone. He told me he was both proud and scared. Then, Bert said he was just gone. High school was over and they never saw him again. I think that caused him a lot of pain. Both him and Sofi. I never met her though. Just him, after work, mostly after the midnight shift."

"They never heard from him again."

"It wasn't long after that, maybe ten years later that he retired and stopped coming on a regular basis. Sometimes, he'd show up with his other son, the biological one. Danny, I think his name was. They sat at a table usually and ate cheese steaks they had bought next door. Bert would wave and I'd bring them a couple of Rolling Rocks. There was a daughter. But he never really talked about her much."

Arianne had stayed with her father for those last days,

sitting by his bed while organ after organ failed him. He never mentioned Bert or Santo again and she never asked. He had used their story as a backdrop for his own unexpected fortune at having a daughter who was not trouble. Umberto Aretino had died several years before and from what she could gather, Sofi followed shortly thereafter. She wondered if Santo knew.

Her travels plans had come to a halt when her father became ill, the hapless direction of her life was suddenly altered for the weeks before and after she came back to Chester. But she was determined to leave soon as the funeral was over. She wondered now if her journey would be changed. What had seemed like an escape from everything she feared she wasn't was now evolving into a search for a person she was sure didn't want to be found. How hard she would look would depend on the next step she would take, which direction it would lead her and whether she would surrender to it.

She had the one address, sent to her old employer and forwarded to her ex-husband who delivered it to her father. The envelope contained a single piece of paper with an address in Lititz. She never asked why or even who had sent it.

She thought she should go there but she suspected that he wouldn't be there when she did. So she began writing, wondering only occasionally if he ever read them. Some letters were long, rambling descriptions of her life in transit, or as she sometimes thought, in shambles. Some were simply lines of poetry or a thought that seemed immediate and important. For almost thirty-five years, she wrote at least a letter a week.

She told herself that it was helpful.

*****

Seamus would wait until he had assembled ten letters and would drop them unread into a larger envelope and mail them to Santo at a post office box in Portland, Oregon. When he spoke to him, mostly about the business of the farm, he never mentioned the arrangement and Santo never brought it up.

17

"Swerve? Me? The path to my fixed purpose is laid with iron rails, whereon my soul is grooved to run." Nick had been staring blankly into space when the old man sitting next to him at the airport in Seattle spoke those words. Roused from what appeared to be deep thought, but in reality was the absence of any, he turned to the man sitting one seat away from him in terminal C.

"I'm sorry," he said, regretting the apology as soon as the words escaped his mouth knowing that this was the exact kind of opening the slightly hunched over octogenarian needed. Nick was aware of the loneliness that often encompassed a life that was lived too long, the demise of old friends and estranged family that often left some gregarious individuals at the mercy of conversations with strangers. He always felt a bit sad for their plight and disappointed in his reaction to it. By apologizing, he was leaving himself open to become the man's new best friend.

"Not a problem." And with that, returned to his crossword puzzle. Nick sat looking at him. If hair was any judge of vigor, his was still full and tightly woven around his head, which seemed to jut precariously over his neck, as if craning to get a better view. He was casually dressed but his clothes were relatively new. Most of his experience with the elderly was from the other side of a reporter's notepad, interviewing them as victims or witnesses, often caught in their most vulnerable moments. These people often had the look of terror in their eyes, not from the fear that something else would happen but more it seemed from the wasted heart beats.

"I was apologizing because I didn't quite hear you."

"Yes, you did. You weren't listening but you heard me because I was talking about you." He turned towards Nick, blue eyes with only a slight rheumy-ness clouding what was otherwise vibrant.

"You were deep in thought or at least you thought you were and you were wondering what you should do next. It's not about a woman or you would have been a bit more anguished looking. No. It was about a direction. I just thought a quote from Melville, chapter thirty seven of Moby Dick might help. Not that I find Moby Dick my go-to for quotes but it seemed to be apropos." He smiled showing a mouthful of his own teeth, slightly stained with age. "You've got yourself a purpose and you don't want it. But it's yours. "Naught's an obstacle, naught's an angle to the iron way."

The man slipped his newspaper into his carry-on and stood. It was a slow steady motion that showed caution accompanied by halting ability. "I have to catch a plane." He was taller than he thought, and walked with authority away from him.

Nick tried to return to his thoughts, which he realized were exactly as the man said they were: Protests against what he knew better than to protest against. The flight he had taken to Philadelphia and then a car on to a has-been city downwind from the city of brotherly love in search of Santo Aretino created a landscape rich in diversity, a story within a story that may not be much of one at all.

He had made his way to visit his late father's sister, who had lived alone since her divorce decades ago. They enjoyed appetizers on her patio and later, drinks in her living room. She was captivatingly beautiful for a woman her age as she sat curled up on her couch. It was there that he found out that she had been lovers with Santo Aretino when he was younger, jailbait younger. It was here that he discovered Santo's talent as an artist, with three very well done paintings still hanging in her hallway. It was here that she found out what kind of a man he was, as she told him, "One of the most fully developed people I have ever met, then and since. He was an old soul inside a youthful prison." Nick remembered asking her what she meant by prison, she responded in a disarmingly matter-of-fact way: "He will always live alone and he knows this. I don't know how but he seems resigned with the sentence."

He left her the next day promising to stop by before he headed back to Portland. She hugged him and wished him well, the kind of farewell that suggested she knew she would never see him again. She had given him a couple of her friend's names, also former sexual liaisons but she would not comment to more than a suggestion of such activity, who might give him more information, but she said she had lost touch with them years ago.

From there he met the cop that John Bates had told him about, the man who repeatedly asked the parole board to inquire about the relationship that Santo Aretino had with Matteo DeSilva, prisoner 76-R-3224. DeSilva had been locked up on drug charges three decades ago, just as the war on drugs was beginning its offensive. The drug bust gained national attention and gave the arresting officers some short-lived notoriety and numerous promotions as a result. The officer cum detective, John Tell had long since retired and in an ironic twist, bought the house where the drug bust had occurred.

The man was affable and talkative. They drank beer and grilled steaks as the late summer rain hammered the woods surrounding the house. He spoke of Santo in affectionate tones but with caveats. He had never succeeded in catching the boy doing anything. He told him about a deceased roommate of his, a Brother Connors who had taught at the Catholic high school Santo had attended. Tell had taken care of his friend in his last days. "Connie would have loved to fill your head with his speculation," the cop told him, laughing at the thought of his friend's venomous disdain for the boy being told to a stranger. "The kid wasn't that bad. Clever as a fuck, but not a bad kid."

"Are you suggesting that every kid is good until he's caught?"

"I am," he answered. "Connie was convinced and in a way I kept trying to find out more about him. I knew he was tangled up with that DeSilva guy and his partner but we never uncovered nothing. DeSilva turns out, was not your model prisoner. So, I had lots of parole hearings and more than my share of attempts to find out if there was any connection between the convict and the suspect."

Interview two was no better than the conversation with his Aunt Dina. Both showed a reverence for the man, still a boy when they knew him, and yet, they knew something he possessed would never be theirs and yet they were comfortable with it, almost resigned. As Nick drove off, he wondered if this would be the course of all his interviews, in which case, he didn't see the Pulitzer Zoti had suggested should have been his. There was however a curiosity that Tell suggested was the driving force behind the Brother's focus on Santo as a boy: His penchant for violence.

This violence was unusual because of its delivery. A scourge of bullies, he directed his dark side towards those that sought to overpower the weak turning into a peer hero. The more the retired cop talked about Connie's obsession, the more he learned about how his late roommate had attempted to use the officer to end his relationship with Santo and remove him from the school he lorded over as the Dean of Discipline, the more it seemed as if Santo was actually being bullied in return. If anything, Nick was beginning to believe that the boy who grew into the multi-billionaire, humanitarian award winning man that he knew, was somehow shaped by these incidents. As he sat in the airport waiting for his return home connection, he wondered how those events might have changed him.

Following the road north out of Chester, he fell into an accidental interview with a former internet millionaire who had retired his budding career to manage his father's motel. The man, who had been "saved" on numerous occasions saw the boy Santo as he hoped he was, the man they knew he was, and a person who came of age too soon, as a sort of demigod. Nick might not have stopped at all if he hadn't spent the whole afternoon with the cop.

Melvin Mistone offered another look at the boy that further deepened the confusion. He described Santo as a savior, an enigmatic personality who somehow was always there when the scrawny, high school aged Melvin was on the receiving end of the senseless violence of a bully. "Santo," he told him, his voice sounding excited as he relived those moments, "would just show up and dispatch those fuckers and most of them were bigger than he was. Dude had a reputation," he added, "and no one, I mean, no one fucked with him."

Even as Nick was fascinated, he was also becoming nauseous. Everybody loved the boy in their own way but it seemed as if their sometime saccharin description of how he impacted their lives was more fiction than fact. It was how legends are developed, tidbit upon tidbit over time until the subject was elevated to a status so far removed from reality as to be something else entirely. Survivors write the history. Just ask the Indians, he thought. He knew that any interview could be conducted at a later date and would, based on how the person felt, possibly yield a different telling of the story. Each time the video played in their head, the stored loop of personal experiences, they made editorial changes to the memory. But these memories seemed baked into concrete.

Even Santo's brother, someone who was technically estranged, had nothing bad to say about him. Nick had taken his initial rebuff for an interview and turned to leave. His experience with family, some centered on his own familial misunderstanding surrounding his mother and late father, was not one of empathy or compassion. Families either told more than they should have or less than he needed to hear. It was the 'throw-the-bastard-under-the-bus' approach or no comment. When it came to these arrangements, there was no middle ground. It was either love or indifference. The brother's initial refusal to talk was not all that shocking. But his revelation about the man's beginning, his Italian birth to a wanna-be nun stepped him back a notch.

But Santo's brother had a change of heart as Nick turned to leave his tiny storefront office. The information he revealed had value to someone somehow, all he needed to do was figure out what and how it mattered to this assignment. As of that moment, the dots could not be connected. In fact, they didn't even seem to belong to the same graph.

The trail to the farm in rural Pennsylvania further muddied the waters and did not reveal any additional clarity about the person he was trying to profile. He knew that people could not be summed up in several words, as many attempted. It always seemed a disservice to everything that happened to a person to merely surmise the "she was a nice lady" or "you could count on him" as the default, past-tense description some people offered.

Of course there were the negative comments that held greater sway in people's minds and were much harder to discard and easier to obtain. Given the opportunity to speak ill about someone not present, or even better, far removed, gave people the opportunity to embellish the truth. Nick knew that once the conversation turned to "how bad" someone was, the interview should end.

The Santo Aretino he was chasing seemed to find equal weight on either end of the spectrum. Everyone remembered him it seemed and all were willing to discuss this enigmatic man. But few described him.

Louise and Seamus were an odd couple. Louise was Dina's friend, a drifter of sorts who after meeting Santo found her life disjointed so, as she put it, "I dislodged." Her "dislodging" was a way of saying that after meeting, and apparently not sleeping with the young Santo, she couldn't take her current life choices any longer. Like many people Nick had met on this short trip, she never fully left Santo's life, orbiting in an irregular pattern, working first a record store he had financed as a retail drug front and then eventually as the caretaker of this small farm. It was a desperate attempt to be anywhere that might one day put her in close proximity. She was both gregarious and willing to discuss the details of her former lover and current sponsor's life and did so as she was organizing a Woodstock like festival on the property.

Seamus was just as friendly but more cautious in his openness. Clearly, the man owed Santo a great deal and his hero worship was of a different sort. He didn't just step up and help him in his time of need like so many of the people he had spoken to. Instead, he gave Seamus a sense of purpose that according to the man, "change me it did and be settin' me straight." Nick decided to not ask about his missing ear, a tangle of scars that still had a pugilist puffiness to it. He did find the Irish brogue charming though.

*****

He sent Che a text with his arrival time in the minutes before he boarded the connecting plane to Portland. He would take the Max train back to their downtown studio when he arrived. He was more interested in meeting her someplace. She hadn't answered by the time he boarded.

*****

John Bates had driven east to see the mountain the pilot had mentioned on the plane's swooping descent to PDX. It stood like an august sentinel, rising straight up, an arrogant rock slicing the belly of the clouds. Unlike the mountains to the east, the Cascade range seemed to stand majestically in isolation, each peak standing in relief of the sweeping vistas. He had no doubt why someone like Santo Aretino, or anyone for that matter, would choose to live in this part of the country.

He too had visited the hometown of his subject, a place that had seen its glory days pass and not return. Three decades ago, it was the home of working class people who did little work inside in the city limits. Those that could afford to moved closer to their employment. Those that couldn't, stayed and grappled with the steady decline of the city aided by the trickling migration of taxpayers and prosperous citizens that always precedes such a slow death.

He had hoped that the place would reveal something about the man he had chased fervently when he was younger and passively in his retirement. He also spoke to the retired cop but managed to garner a wholly different set of opinions from him than Nick Heath had. John Tell was comfortable expounding on his assessment of the man, who was a boy at the time Tell first knew him, and making broad assumptions that in more than half of the time proved incredibly close to the outcome.

Tell talked about the first time he had met Santo and the impact he had left. "From a distance of maybe 500 feet, my partner and I saw him dispatch about twenty kids."

"What do you mean by dispatch?" Bates asked, leaning forward on his elbows. Tell leaned back in his chair, which looked out over the tops of a forest of undeterminable size. It was an amazing greenspace tucked inside the decay of a city that felt forgotten, a stain on a shirt that you weren't aware was there until you thought to wear it again.

"It was really something to watch. We were trying to bust the kid for dealing, based on a tip that Connie had given me." Bates could see the loner in the officer, and in many of those personalities often resided an empathy that went far beyond what normal people might have. They were loyal to a fault and doing the right thing was the only option worth considering. When his lifelong friend became ill, he took him in. Both men had devoted themselves to the same path, with different masters. One became a Brother, a religious teacher without the power and responsibility of a Catholic priest while Tell chose to uphold the law. Santo Aretino seemed to be the overlap in their lives, as a source of discord and unrest.

"He was smoking what we thought was a joint but we were hoping for something a bit more substantial than a simple possession bust. So we waited. It wasn't long before a parade of cars pulled into the school yard where our boy was standing, alone." Tell paused as he ran the mental video in his head.

Impatiently, Bates asked, "What?"

"Like I said, we were pretty far away so we never actually heard the gist of what was said but the kids were from the west end of town, an even more impoverished neighborhood that Aretino lived in. Those thugs didn't usually venture this far so both of us were kind of curious how it was going to play out. And it played itself out in a very dramatic fashion."

Tell explained in excruciating detail the minutes that followed: the cars emptying; the boys menacingly surrounding him; the hasty, frenetic departure which took place a minute later; Santo throwing something; the west end kids driving past the parked patrol car; a kid in the backseat holding his head with a lot of blood; Santo burning his t-shirt. "Even we were not sure what happened. So we went around the block to stop him as he left. And, well, he wasn't exactly forthcoming about what had happened."

"What else? How did he look?"

"Excellent question and one that bugged the shit out me at the time and still does and infuriated my partner: He was a cool as the other side of the pillow. Something happened back there, we told him. We found the ear, we told him."

"You found an ear?" Bates was smiling and felt no less perverse doing it than Tell felt confused. The boy had left a trail of isolated instances of often incredible violence everywhere he went, or at least in the places that Bates had visited. Tell was unaware of Santo's history after he fled this downtrodden hamlet and the private detective felt no inclination to share what he knew. Bates was beginning to conclude that this is a lifestyle, something the boy did without remorse. It was not his place to judge whether it was happenstance or intentional, nurture or nature. In fact, he didn't care. But Bates was intrigued by the developing pattern.

"We kind of put two and two together with a few interviews, the very few we could get, and determined he had ripped the ear off of a kid named Seamus, the last name eludes me, and acted as if nothing had happened." Tell paused and ran his hand through his thinning hair. "I tell you, it was something to watch, the way he just folded the incident away like it never happened."

Bates asked him if ever spoke to the kid with no ear and Tell told him that they had tried. "McCleary. That's what his last name was. And yes. He was pretty roughly bandaged, like a homemade dressing. The kid was really defensive at that point. It wasn't the typical west ender mistrust either. They were bad boys mostly. But this one seemed more docile. It was like he was, I don't know, paid to keep quiet. I knew it wasn't the group he ran with."

Tell sort of drifted off in the memory and Bates allowed him to pause. Cops had an attention to detail and you could almost see him struggle with the notion of intertwining emotion with the facts. He wanted to tell a clear and concise tale but Bates could see a seasoned empathy slipping in. He continued, "We never really went back after that. It just sort of slipped away from the priorities. I got a promotion a short time later to narcotics and Seamus never crossed my path again. I did find out a couple of years later, from a friend who was working that neighborhood that after the kid's mom died, that he moved up north to some little farm near Lancaster. I never did find out why."

They spoke about the arrest that seemed to set the whole thing in motion, although Tell had no idea what those ripples had caused. The world was full of unintended consequences and in this case, the arrest of two drug dealers sent Santo into the void, an unleashing of the beast into the general populace.

Bates had come to believe that there was no plan, not so much from proof but intuition. The boy reacted to the situation and he simply left. The problem the investigator had was the boy's complete divorce from his hometown and the people he knew. As far as he could determine, he never came back. Not once.

But Bates had. The first time he found the trail leading back to here was quite by accident and shortly after his employer had hired him. The boy that Santo had sterilized with the swift swipe of a curtain rod had mentioned a car and Bates had found it. It was still parked on the campus where he had dismantled three boys named Sid, Harry, and Trevor in their dorm room, punishment for the terrorizing of two Amish girls. Bates traced the boy's actions to the hardware store where he bought the items needed to disable the boys while posing as a maintenance man sent to hang drapes, and then backward to the diner, to the gas station and eventually all the way back to Lititz. This is where he met the boy with no ear although he never mentioned this to Tell, an old woman who owned the farm and a younger woman who seemed to be there to help. He didn't bother with trying to talk to the Amish family though; the old woman told him everything he needed to know about the incident but nothing about Santo's whereabouts.

The older woman, Eva appeared genuinely concerned about him but wouldn't ask Bates to update her if he knew anything. She had spent considerable time with the young man and knew the truth about him, as much as anyone could ever know, learning to read the silences, the stretches of thought-filled consideration as they sat with dogs on the porch. She had never met a man or another person who could sit as comfortably in the quiet as he could.

Bates was not used to reporting to a client that every trail he had pursued had reached a dead end, even as many of the people he spoke to had no problem answering his questions. This was curious in itself. He offered no pretense about his intentions and yet, they seemed comfortable answering him.

The trail went cold after St. Louis and soon after, he retired. But the unfinished business of Santo haunted him, an apparition that became elegant in its mystery, a ghost that people welcomed like a long-dead, beloved relative. He was out there, he knew, hiding right in front of people who loved and hated him.

And now the apparition appeared on stage in front of thousands of people and yet, he managed to be as obscure as ever. While some found the theater of the invisible intriguing, it simply angered Bates. For thirty years he had let this one unsolved mystery fester in his portfolio. He knew that he needed to reorganize his thoughts, regroup his strategy and ultimately rearrange his approach.

He drove up to Timberline Lodge, lunched on brewery salami and local artisanal cheeses, and returned to Portland invigorated and focused. His client had long since passed away and the son went on to become a land baron in Pennsylvania, refocusing what should have been sexual energy on fucking poor farmers out of their land.

*****

Seamus allowed his guard to drop as soon as he saw Arianne smile. Although her path to the farmhouse was less direct that John Bates early on and Nick Heath decades later, she found it nonetheless. She had been in no real hurry to do so. Her father needed to be buried and his estate needed to be settled. The information she had received from him needed to be processed. In those waning days, he had unleashed a flurry of pent-up secrets, including information about her mother, a family on her father's side she didn't know existed and of course, tidbits about his favorite patrons. But for some reason, she was focused on Santo.

As a result, the story of Umberto was the most difficult to process. She didn't dare mention to her father that she knew the boy in the story and certainly didn't want to tell him that she had slept with him, even if it was only once. She hoped that her expression remained concerned and accepting, as if she was fully capable to be the new caretaker of these memories. She reasoned that it was cathartic for him to relive these thoughts and revisit the people who were stored there in his slowly dying mind. His confession to the sin of serving alcohol to a minor was done with regret, and as far as she could tell, the only time he had broken the law.

She had already moved on even if the plan to do so was still half-baked. She wondered if she really wanted to see him again or simply know that he fared well. She wondered how she should approach their meeting, or even of they'd ever meet. It had been almost two years since he had left and she had written six letters, each with no address on the envelope, a small numeral was placed where the stamp would go to preserve the sequence. She wondered whether looking for him would be wise but she never questioned the letters.

But she listened intently to the story of the young Santo. He told her that Santo's father had said that the last correspondence he received was from the Jersey shore, a popular destination during his youth. Arianne found this curious. Santo did go to the shore a lot but never really expressed a longing to be there for much more than a couple of days.

As she recalled the details of her father's journey into death, she retold the stories about his father, intertwined with her inability to control her own emotional comport. The list of things she didn't know about the young man had grown. She was becoming aware of the silences Eva enjoyed, the gaps in the story he never mentioned.

"Did his father follow him or try to look for him?" she asked fishing for a clue in the story that he might have failed to reveal.

"Seriously girl? He was happy to be rid of him I think. But then again, he was also saddened by his departure." The nurse had come in and was adjusting his I.V. drip. He turned to the nurse and smiled, "Excuse me if I just keep right on talking to my daughter here. I've been told I'm on a limited timeframe with a short expiration date."

She cutely turned to him, "I'm sorry Sam, were you saying something? I did hear expiration but you aren't in the right room if you're expecting to expire on my watch. I'm just going to fuss around with the stuff your attached to and jot a few notes." She smiled towards Arianne. "Just carry on, honey."

Arianne did as if she was waiting for the exchange to be

over, a hard bookmark on the last part of the conversation. "I suppose you're right. I just find it, I don't know, odd. I know his father knew who he was but you would think he'd try to tell him when he got older. Not with a vengeance, but as some kind of release."

"There is always a less than honest relationship between fathers and sons, Arianne. Sons remind the father of who they were and fathers remind the sons of an authority they don't have and one that won't be had anytime soon." This made her smile. For a brief moment, something Santo had said moved to the forefront of her memory: "Fathers feed what they should starve while sons serve the thing they should rule." She knew he didn't know who his real father was, always assuming that Umberto was not his, but what would he have done had he known?

"That's why I'm glad I had a daughter." He squeezed her hand gently. "Daughters, even if they don't care will come and visit, will tell you what you don't want to hear, and lie only to protect their old man from the truth. Daughters are much more painful. Sons can be dismissed for their idiocy."

"Really? How so?"

"We, I, walk you down the aisle to get married to a man who is not as good as I am and although we, I, know this, we hope for the best and are confident in only one thing." He paused and took a sip of water. He swallowed with a bit of difficulty and made a slight grimace.

"Not your brand?"

"Not even the right color. I prefer something a bit more amber."

"You said you are confident in only one thing."

"I did, didn't I. That when a parent needs his daughter, when I need my daughter, she'll come and sit and listen like she cares no matter what."

"Not all daughters are like that. You just got extremely lucky with me. Anyway, you were talking about why Umberto didn't tell Santo he wasn't, or better, who he was." She felt the weight of this knowledge and didn't feel she was the right standard bearer for this kind of news. But she couldn't resist.

"Umberto didn't feel as though the boy owed him any explanation. He may have felt as though it was quite the opposite and he owed him, if only to forgive himself for not trying hard enough. He was a hard man but I think there was something inside of him that wished he was different somehow. You know, more accepting."

"I think he did owe the boy that."

"No. He did what he could, or should I say, what he was capable of. He didn't come from that generation." The two paused as the nurse finished marking his chart and left the room without a remark. "I will tell you this though: Someone did come along about a month after he left. Umberto had never seen him before and kind of knew he wasn't from the neighborhood. Big man, young though, with half of his ear missing. Just showed up one day with his mother. The woman was frail but she had one of those determined attitudes old country people have."

Arianne was quiet, hoping that somewhere in the next few words would be the elusive clue to finding Santo. Her patience was rewarded. Umberto told her father that the woman needed to talk to him because he was a parent, "and if it was my kid she told him, she'd want to know."

"Apparently the kid, the big kid with her was her son and he knew Santo and they said that he had run. He said he could barely understand the woman for her accent. Umberto said she sounded like the leprechaun from the cereal commercials. He said she turned to the boy who was three times her size, big Irish railroad worker type he said, thick and muscular by design, not by any exercising he did and she told him to tell the boy's father. Seamus I think his name was. So he did."

Arianne's heart skipped a beat. She tried to hold back to allow him to finish but she was afraid he might have. "Did he go looking for him?" she asked when she really wanted to ask about where Seamus said he was.

"Naw. He wasn't really interested in finding for him. He was disappointed in himself but at the same time, kind of relieved."

"Why not? I mean, I kind of know why not..." She let the sentence trail off. Her brain was frantically trying to ask the right question in the most curious and general sort of way without seeming as if she was too interested.

If he had sensed this, he didn't let on. "He said he went someplace, somewhere in Amish country. Libit. Lutits, something like that. Begins with an L is all I know. Up near Lancaster." And abruptly he changed the subject asking if he could have a cheesesteak for lunch. This made her smile. She had the lead. All she needed was a map.

*****

It had been eighteen months since she had seen Santo. It had been two months since her father was laid to rest. And two days ago, her passport arrived. Ten minutes ago she pulled into the long dirt driveway leading to an old farmhouse just outside the town of Lititz.

So here she was sitting with the man with the damaged ear, chasing the incredible disappearing man.

18

Nick had been back two days before he called his editor. He knew before he even picked up the phone that Zoti would not be happy. Uncharacteristically, he was.

"I tried to tell you that there was nothing there." Sitting in his underwear in their small studio, Nick went on to explain the failure of his journey east. Che was fixing breakfast at the stove in only a t-shirt. Occasionally she would turn and flash him.

"Doesn't matter," Zoti replied. "We ventured down the trail first." That he saw Santo as a polarized figure, either loved or despised by the people he grew up around, and the fact that something like this hardly made for a human interest story let alone one about the richest man in Portland, and among those who commanded wealth worldwide seemed to make little difference to his editor.

"I mean, he's far from normal with his Hughes-like reclusiveness but that doesn't qualify him for a story." He stopped short. "What do you mean it doesn't matter?"

"Lots of people are odd, Nick. Hell, Portland has more than its fair share. Present company excluded, of course. So, I don't need to tell you that." He came short of criticizing his own decision to send him in the first place, instead taking the more comforting road, telling him that "He tried and even though you didn't really find anything, you'll have more to work with once you get everything assembled."

Nick composed himself after the change in conversational direction. "I did find out that he was a two-bit drug dealer in his youth but nothing major and he didn't have a record. Just a pissed off retired cop, who cooked a mean steak and despite years of trying, couldn't pin anything on him."

Zoti sat in his well-worn chair and simply smiled. He let Nick ramble on until he felt the self-chastisement had lasted long enough. He knew Nick wanted to call him an ass for even thinking up such a weird trip and respected him for not doing so. Other members of his staff might have found a way.

"I had a visit from a guy named Bates while you were gone, Nicky." He called him that when he felt smug and more experienced that his brilliant young protégé.

"Bates," he said in response. "Old guy, retired dick."

"That's funny. Did we just enter some time warp? Do you think he's one of the Bow Street Runners? He's got a bit of the Brit in 'im I guess. Retired dick?" Zoti laughed while Nick waited for him to finish. He got the Dick Donovan reference and would have understood the Raymond Chandler one as well. He always saw journalism as a sort of private enterprise, each story a mystery, each conversation a clue with only the most deductive of actors solving the crime. Calling a detective a dick seemed in line with the lexicon. "Anyway. Yes. That's him. He said he had met you at that little coming out party for our good friend Santo."

Nick tried to remember what the man had said but couldn't. He suspected that it must not have been too noteworthy or he would have. Maybe he was more focused on Che at the time. Maybe he was more focused on the interruption Zoti had been that night. All he could recall was the man telling him he was going to rent a car and head to the mountain.

"It was late. I barely remember him."

"He remembered you and thought you might have forgotten him so he came down to our offices yesterday. If you hadn't been avoiding coming into work with your self-pity wrapped in youthful rebellion, you would've been here." This made Zoti laugh again. He had made a guess as to why Nick hadn't come in to the office from the airport. He needed to see that hot little woman of his or possibly he had nothing he thought was worth any value. "My boy, that trip will put you light years ahead of the competition. There's something there and it might be big. Hell, it might be fucking huge."

"What did he say?" he asked, disappointed that he sounded anxious. Zoti was one of those editors that acted as if he was sitting on the back of a troller, rods with strong lines shimmering in the Mexican sun, lines extended in the foamy ocean, waiting for the telltale tug of a trophy. He was known for giving you only enough line to be hooked and then, with a gentle tug, he'd set the barb in the corner of your mouth.

"Let him tell you." He gave Nick the investigator's cellphone number and hung up. The last thing he said before the line went dead suggested that Nick had been duped by the illusion his quarry had created. "Just remember, illusions are hard to pin down: they either don't exist or they exist but not the way you'd expect. Our boy Santo is hiding for a reason, and not behind of curtain of fancy lights either. Bring me back something printable, boy."

Nick jotted down the number Zoti had given and found himself more than a little anxious to speak with Bates. If his editor was convinced there something in what this old man had accumulated, it must be noteworthy. His impression of the man standing on the corner the night of the speech was not one he would have found any promise in pursuing. It seemed odd for the man to be standing on a corner late at night in what could have easily been confused as a stalker pose. His experience with eccentrics, as he assumed Bates was, had not always been pleasant.

The phone rang several times before it connected. "Bates," he shouted into the phone when it connected.

"John Bates?" Nick asked wishing the moment he had said it he could grab it back.

"Who'd you call?" His reply was overlaid with the British accent he remembered, just a hint, as if he'd grown up around the sound but let it evolve into something less British over time. Although the question was meant as an insult, Nick ignored it.

"My name is Nick Heath with the Portland Riverfront Weekly."

"Your boss said you'd be called. Fine man that Zoti and a damned good drinker. Are you a drinker, Nick?" Nick was not but judging by the several abbreviated sentences this man had already uttered, drinking would be involved and he would be judged by his ability to imbibe. Zoti and he could easily have lived in the time of the three-martini lunch, where a man's ability was determined by the strength of his liver. He immediately thought he should bring Che with him. She was a gifted drinker, able to pace herself without seeming as if she was doing so. And she had just enough of a rough edge about her that played to offset, if not compliment her near-model perfect exterior. That he hoped might be enough to distract Bates from the fact that he would be nursing his drink.

He opted for the truth. "I drink like a girl." He waited for Bates to digest that bit of self-deprecation.

"That's alright. I'm still a bit legless this morning. Like I was sayin', Zoti can drink. You should take a lesson from him." This was the last thing Nick intended to do. He drew the line on socializing with co-workers and supervisors were even higher on that restricted list. As much as he enjoyed his job, the actual workplace was defined in his mind as a place he didn't want to be, working with people he didn't want to work with, doing a job he didn't want to do. Not that he disliked journalism, in fact he loved it; he just saw himself doing something grander. And not that he didn't like his co-workers; he did and looked forward to parting ways at the end of the day.

And he still didn't see Santo Aretino as the path to that dream.

"I'm staying at the Heathman but I don't want to drink in their bar. I always feel underdressed and underpaid and I don't be puttin' on any fucking pretense to drink. The room's real nice though."

"If you don't mind walking a little bit, I know just the place."

Nick arrived at the hotel about five minutes prior to the appointed time. He had thought he had taken a spot that afforded him a good view. He wanted to see the man, how he moved, even if he interacted with anyone on the trip across the lobby. Nick had always referred to this as 'the walk', the stride that told him about his subject before the person was introduced.

But Bates still surprised him, sitting down next to him. The sudden plop he made when he sat, the exhaled sigh he made Nick turn suddenly.

"See what I mean," he said almost waving his arm at the people moving about the lobby. "I'll bet that old hag has a dog that sports a bow." Nick looked at the woman who appeared to be old money, grey-haired and elegantly coiffed.

Before he could reply, Bates was on his feet. "Where're we headed, mate?"

Nick didn't reply and just headed towards the door. The street outside was busy, not New York City busy, but for an early afternoon in fall, there were a lot of people on the move. The air had just been washed of five days of consecutive sunshine by a brief shower. It smelled good. And Nick, who had seen more than his share of cities and towns, big and small, clean and dusty, always thought Portland looked good with that glisten of moisture, an aquatic overcoat that gave the edges a welcome sparkle.

As the two of them walked toward a small restaurant known for its year round turkey dinners and Spanish coffee, they made inconsequential conversation. They were somewhat out-of-sync, the old man seemed as if he was struggling with Nick's obviously slower pace, shortening his gait to try and match the younger man.

The restaurant was down a small hall in an old Pioneer Building. It was more of a café than restaurant and Nick thought Bates would feel comfortable in a more formal atmosphere. Bates would have been comfortable anywhere he went. Discomfort was, according to him, some other person's issue.

They were led to a booth along the edge of the restaurant. "Back in the day, you got a turkey sandwich with your drink. And during prohibition, turkey became the cornerstone meal. If you're hungry, it is quite good." Bates wasn't listening. He was watching the theatrics of the tableside assembling of a Spanish coffee.

"I'll take one of those," he said. When the waiter arrived at his elbow, Bates completely ignored him letting Nick do the ordering. All he said was "You're buying; you order." Nick ordered a Spanish coffee for both of them hoping that he could sip his drink during the interview.

"Let's start with," and before Nick could begin, Bates interrupted him.

"What's your interest in Aretino?"

"Not much more than any story my editor gives me. I personally haven't seen the fascination people have with him. Yeah, he's rich. Yeah, he's a recluse and charitable and all that. But that doesn't make him anything but a little odd and in case you hadn't noticed, PDX wears its odd on its collective sleeve."

"I had noticed." He wouldn't say anything while the waiter made the drinks. It was a show that Che really enjoyed, and he suspected, anyone enamored with a handsome waiter working with alcohol and fire might be. Thinking of Che cooking in their kitchen made him lose focus for a brief moment. She had promised a beef stew for dinner. He wished he had brought her instead.

Bates gave the waiter a sideways glance that seemed to calculate the pour of the rum rather than the tableside mixology. Nick was in agreement with him on that though. He was much more inclined to watch this presentation while it was being done for someone else than when it was occurring inches from his elbow.

Nick waited until the drinks had been served and the waiter moved on before he urged Bates to tell him what he knew. He suspected that Bates would pace the story so as to include another drink or two and maybe even something to eat.

"I heard that you traveled east to research the man."

"I did but found a lot of conflicting information that I couldn't or can't yet tie together into anything meaningful." Nick was hesitant in telling this man too much of what he found. He didn't want to jade his version of the story.

"That must've been harder than it sounds. I mean, the trail is thirty years old." Bates has a small amount of foam on his upper lip that Nick looked directly at. Bates wiped it with his napkin and continued on.

"I was hired to look for a young man who had whipped

the living shit out of three college students back in the day. The story I put together about the incident took a little bit of time but I managed to piece it together." He pulled his phone from his pocket to gather some of his notes.

Bates took a long drink of his hot drink, ignoring Nick as he began to recap his trip. "Seems our boy Santo took it upon himself to avenge a couple of Amish girls who had been kidnapped," he started without fanfare, "and scared three idiots nearly to death, the morons who did the deed, one of which became sterile after the beating Mr. Santo gave him." Nick put his phone down wondering how Bates came to these accusations. "And his father, the kid's old man, not Aretino's and whose name shall be withheld from this conversation was all up and pissed because his sacred bloodline ended with that incident. No more little brats to torture the world coming from that moneyed household." The last statement was seasoned with contempt. "So, he hired me to find out who did it and lo and behold, it was the patron saint of cold turtles and whatever else he gives his coin to."

Before Nick could gather himself to ask the next question, Bates quickly added, "I assumed he wasn't going to use the information to sue the kid."

Nick could only say one word: "What? Can you back that up just a bit?"

Bates filled him with some of the particulars he had gathered from his own investigation while the crime was still fresh. But his tone sounded impatient.

"Stay with me, Nick. He basically took these three kids, same age as he was, more or less, nineteen or so, and hogtied them with drapery cords to their dorm room beds and lectured them while whipping them with a drapery rod. Not sure whether it was planned too far in advance or it just came to him, but it was a brutal attack. He faked his entry to get past the monitor or RA, some pimply kid, posing as a repairman coming to hang drapes in one of the kid's rooms. Yeah I know, clever but kind of calculating.

"So anyway, that beating left my client's idiot boy more or less useless for procreating and the old man was pissed because the cops wouldn't do anything because they said it was a campus police issue and they couldn't do anything because their expertise was busting pot parties and judging from the two I spoke to, either reselling what they confiscated or using it themselves." Nick was having trouble catching the rapid cadence of his accent. All he could do was lean in and hope to catch the majority of what spewing form the old man's mouth.

"So, Aretino took out three kids his own age, in their dorm room and nobody heard a thing?" Nick thought a recap might force the man to slow down. All the question did was give Bates a moment to finish his drink. He waved for the waiter to bring another.

"He just walked in and kicked some motherfucking ass."

"And then what?"

"Didn't they teach you anything in journalism school?" Nick cringed slightly but didn't respond. "That's the middle of the story," he said, shaking his head and exhaling audibly. "I had two choices as I saw it. That and a nice sized expense account that I figured I could string out for a couple of months. So I went backwards first. Talked to that big Irishman at the farm, the girl's father, and eventually made my way back to that shithole town he grew up in. Met the cop. Did you meet Tell?" Nick nodded. "Did you meet Connors?"

Nick thought about that for a moment. "No. Connors was dead when I got there. I guess he lived with Tell in those last years."

"Guessed? You didn't nail that fact down?" He stared intently at Nick and realized that each word he uttered would have to be more carefully chosen, edited on the fly for a man who made his living, or did, collecting details like bugs in a jar, turning them in the light to see every angle, memorizing their weaknesses and admiring his own domination of the lowly creature.

"Fuck you." He said and that comment pushed Bates to smile. Nick ignored it. Although he was sure Bates had never played hockey, he recalled something Zoti had told him in those opening weeks of his employment. Zoti told him that when someone checks you against the boards in hockey, they only do it for one reason. That reason Zoti explained was to test your balls. Would you push back, he had asked or would you flee like a pussy? Bates had checked him and he checked back.

"He, I mean Tell, mentioned him as the catalyst for a lot of the work he did chasing him, albeit fruitlessly."

"Tragic character Connors. He had it in for our boy and convinced his cop friend that he was up to no good. Not sure what it was all about but for a religious man he was full of the devil's venom. Or he saw himself as some sort of heavenly crusader and Aretino was the devil." Bates paused for a moment. "Dead huh? Did you talk to the prisoner?"

"It was actually his parole hearing that popped Aretino's name in a search. Tell was still trying to tie him to that crime."

"So you didn't," Bates seemed to conclude. "I know that Tell was convinced at that time that our boy was into something or he probably had a hand in it." Understanding that Nick had stepped into an investigation that was never formally pursued, he said reluctantly, "I suppose the parents were dead by then too. Nice people. Tragic, though. They seemed to carry a fair amount of baggage as well. Didn't have a clue who their kid was. Moving backwards basically gave me just a little bit of an idea who he was."

"I talked to more than one person," Nick began, "who thought he was some sort of god. One even called him the scourge of princes for the way he dispatched their enemies."

"I know that the Amish girls thought so too. I didn't talk to them much and the father was pretty closed lipped. But I got the impression that even though he didn't condone violence and probably didn't trust the police, he was happy the boys got the punishment they deserved. So maybe he is a scourge 'cause my client's kid sounded like a fucking prince."

They paused while the waiter made another tableside drink. Bates looked up at him and handed him a twenty dollar bill. "Next time I wave, just bring the drink and not the theatrics." The waiter pocketed the bill and nodded, wheeling his cart to the next table.

"So backwards didn't yield much?" Nick asked.

"Not really, expect to find out that he was one of those hit and run types. Only he gave the recipient the opportunity to see him first. He wasn't shy about the ass beatings. And apparently it was the second time he dispatched those fuckers. First time he got sucked into their hassling of a crippled gas station attendant and he kicked their asses then too."

Nick thought about these actions, tying them to the profile of the man he had recently investigated. Santo Aretino's history of stepping in and saving the helpless from events beyond their control fit nicely into the information he had gathered. The man was a do-gooder with a violent streak that was both reactive, and in the case of the college kids, premeditated. He wondered how he could easily saunter between crimes without remorse. Or perhaps, he was self-punishing those actions with his isolation. He kept that last revelation to himself.

"You're wondering if that was a bad thing, aren't you?" Bates had asked this question of himself as his research continued. He told Nick about Santo's journey west, first to the small bus stop in Ohio, where he calmly saved a fellow passage from what was certainly a bad ending, dispatching some young, local hoods. The police there tried to care, he told him. The sheriff he talked to was leaning towards treating the mysterious passer-by as a welcome vigilante who removed several blights on society and the inevitable prison sentences which his taxes would help support. "Dead men don't cost society nothing," he remembered the rural officer telling him.

"That trail led to St. Louis where the same blind eye was taken by the law in that town. There was some mumbling about strained resources from the detective I spoke with and lack of manpower to pursue what was clearly a crime, but as one officer pointed out, a crime that had forward rewarding results. I had never heard it put that way: forward rewarding results. Made him sound like they wished he had stayed a bit longer.

"I was unable to tie Aretino to the deaths of the two men on that eastern Colorado ranch. There were no witnesses for that event, either, and the bodies were well on their way to decomposition when they were found with most of the evidence destroyed by any vulture activity. The ranch, the state trooper explained to me was known as an opium den. It had been stripped clean by whomever was present the Statie told me and although he was certain that the people present had done the looting. He said there was always someone there but he assumed that they had nothing to do with the double homicide. Stands to reason though, they were all probably too stoned. He also had added that he was positive that this was an outsider, someone with his wits about him. When I asked him how he got to that conclusion, he pointed towards an anonymous tip that was phoned in." Bates paused to drain the second drink, which Nick had to assume was still very hot. "The trooper said whoever did this was not someone just anybody might want to fuck with. Both men was very bad men and both were armed. Neither one of them it seemed had a chance."

"It kind of sort of fits into the intel I uncovered," Nick replied. As Bates filled him on his journey across country, Nick listened intently. Could the reclusive man on stage really have all of these murders to his credit? Did they haunt him? Would he have found this out had Zoti been more generous with his expense account?

"One thing I didn't tell you about was Matty, or more formally, Matteo."

"Hold that thought for a moment. I need to process this."

Bates looked across the table at the young reporter. He wondered how many murders he covered for his free weekly paper and if he was up to the task of weaving all of the disparate actions of a man who valued his privacy, or was hiding from the truth, of a man who was more generous with his wealth than all of the billionaires in the world, an incalculable gift to civilization, or was just some sort of mentally disturbed person who should, despite all of his achievements be treated the same way as a common criminal, even if Bates had failed to find anyone in law enforcement that shared that opinion beside Tell. In their eyes, he was drifter that they were lucky enough to arrive in their corner of the world, ridding them of a blight they had not be able to remove.

"What you need to process is your own sense of what emotions are. Our Mr. Santo, you know that stands for saint, right? He's doesn't have any. His actions were not born of anger or any other emotional marker you or I happen to have. In my line of work, emotions have a fingerprint, something inside each of us that kicks us into action or inaction, makes us sad or happy, makes us flee when there's danger or step into the fray. While it seems as if our subject is willing to step into the fray, there is no calculation when he does. He's just there and does something. Believe me when I tell you this: Most of us wouldn't. We get scared and have doubts and then, and only then do we do something. Even heroes pause for a moment, a split second before they respond, run into the fire or rescue some hapless bloke. In other words, we do stuff in relation to the context. That's emotion and I don't think our boy has any." Bates turned and waved to the waiter for another Spanish coffee.

"Maybe. Maybe he just gets off on it." That was not Nick the reporter speaking. He had been taught to avoid jumping to conclusions and his editor had emphasized this repeatedly. Zoti had explained to him on his first day with the paper that he never wanted to ask the question "How do you know this?" Once it was asked, the question of ethics came into play, and for someone who was beginning his journalistic career, it would set the stage for the question being repeatedly asked.

Technically, there was nothing worth reporting. Bates hadn't given him any names for verification, although he was certain the man had them, otherwise Zoti wouldn't have entertained him for long. He turned him over to Nick instead. Was he supposed to ferret out this information to support his story? Or was it a story that held little merit and the information Bates had offered nothing more than the inevitable creation of speculation instead?

"So what. He's a little emotionally deficient. From what I gathered, he had kind of a conflicted childhood." He wondered whether Bates had dug deep enough to know this.

"It's possible. Being a bastard can impact anybody, especially if you are never told but always suspect."

"You know about that?" If Bates did, he was more thorough than Nick had given him credit for. He did recognize something in the man that he often saw in himself: The ability to have people tell him stuff, seemingly unrelated information that they may have deemed useless and random but would open another door or point to another path not taken.

"I thought nothing of it for quite some time. Sure, it

probably had some impact on how he turned out. Depending on how he was treated as a child, whether it was a deep dark secret that was convincingly kept covered up or if it was something his parents, or one of them just couldn't hide. I'm betting it was the old man. He was some old country Italian guy and when I spoke to him, he tensed up. Just a little bit but it was one of those emotional fingerprints I was just talking about. But he didn't say anything. I just knew."

"How?"

"Easy there, Mr. Murrow. I found Santo's father, or step-father, or whatever he might have been at a local taproom. His wife, a lovely lady told me where to find him. I would've asked her but she wouldn't let me in the house. So I went there and talked with the man. I got nothing other than that little marker that something wasn't right. So I left and came back and chit chatted with the bartender."

Nick leaned forward. "And he told you what?"

"About the kid and how torn the old man was about his role. He did it carefully but at the same time, he sounded as if he cared. So, it would be easy to conclude, albeit without any evidence, that the kid felt some sort of distance in the house. That translated into trouble at school and more trouble in high school.

"This pointed towards Connie that the retired detective had spoken about, or Brother Connors."

"You spoke to the man?" Based on what Tell had told him, the man had been clearly obsessed with finding some sort of criminal activity surrounding the boy and went to his deathbed without any proof. His obsession held fast years after the boy had left the school and probably, considering the toxic nature of his pursuit.

"He was still alive when I met him, yeah. On his way out, strapped to an oxygen tanks while he lit another cigarette.

Yeah, he thought Aretino was dealing drugs."

"He was. Tell told me that much, even if he couldn't connect the dots." Nick had no proof but thought that he could toss it into the conversation to see where it might lead.

"That was never proven and Tell kept trying, for decades to just tie him to an arrest he had made." Matty DeSilva had been released from prison and by the time Nick's trip took place, he had also passed away.

"Mr. DeSilva told me otherwise." Up until that point, Bates had been relaxed comfortably in the booth. From his vantage he could see the bustle of the restaurant around him, the ebb of the late lunch diners to the flux of early dinner arrivals. He was keenly aware that people came here for the Spanish coffees and the turkey. But when he said this, he leaned into Nick on his elbows.

"Keep in mind, it was early in his incarceration. He was new to the prison system and according to the guards, he hadn't had any visitors up until that point, not even his lawyer. His buddy Sal on the other hand had had a visitor every day, for the brief time he had spent behind bars before Uncle Bruno got him out. So, you've got two partners in crime and one with better connections."

"Uncle Bruno?"

"The mob boss at the time, Angelo. Matty told me that Sal was related. But that didn't help him none. The scuttle at the time was DeSilva was going to be released early for good behavior. So, Mr. DeSilva was more than happy to talk. He was wrong."

Nick wanted to ask the open-ended question "And?" but refrained from doing so. He knew that Bates was waiting for it. The two men had the same goal and if Nick was right, what was once a client's wish was now just a curiosity, a sort of closure for a man who had long since given up the chase.

Bates hadn't given him much of his background. He knew the man came from a long line of Sherlockian wannabes and wondered if the ability to ferret out details and deduce was something genetic or simply the results of experienced hand-me-down instructions. Nick had his own information that he was beginning to suspect was not as unique as he had thought when he sat down.

"You know about the girlfriend, right?" He did and recalled the destitute state she was in when he found her. Bates continued, "She had made the decision to turn in her ex-lover in a fit of anger and from that one action, brought two very guilty men into the legal system."

Nick now knew that her youthful impetuousness had turned into a geriatric regret. Nick could still see her emerging from the shadows of her small house, the yapping dogs, and the odor of death not-coming-soon-enough adding to the faded canvas of her life.

"She was quite the looker, all firm and full up on pointy tits, blonde hair and just about pin-up quality. How does someone break it off with something like that is well-beyond me?"

Nick had spoken to her briefly, the way someone asks superficial questions to someone in the hospital. He was not afraid to ask the tough questions and wished he had pushed her harder for answers. But at the time, he felt pity and in doing so, found her to be a minor player in the drama that had unfolded thirty years prior. By the time he had found her, he was already becoming fatigued by the assignment convinced that there was no news worth chasing here. Santo, if he had been up to anything had managed to cover his tracks.

"If she was, the years were not kind."

"So you met her? I imagine they wouldn't have been. A lover scorned opens a wound that just festers, either on the surface or just beneath it. Sometimes, it goes away with time. I could see that she was on the verge of really understanding what she had done. She turned old Matty boy into the cops hoping that she could make the move on Santo."

This was new. Suzy had told him that she did know Santo and seemed genuinely concerned about his well-being. Nick had mentioned that he was doing okay as far as he knew. At the time he felt as though there would be little gained by sharing his real state.

"I'm not sure I follow. Suzy sent Matteo DeSilva to prison to open the possibility of getting with Santo?"

"She was probably ten years his senior at the time. Fucking unreal how someone who could have anyone, I mean she could have probably sucked the chrome off God's tailpipe and here she was trying to bed a teenager." Nick thought about his aunt and her revelation of the lover the young Santo had been, to more than a handful of older women.

Bates waved at the waiter. Nick thought, 'that's four and the old bastard seems barely impacted.' A couple of minutes later, without the fanfare of the table preparation, the waiter brought another drink, the sugar crystalized around the rim, the liquor hidden inside the deep blackness of the coffee, a crown of off-white foam that made the drink as pretty as Suzy must have been.

"She was a quite the looker and probably could've had just about any man she chose but she wanted that Santo more than DeSilva and for some reason, in some twisted way, she apparently thought getting him out of the way would solve her issue." The idea itself wasn't that farfetched but, as Nick knew from his conversation with her, after thirty years of reflection, it was not the best plan.

Nick asked, "So was he involved with the drug dealers?"

Without hesitation, Bates replied that he was. "There is

that criminal code of conduct which suggests you never rat on a friend and DeSilva wouldn't. He knew that I was not the law and he also knew that it wouldn't have any impact on his sentence, so he didn't necessarily say so. Said he was quite the businessman and left it at that.

"I remember him leaning in and saying Santo, although he called him Sonny, had cornered most of the county he lived in, so much so that all DeSilva and his partner had to do was bring it in and our boy Santo would do all of the heavy lifting. They saw their risk greatly mitigated by the arrangement, which probably made them a bit sloppy. But still, when your girlfriend is the snitch." Bates just shook his head at that thought.

"So, the boy apparently got wind of the bust." Bates interrupted him.

"No. He was there. DeSilva said so. Said he usually took a back way to the house and was in the bushes at the perimeter of the lawn when the whole thing was going down. A couple of minutes earlier would have changed this whole story. We wouldn't be sitting here at all. Just a couple of minutes."

No one had mentioned the drug dealing part but Nick had made a logical leap: No one really knew. If he was as savvy as Bates implied, then he too had a distribution network and when he ran, it probably just collapsed. Two main links in the supply chain were removed and Delaware County was left to its own devices.

"Did DeSilva say anything else?" He was hoping that maybe they had shared a contingent plan, a sort of plan B if something ever happened.

"He said the kid never spent any of his money that he could tell. So he probably left with a bag full of cash. Who fucking knows how much. But according to DeSilva, it would've been a lot. So he had traveling cash and, our prisoner suggested that he probably had an enviable stash. Said the kid was a real connoisseur. Both of those things can get you far if you play it right."

This made Nick wonder, and he did so aloud. "So, if Santo had money, what do you think the chances are that he used it to build his empire?"

"Probably pretty good. His wife said he was an investor of rare acumen. If he is or was, then you can bet he switched from dealing to trading. It kind of makes sense. I would give him the benefit of making that decision."

Nick's phone lit up with a text message from Che. "Got a client coming in after hours, be home after that, love us."

Nick asked Bates if he was hungry. In light of Che's extra work, he thought he'd better get something to eat and felt obligated to feed the old man, who had drunk more than he was capable of and did it on an empty stomach. The two sat and discussed their professions over the restaurant's legendary turkey dinner. Bates was interested in what prompted a man to take up journalism in this day and age and Nick wondered if the profession of private detective had run its course, in the traditional sense. This made Bates laugh.

"There will always be stupid people doing stupid things and people like me who get hired to find out. We don't care why they do it or even if they intended to do it. Now it's mostly working for insurance agencies and flying drones and dinking around with computers. I retired at a good time.

"Nowadays, the business requires college. A fucking degree? I had it kind of easy. I was taught to be resourceful and smart. You know what I mean, Nick. It is the question you ask to the right person, phrased just so, at the right time, that yields the result you were hoping for. I was taught, no, it was drilled in to me to keep my values at the forefront. Not as easy as you might imagine.

"Like the client who hired me to find his son's virility thief. I knew he wanted to have him offed or at least fucked with and I am not the fixer type. But he probably knew someone who was or he was going to ask me if I did. They always figure I have a rolodex filled with the names of nefarious elements who will do anything for a buck. I don't. Never did. But they think I did. Which was fine. Lot of time it let me squeeze a few extra coins out of them."

"But you never found him."

"I told the guy the trail had gone cold and never said anything about the other incidents. That was none of his business because it didn't have any relation to why he hired me. Aretino was as lucky as he was clever. This whole shit would've tied him up for quite some time, all over what he would have seen as nothing more than justice being done.

"You know what an ellipsis is Nick? Of course you do," he added before Nick could reply. "Our boy Santo is like that. A sentence that was not finished but you know what the next couple of words are, or should be."

Bates slid out of the booth and headed to the restroom. Nick watched him walk away; no evidence of his afternoon with Spanish coffees or even his age. He decided to send Che a return text.

"How much longer?"

She replied: "Not much. Guess who I'm cutting?

"Can't."

"Santo Aretino."

19

When Bates returned to the table, Nick had paid the check. "We've got to go. Santo is getting his hair cut and I think we should drop by."

*****

Arianne stood in front of the office building appearing much like the statues in the nearby fountains. Her hair, long since allowed to go grey, whipped gently in the breeze as it circled the building from the west and converged on her figure standing at the base of the pink marble steps. People hustled by purposefully, intent on fulfilling the obligations of their schedules or heading home. The late afternoon sun cast long shadows along the corridors of downtown.

She was stuck on the first words she would utter. She knew that Santo was probably not in the building but his wife was, although for a moment, she was hoping that was not the case. Perhaps that was why she entertained the impulse to meet with her but delayed it until almost the close of a normal business day. She had a history of self-defeat that only recently was something she was willing to admit. Perhaps this was one of those moments, the tragic need to step forward even as the journey seemed ill-advised from the beginning.

They had never met but she felt as though she knew her. It must be difficult for a woman to allow her husband to have a correspondence with another female, no matter how convoluted the process had been over the years. And Marley knew who was writing those letters, Arianne assumed even without proof that they had ever been opened or read. Yet it was hardly a correspondence; Santo had never answered a single letter. He could be forgiven. Could his wife? Did she provide counsel on this subject? None of the letters contained any sort of request to update her on his well-being or doings.

Her letters had been written on a frequent basis in the early years, almost one per week. These long-hand missives, had they been written during the age of the internet, would be thought of as a well-considered blogpost by a frustrated traveler. Without any pre-determined destination or plan, she meandered and so did her account of those voyages. For her, the chronicle was cathartic as she feed some internal need to nurture a kinship with the one reader she thought she had.

Santo rarely read them. Marley did, at his request. Her beautiful flowing cursive allowed the reader, Santo, an open view into the mind of a woman deeply troubled by the ambiguity of the world around her. She felt that the worst thing anyone could say to her was "on one hand" and she found that too many did, straddling the line between what they believed in and what they wanted to believe in. She found this kinship amongst a wide variety of strangers, as if she were broadcasting her own doubts, everyone she met was standing at their own crossroads. The weight of these constant decisions was what drew them together, randomly, often in public places, often in different languages.

So, she had kept moving. After she had buried her father, she flew to France. She hiked from Paris, where she stayed for only a day, intent on spending no more than fifteen dollars a day, guided by her thick Fromer's guide offering tips on how to do so, north towards Normandy. There was no specific reason other than her surname found its origin in the region. She had kept her maiden name when she married and at times she felt that was the first wedge she had driven between her husband and her. She remembered his protestations that included arguments such as 'no one does that' to 'why' to the prescient question asking if she was 'prepping your exit strategy on our wedding day' to 'if you loved me, you'd conform to the tradition', all of which left her more stubbornly convicted to keep the name Roberts.

She made her way to Caen and then to Bayuex and then on to the littoral town of Vierville-sur-Mer. While beautiful and stark, it seemed to exist only for the tourism provided by its recent past and the American name of an historic landmark, Omaha Beach. On each stop, she penned a letter to Santo. Each began the same way, without salutation or even a date. It simply began as if she was continuing a conversation that had been interrupted by a knock on the door: Now where was I?

The question was not anchored by the physicality of a place but instead the state in which her thoughts had traveled that day, the hour before or even in the minute preceding the first mark of pen to paper. Trained in the Palmer method of cursive, each loop carefully and artfully made its way into a graceful swing towards the margin, only to find itself repeating. The information contained within these letters was not intended to be travelogue or history, educational or whimsical. Some letters ran on for pages while other days, they seemed harried and obligatory barely filling only one side of a sheet.

She found work as an agent d'elevage laitier she wrote in one letter, a glamorous sounding name for a person who milks cows and learns to farm. The family she stayed with paid her in room and board and a handful of francs which she didn't need. Even as they appeared to be incapable of paying her anything, she cheerfully accepted the money for fear of embarrassing her proud employers.

She stayed along the windswept north coast for over a month, enjoying the provincial nature of the area, a place that seemed to capitalize on the brutality of the world war that had occurred on its shores and yet, stayed distant from the destruction they had long since repaired. The only tourists she met were war veterans, some of who seemed disappointed to find out she was American.

Her journey around Europe would take almost twenty years and in that span of time, she wrote over sixteen hundred letters, sent to a small town in Pennsylvania and then boxed unread and sent to a man she still saw as unchanged, the youthful exuberance and intellectual curiosity still shining in his green eyes. Still restless and unsolved, she continued. Arianne more or less followed Michener's writings after Europe, jumping from Spain to Morocco, Israel, Afghanistan, and eventually circling back north. She worked in pensiones, bars, farms, and even as a secretary at the American consulate in Kabul. With the fall of the Iron Curtain, she entered Albania.

She drifted, seemingly aimlessly. But if she were asked why, her hindsight would have answered more succinctly suggesting it was as much running away from and as running towards. The object in her rearview was the same on the horizon in front of her: Santo Aretino, the man she would never have, could never really know, and was incapable of possessing, It was like a soccer pitch, with both goals at either end worth her attention. She knew he inhabited the suggestion made by Michener: "If a man happens to find himself, he has a mansion which he can inhabit with dignity all the days of his life." She was essentially homeless and she had begun to worry if this was also some sort of penance, self-commitment to a moving prison.

She knew that he didn't need her, never did and after seeing him command the stage, engineering the theatrical ruse of lights and illusion, he never would. She met numerous men and women in her journey and fell in love with half of them, each offering a peek inside the person she wanted to be. Each time she moved on without a goodbye, sneaking away to her next destination without any closure. She failed to mention these emotional debacles in her letters to Santo. She was fearful that he would understand that action, the impulse to reach out until a person reached back, and then fleeing as if the hand was infected with death by emotional entanglement.

She was afraid and she knew it. She felt as though this was a sort of courage unto itself and a way to protect new acquaintances from experiencing her. Standing at the threshold of meeting Santo's wife, if she would even take time out of her day to meet, caused her breath to hitch in her chest. She wondered if her love story in isolation was vastly different than hers. Did Santo finally find someone he could open himself up to without regard?

She crossed the marble floor of the atrium, a large flowing Chihuly glass sculpture suspended from the ceiling made her stop for a moment. She wondered if Santo had picked that piece out. It was explosive, colors jutting out in various vibrant angles and circling back in on itself. She saw the Santo she knew of thirty-five years ago in it, a complex and artistic mind that was comfortable in its own atmosphere, yet suspended in the moment.

She must have been standing there for too long. A security guard, handsomely dressed, approached her and asked her if there was anything he could help her with. She apologized and made her way to the reception desk. A young girl with the face of a fawn picked up her phone and called what Arianne thought was an assistant.

"Yes Ma'am," she heard her say. "I will send her up. Would you like me to guide her?" A brief pause, and a smile in her direction preceded a reply, "Very well." She turned to Arianne and pointed to a bank of elevators at the far end of the entry. "When you get there, I will summon the elevator for you."

It was at that very moment she felt underdressed. Not once in the decades since she had begun her journey had she felt this way. She wondered if what she was wearing would speak too clearly about the woman she had become, a slow evolution that found her favoring comfort over couture, simplicity over extravagance, restraint over the advertisement of beauty. When she reached the elevator the young girl had pointed to, she looked back. The girl nodded and the doors parted. The man inside welcomed her and pushed the only button available. The doors closed and the car lifted silently, scaling the tower with a whisper.

When the doors opened, Marley Aretino was standing there. "I am so glad to finally meet you." She seemed genuinely excited. She slipped her arm in Arianne's, a very European gesture of friendship and walked her down the long hall. Before they arrived at the room at the end, she turned to her and said, "Look."

It took Arianne a moment to realize what she was seeing. Every stamp from every letter from every post office she had used to send her writing was chronologically glued to a huge canvas, ornately framed in gold.

When she spoke, Marley sounded proud, like a school age child showing off her science project. "It seemed such a waste to simply toss the envelopes and I like to collect things that Sonny would never think of keeping." She folded her arms across her silk blouse and smiled. "The world is full of discarded treasures, mementos that mean nothing after serving their purpose. This means something."

Arianne first felt the emotion well up in her, a feeling that was so alien, she barely recognized it. This was the woman that won the prize she turned away, the person who made the man happy enough to ground himself into himself and stay where he felt safe. She was his sanctuary and it was something she knew she could never have been.

"What does it mean?" she asked herself, surprised at the timidity of her inner voice.

As Marley made her way around her huge burled maple desk, adorned with only a lamp and a laptop. Arianne knew that this austerity said something about the person who occupied this office but she couldn't say what.

She offered Arianne a comfortable chair near a petrified wood table and asked her if she would like anything. Before she could answer, she said, "I'm having tea."

"That actually sounds good." Marley spoke to someone but Arianne didn't see her call anyone or even access any intercom. She added scones to her request for an extra cup. She sat down in the chair next to her swinging her long legs beneath her. The Portland skyline was littered with small clouds that created a pareidolian herd of shapes scurrying across downtown proper.

As she began to talk, beginning the conversation as if they were long time girlfriends from a proper boarding school in the east, "Tell me everything", there was a small knock on the door. A young woman entered with a cart and removed the tea service and a plate of triangular pastries.

"I think tea should be served in boiling water and steeped just long enough, so let's give this a couple of more minutes." This felt as though Arianne had missed more than she thought. In her travels, she had met many people, befriended a few and quickly lost track of those people once she moved on. This seemed like something that was important, something she had read about in countless novels but dismissed as simply a staged plot, two women discussing the world while each took bites of pastries while also taking bites out of each other's troubles.

"So," she began again, "Tell me everything."

"About?" asking not really sure what she thought of as everything. Did she want to know more about her travels, adding edited details that didn't fit in the letters, or perhaps she was asking about Santo. Had she read the letters? Was the collage of postmarked stamps something she had gathered from discarded envelopes or had she carefully preserved each as a notch in a history she experienced with the writer?

She wondered how much Marley knew and how much Santo had shared. The man she remembered was a boy on the verge, and while not burdened with the angst of most teenagers, he could be maddeningly quiet. It wasn't that he was incapable of expressing his emotions. It was instead, as if he simply chose not to, or worse, wasn't blessed with the burden they created. And after many years, she realized his silence was intentional, even symphonic.

"I read all your letters. Sonny wasn't, how should I say this, prepared to do so. When the first batch arrived, about sixty of them, sent by Seamus – you've met Seamus I'm told – Sonny kind of seemed, I don't know, reluctant to read them. You two had something and he said he was afraid, not actually the right word because I've never ever seen him afraid of anything, ever, but it was as if he thought that you were trying to rekindle that relationship and he didn't feel as though that was right. So he told me to read them."

"At least somebody did."

"They were beautifully written and I loved your penmanship. No one writes anymore." She took a sip of tea. "I felt as though I was there but not. You seemed to gradually relax over time, allowing yourself to assimilate in some places, I guess that's the right word. In the beginning, and yes, I read them chronologically, you were lonely. And that didn't change much at all but as time went by, you became more receptive to what these faraway places had to offer."

Arianne shifted in her chair. Marley apologized. "I'm so sorry. I wasn't critiquing you. It sounded like it though, didn't it?"

"Kind of but that's okay." She meant that as well. It was not only nice to know that someone read her letters but that someone could understand what she was doing. She wasn't always sure herself. Sometimes she would remember where she left off in the previous letter; other times she simply put words on the page. She had made a promise early on to not reread what she wrote, allowing whatever hit the paper to be as unedited as possible. The only thing she made a conscious decision to do was avoid mentioning how she felt about Santo.

As she listened to Marley talk, the smoothness of her voice, hitting the right inflection at the right moment, she imagined listening to her read poetry, as if she had written it herself.

"I kind of thought I should tell someone what was going on and Santo was the only one I could think of that might be interested." For a moment, she wondered if that simplification sounded convincing. "When my dad died, there wasn't anyone else. That's my social sentence I suppose. I just wrote. It's nice to know that someone read them, even it wasn't the intended."

"Oh, he listened. I read them out loud while he sat a smoked joint or sipped a bourbon or both. He said he wanted to hear a female voice say the words and he wasn't sure he remembered how yours sounded. Oh and I like the way you call him Santo. Very sweet. We fall back and forth on the subject of which name to use. He proclaimed that he wanted to be called Santo because he did not care for the origin story of Sonny. But, between us chicks, he'll always be Sonny."

Marley had a very comfortable way about her. She first noticed that on stage as she opened for the elusive man. Even now, there was a charm that forced people to calm down, release their anxiousness.

"How did he," she started and abruptly changed the question, "Did he react?"

"Sonny? Hell no. I'm not sure how much time you spent with him, which I'm guessing was significant enough to understand more than most would, but he's more the type that leaves an impression while taking nothing in return. He's like emotional Teflon. He just doesn't get it, or better, just chooses not to. Did you expect that he would evolve over time somehow?"

In fact, the Santo Aretino she knew seemed fully formed, even as the youngster who visited her library, as the boy who grew in size to become a man, even as his nature, far more mature than any man she had ever encountered, stayed the same.

Marley broke the silence when she asked Arianne if she had ever heard of J. Alfred Prufrock. Arianne had not only heard of the poem by T.S. Eliot, it had been the subject of her thesis paper. She could almost feel the physical thrust her mind made at that moment, sending it whirling over forty years into the past. The room seemed to spin slightly forcing her to reconsider her situation. She refocused on Marley who seemed to be watching the episode intently. She sipped at her tea. At the moment she raised her cup, Marley looked away politely.

The Love Song of J. Alfred Prufrock was rich fodder and Arianne had delved into it with youthful enthusiasm. It was odd that Marley brought up the poem. She wondered if she referenced it in her letters. It was a tale told in multiple frames of time, present events were as immediate as those already occurred and moments that had yet to happen. Prufrock was symbolically frozen in his room, convinced that others could not possibly understand him. It was a prison of sorts, she had suggested, a place of hiding from the emotional strictures of the world. He was paralyzed by his own instincts, a place of silence and created imagery.

She pulled herself back into the room. Marley sat patiently, holding her cup and saucer in her lap. Even as she took a sip from her cup, her eyes remained locked on whatever journey Arianne was on. She swallowed dryly, "I do know that poem." Her answer seemed obvious.

"I sometimes think that Sonny is like old J. Alfred. He internalizes so much that he loses track of where he is. And if you do that for long enough, and he seems to have been doing for quite some time, even before I met him and I suspect, before you may have as well, it becomes the devil in your backpack.

"You clearly knew him," Marley continued. "He said you were instrumental in pointing him towards the door. That's what he calls life's options. He's reduced decisions to the twist of a knob, entering a room and finding another door and so on. He said that you tapped that something right away and fed his intellect with knowledge or at least showed him the door to it. It was kind of fortuitous if you think about it: A librarian is or became his very necessary tour guide."

"I remember that curiosity. But I'm not sure I knew at the time what I was actually doing. There was nothing linear about his search through all of those books he read and God knows, he read a vast number of them. And yet, I get the impression that he was," her voice trailed off.

"Opening doors only to find yet another just beyond?"

Arianne had to agree. "But Prufrock was a poem about impotence. And the Santo I knew wasn't anything like that."

"I agree. Eliot's approach to that monologue, I was never sure whether he was talking to me or to himself, was to create a subject who saw sex as tyranny. It seemed to take some time before he got to that point but, and this is where Sonny veers away slightly, is not about sex but time and time is either memory or wants to be one." Marley put her saucer on the table beside her and leaned in with her elbows on her thighs.

"Sonny can't remember."

"And that's his prison?" It made sense to her. Here was a man who approached each situation as if it had already happened and didn't need to be stored for future use. "Because it would happen again?" She paused and the thought of J. Alfred, all of his supposed teenage angst and withering body, for all of its confused verbs and failure to ever identify the purity of grammatical theme, a line from the poem surfaced, "Would it have been worth while/ To have bitten off the matter with a smile/ To have squeezed the universe into a ball"

Marley smiled. "Exactly. He told me once that memories fail when they are put into words. This kind of shocked me. I'll admit my response was a bit vain. I asked him if he remembered when we met, when we married, anything we had been through. He said that that is different. So I asked how." She laughed at the memory of that conversation.

"He told you that memories are inaccurate, right?" Arianne asked. He had told her this as they spoke for what would be the last time. That moment was emotionally charged, providing her with the mental marker to review it over and over, consciously or not. It was actually him that moved on and did so without another word.

"He told me that the story has no end and everything after the moment that just passed is mote if you think about what is happening now or about to because of it. Yeah I know, I was like what the fuck does that mean? But I wasn't listening so he waited. I could almost see him counting to ten, giving me a moment to let it sink in."

All Arianne could do was smile. "It's the reference to time being reversible a minute later, right?" By relying primarily on his instincts, never questioning the course that exact minute would take, he was confident that the next moment would be reversible if he so chose. And if he didn't, the next moment would provide another option. It was the principle of hurling forward, he had once mentioned to her. He hadn't changed.

"He's a good man, at least the part of him I know. You had a piece of him as well and your letters suggest that he put you on an unalterable path as well." It felt strange talking to someone about Santo; it was almost liberating. She had never fostered a lot of female friendships and she wondered if this was the reason why: she had nothing to share. "We just go along with him because we know it will make us, I don't whether better is the right word, but it fits. He's like an enhancement. That's why I think he hides himself away, sending his minions out into the world to do his bidding, which it turns out is not what the world expects. They want to know him and I've been with that man for over thirty years and I'm still not even close. Makes me laugh thinking about that how naïve that thinking even is."

"So it wasn't just me?" Arianne seemed to relax as they spoke about the man they knew and the man they know so little about.

"Maybe Prufrock isn't the best comparison but there really isn't a better one," Marley finally said. "He's sensitive like Prufrock. He sees what most of us don't and when faced with what would make most of us flee in terror, he stays and fights. It is one of those 'the world is a better place with him as long as he isn't necessarily in it'. It's why he hides and I don't ever question it."

"If you don't mind me saying so, he's way better looking than I imagined Prufrock to be." This made Marley smile. The man they both had known in his youth had grown into a man who seemed to age only outwardly. His pepper grey beard belied the childish attitude he kept hidden on the inside and that presence leaked out, possibly, as Marley noted, "from the depths of that voice."

A women entered the room following a soft knock. Marley looked and with that glance, the woman approached, whispered something in her ear and left. Marley thanked her.

"I have an interview with a business channel in a couple of minutes, you know, the fallout I told him we could expect. And I'm still the face of the company."

"I have one more thing, more like a question really?" Arianne was looking at the tea leaves in the bottom of her cup. She almost decided to just leave without saying anything.

Marley was looking at her intently, sitting at the edge of her chair, poised to stand. Arianne pursed her lips and asked timidly, "Did Santo ever answer the question about his parents?"

"You mean did I ever ask, or did he volunteer it, or did he mention it in passing? Never. I figured it was some sort of estrangement he didn't want to talk about. I once tried to hint around at it by asking what made him move to the west coast." At this she laughed. "You know what he told me? He had told me that people from Philly don't move west, they move to Jersey. Which, as you can see, is Santo not answering the question, because he refuses to remember the real reason. So, no, I still don't know." And she wanted to add that she was okay with that, in part because she had him now, had him for years and whatever occurred decades ago, the man she reveled in did not seem to be impacted by whatever had happened.

"That's funny," Arianne replied. Even as she seemed ready to keep her appointment, she added more to the conversation when she said, matter-of-factly, "The shadow he calls it."

Santo actually had many names for this conundrum in his life. He contributed to this inability to clearly focus on where he began the journey that he told her, and probably no one else, had changed everything.

"I had asked him what he meant by that about a hundred different ways but he had dropped the thought each time, said he was unable to entertain an ambiguous debate that neither side could offer any evidence for."

"So he did, kind of sort of say something about it?"

"He said once, and only once, that he would never know the answer to the question that he never asked and no one ever answered."

"I found out. I have the answer."

20

Russell McFarlane survived the five story fall with a broken wrist and what the doctors called a slight concussion. The news followed the story for the required day or so and within a week, it had completely dropped from the rotation when it was determined that it was not negligence on the construction company's part. It was his lack of injuries that made it newsworthy at all. The construction on the new Pearl District condominiums was halted for a day and soon after it was determined that the company was not at fault, the safety equipment was not suspected in the accident and the man who had fell did not intentionally jump, the project was back on schedule.

The man's recuperation stayed on a similar schedule and his follow-up check-ups promised he would be back on the job within weeks. Bedside interviews showed bruises and scrapes and an otherwise recovering patient, alert, surprised by the media's attention but otherwise, unable to explain exactly what had happened. When he returned to work, he was applauded by the members of his crew, a handmade sign hanging from his toolbox. It simply read Lazarus.

The back-from-the-dead pun stuck despite his efforts to have his friends simply call him Russ. They dealt daily with the potential of a similar fall and began calling him the biblical name long before he returned. Only one person had hoped that the ground and gravity would have done the job she had dreamt about for almost the entire length of their marriage.

Rochelle had felt some disbelief from the moment he approached her. She was her girlfriend's wing person, a slightly overweight girl who, by her own admission accentuated the beauty of her more slender companions. Any and all attention she did receive was suspect, convinced that the person she saw in the mirror was not the desirable woman she had hoped she would have become.

Russell had worked hard to convince her otherwise, exhibiting a wish to worship her that she had never experienced before. But his falsehood found its footing as it slipped from the promise of submission to the reality of domination, her marriage vows turned from the hope of a future to the cruel sentence of the present.

The fall was indeed miraculous. However, the bang on the head, which could not be blamed on his erratic and domineering attitude he had developed soon after they married, accentuated it. Rochelle noticed the difference within weeks, his roiling hatred for almost everything seemed to deepen, his breathing beginning to resemble a huff, chest expanding as if warning adversaries of his impending violence. He was meaner than before the accident, if it was possible. It also delayed her long hoped-for plan to exit this tragic union. She now felt an obligated, perhaps guilty of some unspoken infraction to help him with his recovery and stayed beyond the day she promised to leave.

Prior to the fall, his abuse was focused on a verbal assault, a never-ending stream of criticism that made her wonder why he wanted to marry her at all. Outwardly, they were doing well by most measures of middle class success: they both had jobs, a nice apartment and were on their way to solid financial footing that so many of her friends were struggling to achieve. But he had grown restless and the fall created a doubling effect. He had now turned from merely abusive to violent.

The embarrassment she was feeling forced her to keep this uptick in bad behavior from her closest friends. She was unsure that she really had their confidence and support. Instead, she worried that the women she knew would instead pass judgement on her rather than bestowing empathy, kept her from saying anything about her abuse. But the one place she felt comfortable discussing the events in her marriage was with her hairdresser.

Che was not your average stylist and Rochelle could tell her things without fear that it would eventually seep into her circle of acquaintances. Listening intently over the years for signs of actual physical abuse and absorbing this sort of information was not easy on her. Until recently, the mental abuse Rochelle spoke about, a much harder to prove situation and one that her client did not have the fortitude to confront let alone overcome, was difficult to listen to and even harder to counsel. Women in these sort of situations tended to blame themselves for the abuse. Rochelle was no different.

But when she told her about life after the fall, Che could tell this damaged relationship had reached a pivot point. He began swinging, she told him. His temper tantrums, previously loud and threatening had moved to the next level. At first, they were body blows. By the time she arrived at her appointment, the bruise on her face had blossomed into something that could not be hidden. Che's advice was straightforward: You have to leave. Of course, she knew that was easier said than done.

*****

Che received the call as she was sweeping the fallen hair from her last scheduled client. She recognized the number immediately. She had not entered it into her contacts at his request. This was reflected her response.

"This is Che," she answered without acknowledging the identity of her caller.

"Any chance I could come in and get a trim?" Santo enjoyed this dance in anonymity. She asked if he wanted to make an appointment adding that she was closed for the evening. He sounded disappointed and meekly asked if she could perhaps squeeze him in sooner. She paused, allowing a smile to cross her face and making every attempt to keep it from influencing her reply, and then suggested that she had other plans for the evening. She sat down at her station and looked at herself in the mirror. He told her he understood and almost as if it was rehearsed, she sighed and gave in.

"Alright," she said with the sound of resignation in her voice. "When can you get here? I don't want to wait all night." Within a minute, the door opened. His afterhours haircuts had occurred weekly since his speech. In almost every meeting, she allowed him to talk about whatever he chose. The topics were often wide ranging and always fascinating. She sensed he was happily married from the way he spoke of his wife. He was a voracious reader, able to quote all sorts of writers in the right context and yet, when he did, instead of making her feel as if she underachieved, had not read enough or was not worldly enough, it made her feel smarter. He had a graceful intellect that seemed to roam to all corners of thought. But tonight, she had something for him.

"My boyfriend is writing a piece on you." The gentle snip of the scissors filling the gaps in their conversation.

"In hindsight, I should have never done that speech. But what choice did I have?" Social media had caught him unaware and the way it seemed to box him in made him realize that isolation would take much more effort than it had in the past. As pressure seemed to mount, with his company's public relations doing the best they could to thwart the onslaught, he agreed, or as he told her, "reluctantly acquiesced" to his wife's "increasingly strong suggestion" to be the public face of the company and step out of "my self-made and very comfortable personal prison." He added, "I'm not so sure it was a good idea though."

"But you did and it was a good idea and it was effing inspiring. The core of your beliefs is so refreshing. I mean, you didn't just focus on making money and when you acquired billions, and only then, would you make some charitable contribution. You had it as part of the plan. Too cool, my friend, too cool." Hearing it voiced in such a way gave him some comfort.

"So, being investigated, or better, reported on is part of the unavoidable fallout?" In Santo's mind, this public airing of what he believed in seemed vain and the resulting media swarm presented yet another decision: How to move forward once the theater was over. The reviews were mixed at best, the vast majority applauding his mission while skeptics bemoaning his anonymous approach. Those skeptics believed in celebrity and the additional dollars it would attract. He was a celebrity that refused to be one.

Some outlets began with a confirmation of his efforts. News outlets would clamor for more information in light of this recent public event. His company had anticipated this and had released several documents about many of the previously covert efforts to save the world from itself. His company, held privately offered a press release to the business channels outlining the way Santo's investments were directed. Several network and cable news anchors were allowed to interview Marley.

Fifteen journalist from the New York Times to the San Francisco Chronicle to the Oregonian began compiling the requisite draft of an obituary. All were faced with the challenge of finding two thousand words about a man no one knew.

Downstream, some of the businesses he dealt with were

obligated to send a spokesperson to talk about the influence his company may have had on their decisions both philanthropic and financial. His green investment strategy, a method of built on a socially responsible foundation of principles had involved strongly worded directions on how his investments were to increase their profitability while doing the right thing by their workers, their environment and their marketplace. That 'right thing', if followed, did produce profits. And even as Wall Street protested, his approach was increasingly mimicked, the true sign of financial affirmation.

Other news outlets twisted the story to suggest that he had other reasons as to why he was hiding. These requests for more information were simply ignored, increasing the speculation that the media had become known for of late. That speculation began showing up in publications built on supposition instead of facts. No effort was made to squash any reporting or even control the events that would take place in the days and weeks afterward. To Santo, it didn't matter. It did to the PR team at SA Holdings, but the instructions, much to collective chagrin were simple: "Let 'em talk."

"I've got to tell you Che, the world will figure out whether they like the arrangement I've set up or not. I'm not planning on changing how I do things any time soon and neither is my company. Or should I say Marley's company."

The success that Che had was due in large part to her respect of the silence that could fall between barber and patron. She would go about her business and if the person sitting in the chair wanted to talk, she would engage. Santo had been the kind of customer who would allow long stretches of silence to ensue between their small talk. She had incorrectly assumed that it would be different. Che had imagined that living in isolation would create a pent up need to speak.

"So, has Nick found anything about me I don't already

know?" he finally asked.

She immediately recalled her father, a renaissance man of sorts who seemed to her to be the smartest man alive, asking the same question of her. "Okay Charlotte, what'd you learn in school today that I don't already know?" As she grew older, the question was answered less frequently. This disappointed him. It was his way of opening the discussion up to something greater than what she was. She would only appreciate the vast storehouse of knowledge that he accumulated over the years but had nowhere to go but to her years after they parted ways. And while she loved and respected him, his personal isolation since the childbirth death of her mother never dissipated. It hung like the moss on the trees surrounding them, a rain forest of lushness and verdant solitude, the perfect environment to feed on his loneliness.

The more isolated her father felt, the more she realized it was her only inheritance from him. Try as she might with Nick, she couldn't break through the mist of disaffection. Leaving was supposed to be hard, he had raised her since birth. But the idea had foundations laid long before they said goodbye.

"He kind of sort of did." She did not intentionally leave that statement suspended to create the next question. She simply wasn't sure he wanted to know or if he did, wanted to be reminded. He had told her during the last visit that he had made a conscious decision to not access the memories he supposed he had. "If I haven't thought about them, do they even exist anymore?" The world he told her is always too anxious to put things into perspective. "Looking at or even mulling what happened over and over, turning it to expose every angle," he explained, allows for a real time editing that changes everything. "If we are influenced by what happened once, how can reviewing it alter whatever it was about us that was forever changed because of it?"

Each event, every minute, is like an independent discovery built on a previous experience he had told her. She had told this to Nick when he returned from his trip to the east coast. It made him pause for a second. "Then, he is either a very bad man, a good man with a bad streak, or a good man who has tried to change his bad ways. If what everyone I spoke to was to be believed, he is a monster who spends all of his time atoning for his sins while avoiding answering for them."

"That's kind of fucking harsh," she said without considering that he may not have divulged everything he knew.

"Look. Zoti didn't send me packing three thousand miles because he thought I needed to see the east coast. If Aretino's the story he thinks he is, there is more to this than meets the eye." He didn't like to talk to her about his work. She was often a differing opinion, the kind of sidebar comment that would enhance a story by detracting from it, by offering a conflicting point of view or worse, acting as clarification where none should be needed. Most of his work was done without any solicitation from her for comment. But he allowed her to do so because deep down, despite not wanting to know, he wrote for her, a muse of unparalleled clarity. And although she would never tell him "I told you so" he knew she would be right if her suggestion was ignored.

He surprised himself with the outburst and he could clearly see her shock. Not the shock of hearing him take such a firm stand. For her, it was the possibility that he was right. The man she had enjoyed at dinner, become enthralled with during that TED Talk, and had quiet intimate conversations during her after hours barbering gave her a different opinion of the man he was beginning to despise. Although, he would admit to himself that this negativity was uncharacteristic, he couldn't help himself. Worse, he couldn't seem to frame the argument for his side. His creativity he kept reminding himself, was borne of his skepticism. This, somehow was different. This time, she had to be wrong.

"Perhaps you can kind of sort of share what I don't know." Santo looked at himself in the mirror. He was a head protruding from a long black bib, hair turned oddly to one side of his head, while she combed and snipped. At this statement though, she stopped and looked at his reflection.

She sighed first before answering. "You know how he knew to go back east?"

"Probably something to do with someone I once knew, or sort of knew. Possibly just chasing a ghost? I'm not quite sure how much your boyfriend found out, but there was a cop who had a hard-on for me during my formative years and just couldn't let it go. Am I close?"

"I'm not even going to ask you if it's true. It is none of business. Fuck knows, I have a few skeletons in my closet." That same look crossed her face again, an expression that fell somewhere between discomfort and curiosity. She stepped around in front of him and leaned on the counter behind her. She opened her mouth to speak and stopped.

"Go on. Please. I left that area a very long time ago, so long that the majority of my life has been lived without the shadow of those days hanging over me. Che, that was then."

"He found out something about you parents." His expression didn't change with this statement, a revelation that she was certain would have brought some response.

"Umberto and Sofi? Not so sure there is anything of interest there. It wasn't the most affable of relationships, not that I recall or want to recall all that much. They've been dead for a long time. So, I'm pretty sure your reporter boyfriend didn't interview them." He paused and smiled. "My long estranged brother. He found him, huh?"

"Nick did Santo and, I'm not even sure I should tell you this, he told him that he wasn't your brother at all."

"That's clever. But not unexpected. What makes that so newsworthy that you're all bunched up about it?" His gaze was fixated on the woman. She was quite attractive as she stood there, like a modern day Edward Hopper scene, the barbershop, the counter she was leaning on with the carefully organized the tools of her ancient trade laid out, and except for the reflection of her Pantera t-shirt reversed in the mirror, it seemed so noir. It could have been anywhere and he could have been anyone. He watched her struggle with something but wanted to be gentle as he could be helping her extract it.

"They weren't your parents. So technically, he wasn't your brother." The moment the words slipped from her mouth she made note of the how blunt that sounded. Judging from the look on his face, the sudden blankness of his response gave her reason to apologize as fast as she could.

"Really?" he asked, his eyes locked on hers. She looked away and stepped to face him, standing between him and his reflection. There was always a certain boyishness men had when draped in the body concealing fabric, the way the head seems detached, that first-time apprehension never seeming to fade with each haircut that would follow. Many of Che's clients were old enough to be her father, as Santo was, locked in a grooming ritual from the first time they sat in the chair as boys. The youthful sense of the unknown always remained and she played to the historical importance of her chosen trade, the huge ceremonious matador sweep of the apron as the body disappears, the assumption that the barber knew what was needed, the keeper of your future appearance to the world. She often felt the power of her station, the way they gave themselves to skill of her straight razor or the swiftness of her scissors. Women were different. Yes, they all sat in the same chair, disembodied, however woman retained their sense of expectation.

"I'm so sorry," she said again, repeating herself. "That was a bit abrupt and although I'm not a student of human emotions, I'm guessing you didn't know."

His first inclination was to lie, telling her that he knew all along and had simply lived with it. But that was not him. He had always confronted the truth, the inevitability of its ownership of every situation made him wonder why people bothered with attempting any sort of falsehood. Each lie came with its own set of facial affectations and ticks, a social broadcast that shouted "you're not worthy of knowing" with each misleading word.

"Supposing that was true, and it might just be..." His voice drifted off, leaving the question unasked.

*****

The man nicknamed Lazarus burst through the door before Santo could finish his thought. Twenty minutes earlier, he had grabbed his car keys, bursting from his house intent on finishing the disturbance his injured brain had prompted. He left his wife crumpled on their bedroom floor, the contents of her half-packed suitcase scattered around her. Discovering her efforts to leave him and beating the source of this new-found courage erupted as it had never done in the past.

As he recklessly swerved through traffic, he muttered curses toward the unsuspecting and as yet absent hairdresser. His rage possessed the unconquerable soul of Invictus, unafraid and self-absorbed in the belief that his fate was never to be questioned. He was captain of his soul and as he hurdled towards what he had convinced himself was the roadblock attempting to derail his carefully cobbled together relationship, he was felt invigorated by his anger.

Che reacted first and instinctively, still positioned between Santo in the chair and the mirror, facing the door. It swung open with such violence, the window shattered. Santo's reaction was much more measured. He could see the man behind him and the terror in the young girl's eyes. She was quickly assessing her escape and, for a moment, the thought of how to protect her client crossed her mind. Her inaction was encompassed in a swirl of options she had never considered.

He watched the man cross the small shop in the reflection of the wall length mirror. His eyes followed him without moving his head, keeping it still as if the scissors were still circling his ear. He crossed the floor in four purposeful strides until he was standing next to Santo.

"Get the fuck out," he yelled to him without looking at him. Che stepped further back, halted only by the counter. Her hand reached for her phone, knocking the blue Barbicide container. Combs were released in a torrent of disinfectant across the surface. Lazarus' eyes shifted from the task at hand for just a spit second.

In what Che would remember as one motion, Santo moved from the chair throwing the cape over the man's head. He pushed him back hard and fell on top of him. As he launched one solid blow to the place where Lazarus' shocked expression was, he was unaware that the floor had done what his fist intended to do. He paused inches before impact, struck by the sudden absence of motion beneath the apron.

He jumped to his feet and in doing so, pulled the cape with him. Russell McFarlane may have survived the fall at the construction site, he may have tolerated the nickname, and may have come to dominate the weakest person he knew, but the single motion done with incredible force had driven his head squarely to the tiled floor. Blood began to pool beneath his head.

"Jesus fuck," Che said trying to replay the last seconds in her head. "What the fuck was that about?"

"So, you don't know him?" Three thoughts ran across Santo's mind, simultaneously crashing into one another: Should he leave; should he stay and confess to what would most assuredly be a media shitstorm; should he insist she finish his haircut?

"I have no idea who that is," she yelled as she stepped around to look at the man whose claim to fame was once denying death. She had never seen a dead person, choosing to avoid the few funerals she was obligated to attend.

The two were still standing over the corpse when Nick and John Bates entered the shop. It was a scene with robust with more than obvious clues of what had happened and yet, not a single revelation present as to why. Santo Aretino, the recluse billionaire was standing with his barber cape still affixed around his neck. Che was still holding her scissors, thumb and forefinger holding the tool as if she was mid-cut when a corpse suddenly appeared at her feet. They both looked up at the same time.

Nick crossed the short distance in a flash and took a defensive stance between his girlfriend and the client. "Are you okay?" he asked.

Bates, moving much slower and in carefully, Spanish coffee induced steps, walked toward Santo. "My name is John Bates, Mr. Aretino," he said with extended hand. Santo pulled his hand from beneath the cape and shook the stranger's hand. He turned towards the man on the floor and made a quick assessment. Bates made a tisking noise with his mouth and offered a single observation: "This doesn't look good. Not at all."

Nick pulled his phone from his pocket and moved closer to the man on the ground. "We should call the cops." The nature of the statement, made without any action being taken offered insight into the complicated nature of the situation. He looked to Bates to confirm the idea.

"Maybe we should just take a moment and figure out what happened here before we involve the authorities." The older man said this knowing that one thing was certain: The scourge of princes, the man he had hunted for three plus decades had done it again. It wasn't a crime of passion nor was it an instance where opportunity presented no other option. Aretino didn't look injured, so self-defense could be ruled out. It also appeared the young woman was unharmed. If anything, the crime could be reduced to a random man protecting a random woman from a person intent on doing harm, even if the reason for the attack was still unclear. Or, no crime.

The police would quickly ascertain the difficulty in sorting out what had happened but it would take time. It might possibly involve the ceremonial arrest of the man who had actually done the killing as they made an attempt to piece it all together, a retracing of each step that would take an extended amount of time was more or less inevitable. Bates doubted that would happen. If it wasn't for the body, it was something everyone could have walked away from, no harm done. But harm was done and laws were broken. Or was it that justice was served without premeditation, another good deed done by the man he had once pursued vigorously without resolution, his career suspect, his cold case, the elusive goal he had assumed he would never actually score. This made him smile.

Nick was less patient, his phone still in his hand. "What do you mean we should wait?" he shouted in Bates direction, his voice attempting to break the momentary daydream the old man was experiencing. He had listened to Bates tell his story for most of the afternoon and had already understood what he was looking at. The man had chased his quarry while at the same time developing an offhanded admiration for the efficiency in which he dispatched bad people, the so-called menaces of society. There was no indication that this was the case here. The motionless man on the floor was not innocent.

"He saved my life, Nick. We need to figure out what happened here." Her voice sounded urgent and small as Che tried to get the men's attention. Nick's sense of moral rightness was conducting a vicious internal argument with her logic, his face twisted with indecision. While the situation was not good, each moment that ticked by created another potential mistake and question that could not be explained to the authorities that would eventually arrive.

Bates took a deep breath and looked around the corpse. "He slipped," pointing at the hair on the floor. There wasn't much to support the argument but if Che could confirm the way the events unfolded, it might be plausible. "The man burst in through the door, the broken glass tells the tale of intent to do harm and in his hurried state, simply lost his footing as he approached the chair. The skid marks that you would assume would have been there are non-existent, the follicles acting like ball bearings. In the fall, he hit his head."

The three of them looked as the old detective suggested the alibi. Then he added, "Your girlfriend," and as he said that, he extended his hand to Che, "John Bates." He took her hand daintily in his, a remnant of his upbringing several generations removed. She allowed her hand to partially slip into his. "She'll just have to say that it happened too quickly to register. The police will reconstruct the scene with the element of surprise factored in and they won't be doing a lot of cross-examinations. It was clearly rage gone bad. Perhaps he was some drug-addled bloke without a home. I've seen them howling at the streetlights of your city, or panhandling in a very assertive manner. Beggars can be a bit more couth" He seemed satisfied with the explanation. He then turned to Santo.

Nick asked an uncharacteristically civilian question: "How will they know it was rage?"

"Not the first time down this path, eh Mr. Aretino?"

Bates said ignoring Nick. He didn't expect any answer to his question. But he did expect the statement phrased as a question to register. Santo simply returned a look of confusion.

"Which path are you referring to, Mr. Bates?"

Before Bates could answer, Nick asked, "So now that we know what happened, I still have to call the cops." He looked at Bates for affirmation but he looked at Che.

"Depends on the lady's opinion." He looked at Che. "It will protect everyone here from needless inquiry and instead shift the focus of the investigation on the dead man. You didn't know him." He turned to look at Santo. "And we know you don't know him. We arrived after-the-fact. There's no weapon and no obvious motive. Yes. Call the police."

The police did a quick assessment of the situation and it all seemed to align with how Bates suggested it might. Santo had asked that the press be excluded until they were done with him. They extended that courtesy and took his information. It would appear in the record and the press would report it. They would ask about the time of the death and whether the fact that the richest man in the city preferred to have his hair trimmed after hours was something they should just ignore. It was the first time Santo's name appeared 'on-the-record'.

He paid his bill and tipped Che extravagantly. He thanked Bates for what was surely, at least in the old man's eyes, a wink-wink arrangement. Nick however pulled Santo close in when they shook hands.

"You owe me an interview." His voice had regain its composure, shifting from the frightened boyfriend to the more forceful, seasoned reporter, surprising himself with its unfamiliar strength of tone.

"I would be more than happy to speak with you, Nick. But I don't owe you anything."

21

T he assistant opened the door quietly and stood waiting to be acknowledged. When Marley turned, she reminded her of the interview.

"Can you wait here?" she asked Arianne. "This should only take fifteen minutes or so." She stood straightening her skirt. She was the image of contented wealth, earned with her savvy and expertise even as the firm's investment choices were guided by her husband. His powers of selection had seemed mystical in the early years of their relationship. His ability to predict where markets were going to move put their enterprise on the right side of trade after trade. This did not go unnoticed by other traders and their muttering attracted the requests for interviews by all of the business channels. This interest was not greatly accelerated after the 'talk'.

The firm they created centered on the ability of Santo to move enormous profits to philanthropic endeavors. Wealthy investors soon prodded the firm, the face of which was the beautiful woman standing before her, to open a hedge fund. They eventually decided to offer a scheme, albeit reluctantly, charging the usual 20/2 agreement that had become the industry standard. The fee, two percent of the total assets under management and twenty percent of the profit earned was willingly accepted by investors who seized on the opportunity to invest with this young legend. These fees, as were all but 20% of any profit from any SA Holding endeavor were channeled back into the funding of the company's special projects.

The firm's reputation grew further as the SMA Special Interest Hedge Fund swelled with investors and profits, beating the market in all but six quarters since its inception. The clever arrangement allowed Santo via Marley to take an activist role on eighteen corporate boards, herding them gently into a sustainable outlook for their companies.

"We'll go back to the house when I'm done and see Sonny." She stepped closer to Arianne, who stood to meet her approach. Marley hugged her. "I am so glad to have finally met you." Her embrace was both firm and reaffirming.

Marley had given four of these interviews since her husband gave his speech. Two of them had been done remotely and one was conducted by a local public broadcasting station on behalf of their network. These were quick and because of network time constraints, succinct. She had little offer in the way of new information about the company, allowing the interviewer to merely peek behind the curtain without ever meeting the actual wizard, but they asked nonetheless.

They were not a publicly traded company, so she could have hidden behind that lack of obligation to the world at large. It would have been easy to do so. However, almost as if he wished he were discovered, Santo had urged her to meet with a select few outlets and give them the courtesy of the interview. He imagined that every journalist once asked the why-is-the-sky-blue question and although that curiosity could have taken them into science or some other field where questions are part of the process, they instead became enamored with doings of people, famous, not-so-famous, the human existence that was waiting to be discovered. He had reasoned with her, "That if you give them some answers, it is better than hiding without ever answering any."

"It's different now, my reclusive celebrity. They want

more. You've chummed the water and now you think it won't attract every fish in the sea?"

"Chummed the water?" There was a brief moment of levity as she considered her own choice of words. They laughed, that warm intimate exchange that they shared, the running joke that would last for days, or weeks, as they ironically poked the phrase into wildly different situations.

While he argued that he had done the speech at her urging, he could respect the fact that it was she, and not him, thrust into the limelight. "So, how can you refuse this small request?" he asked with an infectious smile that eliminated any refusal on her part.

The interviewer from Bloomberg had cut her west coast vacation short at the behest of her producers. She did, after all, get the first glimpses of the reclusive billionaire mowing is own lawn, even if they didn't realize what they had at the time.

Ai stood when Marley entered the room. She was made even taller and more statuesque by the heels she was wearing. She and a lone cameraman had been waiting in a room usually used for in-house corporate conference calls. Marley sat at an angle so as to facilitate both women in the shot.

Aside from the regularly scheduled Tuesday call, the room was mostly unused. It had an understated elegance much like the room she had taken her application test at Morgan Stanley all those years ago. The video conferencing equipment was still arranged on the table, which normally allowed employees and investors to participate, although most remained quiet, as they listened around the world to Marley offer the latest direction for the firm.

Ai introduced herself to the camera, flashing a brilliant smile across her Asian features. "It has been a couple of months since we interviewed Marley Cornish, the CEO of SA Holdings and the M in SMA Special Interest Hedge Fund, the wildly successful hedge fund that can boast that it was the first green fund, the first activist fund focused on creating a more sustainable world, and the only hedge fund that I am aware of that charges the standard rate for the service but channels those funds back into philanthropic endeavors." She turned to Marley who was facing the stationary camera just over Ai's shoulder. "Thank you so much for meeting with us again, Marley."

"It's my pleasure," she responded and the interview was under way. During the previous interview, Ai had done a yeoman's job trying to get Marley to reveal some of the secrets to her firm's investing outlook. Her station's viewers, comprised largely of the investor class, a hungry audience that traded based on subtle nuances in verbiage and the often-veiled suggestions opined from the expertise of the guests they hosted. Economists, former and current government officials, various senior analysts from the major Wall Street firms, and hedge fund managers all made their way to the viewers during the course of the trading day. Ai being among the highest ranked in terms of raw ratings was the go-to interviewer for this story.

The commentary from the various network and cable channel talk show hosts and their guests following Santo's unusual appearance did lose its newsworthy traction in about a week, lengthy by some standards. Most of the investment people were uncomfortable with an outsider three thousand miles removed from the canyons of money where they worked and basically discounted the returns the fund posted as potentially Ponzi-like in nature. One actually mentioned Bernie Madoff by name, suggesting that it was impossible to beat the market as consistently as the fund had.

The variety of hosts at the station on both the television and radio fed the criticisms and by doing so, increased the curiosity of investors. Twitter was alive with the hashtag

#unbelievableprofits and although it was difficult to criticize the numbers it was easier to judge the methodology in the minimum amount of characters. Ai was here to channel those questions into fifteen minutes, much of which Marley knew would involve careful editing to just under three minutes before airtime.

"We all know now that the person behind the person sitting with me is your husband, Santo Aretino. What we don't know is who he really is. The questions that have surfaced since that unusual presentation – can I say theatrics?" she asked with a toothy smile. She continued without waiting for a response. Marley was doing her best to keep her expression steady and pleasant. She shrugged instead, with a slight side nod of her head.

She responded, "Theatrics is a good word, no pun intended."

Ai smiled and made a mental note to reference that comment as a reference to the talk her husband had given. It still had not surfaced on YouTube, but she expected it would, in its entirety soon. "We can all respect a person's right to privacy but the ability to protect that privacy in this day and age is quite remarkable. Especially when considering the high profile nature of what your firm does."

Marley was unsure whether that was a question and Ai's slight pause hinted that it might have been. "My husband doesn't or should I say, didn't begin trying to hide. He's got one of the brains that is tireless – I think the word is indefatigable - and he found out early on, long before I met him, that he had numerous talents that didn't rely on inputting his human interaction to the world. Did he do what he did on the backs of other human reactions? Sure. Did he parse the available news in a different manner than the rest of the investment world? His record would suggest agreement with that assessment. Does he care what the rest of the world says? Yes and no. As much as he loves technology, he has purposely avoided social media. If you think about it, he wasn't so much hiding as he was shielding himself from the noise."

"You have to admit that being a recluse raises questions. Mostly why? Or what's he hiding from? And not just noise."

"They would be good questions I suppose but the answer is the same for both: Nothing. He's just a normal guy with a restless spirit and thankfully, at least to the thousands of people that have benefited from his intense focus, this has been the key to his success. There are many other people in the world just like him. Renaissance men without a court might be a way of looking at them. A polymath of enviable talent. My husband became his own court and when that became profitable, he opened up his success to those individuals. It's kind of like taking that expression "If I only had a moment to think" and turning it into a full time event."

The interview hit a wall after that. Questions about investment direction were answered by "We don't discuss that, sorry." Views on the economy – "We don't follow the economy, we try and reshape it" – or about the global condition – "We focus on exceptional companies doing business in the U.S. primarily" – or the Federal Reserve Bank's next move – "Doesn't impact our methodology" – or about currencies or commodities – "While those trends do play a role in our investment decision, the percentage in which they do is minimal" – began to frustrate the normally affable interviewer.

"I'm sorry, Ai that I don't have more," Marley offered empathetically. She liked Ai and her savvy, on-air persona. She offered a crisp review of her topics that was both reserved and even-toned. "Our company thrives on the trickle-down effect and not the crap-rolls-down-hill attitude of those with money. We service the people who are usually left with the crumbs and not by scraping the plates of the princes, and princesses that rule Wall Street. We don't make money on the backs of people; we help people carry the loads they have been given.

"Your viewers and this is not meant as a criticism, should begin thinking of the so-called 'little people' before or as they make their millions and billions and not as an after-effect of their wealth accumulation. I do think it is great and noble of these really successful investors giving away their vast wealth or promising to do so, after they made it. In my mind and in Santo's opinion, it still seems a lot like throwing a life preserver to a person too weak from the effort at trying to save themselves to do any good. Seems counterintuitive to throw someone overboard only to attempt to rescue them."

Ai smiled and sighed. "Will we ever get to interview Santo?"

"I'll ask him. I will," she added quickly. "But I suspect that your chances will be slim to none. It was my idea that he address that crowd, and not because our firm received the Hilton award, which we were very thankful to have accepted and regretfully declined, or because social media seemed to push him towards that one appearance. It managed to appease while at the same time not really revealing anything. But I'll ask. I promise."

Ai seemed disappointed when the cameras were turned off. "Thanks, Marley. I do appreciate your time but really, I was hoping for more." She knew it was the kind of interview that would spur more speculation, industry condescension and more than ample professional jealousy. When the piece aired, it would be accompanied by the comment from the person at Goldman Sachs who had mentioned the potential of a nefarious scheme. The producers decided to bring him pack to opine on the interview.

As Marley made her way back to her office, she called Santo.

He answered on this second ring. "Hey honey," he said, his voice sounding hushed. "I can't talk right now. The police are wrapping up their inquiries."

"Police?" she said too loudly, looking around her quickly to see who may have heard her. "What the fuck, Sonny?"

"It's nothing really. I was getting my haircut and there was an accident. I'm okay," he quickly added. "It wasn't me. Can I tell you all about it later?"

The answer was not sufficient to satisfy her immediate concern. Santo was off the reservation and somewhere in the public domain. And the public domain had dragged him into one of its dramas. She took a deep breath and agreed to hear the details later.

"I've got a friend of yours here at the office and I wanted to bring her back to the house."

Santo almost replied that he had no friends but instead said, "Her?"

"Yes. Arianne is here, Sonny. Get home as soon as you can. Do you need my help?"

Arianne is here was all he really heard.

*****

The police had been satisfied with the initial investigation. As farfetched as it sounded, it made sense. The dead man had a long history of violence with numerous arrests for assault and more than handful of calls related to domestic violence. Another officer had been dispatched to the man's house where they found a badly beaten spouse. Her first question was about the welfare of her hairdresser. Rochelle was taken to the hospital but was not told that her abusive husband was no longer capable of continuing his marital torture.

Before the police released the Santo and Che, they

instructed both of them to feel free to contact them should they remember anything that would help. Nick, who was visibly angered by the attempt on his girlfriend, seemed less than satisfied at the abbreviated investigation. Although they had agreed to the story, he was hoping that someone would question it with more enthusiasm. He knew the man who had meet his demise was guilty of his crimes, both past and present, but the police seemed unwilling to make any additional assumptions.

John Bates finally had found a moment to speak to Santo just out of earshot of crowd. "I was wondering," he began, surveying the group mulling about the shop, not looking at Santo, "do you wear an amulet of sorts about your neck, Mr. Aretino?"

Santo turned to look at the man in astonishment. He had mentioned the gift he had received from Eva during his speech but made no reference to actually wearing it.

"You know, the 1926 nickel. Do you wear it around your neck?" Repeating the question didn't lessen the implied nature of the query.

"I do. It was a gift." Santo wanted to ask the most obvious next question but refrained from doing so. He assumed that Bates had been in the audience. But he didn't reference how he wore it, if at all. The speech he had given was written over three decades and during that time, he had only followed the guidance in the gift, paying little attention to the coin hanging around his neck.

"The reason I mention it, Mr. Aretino," Bates said leaning in closer, "is because that coin hanging from someone's neck, not saying it was yours mind you, was mentioned in a series of similar situations, just like this one, you know, someone swoops in a saves a poor soul and in the process, rids the world of riff raff, a lot like that poor bloke." Santo didn't respond to this. Bates wasn't necessarily expecting an admission of guilt or even a denial of involvement. He was counting on facial expressions to tell the story. But Santo didn't react. He couldn't. He had no idea what the man was referring to or why he had chosen this moment to make such a broad-sweeping accusation.

"I ask," he finally said, "because you were passing through many of the places where these, shall I say, crimes occurred. I mean, what are the odds that your coin was mentioned in other places?"

"If you are asking me to calculate the odds that I was where you think I was thirty years removed, that is possible. I like math well enough that trying to figure that out might be fun, like a rainy afternoon project. But I am more curious, before I bring pencil to paper, is what makes you think there is even a reasonable chance you are right?"

"Because the nickel around your neck made it into the police reports," he whispered. "Granted, there was never any real effort to track that particular person of interest because no one actually attempted to prosecute the crime. Kind of like here, Mr. Aretino. Seems our civic prince in those cases also eliminated a bigger problem for the local law enforcement. So they just sort of let the case go cold. Like this one I suspect."

Bates found the course of this conversation unsettling. A normally guilty man, caught after years, reminded of crimes committed in the past, would struggle to recall what had happened and maybe even get a little defensive. Memories, whether hidden in some deep recess or recently experienced would prompt certain mental efforts to recall and reconsider and in the process create a facial strain that was unique to the process. If it had been him, questioned by a stranger, making vague accusation, he'd of told them to fuck off. But Santo was much calmer than he thought he should have been. Was this the sort of man who felt as though whatever happened was justified?

"And you think that the nickel I'm wearing made an appearance at, how many crimes?"

"I have to apologize. That was kind of forward of me and certainly unprofessional. I retired years ago and when your name crossed my radar, I thought I'd put my cold case to rest, long after the client who hired me fired me. Hell, I don't even think the bastard is still alive. His kid is though."

That caused a reaction. "You had a client?"

"Did I not mention that I was a private investigator? I apologize again. Yes, I had a client." Bates actually smiled at the prospect that he had finally set the hook. Now he needed to be careful.

"I am certain that the whole story is quite fascinating and this little give and take must be amusing to one of us. Do I want to know what you were doing or even who hired you? Not really. Do I want to know what lured you out of retirement to come and find me? No to that as well." His look had gone from calm to steel, and Bates felt an uncharacteristic chill. He had operated from a distance, a witness to the evil in people's hearts, snapping pictures, taking notes, and delivering the results of those observations to the person or persons who hired him. He was a shadow and like a shadow, he was spineless when confronted with his profession. On the few occasions where his quarry had confronted him, Bates visibly shivered with fear. He was good at looking at people, not confronting them.

The question Bates had asked was spontaneous and the result of an opportunity that put the two of them in the same room. That opportunity was quickly dissipating as the investigation surrounding them seemed to be coming to a close. In hindsight, he began to wonder what he had hoped to accomplish by that conversation. But he was convinced, based on nothing but a gut feeling that Santo was there, and probably in many more situations over that time. No one is a total recluse. Nobody just disappears.

The officer approached the two of them and thanked them for their patience. He gave them both a business card, although he was speaking directly to Santo. He promised to call him if he remembered anything.

Santo walked over to Che and gave her a hundred-dollar bill. She balked saying that she wasn't finished. "Maybe you can come out to the house. I'll send a car. I just think it might be safer."

"I'd like to think that this was an isolated incident. God, I hope it is." God had little to do with this, Santo thought. He smiled at her and turned to leave. "Come next week and bring your reporter boyfriend. We'll get this all sorted out and hopefully put to bed."

*****

Marley and Arianne crawled into the back seat of the black Escalade. They rode in silence as they exited the streets of downtown Portland. Arianne was struck by the amount of people on the sidewalk at this hour. She felt like a foreigner witnessing a strange American ritual. Thirty years on the road, traveling the world in what she would call a failed pursuit, had made her reentry into her own country unsettling. It was from this soil she had left, blaming her surroundings for her ennui. She had not once considered traveling the United States in search of her personal ghost.

"It isn't raining," Marley commented as the wound their way through traffic. "We're very dense these days and I suppose many of these people are not relishing the idea of being cramped up in their closet sized studios once the rainy season starts, so they get out and mill about while they have a chance. It'll rain before long and they will all act as if it wasn't there. Portlanders don't carry umbrellas."

"I suppose that's as good a reason as any." The car exited

the downtown and began heading south towards the small estate she and Santo had shared like an island, an isolated piece of paradise that he called Acri di Verde. This made Arianne laugh when she heard the term.

"Green Acres? Really?" So much of the time she had spent with Santo as a youth had been full of these dry observations on the life around him. Never were they sarcastic in nature. Instead, what made her smile was the way he connected those people and events to something he had read, as if everything that happened occurred first in the mind of a writer and later mimicked by the world. His voracious appetite for the written word was unlike hers: he was the kind of reader that followed a thread to its conclusion. It was from this research, and that is what he called it when referencing it, that he drew his reasoning for why people acted as they did. The problem she had with these conversations was not in the results of these laconic observations but the way he drew them. He couldn't physically interact with the very people he was observing. It was as if he allowed the impressions they left as they moved through life, much like the characters in the books he read, to form the whole being. Although he was probably right more than wrong, it was still a semi-formed reality. He was, she knew, one step removed from the whole truth about the world around him. It was even possibly the same reason they had chosen different paths in an effort to retreat from those realities, he fled into himself while she attempted to escape what she was and immerse herself in the strangeness of foreign surroundings.

"I was wondering," Marley began, drawing Arianne back into the car and away from her thoughts. She turned away from her reflection on the car window, now wet with the drops of rain moving sideways, turning the streetlights into prisms. "You mentioned so many experiences in your letters but the people you encountered all seem so one-dimensional. Like you kept them at arm's distance."

Arianne sighed. "That's a tough question to answer. Maybe I'm incapable of seeing too deeply into who people are. I discovered that your company is working with the governments of the countries with still secret populations of aboriginal people who haven't been tainted by the world at large."

"That's true. We do work with some friendly agency looking to protect a way of life."

"So, you already know about the indigenous people in the Amazon hide with good reason. Not because they don't know we exist. They hide because we will kill them with disease or weapons beyond their comprehension. They know we're out there, the beats on the horizon and they can't see any reason to interact. Maybe that's me. Maybe I know they're out there, people who are three dimensional, but I seem to lack the skill set to see them. Or I think they will ruin me."

"Santo's work, or I mean, our company's efforts made Peru acknowledge these people even existed." Marley answered this like it was a bullet point in a presentation. "And they only reason they did is because we agreed to fund protective outposts to put a barrier between poachers who come in a steal lumber and oil and of course, the drug lords. And that was only after Brazil accepted out help." She paused for a moment. "What's that got to do with you?"

"The same thing it has to do with Santo I suppose. I haven't been in touch with your husband in over thirty years and in the brief time with you, hearing that speech, I realize that he hasn't changed. He's as isolated as they are. As he's always been. And I've come to accept the fact that I'm as isolated as well."

Are these the people Santo is attracted to? Marley thought. People who had operated on the fringes of what the world considers normal often felt as though they had an unexplained purpose in life but were pushed to the edges of society. She was like that when she met him, single-minded and young, working in a man's world when he entered it. She asked herself, "Was she still like that?" His aloof nature had attracted her but listening to Arianne she wondered if his isolation was the real attraction. Was he a kindred spirit of sorts, a man who was unfazed, or as she came to find out, clueless of how people acted or thought? Was that who she was?

As she listened to his talk over the years, mined his passions and untethered herself to soar with his relentless enthusiasm, she wondered how he had come to this place in his life. Thirty-five years later, she felt as though there was still so much more to know about him. But they joked about this chasm suggesting playfully to each other the "You don't know nothing about me" to which she would reply with the same phrase. She knew his quirks, what made him laugh and how he thought most of the time. He was brutally honest and at the same time, beautifully considerate of those opinions. She knew that he shared those parts of him with no one but her, and this made her feel privileged. But she also now knew he once shared those thoughts with Arianne and he had impacted her in the same way.

*****

"Fuck. Fuck. Fuck." He said under his breath as he sat behind the wheel of his car. He had left the barber shop and had hoped to walk away unnoticed. He had parked his British green MG BGT about a block away and walked to Che's shop. The coroner's wagon and most of the police vehicles had left. The crime scene tape however remained and the street was still blocked off. He was stopped by a reporter for the local Fox affiliate and asked if he knew anything he'd like to share. He declined but the young reporter and her cameraman followed him for a half-block. Finally he stopped.

She excitedly asked him for his name. Santo ignored her.

"I was waiting to get my hair cut when it all happened. Sorry. Barely had time to look up from my magazine before it was over. But the cops kept me around as if I didn't have anything better to do." He quickly added, "I would really appreciate it if you didn't air this," knowing full well that they would. It was the television station that always seemed to air people who had not seen anything and that significantly increased the chances that his face and comments would make the first broadcast of the evening.

He was unused to his life being guided by another person's plan or intentions. The kid with the turtle, the award he didn't want and now, being at the scene of a crime, one he had an active hand in and as a result, was a witness to. He was certain Che wouldn't say anything. He was uncertain about the motives of the other man with the coffee breath. And Che's boyfriend seemed tenacious, the kind that was restless, not impatient; just possessing a kind of anxiousness brought on by an active imagination and the resourcefulness to ferret out answers. He knew that theories were built on active imaginations and Nick seemed like he was developing several of his own. He had arrived with the private detective and that suggested they were together at some point. Did the old man use the same common sense deductions to tell his story to Nick?

As he drove back, he wondered if Nick understood the scope of what he had become involved in. Santo had found that people rarely, if ever, saw far enough downstream to understand the unintended consequences of every action. Seasoned reporters tended to have a concept of what their job was. They understood that their job was to report what they found and not aggrandize the situation. But Nick might be too young to take such a mature position. Social media had wrapped itself into the local news that made it hard to report quality over quantity. He felt bad for news organizations. The current trend had created the concept of I-reporters, forcing editors to sift through volumes of information that five years ago would not have even been brought to their attention.

When he arrived at the house, he took a hard right as he entered. When they had purchased the fifteen-acre property, he had a perimeter road paved, winding it through the trees, over hills and hummocks and eventually on to a straightway. Towards the end, it opened to a pit stop-like exit that ended at the back of the garage. He shifted the car hard and brought the car around the bend with careful control of the soft rear end this model was known for. He used this road to think when running on it was not enough.

*****

Marley handed Arianne a glass of red wine and told her to make herself comfortable. She wondered around the great room wondering what possessions belonged to Santo and what his wife's. It was tastefully decorated without giving the feeling that it was done by a stranger. It also suggested that they had no guests, or if they did, were not attempting to impress upon them their elevated financial status in life.

From the corner of her eye, she caught the headlights in the distance, blinking in some cryptic Morse code as the trees blocked her view.

"Sonny's home," Marley said walking back into the room in jeans and sweater, carrying her own glass of wine. "He must be thinking about something. He never takes that road unless he's deep in thought, which, if you knew him like I do, means really deep." This made her laugh. The car disappeared around the next rise.

"I get what you were saying. I'm like his outpost." Marley had dwelled on Arianne's description of indigenous peoples half a world away. They wanted to be left alone, using the resources they had used for generations, perhaps millenniums, and the world beyond their encampments had swelled to the point where the land they had cherished became valuable in more than as just a way of life. Civilization wanted what was buried in it, growing on it, living because of it or worse, in the way of things the world wanted.

An outpost was supposed to fend off intruders, the unwanted marauders and the curiosity seekers, those who meant to do harm or intended to, or simply the poachers. Marley acted like his buffer, his protector and in return, he imprisoned himself to make the effort easier. Without the distractions that everyone on the planet seemed to have, Santo thrived and when he thrived, the world at large benefited.

Arianne had found her role in life was defined by her observational skills, her ability to parse the world around her into two basic elemental situations: Happy or not. She embraced the Chinese version of happy believing it to be a person's Fu, or all of the elements of longevity, wealth, health, virtue, and lastly, living those days well was what defined a person who was truly happy. As she traveled, she took both of these descriptions into account, looking for happy while grappling with the frequency of when she was not.

She found that the more rural people were, the more content they seemed. She only deduced this from watching them work, eat, and interact with each other. Language barriers prohibited her from delving into their true feelings, but she suspected that if she had, she would have found they were mostly happy. Mostly. Urban dwellers seemed less so and the older the city, the more the toil of surviving impacted the way they smiled. They did smile, for the most part, and she had noted and often added these wry observations in her letters, but they only seemed mostly happy. It was no different in France, Spain, northern Africa, the Middle East or even behind the Iron Curtain countries: To her, everyone seemed happier than her.

She had at one point considered her life a bad

comparison. She had, in her opinion, made a mess of what might have been a happy life. She divorced a man without giving her marriage and the potential of the relationship to thrive. Her husband had been a catholic as she need him to be, perhaps more than he desired, but the effort to get him to that point had emotionally drained her. His diversification seemed to always be a struggle for him, even as she drifted through life, seemingly happy. When she realized that it was she who was the charade, leaving seemed the right thing to do. Her husband didn't fight her decision.

Her father's quickly downward spiraling health and eventual passing only aided her decision to leave. Untethered in a world devoid of Santo Aretino was unbearable. She had not expected that. It wasn't the sex, although the one time they had slept together, he had scared her with his quiet passion, his almost uncanny sensuality, and his transcendent attitude to the world around him. His ability to remain calm when confronted with the unknown left her feeling inadequate and humbled. It was only her living with herself. The urge to run seemed the only viable option.

And now the man who entered the room, kissed his wife, not once but three times, looked like a slightly more tanned version of the boy/man she had known briefly and had obsessed over was now within arm's length. The sight of him after three decades made her audibly gasp. He had grown into a rugged handsomeness that could only come from the active pursuit of what a person enjoys.

Arianne stood waiting patiently, almost wishing she hadn't come. He hadn't aged and his smile was even more vibrant and welcoming than she had remembered. He released his wife and turned to her. As he hugged her, she fell deeply and familiarly into his embrace. He allowed her. He pulled back for a moment and held her by her shoulders.

"You haven't changed a bit," he said. She could see that

he was not lying. In fact, if he was more or less the same man she knew all those years removed, he was incapable of doing so. He told the brutal and honest truth when asked and often wore it as his default expression. If the situation was better suited to silence, he would simply remain that way, without any reaction. She had told him once that his silence was a kind of falsehood. But he had disagreed suggesting that people talked too much and because of that they began inventing things to say. By not saying anything, or worse, by refusing to answer the question, he was giving the other side of the conversation the ability to seek its own truth, like finding water in a desert.

She didn't argue with him as much as she would have liked. Time and travel had waged a piecemeal war on her, weathering her skin and greying her hair and in some respects, dulling the luminescence that once accentuated her eyes. But the man before her had experienced no such travails. She turned to Marley and said, "Don't you just hate the way they stay the same and never age?"

"Hate is not strong enough of a word." This made both women laugh. Marley said she was going to get her husband a drink and walked over to a bar in the corner of the room.

Santo led her to a large sofa facing the window. The lawn sloped gently into a tall stand of trees that hid his personal racetrack. He was proud of that lawn and mowed it with golf course accuracy. Marley could never be certain if it was the mowing or the looking at the completed job or a combination of both that brought him the most satisfaction. She would laugh when he called himself a blade farmer.

"I don't know which question to ask first," he said. Marley handed Arianne another glass of wine and her husband a tumbler of bourbon. He wasn't much of a drinker but she was unsure how Arianne felt about smoking pot. They didn't entertain much, if at all and they were careful not to insult the sensibilities of any guests. She knew her husband would rather have smoked.

"How about we get the reason for me finally tracking you down? It wasn't easy you know." Arianne felt as though she could dispense with the stories of where she had been and why; her letters had told those tales. She felt as though she could explain how she eventually found him and why she made the effort to do it now; she could annotate her tale after the fact. So she began with her father.

Santo listened as her story unfolded, how her father had known his, his father's anguish at the distance he had felt was insurmountable, his unlikely and until that point, unknown origins, how he had been told a lie, albeit a gentle and protective tale for all of those years, how his self-alienation was actually rooted in some truth and lastly, how the isolation he had felt, the lost affection and misplaced attention delivered to his siblings was not his fault. He had not been to blame for not understanding. Instead he had blamed them for not telling him the truth. But that was then and the events that had delivered themselves to him may have been a result of those situations. She was not there to suggest that a moment of that time should have been lived differently.

She had considered adding her own opinions and comments to the tale but decided not to. She knew that he would be distracted by the commentary. So she stripped the version she told him down to a story that was not much more than bullet points, more or less chronological. Santo never reacted as he sat and listened.

A heart beat passed and then another. "That's got to make you feel better," he said.

She turned to Marley. "That should explain something but I have no fucking idea what. And he hopes I feel better." He reached for ornately carved box on the table and removed a neatly rolled joint. After it was lit, he offered it to Arianne first.

She greedily drew on it before handing it to Marley. They didn't speak as the joint made its way around several more times.

"Do you know anything about the person who gave birth to me?" Santo had never been a strong advocate for titles, perhaps because of the illusion that his father and mother had raised him with. He expected that after a certain period of time, he would accept what they did as the only option they had available, victims of their own generation, torn between doing the right thing by their family and the embarrassment of having a son who was a bastard and worse, the offspring of a crime. It would take more than several minutes to parse this news.

"I know that she did take her vows and became a nun but she never spoke again, accepting a cloistered position in the convent near Genoa. When I arrived there at the Santuario di Nostra Signora del Monte, which by the time I had arrived had turned into a sort of hotel, she had long since passed of a sickness. I don't have anything else on her except her name after she took her vows: Rosa Francis. The mother superior said she recalled her name as Teresa prior to that."

Santo and Marley looked at each other and then at their visitor, a semi-mythical creature who only corresponded by mail up until this point, arrived suddenly at a time when their normally tranquil and well-controlled life had suddenly taken a chaotic turn, with news that was both curious and somewhat unwelcome. Arianne watched their reaction and wondered if she should not have bothered. Over the decades, she had wondered what sort of reaction this news would elicit and despite the scenarios she had mentally created, this was not necessarily the choice she had foreseen. She wondered if he would even care.

"How long have you known this?" Santo finally asked after draining his drink.

"I found out shortly after you left, although I had no

idea you had made your exit, or at least not as abruptly. But I hesitated and almost didn't tell you, even after all this time. I wouldn't go so far as to say I knew how it would affect you but I made some assumptions."

At this point Marley spoke, in the role of that protective outpost, the guardian of her treasured resource: "What kind of assumptions?"

Arianne pursed her lips. Her grimace was only part of the answer they were expecting. "I thought about it, a lot, and if it was me, and that was only part of what went into the decision, I would want to know. But then as time passed, I wondered if knowing would change the person I had become. I mean, you can't go back and fix things you had no control over, right? Maybe that's not really why. Maybe I thought you were fine without knowing."

"So you argued with yourself for thirty years about whether or not to tell him?" Marley asked this even though she respected the power of knowledge and the impact it could have, especially if it was the kind of information that might negatively impact a person. "You poor girl," she added even though she knew Arianne was at least ten years her senior.

"When Santo and I saw each other last, I was the one leaving. But in a way, he was already gone. You know how I knew? He seemed to have lost his will to stay. I'd be willing to bet that if I went back to that shithole town, everyone who lived there thirty years ago is still within an hour's driving distance. That's probably a fact. My father used to say that if his grandparents had had another dollar for gas, he'd probably have been born in Jersey." She laughed at that recollection. "Never saw myself as a Jersey girl though."

They both looked at her waiting. "Santo was, how should I say this, on the edge. He was like someone about to make a breakthrough of sorts, a bundle of nerves but it was not as if you could see it. You would have to have known him. He's always been coiled underneath and on the surface, cool as the other side of the pillow."

Santo wondered if that was how Marley saw him as well. He didn't have to wait long for his answer. "When I met Sonny, he came into my life like a fog: One day it was clear and the next minute, I was completely enveloped by him. Or should I say, I threw myself into him without ever thinking otherwise.

"So I kind of know what you mean. You knew that this sort of info might derail that perfection. But you knew he'd eventually want to know so all you had to figure out was when he should know."

Arianne smiled. "Except the longer I waited, the more it became my burden. And then I couldn't really find him, or should I say, Seamus wouldn't tell me where you were. And frankly, I couldn't put that kind of shitty news in a letter."

Marley put her hand on her husband's knee. "You okay?" He gave her a half nod, the kind of distracted acknowledgment he often gave her when she interrupted a thought he was having. It was as if he was being pulled by the activity in his brain and the need to give her his attention. You could almost see the struggle for control of which part him would win: his wife or his brain.

"Yeah," he answered, "kind of sort of. I mean, I didn't treat Umberto or Sofi badly. I wasn't the best of sons, but then again, I wasn't really their son. I was in trouble at school a lot but it was mostly because I wasn't the open vessel that they had hoped I would be. I mean I was a good student, passed all my tests, stayed out of trouble." He stopped at this statement wondering if his perception of what he thought of as good and bad was also shared by those teachers. In his mind, the most disruptive thing he had done was rescue the hapless from the bullies in their lives and often paid for it with disciplinary action. He had not entertained those memories nor had he connected all of the players and their reactions to what they were presented with. Those memories were now surfacing, unedited.

Finally he said, "I think you caused yourself a lot of unnecessary anguish over this Arianne." His voice was smooth and warm, the kind of voice that comes from the other side of a confessional screen. "I have an incredibly tough time looking backwards. Marley knows this all too well. As much as I love, even bath in the thoughts of history, my own record is not something I review, ever."

Arianne's eyes became moist but she was smiling. Marley could see why he had befriended her or vice versa. She was also a lost soul, wandering the globe without any anchor, and yet, she seemed to be engaged in the same trek her husband was living. He hid; she fled. And she imagined that Santo would have probably done the same for her, bearing the burden of empathy, wondering if knowing was worth the emotional repercussions. They were not meant to be together but they seemed kindred to some degree. It wasn't so much the love of isolation as love in isolation. She now knew Arianne had experienced it with her father but not so with her husband. She knew from the brief time they had spent together and the decades of letters she had written, she was emotionally capable of love but incapable of keeping it. And now, knowing the burden she carried with her all of those years, a truth buried within those letters that was now much more clearer to her, the love she had for Santo was the kind of affection a mother has for a child. She was worried about his welfare, the fact that he was wandering the world on his own journey without the opportunity to know what might have been an emotional game changer for the average person.

Santo looked at her curiously. This was the Santo Marley knew: Confused by emotions, the purity of them, the way some people simply melt into the feeling. She was thankful that Arianne had freed herself of the burden but she also was convinced the information would not alter the man her husband had become. Over the years, she had tried to teach him about the emotions that people had, at the same time feeding his isolation and his need for it. It was not a mental illness as it would be in almost every other instance. Instead, it was a gift, a freedom from the burden of believing that there was always more and in some instances, less. He was always open and honest and caring and she knew that it took every ounce of his energy to love her. Teaching him how was her greatest accomplishment, far exceeding the successes of the business. His greatest accomplishment was trying.

She had wondered how someone who was so moral, so ethical could be so devoid of the emotions that surround those qualities. He always did the right thing and although he had told her everything that he chose to remember over the span of their marriage, she knew there were missing segments that would never be found or revealed.

Marley suggested that Arianne spend the night, a first for the household. She had debated taking her back into town but it had grown late.

After their guest was settled in a bedroom that had never been used, a room that Santo had questioned as unnecessary and Marley had insisted on with the 'you-never-know' argument, she turned to him in the soft light of their bedroom and asked: "What happened tonight?"

"I think I got a piece of my past, whether I wanted it or needed it is questionable," he replied as he removed his shirt. She never tired of seeing him in any state of dress or undress. Clothes wrapped themselves around his frame as if they adored him and when he had nothing on his nakedness seemed more natural than anything she had ever witnessed.

"I can't argue with that. You're okay?"

"I suppose," he said sighing deeply. If knowledge had

weight, she could see it as he slightly slumped on the edge of the bed.

"So," and she paused until he looked up at her, "What happened before you got home?" She didn't want to ask the question. Something had happened. She could hear it in his voice when he called. He had not traveled a road in search of the truth about his past, and she had decided long ago to not press him on the topic. That road was now under his feet and she knew he had to make a choice: to continue or to stop too soon.

"I'm not really sure, Marl," he said, softly. He hung his head and repeated himself. She stroked the back of his neck and decided not to press him on the issue.

*****

She had always envied her husband's ability to fall asleep, and even with all of the revelations he had just experienced, the sort that would keep a normal person awake for hours, dwelling on each new event, turning it over and over, examining it from every angle, within seconds of hitting the pillow, he was out, sleeping deeply with slow methodical breaths. It was always a brief sojourn into his nocturnal wilderness, slipping out of bed hours before any indication of dawn.

Marley on the other hand, was doing the heavy lifting for both of them. She watched his sleeping figure next to him and for what seemed like the millionth time in their history, she wondered who he was.

She picked a book on her nightstand hoping that reading would coax her own slumber. Then he spoke. He said Arianne's name.

She replied saying her husband's name. At the time, she felt as though replying was more of a question, wondering if her husband was awake. His voice was almost a whisper. In the deep shadows cast by her reading light, she could see he was asleep and oddly, dreaming He had always thought he was incapable of it but she had experienced it before, the innocence of the strongest man she knew, revealed in the quiet of their bedroom. She felt guilty for listening but she knew he needed this, and although she never told him what he said, the often-disjointed ramblings, all without reason of context, without any meaning or anchored to anything she knew about him were nonetheless fascinating. It was a Santo she didn't know and one he had never told her about.

"Oh good," he said, "You're here." For a moment, she thought he was awake.

"You were dreaming, my love." He didn't answer.

There was a heartbeat of silence before he spoke. "Something did happen today. You were right about that. And I'm not so sure it was the right thing to do. But it felt right." Over the years, decades they had been together, Santo had reviewed every memory he had stored away, discussed it at length with a person he hadn't seen since he made his exit from his hometown. He was telling Arianne his stories in his dreams. The length of these talks she found out depended on how she replied. The conversation was one-sided. And random without any systematic or chronological order. He'd talk about events in snippets: when it happened with the earliest memories recalled with fewer details, and how he felt in the seconds following each event. The more violent the recollection, the fewer the details he would recall, at least initially. But over the course of the nights they shared, he revisited these incidents often acting as if he was confused at the reasons why he was there at all. She never mentioned these dreams when he was awake.

But she wanted to, desperately. She had too many questions to challenge him for specifics. All the years of laughing and enjoying each other, the successes and the baggage that came with those successes and here was the inner man. This was still uncharted territory, a place where he wandered alone, or possibly walking with Arianne. Initially she had felt jealous and then just a bit guilty about what seemed to be unfettered access to his deepest secrets. She stemmed her curiosity and attempted to forego any opinions or questions that would interject her concerns.

She felt guilty about playing the part of the woman who was now sleeping in their guest bedroom. And he responded. When he seemed confused as to why he was on a ranch in Colorado, she asked him if he could identify the season. When he talked about the students at Franklin and Marshall, she asked him if he attended the school. When he talked about his hometown, she asked if he could remember his favorite food. The conversations would have been handled differently had a professional been contacted but this was her husband and she was his outpost against the world.

As she leaned on her elbow watching his silhouette, she realized that these events predated her presence in his life. Once again, wondering if speaking to a dreaming person was healthy, she spoke his name. His brow furrowed. He didn't seem to recognize her voice. Once, early on in their marriage, that delicate time when emotions are still raw and new and untested by any travail, she tried to tell him it was her. She tried to explain to her husband's sleeping self who he was speaking with but he would have nothing to do with it. It made sense: They hadn't met whereas Arianne had already formed a bond with him at a young age.

She found herself getting frustrated at times, overcome by curiosity and exhaustion. He ignored the tone of her voice and continued speaking about incidents he encountered. A pattern emerged on two fronts: Most of his words were delivered in a matter-of-fact tone reminiscent of an evening broadcast, void of too many specifics, hitting only bullet points. and almost every memory, if that was indeed what they were, violence seemed to dominate the situation. He spoke about his reaction to people who sought to use their strength to lord over the weak but it was in hindsight that took place only moments after the fact, not three decades removed. The stories came out in no particular pattern.

Santo slowly revealed a boy who became man far too soon. As he spoke, she gradually established a chronology of events. He had become the man he was today, a person who had become the protector of the vulnerable at a very early age. He told her, or the Arianne of his dreams, of grade school encounters, often bloody that carried over into his high school years. He discussed how the adults around him at the time reacted, including Umberto and Sofi, a police officer named Tell, and another person referred to as Brother Connors. He had never mentioned these people during his waking hours, but on these particular nights, they commanded recourse. As he spoke to Marley, assuming the role of Arianne, he sought to find the reason why his parents were distant, why the police had focused so much attention on him, and if his ability to remove bullies from the halls of his high school seemed so right, why the person that she eventually came to understand was the Dean of Discipline sought to suggest otherwise.

His conversations with Arianne continued well beyond the time they actually spent together. In these conversations, her husband became increasingly more violent. By her count, there were at least four dead bodies strewn across the country and host of others he had left seriously maimed. His nocturnal confession did not come with any request for forgiveness. Instead, he always, often sounding resigned, assumed that he had been where he needed to be and took the only option the situation had presented.

And then it stopped, abruptly. She wasn't sure whether he had purged himself and was mentally satisfied with the exercise or something else. Tonight's mental visitation, perhaps spurned on by their visitor, was over. His breathing became even as the tone of his slumber seemed to signal an end to this personal review.

The man she had never questioned about where he came from, the man who insisted he had appeared in her life complete, had, as in so many instances before, offered the answers. She realized that the life he was living with her for the last three decades, a marriage that was storybook perfect, had provided him with the hiding place he needed. It was easier, she now realized, for him to insulate himself from the world rather than to try and enter it. His confessional suggested she was complicit in hiding a fugitive, if they were true. Was this why his only forays into the world at large were quick jaunts on the private jet to sites where his philanthropic work was actually in place? It might be an archeological dig or a soup kitchen. But it was always in and out, almost unnoticed and certainly without fanfare of any kind. Was he aware of the tenuous nature of his freedom? She knew Santo would find a nondescript car and drive from the plane alone to his destination. Did he consciously acknowledge the risk of being in the public domain? Was it because he knew it was a risk? What was she supposed to do with this information that felt more like a theft, or worse an intrusion than a shared revelation?

She had cared enough to listen to those ramblings in an attempt to help him with an issue he didn't know he had. He knew that she had forfeited hours of sleep in that effort and when it was done, she was unsure what she had uncovered. The Sonny she knew was the Sonny in his dreams and aside from the details, she didn't feel as though she was sleeping with a stranger. In fact, she felt closer to him despite the fact he had never told her anything about his past.

Then, suddenly, her sleeping husband spoke again. "Let's

put it this way: The cops don't think I did anything."

"Did you?" she asked.

"There was a dead guy."

*****

John Bates waited until Nick and Che exited the building. Nick had grown tired of the man. The evening's events had collapsed any of his curiosity into a heap that he no longer had the energy to untangle and Bates was offering no clue on how to untie this Gordian knot that Santo Aretino seemed to be. His girlfriend had nearly met her maker and the man whom he had been assigned to research, to uncover the truth behind the mysterious billionaire's past had suddenly become someone he was forever indebted to. He didn't believe Che's story but also did not contradict the telling of it. She was safe and he was happy for that.

He stepped from the shadows of a doorway, startling them.

"Jesus fucking Christ, John. Really?" He asked this with more than a little outrage in his voice. Che hadn't even noticed him and when he stepped out, she barely reacted. It was to be expected he thought. She had witnessed a man getting murdered and this was not an event anyone should have seen. The reaction to such an event should have given her a heightened sense of fear, but in her case, she withdrew.

"Sorry," he replied but without conviction. "What are we going to do about this, Nick? We both know that he didn't slip. We both know what happened."

At this point, Che looked up. Nick had not introduced the man he arrived with during all of the confusion. She stepped right up to him and quietly said to the man who was still very much a stranger: "Nothing. We, you, Nick, we're not doing a fucking thing. I'm standing here because of that one man and there is no way I'm changing my story because, that is the way I said it happened. Period."

They both began to walk away from the man who was a stranger to Nick less than eight hours ago and less than that for Che. He yelled to the couple, "What about your journalistic ethics and integrity? What about Zoti?" He saw Nick lean into Che's ear and walked slowly back to the man.

"I haven't been doing this as long as I would have liked to, Mr. Bates, but it has been my life's calling." His voice was metered and emotionless. "And I'll admit that this is the first time a story I was working on landed right in my lap because it was too close to avid." He leaned into Bates slightly but the man stood still, his eyes locked to the young reporter. "So, I may not have all of the, what did you say, ethics and integrity that someone much more seasoned has but, that said, I have enough to know the difference between a story about a man who has hidden more than one mystery about himself from the public and the public's right to know what that mystery is. I will say, no one else seemed to give a flying fuck about Aretino enough to pursue the questions they may have had. So why should I?

"The man lying on that barber shop floor was not a good man and judging from what we know about him now, no one will care much that he's gone. His contribution to the greater world was to give some way to measure the evil in the world, like, I suspect, the people you suggest were maimed or murdered by our reclusive criminal, your guilty-until-proven-innocent quarry. And even that doesn't seem to fit."

They were now standing almost nose to nose. "It's the stuff of comic books, a Commissioner Gordon versus Batman. But it's not. So we're going to leave it where it is and move on. I'll still have to write my piece but since this whole thing happened, and a fortuitous meeting with the man, might result in allowing me to gain better access. But to what end,

Bates? I'm not writing a piece for a check stand tabloid."

The two stood silently considering their options. Bates had the answers he sought, at least enough to prove that the enigma that is Santo Aretino was less so.

"Now let's just part ways, Mr. Bates," Nick said softly. "I've got a pretty rattled girlfriend over there who needs her wounds licked, and that isn't going to happen while we're talking about something I don't want to talk about any more."

EPILOGUE

It began: *If you are inclined to allow the suspension of belief for just one moment, if you get swept up in the mysterious billionaire philanthropist fantasy who has befuddled fellow investors for decades with his extraordinary talent in the stock market, a man who has hidden away in the fashion of Howard Hughes, running an empire worth billions through the auspices of his equally talented wife, Marley Cornish, you can stop right here. Once you embrace a shred of doubt about his elevated status, even as he has shunned such accolades, the illusion quickly crumbles.*

But for those of you who share an unspoken skepticism, where the criticism of people who actually do good things in this chaotic world, where questioning those that genuinely help people and their environment, while protecting national treasures and cultivating young entrepreneurs who share a similar vision, you might feel, for lack of a better word, unpatriotic. Santo Aretino is a national treasure that we have only just discovered, even as he has operated in what seemed like plain sight. Such a treasure requires verification and in doing so, establishing authenticity and provenance.

And so the article titled "Saint Aretino" began. It was Zoti's idea to use the play on Santo's name and strongly suggested the text that had the job of luring readers to venture on between the pages. It wasn't necessary. The special edition's subject was leaked and the social media feedback suggested that the Portland Riverfront Weekly make a plan on producing additional copies. It was a boon for the advertisers who had already paid their fees to the free paper. It would turn out to be most widely circulated copy in the paper's history. The New York Times and Wall Street Journal would request reprint rights.

The cover pictured a shadowy man in a trench coat standing at the gates of an equally shadowy representation of Wall Street. This set the stage to the lead question: "Can this be the place where good is born?" The hope was to offer the possibility that the reader could peak inside a world they knew little about, perhaps gleaning some sort of investment know-how seemingly gifted upon a man who never told anyone how his system works. It had been dissected, modeled by the quantitative analysts, fed into computers, examined at length by math wonks at MIT, mimicked by other investors and investigated by the SEC. But the article's author, Nick Heath would quickly divert these readers from making those assumptions by issuing the following disclaimer: *I profess to know nothing about business or the business of investing.*

But, he continued, *I do know the feeling that something just isn't right. The first time I met Santo Aretino, I had no idea who he was. There was no outward indication that this man held the world of charitable giving forever indebted to his investment strategy. Countless thousands of people were tied to a financial function that few knew existed. And that success was until recently, a closely guarded secret. And still mostly is.*

So how did this all begin? Not the way you might expect. And so Nick began explaining Santo as a young man, his east coast upbringing and the source of his original seed money. Zoti insisted that this sort of background was necessary to establish bias.

The theme of his coming out speech, done under the banner of TED Talks, was centered on doing good. Leaving the world, a better place because, when you are eulogized, your friends and acquaintances will be having nothing but fond memories, awe-inspiring accounts of your efforts and setting the stage for how you will truly be missed. But how does someone who fled his home and parents suddenly, without warning, and head west justify his youth under such criteria?

I don't know. The recollections of the people I could find thirty years later were tainted by time but if these testimonials to the youthful Santo are any indication, he was a divisive young man that fostered a god-like hero worship and on many occasions, the polar opposite, a bothersome disruptor. So an estranged brother, a friend who would never call himself that because he never really knew Santo well enough to use that descriptor, a retired cop, a deceased teacher from his high school, or a former lover(s) might seem like enough to cobble together a picture of who this man might have been. But the real source of who Santo Aretino was came from a man who was a former business partner serving lengthy term in an upstate Pennsylvania penitentiary.

It would be tempting to say you don't know anything until you speak with someone who held their tongue for years as they rotted away in prison. What did that man know? In truth, I can't answer that question. Nick had never interviewed Matteo (Matty the Knife) DeSilva. This person's drug conviction had actually expired several years prior him visiting the east coast. Mr. DeSilva had recently expired as well, taking his secret to his grave. But Nick had spoken with John Bates and he had taken the time to make notes, all of which was checked as well as it could have been. In most cases, this would have been insufficient to include in a story hoping to pass journalistic muster but Nick had asked the subject of the story to refute it. The moment he hesitated, he answered the question and both of them knew it.

*****

"I still have to write the story," he told Che. "The guy has a past..."

"That should stay there," she quickly added. "C'mon, Nick. It doesn't have to be a puff piece but it could give the world some insight on how a man can reinvent himself, shed his past like an old skin and change the world without being berated for youthful mistakes." She was curled up at the other end of the sofa, wine glass in hand.

"Youthful mistakes?"

"You made them and I'm still with you." He rolled his eyes at that statement.

"Then get me an interview with the man."

"It will cost you," she replied playfully.

*****

But you don't need to know about the man that was, a less-than-fully formed man who became something you and I will never aspire to. And with good reason. We're too emotional. We're too in touch with our inner selves. We want to feel good and look better and we essentially want everyone to know we helped this charity or that cause or volunteered or donated time, energy, money or stuff. This is not necessarily a bad thing. Psychologists are more than willing to point out the happiness that is generated with charitable giving and some have even go so far as to suggest being prompted to do so perverts the happiness that might be attained.

They also point out as well, the numerous incentives that often coincide with acts of charity, such as tax breaks or the campaigns that get celebrities to donate their names to the cause, can defeat that attempt at happiness. These nudges makes us feel better because at the heart of who we are is stroked in such a way that we get something in addition to the happiness achieved with giving and a bauble or keepsake, or Facebook bragging rights.

I was invited to take a plane ride with Santo Aretino to visit a project he was working on. It was during that trip – and yes, it was a very nice private jet, and no, I have never been on one before – that I conducted this interview.

Let me describe this man to you in, and this is his request, vague enough details that you won't be trying to hunt him down.

Of course, there is very little likelihood you will accidentally bump into him on the downtown streets of Portland and because he values his reclusivity above everything but his wife and his projects, you have incredibly poor chances of actually seeing him.

That said, he is a handsome man of formidable size. He's large enough to give you the impression that he can handle himself, the kind of volume you want with you during a bar fight, but not large enough that he looms. His touch of grey doesn't make him look like a man in his late fifties, early sixties but he is. He has a long stride and a fitful presence. In a word, he is unforgettable.

The first thing I asked was where we were going.

Aretino: You heard about that Ebola outbreak in Africa last year, no doubt. Well, like so many things in this world that dismantle the social order, it could have been prevented. Because it was probably begun with bushmeat, gorillas hunted for food, and because a third of the gorillas in Africa have now died from the disease, that's where we're going to start.

The problem was getting a lab up and running and delivering the vaccines to the animals. So we're headed to South Carolina where we're going to airlift the whole operation, lab and techs and all.

Heath: That must be costing a pretty penny (I said without realizing who I was making that comment to).

A: Without a doubt. But what price do you put on a life if you can save two? We save the gorilla from the same disease we've mostly learned to control but what do they have? Are we supposed to give those hungry Africans gloves and face masks? And if people are hungry, who are we to stop what they are doing? Not that we're not trying but we look like the big prosperous west stepping into a situation they strongly suggest we simply don't or can't comprehend.

H: Do you run into this with a lot of your projects?

A: Not really: Maybe more so in third world countries and places where we are trying to save antiquities. In those places, hungry people aren't killing the local big game; they're selling art for pennies.

H: The list of projects still underway is impressive and the ones you've completed would eat up all of the column inches my editor gave me.

A: Let's just say the company's projects. The way it works, Nick hasn't and won't change just because of this interview. They do all of the heavy lifting, the planning and the follow-through under the guidance of the CEO. I just make the money that pays for it.

H: I wasn't going to bring that up until later but since you did: How did you do it?

A: How far back would you like me to go?

Nick paused and told Santo that he wanted to let him know what he had done. "I did some research back east after your TED Talk and there was some strong hints that the money you used to begin your investment career may have been ill-gotten."

"Seamus said you had paid a visit so I suspect you didn't just arrive at the farm on your own. And I'm guessing it didn't take much digging to uncover some truths that I made no effort to hide." As he spoke he looked directly at Nick. The eye contact made him shift his gaze slightly. "So, what do you say we clear the record up and do it right now? Will you be able to separate stories from memories? Or correctness from clarity?"

H: As far back as you think would be of interest to the readers.

A: I left my hometown with about $200,000 in cash, give or take and all of it was, at least in those War-on-Drugs days, ill-gotten. And yes, it was the seed money I used first to buy gold which *allowed me to take the "seed money" off the table and invest what was left. So, purists might argue that the money was tainted but I would beg to differ and so might the people that benefited. When it comes to money, no moralist is ever comfortable, but between you and me, I could care less.*

As to your other question: how did I do it? Someone one said that investors aren't born, they're made. I look at it just a bit differently. I think investors have no other choice. They think differently than the rest of society, and I'm not talking about the people who do it for the thrill or the folks who do it for a living. I'm talking about the people who can combine all of their prior knowledge and distill it into a comfortable decision that just happens to be profitable.

But I think the real animal instincts come into play when you earmark eighty percent of your profits for non-investment purposes. That I think makes it a little bit harder. It is the same sort of thing that happens when you overtax the rich; they just make more money. But charitably taxing my gains before I realize them, I am incentivized to make more.

The year I was born, Ayn Rand published her thinking about this very thing. She believed, and I suggest incorrectly, that the 'prime movers', the wealth creators should stop creating wealth if that wealth was being taxed. And it was, at a rate of about 91% on an income of $400,000 upwards. But the economy didn't slow down. In fact, it gradually accelerated. A guy named Peter Drucker once suggested that the world would not be impacted on iota if all the super-rich simply disappeared. But we are the risk takers. I don't argue for positive externalities or optimal progressivity, a bunch of economic terms that suggest the affluent are absolutely needed. I've just approached wealth as a social experiment instead of a tax avoidance issue.

H: I'll include that answer because it is fascinating and will interest some readers and completely baffle others. And speaking for the others, I'll admit that I don't know much about investing but that seems like it would be ridiculously hard. Do you think of it as gambling?

A: Oh hell no. It is much more sublime than that, if investing can be spiritual. Investing is a reaction to markets and markets are people and people try to bully other people like they were playing some sort of arena sport where the crowd cheers the gladiator. Which is fine I suppose. But think about it. If someone came along and took advantage of those profit thugs, who would care? That's what I do. I wait for the mistake and if I'm lucky, get ahead of it. John Bogle is famous for saying if you are a good investor, there is a bad investor on the other side of the trade. Or something to that effect.

H: So it's luck?

A: No. It's bravado and ego and brash behavior and even the most even keeled investor falls victim and that's when I jump in and profit.

H: So, there was nothing in your background that prepared you for this? Was your father a banker or an investor or something like that? For the sake of the reader, Nick asked the question he knew the answer.

A: (laughs) I have only recently found out that my parents were not really my parents. That's kind of sad in a way. I was always wondering why they didn't seem to get it. You know, not in the teen angst sort of way. It was more like we knew each of us were kind of sort of strangers. Had I known how it happened when I entered into their lives, I might have grown up a bit more empathetic to their lot in life. I know they didn't choose to have me and I wasn't intentionally hard on them either. We just never gelled.

They're long gone and I refused to take anything from them from a very early age. Maybe I knew. Maybe they thought I did. So no, I got nothing genetic from them and the whole nurture thing was, like I said, wholly refused by me. When I found out I was adopted, and never formally mind you, it was about a month ago. So if I was the type that engaged in hindsight, I might have done things differently. But if I had changed a single minute, I wouldn't be sitting here talking to you.

H: What made you come out west?

A: Without getting in too deep in a past that doesn't really matter and didn't impact the future, I would answer that it was time. I grew up just outside of Philly and living there always seemed so monotone, as if washed in perpetual grey. I'm certain that it was probably just me because I'd be willing to bet that most of the people who were there when I left never saw it that way and as a result, never ventured very far afield. I just had to leave, in more ways than one.

H: That TED Talk you gave a couple months back was quite theatrical, more so than some of the other ones I've seen. What gives?

A: That was a series of, how should I say, unfortunate mishaps. Frankly Nick, I am none of your business. But apparently social media didn't think so. Kind of like: How dare he protect his privacy. So, I gave the people what they wanted and kept my privacy in the process. It was theatrical and a royal pain in the ass to participate in. Imagine standing backstage with a bunch of look-a-likes and no one knew who I was. It was kind of creepy but I laughed. I think it was successful in the end.

Look, I have made it my life's work to keep the bullies from preying on the weak. That was the bullies preying on me and they lost. I heard that social media lit up.

H: It did and most of it was good. I took my girlfriend to it and she's a fan for life. Kind of changed her. Now once a week, she makes me carry her stuff to a local park and she does haircuts for the homeless. Nothing fancy, just a quick trim but it's funny, she make me man the hair washing station, which isn't much more than a hose and tub. I get it wet, they scrub and I rinse. It's hilarious but she says she feels better.

A: Eudaemonia.

H: And what is that?

A: Aristotle called it the happiness someone feels when they perform some moral duty without the benefit that we normally expect.

ABOUT THE AUTHOR:

While I offer the disclaimer that no person in this work of fiction is in any way real, the books and authors and other tangible items from the real world, such as the places, are. People close to me might be inclined to read me into the protagonist, and not in a good way; in a possible way, had one thing been different. I am not Santo Aretino.

I think it was John LeCarre who suggested that fiction is life with the dull bits removed. I agree and wouldn't change a thing.

My fate is much better than fiction, with a wonderful wife of over thirty-five years, four kids and three grandkids. This is my third novel. I have four non-fiction books published by McGraw-Hill, all focused on investing for those who know nothing about it.

This is the last book of this trilogy. The first, "Scourge of Princes" and the second entry into this story "Invisible Cities" are available at Amazon and in eBook form everywhere.

Future works will be written under a pseudonym.

www.ingramcontent.com/pod-product-compliance
Lightning Source LLC
Chambersburg PA
CBHW031944260626
47157CB00017B/2196